Fifty Cents
for
Your Soul

Denise Dietz

ISBN: **0-9663397-5-4**

Published by:
Delphi Books
P.O. Box 6435
Lee's Summit, MO 64064
Email: DelphiBks@aol.com
Fax: 816-478-2156

First Delphi Books printing April 2002
10 9 8 7 6 5 4 3 2 1

Book design: Desktop Publishing Ltd., Victoria, BC
Cover photo: Thomas Albany

Printed in Canada by Friesens

This novel is a work of fiction. Although it contains references to actual places, these references are used merely to lend the work a realistic setting. All other names, characters and incidents are the product of the author's imagination. Any resemblance to actual persons, living or dead, is entirely coincidental, and all events are pure invention.

Also By Denise Dietz

Novels:

Footprints In The Butter - An Ingrid Beaumont Mystery
Co-starring Hitchcock The Dog

Throw Darts At A Cheesecake

Beat Up A Cookie

Dream Dancer

The Rainbow's Foot

Anthologies

Journeys of the Heart

Criminal Appetites

Co-authored with Mary Ellen Johnson

A Highwayman Comes Riding

For Rex Anderson...
guide, philosopher, author extraordinaire

A big "THANK YOU" to the following:

Fran Baker, publisher of Delphi Books. Gordon Aalborg, my Canadian Muse. Thomas Albany, Lynn Whitacre, Mary Ellen Johnson, Victoria Alexander, Rudi Aalborg, and Jim Bisakowski.

Most of all, I am grateful to EILEEN DIETZ — a Demon on the outside, an Angel on the inside.

"Hollywood is a place where they'll pay
you a thousand dollars for a kiss, and fifty
cents for your soul."
Marilyn Monroe

"A sharp knife cuts the quickest and hurts
the least."
Katherine Hepburn

"Everyone to his own taste, as the woman
said when she kissed her cow."
Rabelais

Houston

"Now I lay me..."

The woman who straddled Victor Madison had hiccups. They inched up her throat, higgledy-piggledy, and emerged between her moans of feigned passion.

Snakelike, she twisted her face, scrutinized the bedside table, and zeroed in on a book. A portion of shiny red cover was missing and the book's title, above a satanic, sharp-fanged face, spelled out: FOREVER ASMO...

Between the pages, looking like a fat bookmark, a sheet of paper had been folded twice, lengthwise. Every visible line included one word, written over and over, as if Madison had wanted to duplicate a signature. *Piglet*, he had scribbled. *Piglet, Piglet, Piglet*...

Next to the novel were three empty Tsingtao bottles and an empty bottle of champagne. Next to a kidney-shaped lamp, an ashtray held gold foil from pralines dipped in dark chocolate.

Madison had eaten the candies, every one.

She had gulped down the champagne, every drop.

A pessimist might say she was half-drunk while an optimist might say she was half-sober. Drunk enough to endure the tireless beast who lay beneath her spread legs. Sober enough to hear raindrops pelting the window. To her ears, the raindrops sounded like acrylic fingernails drumming *do-a-deer-a-fe-male-deer*...

Madison tiddly-winked her nipples, then compressed her ribcage, and the hiccups evaporated. What a relief.

Her relief was short-lived. He began to hoist her up and down like a carousel horse, impaling her each time, and she let out a shriek. "Sorry," he said. "S'okay," she said, even though it wasn't.

But he was her meal ticket, her Bob-Hope-Bing-Crosby "Road to Fame and Fortune," especially the hope part. So she faked another orgasm, then collapsed against his chest. He smelled of sour sweat and Obsession cologne.

"You're the greatest, Madison," she said, trusting her voice sounded seductive rather than weary.

Hadn't Vivian Leigh, as Scarlett O'Hara, said something about toting the weary load?

Maybe not. Maybe it had been that old-man-river man in *Showboat*. The re-make…a happier ending…Magnolia and Gaylord singing about make-believe while Ava Gardner smiled sadly and the movie's invisible orchestra played…

Jump down, turn around, pick a bale of cotton. Jump down, turn around, pick a bale of… Hey. Could a person die from too much fucking? Or too much fucking heat? Although Madison's hotel suite was expensive, the air conditioner didn't cool good. Cool *well*. Cool *hell*.

Perspiration trickled down her face and thirst clawed at her throat. How could she be so wet on the outside and dry on the inside?

The only other light came from a TV. Disney's *Sleeping Beauty*. But Madison had clicked the remote on MUTE and the Prince searched for Beauty in animated silence.

How could Beauty sleep for a hundred years? Wouldn't the wretched girl have to wake up to eat? Drink? Pee?

Victor Madison wouldn't wake Beauty with a kiss. He'd lick, suck, thrust, prick…

Oh, God, wasn't it the prick of a spindle that had Valium-ed Beauty into her centennial slumber?

Lucky Beauty. Lucky Princess. Now he lays me. Down to sleep. Pray the Lord. My soul to keep.

Madison's first two fingers plunged, and she felt as if a pronged corkscrew had invaded what she, as a teenager, had called her volvo.

Here we go again. Here we go loop-de-loo, here we go loop-de-laid… He stopped. Why? Damn, she hadn't moaned. He liked her to moan. She moaned.

"Shut up," he said. "I hear something."

His fingers twitched nervously and she began to experience her first genuine orgasm of the evening…until she glanced down at his face. It looked skeletal, as if his skin had been knotted at the nape of his neck.

"Elevator," he whispered, removing his fingers. "Elevator. Me."

Elevator me? Was that a sexual innuendo?

The bedroom door dragged against thick carpeting and ruined the visitor's dramatic entrance.

"Come in," Madison said, his voice filled with relief.

"I'm already in, you bastard."

"Come on *down*," Madison taunted.

With another moan (this one ingenuous), she shifted positions and lay on her back at Madison's side. The intruder's expression revealed a jealous rage, and her brain suggested... no, *demanded* that she scream her head off. But the hotel was old, its walls well-insulated, and anyway her spit had dried up.

Hadn't Madison locked the suite? Yes. She remembered him placing the do-not-disturb placard on the outside of the door, then checking the lock...

Had he, or had he not, slid the chain?

"*L'chayim*," he had said, handing her the champagne bottle and stuffing his mouth with pralines.

While she gulped down champagne, straight from the bottle, he'd eased her clothes off. Then, kneeling at her feet, he had pressed his palms against her butt and aimed his tongue at her volvo.

"Bed," she had said, already unsteady on her feet. Earlier, she'd primed the pump with a couple of margaritas.

Without another word, he had propelled her onto the mattress.

She had lusted after Madison, even conspired with the devil to get him, but she soon discovered that making love to him was like running uphill on a treadmill.

Now, watching him prop his head and shoulders against two pillows, she burrowed closer.

Ignoring her, he stared at the intruder and said, "Care to join us?"

His voice sounded arrogant, not fearful. So it was a joke. Right?

The intruder stepped toward the bed, hand held high. Light from the TV brought a knife blade into stark, sharp relief.

This had to be one of Madison's famous publicity stunts, right?

The knife swooped down, aimed at Madison's penis and testicles. At the last minute, it changed direction, driving easily through his neck—a barbecue skewer strung with pharynx, larynx and Adam's apple. The blade slid out the other side, notching the pillowcase and the striped casing.

Dizzy with disbelief, she vaguely categorized the pillows as the feathery kind, not the foam rubber kind, because tiny white-gray feathers stuck to the bloody blade as it withdrew.

Any moment now Madison would yell cut-and-print. Right?

Wrong. Madison's smug smile faded. His mouth dropped open and blood ran from the corners, down his cheekbones, toward his earlobes. His hand snaked out, grasped her breast, squeezed convulsively, then fell away.

Jeee-sus. Victor Madison was dead. Deader than the corpses who populated his horror films. Deader than the movie monsters who always received their come-uppance during the final reel, then resurrected themselves for a sequel.

Would Madison resurrect himself for a sequel?

Using her heels and butt, she managed to bump and grind herself sideways, but the killer straddled her body, knee-pinned her to the mattress like a butterfly, and said, "If you move, I'll carve my initials on your breasts."

The feather-encrusted knife gestured menacingly.

She had to throw up. "I have to throw up," she said. "Can I go to the bathroom?"

"No."

"Can I pray? Please?"

"Not if you puke."

"I won't. I promise," she said, wondering if she could keep her promise. She smelled Madison's blood, the killer's sweat, and her own fear. She smelled the chocolate-covered pralines, too, even though Madison hadn't shared...the pig.

She pictured Madison's bookmark. Piglet.

"Are you Piglet?" she asked.

"No, I'm Eeyore. Look, I haven't got all night. Do you want to pray or don't you?"

"Our fa-father, which art in hev-heaven, hallowed be...hallowed be...I can't remember the words. Wait, oh wait, I know."

This time she recited the nighttime prayer of her childhood aloud, and had reached the line "If I should die before I wake" when the knife carved a smile across her throat.

The murders made front-page headlines, worldwide. Even the *New York Times* and *Wall Street Journal* screamed bloody murder.

For Victor Madison, it was the culmination of a long life of publicity. For Dawn Sullivan, it was her first starring role.

ONE

"In the beginning..."

My spiritualist never mentioned murder. I guess it wasn't in the cards.

On the day after my twenty-fourth birthday, I arose from my bed and contemplated abdominal crunches. Instead, I drowned Captain Crunch in skim milk, then clothed my petite body in denim shirt, faded jeans, and black leather boots. Would a .32 automatic fit inside my padded bra?

Probably, I thought critically, draping a *Les Miserables* sweatshirt across my shoulders and slip-knotting its sleeves at my collarbone.

Except, I didn't own a gun. Or silver bullets. I didn't even own a crucifix. No big deal. A cross wouldn't be much protection against a famous spiritualist. Neither would the Star of David chained 'round my neck. I had a gut feeling guns and silver bullets wouldn't work, either.

My only defense was disbelief.

One hour later, I tethered my sunglasses to my shirt and entered the Ansonia. The ghosts of show biz celebs supposedly permeate the dark, musty hallways, and I wondered who, or what, lurked behind closed doors? Rosemary's baby? No, that was the Dakota.

The Beatles' *Do You Want to Know a Secret* hummed from a room radio, and the hairs on the back of my neck prickled. Hadn't John Lennon been murdered outside the Ansonia? No, damn it, the Dakota.

What the hell was the matter with me? I had nothing to fear. True, I've occasionally used the lord's name in vain, but I've never coveted my neighbor's wife or ass. I've never killed anything except roaches, and I honor my father and mother. Well...my father.

Taking a deep breath, actually, several deep breaths, I rode the elevator to the fourth floor, hesitated, then knuckled my fist and knocked.

The door creaked like a coffin lid and a woman said, "Come in."

Mrs. Carvainis could have been hired by central casting to play the part of the quintessential spiritualist. Her face had accumulated so many wrinkles, it resembled a piece of crumpled graph paper. Below her saggy chin, she wore a long black dress. The oval brooch, pinned to her bodice, looked like an alexandrite stone. Her hair was white and sparse and bunned. Her eyes were very black, as if an ophthalmologist had dilated the pupils. Her plucked eyebrows followed the economy, peaking in the middle then dropping sharply.

She led me through her living room, where a rabbit-eared TV squatted atop a wrought-iron stand. Her ancient on-its-last-legs couch and chintzy armchair would have been laughed off *Antiques Roadshow.* A coffee table held a stack of yellowing newspapers that climbed, like Jack's beanstalk, toward a *Casablanca* ceiling fan. A rickety card table displayed today's paper, opened...inadvertently, I presumed...to the Horoscopes page. A jar filled with potpourri tried to hide the smell of...mildew?...kitty litter? Venetian blinds displayed Manhattan sky-stripes, and I felt like a claustrophobic Peter Pan.

We walked into a gloomy study whose paneled walls reminded me of dark prosceniums. An old carpet covered the floor. Its ornamental scarab design seemed to move in colorful swirls. Oh God, did I really want to do this? No. But I'd promised my best friend, Bonita Sinclair, a fellow actress whom I'd known since kindergarten. Bonnie believed in psychics, and she'd given me half the fee...a birthday present.

Mrs. Carvainis pointed her gnarled, rheumatic finger toward a table and two chairs. The table's sculpted legs ended in lion's feet with mahogany claws. "Please sit, Francine Rose," she said, then peered at me as if gauging my reaction, having apparently forgotten I'd given my name to her over the phone.

In fact, I'd given her my stage name...Francine Rose. An authentic clairvoyant should have known that my real name was Frannie Rosen. I wanted to strangle Bonnie. Instead, I sat.

Mrs. C's index finger squiggled across my palm. I'd felt the same sensation before. Summer. Ten years ago. Lying on the ground, staring at the sky, daydreaming up a storm, I hadn't noticed a parade of fire ants. Until they decided to take a shortcut, beginning at the base of my fingers, ending at my wrist. This time I held my hand steady, but the rest of my body squirmed like a puppy getting its tailbone scratched.

"How old are you, Miss Rose?"

Bonnie had said Mrs. C would need the date and time of my birth. A preemie, I had arrived one month earlier than anticipated, which had set the precedent for a life span of infractions. Mom remembered pain, not time, but Daddy knew the exact second—and now Mrs. C did, too.

"I see good fortune for you," she said, "the answer to all your dreams. Cameras and film. You are an actress."

She pronounced it "ecktriss," but I couldn't determine if her accent was genuine or fake. In any case, "ecktriss" was a safe guess. Who else would be visiting Frank Baum's wicked Witch of the West Side at eleven o'clock in the morning? Who else would be spending grocery money on a psychic who perused daily horoscopes?

"If you keep to your present path," she said, "you will reach the top of your field. Right now I see contracts and money. Lots of money. But be careful. There are negative forces jealous of your success."

"Money? Success? How soon?"

"Everything will begin to happen in a festive atmosphere. I see cameras and people. Travel. Romance with a tall, dark—"

"My boyfriend is blonde, Germanic. Hitler could have used him as a poster boy."

"Romance with a tall, dark man." She scowled, and her brooch stone swirled purple and red. "Keep your faith at all times because there are forces trying to tear you down. Demonic forces."

Her jewel blinked like a stoplight, and my breath caught in my throat as I remembered that alexandrite stones might change color but they didn't blink like stoplights. My father was a jewelry salesman. I had cut my teeth, so to speak, on polished gems. What the hell kind of stone was this woman wearing?

"Trust to whatever forces you believe in," she continued. "You must see both sides of what you are doing in order to take the right path. Satan wears many disguises and can easily fool you. Some people think the devil doesn't exist, just as some people think God is dead. It's your choice, Miss Rose."

Mrs. Carvainis droned on and on about my past. Generalities. Stuff about how I tried hard but wasn't appreciated. Still wrapped in my protective shield of disbelief, I decided she was playing upon my insecurities as an "ecktriss." Until she said something very strange.

"You were named for your grandmother. You are an only child, but there was another. Stillborn."

Wrong and wrong. Named for my great-grandmother, I had been C-sectioned from my mother's womb exactly eight months after her marriage.

She had been a virgin until her wedding night, and I've been told at least a million times, by Mom, that my birth almost killed her. I've also been told…a million times…not to exaggerate, but one thing is certain. During my please-please-make-me-a-brother-sister-phase, Mom said she could never have another child.

So how come my wicked Witch of the West had pulled that rabbit from her ersatz crystal ball? And how come I desperately wanted to question such a strange assumption, but, instead, clammed up?

Dismissing the past, Mrs. Carvainis reached for a pack of Tarot cards. I knew, from Bonnie, that Tarot was subject to numerous methods of interpretation, but all readings involved the questioner, the interpreter, and the cards. Sometimes the questioner asked her questions aloud for the interpreter to hear, at other times not. This was a not. Sometimes the interpreter had the questioner shuffle cards, at other times she did it herself. Mrs. C shuffled herself. And dealt.

Shit, I didn't want to play card games. So why didn't I run like hell?

Because there, right there on the table, lay the Death card.

Mrs. C pointed out an abundance of Pinnacles, portending financial matters, forecasting personal advancement.

With a shaky finger, I gestured toward the Death card.

"That card may imply change or mishap," she said, "rather than physical death."

"Oh, my God. Am I going to have a mishap?"

"Trust to whatever forces you believe in," she repeated. "'I have fought a good fight, I have finished my course, I have kept the faith.' New Testament."

"'The devil can cite Scripture for his purpose,'" I blurted without thinking. One of my really bad habits is combating quotes with quotes. But since I'd already opened mouth, inserted foot, I continued. "That's from Shakespeare's 'Merchant of Venice.' By the way, Mrs. Carvainis, do you believe in spirits? Fairies? Elves?"

"Doppelgangers," she said, her brooch the color of blood.

My skin felt goosebumpy. Doppelgangers…ghostly counterparts of living persons. The Jewish equivalent would be dybbukim; souls who enter (and control) a person's body until exorcised by a religious rite. My stupnagel cousin Charlene had told me all about doppelgangers and dybbukim. I had been knee-high to a Munchkin, and Charlene had scared me to death.

Shaking off the memory, I said, "I believe in fairies. Land of Nod. Oz. Middle Earth. And yet when I saw J.M. Barrie's *Peter Pan*, I thought

Tinkerbell was a jealous little twit. I rooted for Captain Hook."

Mrs. C smiled for the first time. A gold tooth winked from her left incisor section. "'The reason why birds can fly and we can't," she said, "is simply that they have faith, for to have faith is to have wings.' J.M. Barrie."

Her brooch was now blue-gray, so it wasn't an alexandrite. Alex stones never turn blue. It was probably a mood-ring-brooch, absorbing heat from her blunted bosom.

I finally asked the question I had come to ask. "Will I win an Academy Award?"

Rising to her feet, my psychic glanced at her watch then nodded toward the living room. Even a stupnagel like my cousin Charlene would have understood that the session was over, finished, dead.

"God bless," Mrs. C said, in the same tone of voice she'd used for doppelgangers.

TWO

Outside the Ansonia, rain splattered the pavement like hair spray from an aerosol can, and someone had discarded today's newspaper. Fishing the Lifestyle section from the trash can, I scanned the soggy pages until I found Horoscopes.

I'm an Aries.

"No matter how daunting the challenges ahead of you," I read aloud, raindrops beading my lashes, "no matter how tough the opposition you have to face, you will win with ease…you can feel it in your bones. The sun moves into your birth sign on Friday and your courage and confidence have never been higher, and as Mars, your ruler, aspects Venus, planet of Love, your passion is pretty impressive, too. Look out world, you're on your way."

Today was Wednesday. I smootched the paper into a ball and Michael Jordan-ed it toward the trash can. Net-shot. *You can feel it in your bones?* My bones felt wet as I raced a bus to the corner, and won.

Bonnie had decided we'd meet at our health club, following what I had dubbed my "psychic-pathic" appointment. Bonnie wanted to hear every detail. Pinnacles and Wands, I thought, and Death.

No. Mishap. What exactly did mishap mean?

Stumbling onto the bus, I scanned its occupants for serial killers. Several passengers mumbled into cell phones. Quite a few had their noses buried in books. I could see covers; bestsellers by Sue Grafton, Fran Baker, Susan Isaacs, Stephen King and Victoria Alexander. There was one vacant seat, next to a man who looked non-toxic. As I belly-danced past his knees, he kept his gaze focused upon the thick paperback he cradled between his legs.

From my window seat, I watched tall buildings kaleidoscope by.

Then, suddenly, the rain stopped. Luminary streams bounced off walls of glass that sparkled like zircons. Reaching into my meager cleavage, I retrieved the sunglasses that still dangled from the vee of my shirt.

The convex lenses darkened my window-world, so I began to compose rap lyrics, using the multiple cell phone conversations as my background music. I had finished: *Psychedelic psychics rule the world, what the fuck got into you girl?* and was working on: *Mars is your ruler, Venus your passion, Fire is your Sun sign, you wasted your cash on…*when the bus stopped and a young, light-skinned black woman swayed down the aisle. Switching a pet carrier from one hand to the other, she searched for a non-existent seat.

The man in the seat next to mine looked up from his book, glanced at the black woman, then stared at me. His eyes were opaque, devoid of any expression, as if he'd been hypnotized. "Gotta go," he said.

I thought he meant the bathroom because he squirmed the same way one squirms when one has to go potty and one is stranded on a city bus. But then he said, "Yes, okay, no problem."

He stomped to the exit door and tried to walk through it. The bus kept moving, but the man acted like an agitated bird trapped inside a house, beating its wings and beak against a window. In this case, the man beat his arms and face against the door. The bus driver slid to the curb, slammed on his brakes, and opened the door. The "birdman" exited onto West 56th. Street, the bus driver said something about crazy-nuts, and the bus began to roll again.

At the same time, I yelled, "Hey, Mister, you forgot your book."

Snatching it up, I held it against the window, a useless gesture. The man had vanished, as if he'd never existed.

Depicted on the paperback's shiny red cover was a demon's face and the words: FOREVER ASMODEUS by S.B. EISENBERG.

Forever Asmodeus had climbed to the top of the *Times* bestseller list, first as a hardcover, then a paperback. Should I turn it over to the bus driver? Did the bus station have a lost and found? Would "Birdman" retrieve his lost property? Or had he disappeared into *The Mysterious Bookshop*, where he'd find another copy?

My dilemma was momentarily forgotten when the black woman slid her extra-wide tush across the crazy man's seat. Releasing the handles of the pet carrier, she settled it between her white socks and dilapidated sneakers.

"Hi, I'm Frannie," I blurted.

Framed by glossy ringlets, my new seat-companion's face was round, not oval, as if God or somebody had drawn it with a grade school pencil compass. Her coal-black eyes slanted at the corners while a smattering of freckles garnished her nose and cheeks. She wore a long brown skirt, fastened at the waist with a safety pin, and a white tee that stated: IF THE RICH COULD HIRE OTHER PEOPLE TO DIE FOR THEM, THE POOR WOULD MAKE A WONDERFUL LIVING.

Introducing oneself is not a Big Apple custom. Blame my gaffe on the teeshirt's Jewish proverb. My father used to say that. A lot. On the other hand, my mother tends to ignore Hebrew prophets...except during Yom Kippur. Or when she wants to lay a guilt trip on her nondenominational-by-choice daughter.

Compounding my original sin, I said, "What's your name?"

"Tenia," she replied.

"Is that your cat inside the pet carrier, Tenia?"

"Ain't got no cat."

"I've got a cat. He's a pain in the..."

I meant to say ass, maybe tush, but the unorthodox cacophony that emerged from the pet carrier momentarily tied my tongue. A harsh hiss, then...castanets? Baby's rattle?

"What's *that,* Tenia?"

"Snake."

Had she really said snake? Snake didn't sound anything like dog or gerbil, but I must have misunderstood. Then, despite the hum of cell phone babble, I heard the *rrrrrr* sound again.

The bus screeched to a halt at my stop and opened its accordion doors. Tenia stood up to let me pass. "Sorry, excuse me, watch your toes," I said, and could almost swear she gave me a Cheshire Cat smile. In other words, if a smile can be described as smug, Tenia's was.

Exiting into wet sunshine, I strolled toward The Spa's awning-clad ramp. And nearly stumbled when I had a sudden thought: *Holy shit, a snake.*

Picturing forked tongue and fangs filled with toxic Novocain, I wondered if I should call 911.

THREE

Calling 911 sounded like a really dumb idea.

After all, I hadn't actually *seen* a snake.

So I entered my health club and furtively slithered past the front desk, manned by two skinny nymphets. I couldn't sign in and receive a free towel since I owed money. Not quite "this account has been turned over to a credit agency" money, but close.

During a moment of idiotic impulse, induced by Happy Hour margaritas, Bonnie and I had filled out restroom coupons, good for one free week at The Spa. Bonnie had bought discount tights and leotard while I splurged my grocery budget on adorable workout clothes, aerobic sneakers, and leg warmers.

Only one week to achieve miracles.

The first day, a Hugh Hefner centerfold measured and weighed me, then shook her head and smiled sadly. Wondering if she practiced her smile in the mirror, feeling like Old McDonald's cow, I signed up for three years. Bonnie, more prudent, had signed up for six months. To date, I had lost one pound and two inches. The two inches were in my breasts.

A poster boy for natural-fiber-extract leaned against the desk. Since his last name was two syllables longer than Schwarzenegger's, I called him "Mr. Biceps." He flirted with the nymphets, blocking their view. Hunching my head like a turtle's, I rounded the corner, climbed multiple stairs, slipped through a door onto a running track, and stared down at a parquet floor that was partially carpeted with cinnabar-colored mats.

Rock music blared from hidden speakers while the perpetual aerobics class stretched and grunted. Bonnie pointed one leg toward me and saluted with her toes. Her body glistened with sweat, but not one strand of her long blue-black hair looked mussed. When I aerobicized, I could swear Little Orphan Annie had reached puberty, screwed fight promoter Don King, and given me up for adoption.

Except my hair is pale gold, not red-orange.

Bonnie mouthed something that looked like, "Frannie. Gobbledy-talk-yoohoo. Hadda drimpk."

I nodded anyway and headed for the whirlpool.

Secluded inside the "female" locker room, The Spa's whirlpool is the size of a small pond. From behind sloping bucket seats, hot water jets spurt and blow like agitated whales.

All other "females" were still conditioning their respiratory and circulatory systems with oxygen consumption, so the whirlpool was unoccupied. Its steamy fingers beckoned. Dropping my sweatshirt, sunglasses, and *Forever Asmodeus* onto a dry bench, I shed my blouse, boots, jeans and underwear. Then I slid into a seat and let pressurized bubbles soothe sore muscles and stressed shoulder blades.

I turned, knelt, and grasped the whirlpool's tiled edge with both hands. Thinking about success on the stage and my boyfriend Andre, I positioned myself so that the gush of hot water honeycombed the region between my spread legs. It felt like a monster tongue osculating.

Baptismal masturbation, I thought, shuddering with orgasmic delight. Then I turned, leaned back against the seat, and closed my eyes.

I see the answer to all your dreams. Cameras and film. You are an ecktriss.

You betcha. I could have told Mrs. C about my first starring role. Creative nursery school. I had played Jill, tugging a reluctant Jack up a papiermâché hill. Instead of breaking his crown, Jack wet his pants and fled the stage. Despite laughter from the audience, I finished my verse. Then, after the applause had died down, I tried to crush my partner's unbroken head with our prop, a metal pail.

Grade School. I played Martha Washington. A boy who stuttered was cast as George. Since the scene had been planned for seven minutes, I ad-libbed, stepping on his lines. Thus, we rewrote history and created the Mother of our country.

High School. While other kids took French or Spanish, I studied Southern. Triumphing over a classmate's relationship with the director (they both hailed from the same small Louisiana town, where everybody was somebody's cousin, spouse or sibling), I captured the role of Maggie in *Cat On a Hot Tin Roof.*

Syracuse University. Two years, and I'd had my fill of cheering at football games, recuperating from my first, second and thirteenth hangovers, losing my virginity, and cramming for final exams. My best role was "Martha" again, this time in *Who's Afraid of Virginia Woolf?*

I dropped out of college and performed six weeks worth of "bit part" on a soap. After that, I had ten lines…eleven if I paused in the delivery…in an Off-Off-Broadway play. I did lots of movie-extra work. Pick a NY cop show, any show, and there's me, looking horrified, standing behind the yellow crime scene tape. I once considered leaning forward and projectile-vomiting over the tape, just so I'd get noticed, but sanity prevailed. Then came my lucky break. A commercial for a new bubble bath product. Except no one ever saw me, covered by suds, reclining in an antique tub, because the FDA refused to OK the formula. The bubbles, it seemed, were herbaceous; probably contained poison ivy; my tush itched for days.

Single, independent, I shared rent and groceries with my friend and lover, Andre Vaughn. We met when I played a homely teenager, during my six weeks worth of soap opera. The way we fell in love was one big cliché…or a movie script. Framed by an open dressing room door, I took off my fake glasses, fake overbite, body padding, and the stupid wig that hid my long, curly, palomino-gold hair. "Frannie?" Andre said, skidding to a halt and staring into the room. "Andre," I said. "Frannie," Andre said, moving closer. Fadeout…

Later we both swore we heard background music; piano and violins, maybe even a harp. We even swore we heard James Brown singing *I Want You So Bad.*

So yes, Mrs. Carvainis, I'm an ecktriss. Even though I wait tables at an Italian restaurant, my agent tends to forget my existence, and my mother thinks I should finish college and teach school.

If you keep to your present path, you will reach the top of your field.

The Death card may imply mishap rather than physical death.

Ain't got no cat. Snake.

"Frannie, are you asleep?"

Opening my eyes, I watched Bonnie slide her perfect body into the whirlpool.

"Wool-gathering," I said. "What were you trying to tell me before, during aerobics class?"

"Last night I had this really weird dream."

Wisps of steam swirled around Bonnie's chin.

"I dreamed about you and demons," she said.

FOUR

Before Bonnie and I could discuss her dream, a gaggle of sweaty, giggly, white-footed gooney birds invaded our whirlpool.

Bonnie showered, whereupon we headed for The Spa's snack bar.

After avidly consuming two all-beef hot dogs snuggled inside two whole-grain wheat buns, I crunched a frozen Cappuccino between my teeth. Bonnie drank what The Spa calls an "Orange Julia"—named for Roberts—and I call an "Orange Environmentalist." Filled with a virtual alphabet of vitamins, nothing had been killed to blender Bonnie's brew, not even an orange.

We didn't talk about demons.

I didn't mention Tenia's snake.

We might have picked apart Bonnie's dream if "Mr. Biceps" hadn't squiggled his taut butt between our stools. When he offered to pay our tab, I swallowed my pique, but that meant we had to endure his inane chatter. At least Bonnie did. I needed Andre to finish what I had started in the whirlpool.

Or maybe, instead, I'd sit and visualize the phone call that would confirm Mrs. C's "contracts and money" prophecy.

I said goodbye to Bonnie.

Then, pausing at The Spa's doorway, paraphrasing J.M. Barrie, I said, "Clap three times if you believe."

Exiting The Spa, I clapped three times.

FIVE

Upon arriving home, I changed into my favorite Betty Boop teeshirt, sat on the edge of my favorite piece of furniture (a barber's chair), and stared at the phone.

Andre had signed the lease on our apartment five months before we met. He says I moved in at noon-thirty and by 1:15 had redecorated. A slight exaggeration. It was probably more like 3:15.

Be that as it may, I suspended several plants from any rafter I could find, brightened a few corners with potted palms, and covered the scarred wooden floors with what my mother calls "ersatz Oriental." Wall fissures were hidden by framed theatre and movie posters, hung haphazardly because the cracks had no perceptible pattern. For example, *A Star is Born* (Garland's version) rested two inches below the ceiling's molding while *The Graduate* was eye-level, assuming the eyes belonged to whomever reclined on our ersatz leather couch.

One week later I added *The Diary of Anne Frank,* Mom's housewarming gift.

"I've heard," Mom said during her first and last visit, "that you can get cancer from dry-rot-fungus."

I hung Anne above the ersatz fireplace, the only lump of matter that had received Mom's seal of approval.

"Use it in good health," she stated, just before she stepped into the hallway, gazed pointedly at the fifth-floor stairwell, then shot me her patented Jewish sacrifice look. Mom has varicose veins.

"Frannie, ah, Fran, why do you, ah, keep staring at the phone?" Andre said, sounding like James Cagney. He—Andre, not Cagney—sat in our living room's overstuffed armchair, a script in his lap.

We have phones in our kitchen, bedroom and living room. This phone, the one without an answering machine, squatted atop my second favorite piece of furniture; a miniature merry-go-round horse, topped by a circle of smoked glass.

"I'm visualizing a call from my agent," I said.

"You're practicing A T and Telepathy? Trying to elicit a call by thinking 'ring' inside your head? Oh, I get it. The fortune teller."

"Not fortune teller, Andre, spiritualist."

"How could you waste grocery money on that shit? Speaking of groceries, I hate generic peanut butter. Please buy Peter Pan."

"Peter Pan was a damn chauvinist," I said. "He never saw Wendy as a real woman. He wanted her to mother the Lost Children and sew his shadow back on."

Andre winked. "He taught Wendy how to fly."

"Big deal. I think I read somewhere that an airline has added a direct flight from Kennedy to Never-Never Land."

"Jesus Christ. An innuendo goes right over your head."

"It does not."

"Next you'll tell me that Peter Pan wanted to screw his mother."

"I will not. I left Freud and his dissident friends at Syracuse University, and I'm not into kinky."

"Really. What about Mickey Roebuck?"

"What about him?"

"He wears ladies' underwear."

"He does not."

"Have you ever seen him in his underwear?"

"No. Have you?"

"You never saw his panties, not even when you shared his loft?"

"Our relationship was platonic and…you're joking, right?"

"Maybe."

One thing I hate about Andre is what I call his enigmaticism. Had he seen my friend Mickey in panties? And if so, where? "Maybe" meant I'd never know because Andre would simply change the subject.

Extending his hands, he molded them around an imaginary crystal ball. "I see Oscar on the mantel," He said, sounding like that kid in *The Sixth Sense,* the one who saw dead people. "Watch out for the flames, Oscar, we have no fireplace screen. Too late. I see Oscar melting, mellllting."

I felt my temper simmer. "Our fireplace is dysfunctional, you idiot, just like you and me."

"I see travel…a plane…destination Never-Never Land. I see romance with a boy who wants you to sew his shadow back on."

"A boy who won't grow up."

"I see a Kansas tornado and Auntie Em."

My temper boiled over. "Knock it off, Andre. Bonnie recommended Mrs. Carvainis and—"

"I see danger, but you will give in to it, even enjoy it."

Tempering my temper, I said, "What kind of danger?"

"I see a tall man, a soap star."

"How tall?"

"Six foot one."

"And a half," I said, because halves are very important to people who are five foot two and a half.

"I see him ripping off your clothes and kissing you in places you've never been kissed before."

"Go on."

"I see the tall superstar—"

"How'd we get from soap star to superstar?"

"—taking a break and fixing himself a tuna sandwich." Rising, Andre placed his script on the chair.

"It's almost supper time," I said. "You'll ruin your appetite."

"Jesus, Frannie, you sound like your mother."

"What an awful thing to say."

"Sorry." He humped one shoulder, then the other, rotating sinewy back muscles. "A hangman has knotted a goddamn noose *in* my neck."

"When we're rich and famous we'll buy a Jacuzzi."

"Speaking of famous," Andre said, glancing toward his script.

"Big scene tomorrow?"

"I get shot saving Trish from bank robbers. There's this great bit in the hospital where I express my love for that gorgeous slut...if it was a movie I'd win an Academy Award. Then I pass out."

"Your love? But I thought Trish was pregnant. I thought what's his face is the father. I thought...never mind. I'll fix you a tuna sandwich, Andre, then cue you until it's time for me to perform my waitress bit."

"Shit, I forgot. Your boss called. There's a private party tonight, so New York's finest Italian restaurant won't need the services of Frannie Rosen, Long Island's consummate purveyor of matzo ball soup and gefilte fish."

"Oh, good. I need the money, but my waitress uniform reeks of garlic, parmesan and Chianti, and this nutcase left *Forever Asmodeus* on the bus seat next to mine."

As I paused for breath, Andre said, "Forever who?"

"Asmodeus. Some kind of demon. *Forever Asmodeus* is a sexy horror novel, honey, and I've been dying to read it. So I'll spend tonight at the Laundromat. But first…"

Pushing Andre to the floor, I straddled his long, lean body.

"He rips off all her clothes," I said, as he began to peel denim down over my tush. "That's what you call rip?"

"Your jeans are skin-tight, Frannie. Maybe you should spend the night with a diet guru."

"You dirty rat." Rats. My enunciation sounded like Bette Davis, not Cagney. Rolling away, I wriggled out of my jeans.

"Tell me what you want," Andre said, "and then I'll tell you."

"I want to make mad, passionate love."

"Say the words, baby."

"I love you," I said, kicking my jeans toward the fireplace.

"And I love you. Say the words, Frannie."

Andre got turned on by explication, but I didn't. "You're supposed to kiss me in places I've never been kissed before," I said. "Good luck."

He kissed Betty Boop.

"Wait a sec," I said. "Let me take off…hey, what's the matter?"

He had propped himself up on one elbow. Between his eyes was what I called his White Anglo Saxon Protestant crease.

"What's with your WASP crease?" I said. "Is something wrong?"

"No."

I tend to blurt out every catastrophe, from a broken fingernail to a broken water main, but Andre keeps his mouth shut…like an unsteamed clam. "You look underwhelmed," I said. "Why can't we make love?"

In a Jerry Seinfeld voice, Andre said, "It's almost supper time. You'll ruin your appetite."

He turned his head sideways. I took a moment to admire dark blonde hair falling into blue eyes shaded by lengthy lashes. Perhaps his nose was a tad aggressive and his mouth too generous, but all the ingredients came together to produce a classic profile. On the other hand, he claimed my nose was impertinent and my mouth pouty. We had selected our black cat, Snowball, from the animal shelter because Andre insisted the cat's eyes looked like mine.

"Andre," I said, "do you want to hear about the whirlpool?"

I told him…showed him. Show and Tell, and I could tell he was getting turned on. This time he straddled *my* body. Then he lowered his face to my breasts and sucked Betty Boop's expressive eyes.

My nipples responded to the wet warmth while my vagina began to generate its own moisture. I could feel it on my fingers, still teasing in order to tease Andre. His penis pried my fingers apart, discovered the dampness, and thrust.

"Suck Betty," I said. "Suck…yes…more…yes…Betty Boo…yes."

Instead, he pulled out and shifted positions, until his erection was level with my chin. "Frannie, c'mon, please," he urged.

"I can't. You know I can't."

"Yes, you can. Forget Jewish inhibitions."

"Inhibitions have nothing to do with it. I can't put it…you in my mouth, Andre. I'm sorry."

He changed positions again. "Someday," he said, then penetrated.

Penitent, I lifted my legs onto his shoulders, giving him easier access. Damn my mother all to hell. She'd told me a gazillion times that Good Jewish Girls didn't ingest a man's you-know-what.

I gasped, shuddered, writhed, moaned.

Andre moaned.

I came.

Andre came.

I sighed.

Andre laughed.

I said, "What's so funny?"

Andre said, "There's a Peeping Tom at our window."

Turning my head, I saw a black face with tufts of hair protruding from its ears. An ethnic nose. Unshaven, whiskered cheeks…

A black demon.

Green-tinged amber eyes stared, unblinking. Lithesome rather than lecherous, the Peeping Tom stuck out his tongue, then lifted one foot to cleanse the callused pads between his needle-claws.

I looked at Andre. "Who let Snow outside on the patio?"

"You did, Frannie, and it's not a patio. It's a goddamn balcony."

Last summer I had decided to convert our patio…balcony…into a greenhouse. When I was a kid, *The Secret Garden* was one of my favorite books. However, since I killed our house plants with disturbing regularity, the plan had never materialized. Sometimes Andre cooked hamburgers atop a tiny Hibachi grill. Sometimes I tossed our fat black cat out there so he could fill his lungs with polluted city air.

After we had the cat neutered, we changed his name from Snowball to Snow, and Andre swore Snow's I-need-pussy meow had mutated.

According to Andre, Snow now sounded like Streisand. To me, he sounded the same as always. Screechy, as if his whiskers were being zapped by an electrologist.

Rising to my feet, I walked to the window, opened it, and watched my fat cat leap from sill to radiator to rocking chair. A window philodendron tottered and fell. "I planned to trim the leaves anyway," I said, staring at dirt, tangled roots, and stems.

"What leaves?" Andre said.

The phone rang. I recognized the ring. It was strident. It whined. It procrastinated and justified. It was my agent.

It was my mother.

"Daddy wondered if you'd like to bring your boyfriend over for a Sunday cook-out," she said. Although she had lived on Long Island for twenty-five years, her voice retained her Chicago syllable stress. In fact, she could have announced home games for the Chicago Cubs.

She knew how to phrase a question, too. The invitation came from Daddy. Mother couldn't care less.

"My boyfriend has a name, Andre Vaughn," I said. "Gee Mom, I think we're busy Sunday."

"You think? Why don't you check your calendar, Frannie? Your father hasn't seen you in weeks. He misses you, worries about you."

Daddy misses me. Daddy worries. Jewish guilt. Talk about passing the buck. On the other hand, Daddy passed me bucks while Mom mailed me wedding notices clipped from local newspapers. Birth announcements, too. And self-stick memos. "Remember your stupnagel cousin Charlene?" Mom had once written, her microscopic handwriting embellishing the sticky square. "Charlene is married to an accountant, teaches junior high school, and just had a baby girl." Jewish subtlety.

IT'S A BOY read the card I mailed when Andre and I adopted Snow.

I ran to the bathroom and washed away Andre's proof of desire, hoping Mom would believe I was checking my calendar.

"If you have to go potty," she said when I returned to the phone, "you could at least offer to call me back."

"Sorry," I said, thinking that my mother was more clairvoyant than Mrs. Carvainis.

"How's Anne Frank?"

It took a moment. "Fine," I said, glancing toward the movie poster.

"What about Sunday, Frannie?"

Okay. I got the connection. Anne had been shut up inside an attic, and would have given anything for freedom and fresh air. Anne Frank didn't let weeks go by without an obligatory parental visit.

"I'm scheduled to work at the restaurant," I fibbed. "Big church crowd. Italians eat humongous meals after church. Mussels Marinara, calamari …that's squid, Mother…cannelloni, veal parmigiano, yum."

Mom exhaled her martyr's sigh. "I'll tell Daddy tonight, after pot roast and marzipan, when he's relaxed and his blood pressure's not too high. He canceled his business trip so he'd be home. He's getting older, Frannie. Soon he'll retire and we'll move to Florida."

Shit. Four guilt zingers in four sentences. "Maybe the manager will change my shift," I said.

"Daddy said to tell you he'd pay for Long Island Railroad tickets and pick you up at the station."

"Mom, did you…" I hesitated, the question on the tip of my tongue. *Did you have another child? Stillborn?* But I couldn't ask. It would be like one of the Brady Bunchers asking Florence Henderson if she'd ever had an abortion. "I'll, um, see you Sunday. Bye."

Andre watched me wait for a dial tone before I slammed down the receiver. Then he said, "Why do you do that?"

"Do what?"

"Purposely irritate your mother. She hates it when you talk about waiting tables and, eventually, you cave in."

"You're a WASP from Wisconsin, Andre. What do you know about Jewish guilt?"

"I'm learning."

"We could make my mother happy and get married."

"Do you want to get married, Frannie?"

"No. If we were married, she'd start nagging about babies and job security."

"Speaking of job security…" Andre said, returning to his chair and script.

The phone rang. My mom has a habit of calling back a few minutes after hanging up. Usually she says something like: "Do you dead-bolt the door, Frannie? I don't want you getting raped in your sleep."

I've heard that getting-raped-in-your-sleep crap at least a million times, and I've always wanted to tell Mom that I'd definitely be awake.

Pressing the phone's receiver against my ear, I said, "Andre and I are talking marriage and two-point-four children. We'll name them all after Grandpa Irving, even the girls. Then I'll finish college and teach junior high, just like my stupnagel cousin Charlene. Okay?"

"If you plan to be a teacher, cookie, you won't be interested in my news," said a male voice. Harris. My agent.

"What news?"

"They want you to audition for *The Exorcist*."

"They've already filmed *The Exorcist*. Is this a re-make?"

"Did I say exorcist? I meant *Forever Asmodeus*. They want you to audition for the part of a double."

"A stunt double?"

"Not a stunt girl, cookie, a—"

"Stand in? No way."

Harris exhaled my mother's patented martyr-sigh. "If you'd just zip your mouth shut and let me explain. *Forever Asmodeus* is about a young teenager who becomes possessed by a demon. They're testing a thirteen-year-old girl for the role, but they don't think she's capable of performing a certain scene. They want someone her size and shape to play the scene. Are you following me?"

Ignoring his discourteous thirteen-year-old shape clarification, I said, "What a funny coincidence. I found that book on a bus and planned to read it tonight. Maria Shriver and Barbara Walters both interviewed the author. Sex, religion and exorcism…yum."

"Want to hear another funny co-inky-dink, cookie? I didn't even know the part was up for grabs until this African American lady delivered a memo to my office."

Harris always calls white women "girls" and black women "ladies," as if he's afraid a black revolutionary will picket his office, holding aloft a signs that says: YOU CAN'T RUN FASTER THAN A BULLET.

"A memo?" I said.

"Yeah. A casting memo. Straight from the horse's mouth."

"Whoa. You've lost me, Harris."

"Maybe you met some big shot at one of your bars—"

"One of my bars?"

"—and made a good impression, because the part fits you like a glove. They even want your color hair. Look, cookie, that Asmodeus book is trash," Harris said, as if he ever read anything except *Variety, BackStage,* and an occasional Jackie Collins excerpt. "But they're looking for a good actress, and it could lead to other roles."

"Who is *they*, Harris?"

"Victor Madison."

Victor Madison. The most famous horror film director in Hollywood.

"First," Harris said, "you have to get past Suzanne Burton."

Suzanne Burton. The most famous casting agent in Manhattan.

"You have an interview with Burton tomorrow, cookie, at three o'clock. Don't be late."

The appointment had already been set. Like my mother, Harris knew I wouldn't say no.

I hung up the phone and turned to Andre. "That was my agent."

"I'm not deaf, Frannie."

"I have an interview with Suzanne Burton for a Victor Madison film. What do you think of that?"

"I think you promised to make me a tuna sandwich."

"I mean Mrs. Carvainis, Andre. She mentioned demons and Bonnie dreamed—"

"Can't we discuss demonic conjecture after lunch?"

"It's way past lunchtime, and why are you so cranky?"

"Because it's just an interview, Frannie. But you'll get your hopes up, buy something stupid, brag to your mother, and crash big-time if they cast someone else."

"The interview is tomorrow, Andre. I don't have time to buy something stupid."

"When you make my sandwich, don't cut the crusts off the bread."

"And I won't call my mother."

"Not too much mayo, please, and no celery."

"Hey, I'm not Wendy."

"I said please." Andre grinned. "If you make my sandwich, I'll sew your shadow back on."

"Okay, deal." Scooping up Snow, I headed for our kitchenette. Then, dicing celery, I thought about Andre.

He knew everything about me, including my Mother Goose debut. But he was reticent about his background, and I would have discovered very little had it not been for his soap opera contract celebration. He had become roaring drunk and talkative, repeating what his father (roaring drunk and talkative) had once told him. Later, I wove together the bits and pieces.

The first of seven children, thirty-one-year-old Andre had been born and raised on a Wisconsin dairy farm. His mother, a farmer's daughter by the name of Joan Cunnings, had succumbed to a traveling salesman named Henry Vaughn. Joan Cunnings would cover her calendar with big red X's, marking the days until "Hank" would visit the farm and lead her up into the dusky hayloft. One month Joan's period never came and Hank, unfortunately, had...and did.

With regularity. Soon seven little Vaughns, like seven little Foys, were performing inside the barn, underneath the hayloft where Mommy had gotten screwed. The infamous hayloft became Andre's casting couch for any pretty neighbor who wanted a starring role. When the prettiest married his brother, he packed his bags and fled to New York.

"Where's my sandwich, woman?" Framed by an archway, Andre gave me a smile that would melt Oscar.

"Almost finished, man. I just have to cut the crusts off."

"Frannie, I like crust. Is sandwich circumcision a Jewish tradition?"

"No, Andre, my mother always made me eat my crusts."

I took a bite of leftover tuna, thoroughly enjoying the gobs of tart mayonnaise and the satisfying crunch of celery. "Andre," I said, "did you know that Clark Gable made love to Carole Lombard in a duck blind? Gable also bragged that he had made love in a canoe, phone booth, swimming pool, and on top of a fire escape."

"Frankly, my dear, I don't give a damn."

"Do you think they named Clark candy bars for Gable?"

"Frannie, you ask such stupid questions."

"Let's find a duck blind, or a canoe, and you can teach me how to fly. Do you think Wendy Darling wore panties underneath her sedate nightie? Disney's artists have no guts, no *chutzpah*. Don't you think Peter Pan's green tights should have flaunted an animated penis?"

"Grow up," Andre said, spitting pieces of celery into his hand as if they were cherry pits.

Lured by the smell of tuna, Snow jumped up onto the counter, pressed his furry face against Andre's palm, nosed each discarded leafstalk chip, then gave me a haughty cat-glare.

"I'm sorry, I'm sorry," I said, first to Andre, then Snow. "I always forget how much you hate celery."

"Maybe when you grow up you'll remember," Andre said, cranky again.

Low blow. I'd show my WASP lover how ageless I could be, after I auditioned for the part of a thirteen-year-old.

SIX

Suzanne Burton, head casting director for one of the most exclusive agencies in New York City, was in her early fifties. She looked forty. I had a feeling she had always looked forty, and always would. She wore black-and-white plaid slacks. A chrome-colored blouse rode over the slacks, cinched about her waist by a Sterling belt. Her short hair had been frosted silver. Her eyes were squirrel-gray. I wondered if she color-coordinated her hair and eyes to match her clothes.

Her office surprised me.

I had anticipated a testimonial wall, cluttered with autographed photos. I had pictured phones galore, blue-penciled scripts, and an open window for the occasional swan dive.

Instead, her carpet was salmon, and her beige walls boasted one Wylie Jamestone painting. Across from her computer desk, atop a Lucite desk, were CD, TV, VCR and fax machine. And her picture window, closed, had no sill.

She studied me for several moments, taking in my tweed jumper over thin white turtleneck, my black tights and Capezzio slippers. My hair, in one thick braid, fell to my shoulder blades, and I'd shunned makeup ...except for mascara and pale pink lipstick.

Had I overdone the teenage bit?

"Sit down, Ms. Rose," she said.

"Please call me Frannie, Ms. Burton." Sinking into a gray leather chair, I hoped she'd tell me to call her Suzanne.

"How tall are you, dear?"

From Ms. to dear...a good sign? "Five three," I said, adding a half an inch.

"We're looking for a small actress. Your agent...uh..."

"Harris, first name T. Murphy," I supplied.

"Yes. Of course." She looked as if she was Rolodexing the name, filing it sequentially—Harris Julie, Harris T. Murphy, Harris Tweed, Harrison George. "I've seen quite a few young women, Ms. Rose, but they didn't have the strength to play our demon-girl."

"I've got strength, Ms. Burton. I've had horseback riding and ballet lessons, and I belong to a health club."

"The young woman we cast will probably do two scenes, but the scenes are very important. Have you read the book, dear?"

No. Last night I shunned the Laundromat, re-read The Secret Garden, and doodled a patio greenhouse. "No," I said. "Not yet. I wanted to audition cold. I mean, fresh. Without any preconceived notions. I mean, um, impressions."

Shit, I sounded like a stuttering thesaurus. Darting a glance at the window, I wondered if it opened. Maybe I could make a quick exit and hit the pavement.

"Read the book and come back…" Suzanne Burton consulted her appointment book. "I'll squeeze you in tomorrow, same time."

Whereupon, she dismissed me via the door.

Forever Asmodeus recounted the story of a fat and frumpy teen who strikes a bargain with a demon. Physical transformation occurs, and Robin, the protagonist, possessed by Asmodeus, sets out to be promiscuous. The deal includes an heir, and the demon isn't choosy.

After her metamorphosis, Robin looks like a pretty teen, unless she's near a mirror. Her reflection is grotesque. Naturally, she tries to avoid mirrors. This is difficult in places like the school locker room (cheerleader is a given) and a shopping mall's boutique.

Her parents discover the transformation. They get in touch with a TV evangelist who is being touted as a Presidential candidate, and beg him to exorcise the demon. After approximately five hundred pages, Robin's parents are satisfied, never realizing that Asmodeus—sneaky devil—has possessed Robin's infant sister, paving the way for a sequel.

Harris was spot-on. Trash. Yet, the book was a page-turner. And the author had struck at the heart of this adult's childhood fantasy. During my overweight, insecure youth, it would have taken me less than the blink of an eye to accept Asmo's demands. Internal possession for physical beauty and popularity? You betcha.

* * *

Suzanne Burton's receptionist greeted me like a long lost stranger. Her expression fairly shouted: "Gate-crasher." Obviously disappointed that I wasn't Russell Crowe, Cameron Crowe, or even an animated crow in *Dumbo*, she handed me a script and returned her myopic gaze to her computer screen.

Suzanne had meant it when she said she'd squeeze me in. I waited five, ten, twenty minutes, then began to compose rap lyrics. The receptionist's ersatz fingernails-on-keyboard made great background music. I rapped three verses and was working on the fourth. *I want this job, I need some dollars, I bought something stupid, and Andre will holler. I want this freaking job, I need the bucks, I called my mother...*

"Thank you for your patience, Ms. Rose."

This time Ms. Burton wore a gray dress and matching suede boots. "I want improvisation," she said, once we had entered her office. "Use the dialogue if you wish, but focus on action."

Tossing the script sides toward her desk, I fell onto the salmon carpet. Inside my head, I heard a real rap song, a song The Spa often used for aerobics sessions. I twisted, turned, writhed, grunted, and the pain was real. Playing Robin-Asmodeus, I gave Suzanne two-for-one; a shy, giggly teen and a growly demon. Then I looked up, craving strokes, having just given the best audition in my so-called career.

"That was fine," Suzanne understated. "Monday I need you to meet with Sol Aarons at the CBS studios, inside the makeup room. Have you heard of Aarons?"

Sol Aarons. The most famous makeup artist in the world.

"Who hasn't?" I said.

"I'd like you to lose a few pounds, dear."

"Lose a few pounds," I parroted.

"We're considering a nude scene for Robin. Do you have a problem with that?"

Oh my God. Mom would plotz. Or else she'd nag Daddy into early retirement and move to Israel; a desert kibbutz with no movie house.

I shrugged, playing it cool. At the same time, I wondered what Andre would say. He'd probably say, "Forget Jewish inhibitions."

Suzanne gave me a have-a-nice-day smile. Then she said, "Next Thursday I'd like you to audition for Victor. Victor Madison."

The name wafted through her office on gossamer wings. Vic-tor Mad-i-son. The name floated like a helium balloon. No. A kite. No...

I scratched my brain for the perfect interpretation. How about syllabic light beams sculpting symphonic cobwebs?

In other words, Suzanne verbally caressed Victor Madison's name.

Weren't cobwebs sticky?

"Frannie, you ask such stupid questions," I said, after I'd hit the pavement.

SEVEN

Makeup artist Sol Aarons, 50-something, looked so rogue-ish, I imagined him as the kind of kid who drew caricatures of his teachers and pulverized the school bully. I hadn't sketched my teachers, but I'd pulverized the school bully. And for one brief shining moment, around age twelve, I'd seriously considered a career as a fashion designer. To that end, using lined notebook paper, I'd tried to turn Little Lulu and Sluggo into Archie and Veronica, complete with avant-garde wardrobe.

Sol and I became pals in the twinkle of an eye.

"I have to make a full mask of your face," he said, his blue eyes twinkling, "to see if it matches the face of the girl Suzanne wants for Robin. Her name is Lynn. Lynn Beth Sullivan." After fishing a Tsingtao from a Styrofoam cooler, Sol's expression turned rueful. "One of my addictions," he said, hefting the bottle. "You can have a beer later if you like, Frannie, but right now you must sit very still. The procedure is uncomfortable, but I want you to try and keep your teeth apart so the mouth is structurally sound. Okay?"

"Sure," I said, instinctively flexing my jaw.

Sol's studio looked like Bloomingdale's cosmetics department, except for the two bald swordsmen who stood next to large tubs of colorful base. Their names were Oscar and Oscar.

I had seen them on TV, having only missed the Academy Awards once, at age thirteen, when my appendix began rupturing. But now, for some dumb reason, I noticed that Oscar had no genitalia.

Seated in front of the dressing room mirror, I scrutinized Sol's reflection. A full mane of brown hair, a Wyatt Earp mustache, sapphire eyes, and ears studded with diamonds filled in my mental Etch-a-Sketch.

I felt comfortable but grungy in my faded Levi's and waitress tuxedo shirt, eternally stained with Caesar salad dressing. Although laundered at least a million times, the shirt still smelled of anchovies.

Sol met my eyes in the mirror. "When I was a boy I used to put on scary makeup to fool my friends," he said, smootching grease all over my face. Then he had me close my eyes and breathe through a straw while he told me about his makeup sessions with Marlon Brando and Dustin Hoffman.

"Well?" I said, after Sol had removed the outer plaster mask and some loose, floppy silicone.

"Well, what?" He gently dislodged tiny shreds that still garnished my eyelashes, then handed me a Tsingtao.

I sneezed and wiped my nose on my rolled-up sleeve. "Will my face match the other girl?"

"I don't know, darling, you were first. Lynn Beth is due here Wednesday."

"Then I guess I'll find out Thursday, unless…" I knocked on wood and clapped three times. "Unless Suzanne calls…" I tried to sound like the witch who'd worn a prom dress and burst onto the screen in a bubble; the Oz Munchkinland witch. "Unless Suzanne calls and cancels my audition with the great and powerful Victor Madison."

Was it my imagination, or did Sol grip his beer bottle as if it had become the only tangible object in the room? However, I was unable to read the expression in his sapphire eyes.

Resentment? Defiance? Bitterness?

His demeanor suddenly turned normal again, assuming normal meant cautiously placing his Tsingtao on the table, picking up his two Oscars, and hefting them like dumbbells. Then he handed me one.

I gazed into the mirror and visualized my acceptance speech.

Holding Oscar against my face, I felt heat radiate from its Charlton-Heston-Ben-Hur body.

Even without the genitalia, Oscar generated desire.

In other words, I felt horny.

Wasn't Hornie a Scottish nickname for the devil?

Frannie, you ask such stupid questions.

That night, while moisturizing my face, I discovered an almost imperceptible half-moon-shaped burn on my right cheekbone.

I wanted to tell Bonnie about my makeup session with Sol, but I got her answering machine. Trying not to sound like my mother, I left Bonnie a message. Then I called my mother.

"Make sure you wash every bit of that greasy gunk off," she said, "or you'll get pimples."

EIGHT

"Damn, damn, damn. I don't know what to wear."

"Frannie, what's the difference? If you hurry, we can share a cab." Clothed in sockless sneakers, jeans, his/our *Les Miserables* sweatshirt, and a Mets warm-up jacket, Andre paced up and down the bedroom.

"I want to make a good impression on Victor Madison," I said, "but I'm supposed to double for a thirteen-year-old girl. Don't you think I should look young and innocent?"

"Absolutely. What did you wear when you played Jill?"

It took a moment. "Overalls and a beanie. But Jack peed his pants and exited stage left. God forbid Victor Madison should pee his pants and exit stage left. Please, Andre, please. Tell me what to wear."

"Why don't you call your mother and ask *her*?"

That shut me up. I stared at my empty closet. Then I stared at every piece of clothing I owned, spread out across the waterbed.

"Andre, you have a part in a soap," I said. "You shot a shaving gel commercial that was actually shown on TV. I make tuna sandwiches and clean Snow's litter box and vacuum our ersatz Oriental carp—"

"Enough, Frannie." He tossed me a pair of pink linen slacks and a white blouse. "Too bad you're not auditioning for the part of a Jewish demon. Guilt is definitely your forte."

I tried not to wail. "This stupid blouse is wrinkled."

"A blouse isn't stupid, Frannie. A person who refuses to iron is stupid."

"If God wanted me to iron, She'd have given me hot hands."

With exaggerated patience, Andre sorted out the mess on our bed. Then, like the butler in an Agatha Cristie movie, he handed me a short-sleeved sweater crocheted in pink and white stripes.

"Nice," I said, "but it's tight and shows too much cleavage."

"What cleavage?"

He had a point. "How should I fix my hair, honey?

"Christ, I don't know. Shave it off or mousse it into Shirley Temple curls."

"All right, be that way. You have a part—"

"Gotta run, Frannie. My producer called. She has new scripts. With luck, I'll emerge from my coma. I hate breathing through that nose plug. Good luck, babe."

Andre gave me a quick kiss and exited stage left.

I wondered if it mattered what I wore? Suzanne had called. Sol hadn't finished the face-masks yet, and Madison wanted my audition to take place inside his hotel suite. Why? Did he want me to perform the nude scene she'd mentioned? If yes, clothes wouldn't matter. Suzanne would be there, too. I remembered telling Andre I wasn't into kinky. Were Suzanne and Madison into kinky? I tried to erase that thought because, to be perfectly honest, ever since my meeting with Sol I'd been feeling hungry, passionate, inspired. Andre hadn't made love to me since my psychic-pathic visit, and a threesome sounded…intriguing.

No. Never. I was monogamous, would always be monogamous. Asmodeus had nothing to fear.

Asmodeus? Christ, I'd just had a brain-glitch, probably because I had re-read the book last night and Asmodeus, sneaky devil, was on my mind. My mind recovered the fumble. *Andre* had nothing to fear.

I brushed my hair into a ponytail and cloaked my cotton-candy-colored outfit with a vintage Brooklyn Dodger's warm-up jacket. Then I locked the apartment, navigated five staircases two-steps-at-a-time, and waited impatiently for the bus. While waiting, I tried to conjure up an image of a demon, but all I could visualize was Tenia's rattlesnake. So I'd use the snake, if Madison wanted a Robin-Asmodeus improvisation. Hissing through my teeth, I began to feel malevolent.

Madison's hotel fronted Fifth Avenue, across from the park, and I was too early. Seated atop a grassy knoll near a duck pond, I watched molten sunshine accentuate drake feathers. The ducks quack-quacked, and it was difficult to sustain malevolence. Until I pictured fangs between their bills and claws between their webbed feet.

I wouldn't collect one of Sol's Oscars for the role of a double, but Harris had said it could lead to other parts if Victor Madison liked my work. I wanted to be good, and good meant bad.

Once upon a time, while wandering through the city, I had walked into an art gallery and seen a portrait of Madison. The exhibit included photos of Marilyn Monroe, the Beatles, Walt Disney, Alfred Hitchcock, Garbo, Janis Joplin, Steven Spielberg—legends in black and white.

Especially black. Against a pure black background, Madison had stared directly into the camera. His hair was so dark, you couldn't see the shape of his head. His face was a pale mask, with onyx eyes and a cruel, sensual mouth.

Under each framed portrait, the photographer had included a quotation.

Marilyn Monroe: "Hollywood is a place where they'll pay you a thousand dollars for a kiss and fifty cents for your soul."

Disney: "Every time they make a pornographic film, I make money."

Joplin: "You can destroy your now by worrying about tomorrow."

Victor Madison had quoted Shakespeare. *King Lear.* "The prince of darkness is a gentleman."

Madison's photo also graced my friend Mickey Roebuck's loft, but Madison's face had been distorted by dart punctures, leaving the impression that something (greasy gunk, maybe) had induced pimples.

My watch said it was time to meet a living legend. I felt like Alice in Wonderland. Only instead of cartwheeling down a rabbit hole, I was about to fall through the pages of a movie magazine. I remembered Alice's "Oh, dear" upon meeting the Queen of Hearts.

That broke the spell. I would have said, "Oh, shit."

Riding the elevator, I listened to Manilow Muzak.

NINE

Suzanne responded to my knock. I didn't cartwheel or fall, simply marched into Victor Madison's suite, the last notes from Barry's *Copa* still inside my head, establishing my rhythm.

Oh, dear. Shaking the famous horror film director's hand, I mumbled, "It's a pleasuretomeetchca."

Andre would have compared me to Snow during a thunderstorm. I felt as if someone had handed me Alice's eat-me-drink-me potion, except my eyes, rather than my body, had grown too big.

Madison wore black jeans, basketball sneakers, a charcoal-gray Oxford shirt, and a black V-neck sweater. With his short dark hair and black-rimmed glasses, he looked like Clark Kent. Where was my man in the art gallery? Where was my Prince of Darkness? Only his eyes retained that sinister, brooding quality.

Without being obnoxious, he examined me from head to toe, and I wondered if he had X-ray vision. Could he see my breakfast bagel and ersatz cappuccino—half Maxwell House coffee, half 2% chocolate milk?

As if she'd read my mind, Suzanne said, "Do you want something to drink or eat, Ms. Rose?"

"No, thank you."

"Then I'd like you to reenact the scene you performed for me in my office," she said.

"Here?"

"No, the bedroom." Madison tapped the ash from his cigarette into a water glass. "That's where Robin has her confrontations with Asmodeus, and a bed has to more comfortable than the floor."

His voice was deep, with a slight Brooklyn accent. I had expected Cary Grant, and felt somewhat soothed by the regional diction.

Madison offered me one of his Marlboros. I've never smoked but my shaky fingers needed a provisional prop, so I put the cigarette between my lips a la James Dean, then watched Madison reach toward a nearby table and pick up a silver lighter engraved: **TO M FROM S**.

M...Madison. S...Suzanne?

As he flicked the lighter, Suzanne said, "Are you ready, dear?"

Shedding my jacket, I killed my un-smoked cigarette in an ashtray filled with gold candy foil. Then I entered the bedroom and glanced around.

An ornately-framed Isabelle Copley painting enhanced one wall. The window view looked like an illustration for a Big Apple postcard. A lawn-mower wouldn't have sneered at the plush carpet, and the dresser beneath a beveled mirror had so many drawers, Madison could have opened a *Gap* franchise. Dominating a small table was a steel sculpture that resembled a winged baboon.

Striving to sound worldly rather than dumb, I said, "Who made, uh, sculpted the sculpture?"

"Picasso," Madison replied.

"Really?" My Picasso encounters included my Aunt Brenna's coffee table book, several visits to the Museum of Modern Art, and one Picasso quote: "Art is a lie that makes us realize truth."

"Really." Madison smiled. "It's a replica, of course. The original struc-ture stands 50 feet high and weighs 163 tons, but I like to take this one with me when I travel."

"Why?" To me, it still resembled a baboon. Or a gargoyle.

Madison smiled again. "It soothes my soul."

I wanted to ask him why his soul needed soothing, but Suzanne said, "Shall we begin?"

Taking a deep breath, actually several deep breaths, I hit the bed.

Madison watched.

Suzanne watched.

I could almost swear someone else was watching, too, even though there was nobody else in the room.

The mirror. It had to be the mirror. Somebody, or some *thing*, was in the mirror, watching me.

Was I nuts? Or had I seen too many Wes Craven movies?

I tried to ignore the mirror. I remembered the book; Robin trying to avoid mirrors. She hadn't succeeded. Half of me said this was good, I could use Robin's tension for the audition. Half of me said this was bad, crazy, scary. The third half told me to run like hell.

I don't know why I didn't run. Maybe because I had blabbed to my mother, telling her about the audition ("Promise you won't say anything, Mom."), knowing she'd call her sister, my stupnagel cousin Charlene's mother, as soon as I hung up the phone. Or maybe it was because half number one sounded a lot more persuasive than half number three.

Almost instantly, I realized that implementing the mental picture of Tenia's snake would never fly. I wanted Robin to be terror-stricken, but the image of a rattlesnake would render her motionless, unable to flail out at her adversary.

"Take your time," Madison said.

"Do you need to use the bathroom, dear?" Suzanne sounded impatient.

"No." A shiver traveled up and down my spine. The bedroom felt cold, almost frosty, but that wasn't the reason for my shivery sensation. Fact was, I didn't need to use the bathroom. I needed to *hide* inside the bathroom. Because, to my chagrin, I couldn't perform. I couldn't do that scene, or any other scene. I didn't give a rat's spit if Suzanne and Madison critiqued my presentation, but I was paralyzed by whomever, or whatever, lived inside that mirror.

Suddenly, I heard clicks.

Slanting a glance toward the mirror, I saw beetles avalanche from its scrolled wooden frame and tumble to the dresser. Most landed upside-down. As I watched, unable to look away, they righted themselves with a click.

Christ. If I opened my mouth the click-beetles would crawl inside.

Fuck the improvisation. I wanted to go home. Fuck Asmodeus.

Without warning, ice-cold fingers unzipped my fly and tugged my slacks down my hips.

"No," I screamed.

"Good," Madison said. "I like that interpretation."

His voice seemed to come from far away. But the clicks sounded closer. Had the beetles tumbled to the floor?

Still on the bed, I felt my body flop like a grounded fish. My slacks and panties were down around my ankles, shackling my feet. Icy fingers rubbed back and forth, back and forth, in a mesmerizing rhythm of continuity. I was burning up and shivering at the same time.

"Don't," I begged. "Please. Leave me alone."

"Good," Madison said.

CLICK. CLICK. CLICKCLICKCLICK.

"Why are you doing this?" Even to my own ears, my voice sounded plaintive, the whimper of a young, scared little girl.

With the greatest effort of my life, I moved my hands toward the icy fingers between my thighs.

Nothing. No icy fingers.

CLICK. CLICK. CLICK. CLICK.

"Get away from me."

"Good," Madison said.

Now *my* fingers were rubbing…and I couldn't stop. I began to shudder. On the verge of an orgasm, I squeezed my eyes shut.

The clicks diminished, but behind my closed eyelids I saw a tidal wave of *animals.* Carnivorous. Herbivorous. Insectivorous. Omnivorous. Equine. Bovine. Canine. Feline…

And they all wanted to feast on the moisture between my thighs.

I tried to raise my lashes but they seemed glued to my cheeks, and all I could do was blink with my eyes closed.

"Good," Madison said. "Very good."

And very good meant very bad.

I must have blacked out, at least momentarily. When I became fully aware of my surroundings, Madison was leading me from the bedroom. He announced that he'd screen-test me right away, how about tomorrow? When I nodded, he said, "I've never seen an improvisation like that before. It looked real."

I wanted to ask him if I'd really masturbated, but I couldn't. It would be like June Cleaver asking Wally if the Beaver had locked himself inside the bathroom with a copy of *Playboy.*

"Yes, oh yes, that was terrific." Suzanne sounded stunned and smug at the same time.

Jesus Christ. Everything looked and felt so normal.

Did I imagine the click-beetles?

Did I imagine that whole orgasmic sequence?

Maybe I had performed an erotic aerobics session.

Comedian Mort Sahl once said his life needed editing. I edited my audition. I had used The Method, I decided, which I'd learned, studied, memorized in college. Igor Stravinsky. Good old Iggy.

The door to the suite opened. Sol Aarons, a woman, and a young girl entered. There were introductions.

I stared at Lynn Beth Sullivan. Like the first initial of her last name, every descriptive adjective began with S. Slinky. Sexy. Sensual. Seductive. Sinfully superb.

Sunk. I was sinking fast. She was only thirteen, yet my pink and white sweater emphasized breasts one third the size of hers.

Beneath a fake fur jacket, she wore a blue Cashmere sweater, white, butt-tight jeans, and high-heeled boots.

Her mother, Dawn Meidam Sullivan, was pretty. Dawn's brown eyes were a tad too small, but her auburn cloud of hair was lush, her nose and mouth patrician. She had clothed herself in a dun-colored, shapeless, too-long dress, and a pair of dreadful canvas shoes. Could she have chosen that outfit on purpose? Maybe, wanting the spotlight to shine on her daughter, she'd sacrificed her own curves. Maybe she was color-blind.

Madison told me to stand next to Lynn. Her ginger perm blended nicely with my pale gold ponytail. She was half an inch taller, but we both had cat-colored eyes and cleft chins. We could have been sisters.

Except for our bodies. In my youth, I might have bargained with Asmodeus for Lynn Beth Sullivan's body.

Sol Aarons said the makeup tests were working out fine.

Scratching my brain for an exit line, I glanced toward Suzanne. She twined her arm through Madison's while he tried to flick his silver lighter and light Dawn Sullivan's cigarette.

M...Madison. S...Sullivan?

"We look alike, don't we?"

I turned to Lynn Beth and said, "We sure do."

"This is my first movie," she said. "You probably have a list of credits a mile long."

Right. Jill the Aquarian, two aging Marthas, Maggie the Cat, a fat and frumpy soap teen, and eleven lines in an Off-Off Broadway show. I told Lynn about the "Broadway" show.

"I've never been on the stage," she said, "but my agent sent me to an Annie audition once. I didn't get the part. My voice sucks."

"Who's your agent?"

She mentioned one of the biggies, then said, "My first agent was a friend of Mommy's. He signed me when I was a child."

Mommy? I tried to remember when I had gone from Mommy to Mom. Around age eight. By thirteen it was Mother, with two syllables.

"I did some commercials...Kellogs, Nabisco, Campbell soup, Kraft cheese and macaroni," Lynn Beth said, as if rattling off a grocery list. "And I played a kid on a series pilot, a sit-com, only it wasn't picked up by any of the networks. Then I grew."

"Too old?"

"Too big," she said, and I knew she meant her cleavage. "Mommy met

Madison a long time ago. When she heard he was looking for a someone my age to star in his new movie, she wrote him a letter and sent him a picture. Isn't that lucky?"

Her voice lacked…intensity….so I said, "Do you like acting, Lynn Beth?"

"I guess so. I'm not very good."

Not very good meant not very evil. I couldn't help thinking that if Lynn Beth couldn't play the possession scenes, I could.

"Mommy says it doesn't matter. She says directors like to direct, so even if I'm not good but look the part, I'll get cast. She was wrong about Annie." Lynn Beth shrugged. "Mr. Madison wants Jeremy Glenn for the evangelist. And they've asked Paul Simon to write a theme song. Isn't that awesome?"

For the first time she sounded like an enthusiastic teen. Paul for the music. And Jeremy Glenn…dear God, how many times had I stood behind that yellow crime tape, looking like Ellen Burstyn in *The Exorcist* or Jamie Lee Curtis in *Halloween,* when all I wanted to do was sidle up next to Jeremy and hand him my apartment key?

Correction: my loft key. I had been sharing Mickey Roebuck's loft when Jeremy, who's Canadian, played a New York Cop. Jeremy still plays a cop, except now they shoot his popular TV show in Canada.

Jeremy Glenn. Tall, dark, handsome, and—from what I've heard —straight. Very.

Bringing my attention back to Lynn Beth, I agreed that Jeremy and Paul were awesome.

"They've asked Catherine Lee Sands to play my mother," she said.

"Lynn Beth." Dawn Sullivan cupped her hands around her mouth like a megaphone, even thought she couldn't have been more than a few feet away. "Mr. Madison wants you."

"Okay, Mommy. Bye, Frannie."

Dawn stared at me, but I couldn't read her expression.

Jealousy? Hostility? Resentment? Contempt?

"I suppose we'll see you at the screen test tomorrow," she said, giving me my exit line.

"Tomorrow," I said, never realizing that Alice had just taken a giant leap through the looking glass.

TEN

Three hours later, Mickey "Samson" Roebuck let me off in front of my apartment building, then un-cinched my bulging pocketbook from the back of his motorcycle.

Texan to the core of his six-foot-four-inch body, Samson had been born in San Antonio. Half Mexican, half Irish, he wore his red-black hair in a thick Willie Nelson braid. Despite his obvious physical attributes, it was the hair that had contributed to Samson's nickname. Turquoise eyes matched his choice of jewelry.

Samson "dabbled in professions." Among other things, he'd been an actor, a nightclub stripper, a sommelier des vins, and a model. When his wealthy parents died, leaving an inheritance, he resolved to become a best-selling author. Since he didn't have a starving-artists-live-in-cheap-garrets perspective, he leased an expensive loft and shared it with a variety of homeless cats. Andre and I sometimes teased each other with movie dialogue. Samson and I liked to play *Jeopardy*.

I had run into him at the library, where he had been researching film erotica. I, of course, wanted to research demons. When I told him why, he looked pensive. Then, like a dog shaking water out of its fur, his attitude changed. Whereupon, we'd gleefully harmonized *Ding-Dong The Wicked Witch Is Dead* until people shushed us.

Now, he kissed my forehead and said, "Good luck."

"Thanks," I said. "Hey, wait. Didn't you once work with Madison?"

"Yes, ma'am. I was an extra in his first film."

"What did he look like then? I mean, in his misspent youth?"

"We extras rarely saw him. When we did, his eyes seemed to flash black lightning."

"A prince of darkness?"

Samson grinned. "Ah, *King Lear*. Yes, ma'am, that's a good way to describe Victor Madison. Don't forget to say hello to Andre for me. How is your hunk?"

"Hunky."

Samson doesn't like Andre. I'm not sure how Andre feels about Samson, except I think Andre thinks he's gay. But while Samson has never been romantically involved with a woman, I never saw him bring another man to the loft, and I sponged off my darling Samson for nine months. My mother disapproved. And approved. The downside was that Samson doesn't have a Jewish bone in his body. The upside was his money and his loft, which has a kitchen to die for and *two* dead bolts.

He tucked an errant curl behind my ear. "Frannie, I hate to sound like a Greek chorus, and I rarely spread rumors, but the grapevine says Andre will soon be gearing up for trips to the unemployment office."

Aha, I thought. *That's why Samson seemed so cerebral when he bumped into me at the library.* Aloud I said, "That's bitchy, Samson. Your grapevine must be full of jealous raisins."

"I'm glad for your sake, darlin'. Keep the faith."

"'To have faith is to have wings.' Quote, unquote."

"The Wright Brothers," Samson said.

"You forgot to put it in the form of a question," I said.

"Who are the Wright Brothers?"

"Wrong," I said, trying to sound like Alex Trebec. "J.M. Barrie."

After Samson's small puff of pollution had turned the corner, I entered my apartment building. Slowly navigating the stairs, I wondered if it could be true? Unemployed? Andre?

I greeted Snow and saw that my other roommate was missing. So, after going potty, I checked my answering machine.

The first message was from my agent, Harris, who last week couldn't remember my name.

"Frannie sweetheart," he said, "you're not home."

The second message was from Mom, another one-liner: "I guess you're not home."

The third message was also from Mom. I had left my sweater at the cook-out, did I want her to mail it back?

The fourth message…Mom again. I was to tell Anthony thanks for the flowers, it was very thoughtful but not necessary. And I should NOT tell him the flowers were almost dead already.

Andre, Mom, not Anthony.

The fifth message…Mom. She forgot to tell me Sunday that my stupnagel cousin Charlene was pregnant again, maybe twins, and her husband had just gotten a raise, thank God, since soon there'd be four, maybe five mouths to feed. And I should tell Anthony he should eat more, people in Ethiopia were starving.

Mom was number six…why was I not surprised? She hadn't said her dead bolt bit yet. This time she wanted to know what Victor Madison looked like, was he as scary as his movies? And I shouldn't forget to lock the door because she didn't want me getting raped in my sleep.

Nothing from Andre. Mister Sun was sinking fast, and so was I. Wouldn't my "hunky hunk" be mildly interested in my audition? Maybe he meant to surprise me with Chinese take-out.

Whoa. Could Andre's contract be up for renewal? He had been so cranky lately, and his soap had just shot a hospital sequence…

"I'd better get this part," I said to Snow, then grabbed a Diet Pepsi from the refrigerator. "Maybe Samson lied, the snake. He'd love to stir up trouble in Paradise."

I was still in the kitchen when I heard: *click-click-click.*

Oh my God. Beetles? No. Snow was scratching at the patio door. I let him outside and watched him prance nimbly to the railed edge. "Be careful," I said. "You have tons of faith, but you don't have any wings."

Bonnie had called last night, warning me again about dream-demons. Despite Bonnie's admonition, I decided to rehearse for the screen test in my usual way. Turning off the lights, I scrounged together all my candles, creating an altar, wanting atmosphere for a personal seance. If I had been rehearsing for *South Pacific,* I would have covered my living room floor with sand and washed my hair.

For this screen test, I needed spiritual vibes.

Digging into my pocketbook, I retrieved illustrations of Old Scratch, Clootie, Beelzebub, and other demons, run off on the library's copy machine. Different sizes and shapes, they grinned with pointy teeth and fangs. I taped the prints to the wall. They had seemed harmless, even amusing, at the library. In my bayberry-scented, wick-lit room, they looked evil. Nevertheless, I became engrossed.

Remembering this afternoon's cavalcade of animals, I worked on primitive intonations; barking, oinking, hissing. I let the sounds distort my face. I felt hot, cold, hot again. Itsy-bitsy sweat-spiders trickled down my forehead, my cheeks, my chin, my neck, between my breasts. Whimpering, growling, crouching, crawling, I watched the candles flicker. Demons danced a wild jig, their bodies swaying, their mouths agape in silent glee.

The candles' oscillating shimmer became hypnotic, soporific…and hallucinogenic. Recent images merged. Pinned to Victor Madison's forehead, my psychic's pulsating brooch looked like a third eye. A white rabbit chanted, "Frannie, follow me, follow me." Instead, I followed Tenia through a mirror, then plummeted toward a snake pit at the bottom of a rabbit hole. Jeremy Glenn reached out from a TV screen and caught me. A demon fiddled *Bridge Over Troubled Waters* while I snuggled against Jeremy's heroic chest. Gazing up into his face, I watched his features blur into the red-eyed, shadowy devil who'd screwed Mia Farrow and spawned Rosemary's baby. Beetles clicked…

The front door opened and my candles went out, leaving darkness and the vague scent of bayberries. I heard footsteps and felt fingers touch my shoulder. Icy? No. Sweaty. On my hands and knees, I scurried to the room's corner, and cowered.

"Frannie?"

It knew my name. The demon knew my name.

"Frannie, what the hell? It's me…Andre."

He strode across the room and hunkered down. Burrowing my head beneath his un-zipped Mets jacket, I said, "Make them go away."

"Make who go away? Wait a minute. I'll turn on some lights."

"No. Don't leave me alone. They'll get me."

"Who?"

"The demons and the beetles."

"John, Paul, George and Ringo?"

I swallowed an hysterical giggle at the image of Beatles clicking and hundreds of beetles chorusing *Hey Jude*. "Not Beatles, Andre, beetles. Deathwatch beetles. Click-beetles."

"There's some bug spray underneath the kitchen sink."

I assumed a normal position, if normal means tush on heels, feet and tush scrunched against the wall. "My cousin Charlene is pregnant again, Andre. Twins."

"She can name them Beetle-de-dum and Beetle-de-dee."

"That's not funny. Maybe I had a panic attack. Maybe I'm stressed because my biological clock is ticking."

"Frannie, you're only twenty-four."

Scooping me up into his arms, Andre staggered toward the couch. I gave him a kiss, tasting liquor on his breath.

Andre said, "Who are your friends?"

"Friends?" I whipped my head around, scared again.

"The pictures on the wall."

"Oh, them. I was trying to get in the mood. Rehearse."

"For what?"

"For 'Forever Asmodeus.'"

"You got the part?"

"Not yet. I have a screen test tomorrow."

"That's great, Frannie, but couldn't you rehearse by memorizing a script?" He flicked a lamp switch. "A script doesn't bleach all the color from your face. You look like a reverse negative of Snow."

"Oh my God. Snow. I left him out on the patio."

"Balcony," Andre said, dumping me onto the couch and letting our fat black cat inside.

I suddenly realized that Snow's face had been at the window for a long time, next to a picture of Moloch. I also realized that Andre wasn't exactly walking straight.

"Andre, are you drunk?"

"Who, me?"

"You *are* drunk. You can hardly stand up. How did you carry me to the couch?"

"Emergency. Damsel in distress."

"What's wrong, honey?"

"Come with me to the Casbah," he said. Sliding down the wall, he belched twice, then swallowed convulsively.

"You can't make it to the bathroom," I said, watching his face turn one shade lighter than the Jolly Green Giant. Whatever Andre had consumed, it was making a gigantic effort to exit his body via his throat.

"I have concupiscence," he said.

"Concu-what?"

"Concupiscence. Hah. You can't even say the word sober."

I was tempted to reply, "Yes, I can. Sober"…but now was definitely not the time or place.

Andre said, "Not bad for a WASP from Wisconsin, huh? Means strong sessual…*sexual* desire. Concu…pis…oh piss, now I can't say it."

I sat next to my intoxicated hunk, who issued forth several warning burps. His body slouched like a rag doll on a shelf as I struggled to remove his jacket, my hands all thumbs. If Andre vomited on the Mets, he'd never forgive himself. Or me. I moved a dehydrated palm closer.

"Tell me what happened, honey," I said.

"Celebration. Lotsa grapes. Madeira, m'dear. Goodbye party. Everyone bought pitchers. Ohshit. Sorryfrannie. Gonnapuke."

Grapes, I thought, shoving the palm directly beneath Andre's heroic chin. *The grapevine. Samson's bitchy remark.*

"Those fuckin' writers killed me," Andre said, lifting his face. "Remember the new script? Today I died."

"But the death card was meant for me," I said.

A Brooklyn Playground - 1969

Staring up at his six-year-old sister, Chaim Mostel could feel wood beneath his butt and cement beneath his feet.

This morning his mother had said the sidewalk was "hot enough to fry an egg on." The playground's concrete was even hotter, but Chaim's bare heels and toes didn't budge.

His pretty sister was etched against the blue and white sky, just below a dark, evil-looking shadow.

The shadow of…*a giant bat?*

No.

A bird?

Maybe.

What kind of bird? How about…*a vulture?*

A vulture chewing ruby-red carrion.

"Yeah, perfect," said Chaim, sliding off the end of the seesaw.

Peggy Mostel squealed, pedaled the air with her Keds, and clutched the seesaw's handle. Her end hit the cement with a thud, and she smelled wee-wee, having peed her pants on the way down.

"Jeez, I'm sorry," her thirteen-year-old brother said, but he didn't look sorry. He looked nasty. The Rabbi had once showed her and her friend Patsy a picture of a man watching skinny Jews get shot by other men. Chaim looked like the man who watched.

Rising to his feet, he helped her stand up, brushed off her shorts and Winnie the Pooh teeshirt, then carefully placed her Dale Evans cowgirl hat on top of her head. When he finished fussing, he stretched his fingers into the shape of a pretend-camera and said, "Click."

Then he said, "Perfect, Peggy Piglet, I like the way that red hat matches your cheeks. I wish your eyes were black like mine, 'stead of gray, it would make a better picture. Oh jeez, did you hurt your tush?"

She felt as if she'd been spanked, but she didn't want to tell him that because she knew he'd look nasty again. She tried real hard, but couldn't stop her hands from moving to her sore tush, and she couldn't hold back the tears that rolled down her face.

"Aw, don't cry, Peggy Piglet," her brother said. "There's snot coming out of your nose and that ruins the picture."

What picture? she thought, as her brother wiped her nose with the hanky he carried in his pocket. The hanky was new and had 'nitials.... V.M. Most kids wore blue jeans and teeshirts with an upside-down Y in the middle of a circle, but Chaim always wore black slacks and a black shirt, even a black jacket when it was cold. He hated shoes, but when he had to wear them, he put on black socks and black penny-loafers.

Sometimes Mama let Chaim use her camera, but Peggy didn't like the scary pictures he took. Once she and Mama stood on the porch and her brother said, "Say cheese." But when the picture came back from the store, the porch looked big and Mama and her looked little and the window looked like it wanted to eat her and Mama.

"If you stop bawling," her brother said, "I'll take you to the movies. They're showing Disney this afternoon, *Lady and the Tramp* and some Pluto cartoons." He held his Mickey Mouse watch up to his eyes so he could see the numbers better. Mama said he needed glasses but there was no money for glasses. "If we hurry, we'll make the previews," he said.

"I can't go," she said, new tears brimming. "I peed my pants."

"Oh, wow," he said. "Ma's gonna kill you."

She poked her thumb inside her mouth.

"Unless we stay here 'til your pants dry," he said. "Wanna swing, Peggy Piglet? I'll push you."

She looked at the swings and thought how nice it would be to fly through the air. The sun would dry her shorts and panties. The wind would dry her tears. And if you swung high enough, you might even touch a cloud with your toe... She stared at her big brother. He looked nasty again.

Her mouth opened and her thumb fell out. Windmilling her arms, she raced down the path toward home, her legs churning, her sneakers scattering leaves, pebbles and popsickle sticks. Wee-wee trickled down her thighs; she'd peed her pants again.

Chaim squinted toward the swings.

Three...no, *ten*...vultures perched on the overhead support, their beaks ripping at the flesh of the corpse who swung back and forth...

Shit. The dead body would fall off the swing.

Unless another vulture…the giant vulture who'd flown over the seesaw, maybe…stood on the swing…no, hovered directly above the swing…its barbed talons digging into the corpse's rotting shoulders, keeping him…her….stationary. Her dead eyes would be open, and as the swing swung, millions of people would see her white panties…like Marilyn in *The Seven Year Itch*.

Yeah. Perfect.

Too bad he couldn't un-crypt Monroe's body and put *her* on the swing. Except the goddamn autopsy would have left her empty inside and the vultures would have nothing to feed on.

He strolled toward a nearby park bench, where he'd left his shoes, a small portable radio, and a dozen comic books—one Lone Ranger, one Superman, the rest horror. New York State had passed a law banning the sale of horror comics to anyone under 18, but Chaim knew the law couldn't be enforced, especially in Brooklyn.

Every morning, riding his bike, he delivered newspapers. Every weekend, riding his bike, he delivered pizza for Moon Pizza Pie ("When the moon hits your eye"—stupid slogan) and people tipped him good because he was good looking and there was something in his eyes and it wasn't fucking moons.

Even working both crummy jobs, it had taken him over a year to save the money for his movie camera, safely hidden inside his bedroom closet, on the top shelf, behind some old shoe boxes. Ma would kill him if she found the camera. He was supposed to be saving his paper-pizza money for college, except he wasn't sure he'd go to college.

Some kids wanted to be actors, like Brooklyn's own Tony Curtis. Except for the color of his eyes, Chaim looked like Tony Curtis, but Chaim wanted to be a famous director.

He didn't mind using his own name, but sometimes people couldn't say it right so he'd picked out a new name…Victor Madison.

Six and a half weeks ago, his half-Russian, half-German father, soused on cheap wine, had been plowed down by a truck while staggering across the street. Wearing a moth-eaten cardigan sweater over an undershirt, Isaac Mostel's trousers and underpants were missing, and his last words were: "*Wo sind die toilettenpapier?*"

Chaim had "borrowed" a roll of toilet paper from a neighborhood bar, but he hadn't gotten back home in time. So, in a way, his father's fatal accident was all Chaim's fault. Not that he felt guilty or anything.

"Isaac Mostel was *meshuga*," said the Jewish neighbors.

"Motherfucker had a few screws loose," said the black neighbors.

"Mr. Mostel was tetched," said the Irish-Catholic crone who lived next door and always mispronounced Chaim's name.

Kiang she called him, so he'd looked "kiang" up in the dictionary, and since it meant "a wild ass" he'd never corrected her pronunciation.

His neighbors, however, were right-on. Papa was *meshuga*, had a few screws loose, and was definitely tetched in the head.

So be it. Chaim Mostel was the son of a madman. Mad-i-son.

Every night he scribbled his signature…

Tony Madison

for Tony Curtis. Then he changed it to…

Victor Madison

for victory.

Now, seated on the park bench, he listened to his radio belt out *Those Lazy-Hazy-Crazy Days of Summer*. Flipping through the back pages of his comic books, he scanned the ads for horror paraphernalia. By next week he'd have enough money to order the blood-stained rubber knife and the werewolf mask. Wouldn't that scare Peggy Piglet to death? Especially if he arranged the bedroom lamp so that only the knife and mask were visible.

Before Isaac Mostel had tempted fate by drunkenly jaywalking across the street, he'd often been heard to say: "If you were born lucky, even your rooster will lay eggs."

Isaac Mostel had cashed in his insurance policy for booze money rather than toilet paper money, so the Russian proverb turned out to be Chaim's only legacy, which was fine by him.

Because he knew he'd been born lucky. And smart. And talented.

And bisexual.

On the day of his bar mitzvah, he had fucked the Rabbi's daughter. Then he'd fucked the Rabbi's son.

ELEVEN

After Andre had puked approximately four quarts of Madeira into our potted palm, I helped him to bed, wrangled the sneakers from his defiant feet, and covered his body with an eiderdown quilt.

The drunken snores of my beloved vibrated in my ears as I slanted a glance toward the dresser that Nana Jen's mother, my great-grandmother Frances, had ordered from a 1909 Sears Consumers Guide. According to Nana Jen, the dresser had cost a whopping $6.95. Mom hated it. I loved it.

Jenny Rosen had been born in 1909, on the one hundredth anniversary of Abraham Lincoln's birth. She died in 1989 and some of my memories are vague, but I can still recall the perfume on her breath...Cherry Lifesavers. When my dad bought his first convertible, Nana Jen used cucumber slices to smooth her "automobile wrinkles." And once, while pointing to her dresser, she said, "That's a genuine, hand-carved, French bevel mirror, Frannie."

Would click-beetles emerge from its genuine, hand-carved frame? Not a chance. Rescued from my parents' attic and U-Hauled to the city, Nana Jen's dresser had possessed buggy residue. But every single spider web had been carefully and thoroughly feather-dusted away.

I returned to the living room, wrapped dry cleaners' plastic around my vomitus palm, walked out the front door, strolled halfway down the hall, and shoved my corpus delicti into the chute that ended in front of a basement crematorium. Then I rescued a Diet Pepsi from the benign jaws of my refrigerator.

The phone rang. It sounded unobtrusive and congenial. Definitely not my mother.

"Frannie," said Bonnie, "I saw a shadow pass into your body."

"Peter Pan's," I said, feigning laughter. "He has this habit of losing his shad—"

"I saw you sitting in a dark room with candles and an altar, and I was scared because I couldn't tell if the spirit was good or bad. After the form passed into you, your face and body looked strange, all contorted, but then I saw a glow around you, an aura, so I called to tell you that everything's okay. Your good angel is protecting you. Don't be afraid. The bad spirits will leave you alone if you trust to loving forces."

"It's my choice, right?"

"Exactly."

Immediate assumption: Bonnie had visualized my personal seance because she knew about my *Forever Asmodeus* interviews. She knew how I rehearsed; had been with me inside Samson's loft the morning of the day I tried out for *Grease;* had helped me tape Travolta to the wall and zip up my old high school prom dress; had put the movie's soundtrack on Samson's CD player…"Wella, wella, wella…*oomph*," Samson's speakers had blared while Bonnie tried to cue me.

"Thanks for being tuned in, for caring," I said sincerely, then told her about the screen test. "Hey, Bonnie, there's this character in the book who befriends Robin before her transformation. A young teacher. French. Her name's Martine. You speak French."

"I do not."

"You do, too. Every time we watch *Gigi,* you parrot Leslie Caron."

"I speak high school French, Frannie, and I don't parrot Caron, I sing along with Caron. In English."

"Right. Okay, here's the game plan. Meet me at the studio and I'll introduce you to Victor Madison. Maybe the role hasn't been cast yet."

"No can do. Tomorrow I have an audition for a new diet cola."

"Spokesperson?"

"Crowd scene."

"Madison's movie will be more fun. And more profitable," I said, appealing to Bonnie's pragmatism.

She heaved a deep sigh. "If my horoscope agrees, I'll meet you at the studio. Tell me where and what time."

I gave her the address. "I have to be there at eight, for makeup. The testing should take place around eleven."

"Then I'll see you tomorrow…maybe. Meanwhile, sleep tight and don't let the bedbugs bite."

Shuddering at the thought of bugs, bed or otherwise, I told Bonnie about Andre's soap opera demise and the potted palm's demise. But I didn't mention the click-beetles or my erotic aerobics session. I guess I didn't want my best friend to think I'd totally lost it, so I finished my brief recitation, said good night, and hung up the phone.

Noises drifted up from the street, filtered through an open window. Dogs barked and sirens wailed and the cadence of falling raindrops hit my patio like the plop of hollow Ping-Pong balls. The city sounds were soothing. Why hadn't I heard them during my spiritual reverie?

I curled up in front of the TV for the eleven o'clock news. Watching our esteemed President mouth clichés, I wondered if he had ever bargained with a demon for popularity and/or campaign donations.

My mind strayed, tuning out the usual reports of Manhattan's murders and mayhem. Mom had accurately forecast each catastrophic event during last Sunday's cookout, in between bites of her Kosher hot dog and homemade strudel.

There was a brief intermission...Andre's old shaving gel commercial...then the screen's image changed to an enlarged weather map as the weathergirl predicted rain. *No shit,* I thought, glancing toward the patio. The weathergirl looked like an ebony version of the smiley-face sun that now graced her map as she stated, with authority, that tomorrow would be clear and calm.

"Well, hell, Scarlett," I drawled in my best high school Southern. "After all, tomorrow *is* another day."

TWELVE

The weathergirl was dead wrong. Clear and calm? Maybe she'd misread the cue cards and had meant to say, "Overcast and flatulent."

Last Sunday, while Mom chattered on and on about my cousin Marlene, sister of the fertile Charlene, Daddy had furtively slipped me an envelope filled with grocery money. So I splurged on a taxi.

Silently cursing the driver, who navigated corners like an Indy 500 reject, I blessed Marlene, who'd recently become engaged to a "Negro" named Fahd Kareem something. Poor Mom. She didn't know if she should play up the pending marriage or critique the racial-religious diversity. So she settled for Sammy Davis Jr.—a "Negro" whom she'd unequivocally admired. Looking pointedly at me, then Andre, Mom said she hoped Marlene's fiancé would convert, too.

It isn't every day that one has a Victor Madison screen test, and I felt nervous. No. Panic-stricken. When I'm panic-stricken, I compose rap lyrics. I'd barely chosen the lyrics for Charlene, Marlene, Fahd and Sammy, when my cab pulled up to the curb and I woefully discovered that Daddy's grocery money had shrunk faster than a wool sweater inside a Laundromat dryer.

It took Sol Aarons three hours to apply my makeup. As my nervous panic dissolved, I tried not to yawn.

Hair grew out of fake eyebrows while my real brows were covered with latex. Greens and purples were blended into my skin until my cheeks looked sunken to the bone. The makeup built up, layer by layer. Each piece of latex had to be smoothed without a wrinkle. I pictured my Nana Jen's porcelain complexion, remembered her remark about automobile wrinkles, and made a mental note to buy cucumbers.

Sol used a special glue that burned wherever my skin was tender. I silently damned Andre for sandpapering my fragile jowls with his unshaven chin during his brief good-luck mumble and kiss. Very brief, because Andre's breath smelled like dead chicken breasts. Correction: the rancid Styrofoam the breasts came packaged in, trashed under our kitchen sink while waiting for cremation.

When Sol finished, I couldn't move my mouth. "You'll get used to it," he said. "Eventually it will start to move with your face."

What face? My features were hidden beneath a grotesque latex mask. Even my hair had been vaporized with black atomized spray.

Clothed in a Wendyish nightgown, I walked onto the set…and the crew laughed. Damn. If I wanted to be taken seriously, I'd have to play Robin from the inside out.

Madison had left instructions for me to test a few special effects. In the book Robin projectile vomits all over her parents and Joe Bob Lancaster, the evangelist. Madison's hand-picked crew set out test materials—bowls filled with cottage cheese, marmalade and peach preserves. Following directions, I spooned a mouthful from the first bowl and spit toward the camera.

Cottage cheese dribbled down my chin.

"No, no, no," screamed the Assistant Director, Sheldon Giglia, who had clothed himself from head to toe in plastic. "Don't you know how to spit, missy?"

"A'course," I said. Of course I knew how to spit. What baseball addict doesn't know how to spit? But spitting through Sol's latex mask was more difficult than whistling through a mouthful of crackers.

Instantly hating the Ass. Director, I spooned all three ingredients between my lips and launched cottage cheese, marmalade and peach preserves at Giglia and the prop man. I tried to grin, but my mouth wouldn't stretch that far. *Missy* would never miss again.

With an enthusiasm once reserved for childhood excursions to Jones Beach, I re-dug my spoon into the bowls and shoveled the test materials between my lips until my cheeks pooched like a chipmunk.

Victor Madison walked onto the set. I swallowed, and knew how it felt to ingest a cheek full of tobacco.

Although the soundstage overflowed with filming apparatus, there was no orchestra. And yet an imaginary musician issued forth an imaginary drum roll. An imaginary spotlight seemed to follow Madison, blending his face and form into the room's shadows. The crew watched his every move. So did I. He possessed a magnetic charisma. In other words, Victor Madison could easily play Asmodeus, the devious demon.

He greeted me, then turned to Sheldon Giglia, who was trying to shed his plastic without touching it. "Stand in for the preacher, Shelly," Madison said. "I want Francine—"

"Frannie, sir. Francine's my stage name."

"Okay, no problem," Madison said. "I want you slap Shelly's face, Frannie, just like Robin does in Chapter Thirteen."

Okay, no problem, I thought gleefully, hauling back and hitting Giglia the same way I'd once clobbered the school bully. Giglia reeled to the wall of the set and fell, tush first. After several repeats, he began ducking before impact.

"Take a break," Madison told his crew. "We'll shoot the screen test in fifteen minutes." Leading me toward a small bed, he said, "Do you remember the segment in the book where Robin holds a crucifix aloft, then drives it viciously between her legs?"

"Yes, sir."

"She screams obscenities, her parents come running, and they discover her transformation."

"Yes, sir, I remember."

"Christ, don't call me sir. In the film, the camera will pan in on Lynn Beth's contorted face, supplemented by an insert shot…your hand plunging the icon beneath a bloody nightgown. Right now, I want you to play both parts. The girl and the demon. Go as far as you can with it, push the envelope, and don't worry about overacting. The audience has to feel disgust, but they must also feel empathy. Do you understand?"

"Yes, sir…uh…"

"Madison. Not Mister. Just Madison."

Ten minutes later, a prop man handed me a papier-mâché crucifix, a foot long and maybe three inches thick.

"Ready," I said, gripping the prop.

"Action," Madison said.

First, I used all the animal sounds I had practiced. Then…

"You're a pig…a sow…a glutton," I shouted, playing Asmodeus. "Please leave me alone, p-p-please," my Robin sobbed.

I drove the crucifix between my thighs. Rather than sexual, I made the motion angry, triumphant. My demon was trying to mentally destroy the young girl and reinforce his possession.

"Help me. Won't somebody help me?" my Robin pleaded. "No one can help you," my Asmodeus said.

I didn't need an unseen presence in a mirror.

I didn't need click-beetles or icy fingers.

I was performing *good*. And good meant bad.

Evil.

Tears brimmed as I altered my inflection for each character; high-pitched, frightened shrieks; low, demeaning growls that included every profanity in my vocabulary. I scurried across the bed on my knees, crawling from side to side, tossing pillows toward my demonic adversary. Stiffening my arms and shoulders, I held the papier-mâché crucifix at arm's length.

"No. Please. Oh my God. Nooooo…"

"Cut. Okay, Frannie, cut," Madison said.

His loud voice perforated my focus, my intensification, and I forced my body to relax. The set was very quiet; you could hear the proverbial pin drop. Then the crew applauded and I started to cry…Frannie tears, not Robin tears. The crew…the film world's toughest audience…and Madison came out from behind the camera and kissed me on the forehead…very good…very evil…you betcha.

Lynn Beth Sullivan arrived, wearing identical makeup, and we tested together. They shot us duplicating each other's facial expressions. Eyeing Lynn Beth, I felt as if I stared into Alice's looking glass, only I knew that Hell's demons, rather than Wonderland's allegories, prowled behind its smooth, polished surface.

For some dumb reason, I assumed the makeup removal would be fairly simple. Wrong. Each piece had to be lifted as gently as possible. Greens and purples merged, solvent ran into my eyes, and my poor skin resisted the tug of latex. Sol Aarons kept sneaking sips of Tsingtao. Still tense and stiff, I wanted to drink a six-pack…with tequila chasers.

Bonnie entered the dressing room, Madison's arm around her shoulders. She looked beautiful. Her blue-black hair had been plaited in one long braid, thick as a Sumo wrestler's wrist. Sooty lashes framed violet eyes. Straight white teeth nibbled at her generous lower lip.

I raised one latex-free eyebrow. Bonnie shrugged and nodded, which in Rosen-Sinclair shorthand meant she'd be considered for the role of Martine. The way she glanced up at Madison's face meant all kinds of interesting suppositions.

She and I left the studio together. Timed street lights glared yellow, their sparkle reflected in muddy, guttered rain water. Soon Broadway's neon marquees would disguise decadent glitz. Carriages would glide through Central Park, leaving horse shit in their wake. The Knicks would host the Celtics, and pickpockets would work the crowd. Greenwich Village would put on a show for tourists, then count profits. At least two suicides would leap from the Brooklyn Bridge.

New York City, my city. I felt alive, full of hope and promise. I was so damn happy to be a part of it...if I could make it here, I'd make it anywhere, thank you Frank Sinatra.

Bonnie had "positive vibes" about the part of Martine...and a dinner date with Madison. But it wasn't a casting-couch date, she quickly explained. Her agent was supposed to call Suzanne Burton immediately if not sooner.

"Be careful, Bon," I said. "I think Suzanne has a *thing* for Madison."

I told her about the S&M lighter and the way Suzanne had verbally caressed Madison's name. "I wouldn't mention the dinner date," I said. "What's the matter? Why do you look so funny?"

"Victor told me not to mention our date, too. Emphatically."

Victor? A stab of jealousy entered my brain and exited just as quickly. I had Andre. Last month Bonnie had severed her "forever and ever" relationship with what my psychic would have called an "ecktor."

An eclectic ecktor, no less, who believed that performing Camus for zero dollars was more spiritual...and visceral...than paying his share of the rent. But what really bummed Bonnie out, the straw that broke the carnivore's back, so to speak, was his dogmatic insistence that fast-food hamburgers were not only cheap, but healthy.

Forever love, I thought. *Forever Asmodeus. Both fiction.*

Damn, another brain-glitch. Andre was my forever love. Wasn't he?

So why did a stupid childhood verse supplant my mental faux pas?

Fuzzy-wuzzy was a bear, Fuzzy-wuzzy had no hair, Fuzzy-wuzzy wasn't fuzzy, was he?

THIRTEEN

A storm cloud followed me home, then headed for Canada.

Less than an hour ago I'd felt euphoric. Now, as I trudged up the stairs, all I felt was the stress on my calf muscles.

Inside the apartment, a clean-shaven Andre sat on the couch. Bare-chested, he wore denim cut-offs. Our goose-neck lamp's 75 watts bounced off his shoulder, traveled down his pectoral muscles, halted briefly at the concavity below his rib cage, then pooled near his groin. Had he heard my footsteps in the hall? My key in the lock?

He knows exactly what he looks like, I thought. *He's posing for me, giving me his gee-I'm-so-sensitive, Daniel Day Lewis façade.*

Then I saw the paperback clutched in his fingers, which should have dispelled my cockeyed notion…except Andre never reads books.

Ella Fitzgerald sang from our stereo speakers, coating the furniture with layers of blue. Louis Armstrong joined her for one duet, and my guttered candles, still decorating the room, dripped waxed tears.

I sniffed, but all I could smell were incense sticks. Andre, bless his intuitive heart, had dispatched the noxious, chicken-blood-soaked Styrofoam to the basement. At the same time, he'd trashed my demon pictures.

Snow looked very black against the white baseboards. Casting a humpback shadow on the wall, he slept, a cat grin and slight undulation of his tail implying that his dreams included memories of an un-neutered Snowball and nights of free pussy.

I walked closer to Andre, who wasn't precisely reading; who hadn't suddenly converted to Judaic Literaryism; whose brow was still low; whose spots remained unchanged. Feeling cranky, not knowing why, I watched him flip through the pages of my *Forever Asmodeus* paperback, a bottle of Sterling Chardonnay at his elbow, a bouquet of thorny red roses near the wine.

"Those flowers are for you," he said, still looking down at the book.

"Andre, that's so sweet."

"They're from your friend, Mickey Roebuck."

I read the card. "All it says is 'Thanks.' Why on earth would Samson send roses?"

"Supper's in the crock pot," Andre said, looking up from the book. "Damn, this Joe Bob Lancaster role is terrific."

"Do you think the author named him for Burt?"

"Huh?"

"Burt Lancaster, who won an Oscar for his role as Gantry...Elmer Gantry...in 1960. No, 1961. Hey, I just thought of something. If you turn 1961 upside down, it's 1961."

"Frannie, what the hell are you babbling about?"

"I'm not babbling, Andre."

Actually, I *was* babbling, yes siree Joe Bob. Because if I rattled on long enough, I might banish the foreign sentiments that splintered my brain. Love wasn't fiction. Andre hadn't been posing. And just out of curiosity, what the fuck had happened to Fuzzy-Wuzzy's hair?

"Victor Madison wants Jeremy Glenn for Joe Bob Lancaster," I said.

"Sure. That makes sense. A TV supercop playing a presidential evangelist. I suppose Glenn wants to broaden his scope or something."

Christ, I didn't need Andre's petulant sarcasm. I was so tired my bones ached, so I didn't say the role would broaden the scope of a soap star, too. "Hi, Frannie, how did the screen test go?" I said, instead.

"Sorry. Hi Frannie, how did the screen test go?" Andre gave me his melt-Oscar smile, and I couldn't help wondering if he practiced that smile in front of Nana Jen's genuine, hand-carved, French beveled mirror.

"I'm fairly certain the part is mine," I said. "It's only a double, of course, but the crew applauded and Madison kissed—"

"Great. That's great, Frannie." He nodded toward the Chardonnay bottle. "Have some wine."

"Hair of the dog, Andre?"

"What? Oh. Christ, I'll never drink again. This morning I felt as if I'd swallowed rusty razor blades, and a wine hangover is *not* my idea of a fun time. Then, while brewing coffee, I detected a gross smell. Following my nose, I looked underneath the sink. I thought there was nothing left in my stomach, but...well, the last of our potted palms, the one you named Elvis, has left the building." Andre's thaw-ice grin reappeared. "I opened that Chardonnay for you, babe. And, to be perfectly honest, you look as if you could use it."

"I look tired, that's all. I *am* tired."

"The wine will perk you up."

"The wine will put me to sleep." I yawned, then sniffed again. "Your stew smells yummy. I didn't have breakfast, too nervous, and lunch was a spoonful of cottage cheese, marmalade and peach—"

"I thought you hated cottage cheese." He placed my paperback face-down on the coffee table. "The wine'll go flat if you don't drink it."

"What's the deal, Andre? Do you want to get me drunk?"

"No, not drunk. Call it an experiment, Frannie. You might loosen up a little, inhibition-wise, if you're relaxed."

Lifting the bottle to my lips, I sampled a sip.

"That's my good girl," he said. "C'mon, drink up. I have another bottle on ice."

"I'm drinking on an empty stomach, Andre. Forget loss of inhibitions. I'll pass out."

The wine, however, was beginning to taste good. It went down smooth, and soon I'd consumed a goodly portion. Andre retrieved the second bottle and a corkscrew. I giggled.

"What's so funny, Frannie."

"Corkscrew." Pressing my hands against my mouth, I giggled into my fingers while tears squirted from my eyes.

"Jesus, maybe you'd better quit while you're ahead." Andre sat on the edge of the stuffed armchair and tapped his lap. "You sound—"

"Buzzed? Yeah. Ain't got no tolerance for spirits." I giggled helplessly, almost choking. Somehow, I managed to say, "Spirits, Andre, get it?"

"Sorry, Frannie, I didn't get the corkscrew joke."

"Oh...oh...corkscrew." New giggles churned. I took a physical and cerebral breath, then tried to explain. "You want an uninhibited screw so you opened the wine with a...maybe it's not all that funny," I conceded mournfully. "I cannot tell a lie, Andre, or a joke, but I can spit. The ass director said I couldn't, but I showed him. Want me to show you?"

"Maybe later. Right now I think you should put the bottle down and sit in my lap."

"No, no, no. You want me to lose my inhibitions." Defiantly, I took a slug from the second bottle. Then, to the tune of *Bye, Bye Blackbird*, I sang, "Bye, bye, 'bitions."

"Frannie, put the goddamn bottle down."

"Party pooper." I put the bottle down carefully, the same way Sol

Aarons had put his Tsingtao bottle down, only my table was Oscar-less, which made me shed a few melancholy rather than giggly tears. "Pack up all your cares an' woe, here I go, flyin' low…" I spread my arms, did a Peter-Pan, soared through space, and landed on the floor. "Bye, bye, 'bitions, good-bye."

Andre picked me up and returned to the armchair. "Speaking of Jewish inhibitions," he said, "your mother called."

"No shit. So how's Charlene? Bet she's havin' tricklets."

"*Triplets* were not mentioned, but your mother forgot my name again."

"Anthony's an okay name, Andre. You could do worse."

"This time I was Artie."

"I dated a boy named Arnie. In college."

"*Artie,* not *Arnie.*"

"Arnie was cute, but very short. My breast used to hit his pocket protector. He was pre-friggin-med. Mom was ecstatic."

"I'll bet she wasn't so happy when you ditched him."

"I didn't ditch him. I engaged him."

"What?"

"We got engaged. Immediately, if not sooner, Mom booked the Rabbi, temple, mailed invitations…she was so afraid I'd chicken out."

"Obviously, she was right."

"Nope."

"You're married?"

"Nope."

"Divorced?"

"Nope. We never finished the ceremony. I oh-deed."

"On *what?* Frannie, you won't even take aspirin."

"On Midol. The night before the wedding I got my period. No one gets cramps as bad as a good Jewish girl, trust me, so I filled a glass with tequila and swallowed a couple of—"

"Jesus, you overdosed on two Midol tablets?"

"Two bottles. Aunt Sylvia organized here comes the bride. I wobbled down the aisle, took one look at Arnie's tuxedo pocket-protector, giggled uncontrollably, and passed out."

"Then what happened?"

"Daddy called the whole thing off. Mom went ballistic…is that the phone or my head?"

"The phone."

"You get it, please. That's Mom's ring. I can't handle her right now, and if we let the machine pick it up, she'll keep calling back."

"It's your agent," Andre announced in a Liberace voice. Handing me the receiver, he walked over to the CD player and turned Ella's volume down.

Suzanne Burton had phoned, Harris said, and I wondered why he didn't sound like a balloon about to burst. *Maybe she forgot his name again,* I thought, my head about to burst.

Nope. Mystery solved. Suzanne had called yesterday, after the audition, before the screen test. If Madison liked the screen test, I'd get top money and a guarantee of five weeks.

"The test was incredible," I said. "Unbelievably terrific. The crew applaud—"

"Don't get overconfident, cookie," Harris said. "Talent means zilch in this business. A director will enthuse over what you did on the set, but one of a thousand things could happen. For instance, what if your makeup doesn't match the other girl?"

"It'll match. Lynn Beth Sullivan looks more like my mother than I do."

"Yeah, sure, but maybe they'll decide they don't need a double."

"Harris, Lynn Beth's thirteen years old and there's this crucifix—"

"Okay, cookie, okay," he said, and I could visualize him forking the peace sign with his pudgy fingers. "Don't get your knickers in a twist."

"My what in a what?" I said, and could almost *hear* him blush; Harris has to be the biggest prude in the history of the world.

"I've got this new client," he said. "From Australia. Her name's Sherry-Anne, one name, like Madonna. Knickers are…" he lowered his voice as if he were about to cuss "…panties."

I didn't want to hear about a new client. It made me feel like an old client. So I said, "What happens next?"

"They'll messenger the preliminary contracts to my office." Harris exhaled his (and my mother's) patented martyr-sigh. "There's a clause….there's always a freaking clause."

"Which says?"

"Suzanne can drop you if the screen test is bad."

"Bad is good, Harris."

"Huh?"

"Nothing. Forget it."

"Can you sign the prelims on Monday, cookie?"

"Sure. I know it's only a double, Harris, but at least I'm the star's double. That makes me a star-by-proxy."

"They'll messenger your check for the screen test, too."

"Good. I can use the money."

"That doesn't mean you got the part."

"Bye, Harris, have a nice day," I said, glancing toward the window. Nightfall chomped away at daylight, missing skyscrapers by inches, and I thought: *It's too cloudy for stars.*

Rising from the armchair, I staggered to the merry-go-round table, slammed the receiver into its cradle, and stared down at some long white envelopes. Correction: I knocked over some long white envelopes. Sinking to my knees, I said, "What are these, Andre?"

"Résumés," he said. "Applications for regional theatre. I figure I'll parlay my soap stint into a summer run."

I looked down at the envelopes. "Toronto? Galveston? Miami? Tulsa? You plan to leave New York?"

"Manhattan isn't exactly regional, Frannie."

"Long Island is." He hesitated so long, I knew he'd already called his L.I. buds. "I'll bet you could get another commercial, just like that." The snap of my fingers sounded like the snap of a dry twig.

"What's the big deal, babe? I'll be back this fall."

"No, you won't. What about California? You said—"

"*You* said…" He took a deep breath, sank into the armchair, and patted his lap. "Frannie, from the very beginning you said we wouldn't let our living together interfere with our careers."

"But that was when we were both based in Manhattan," I said with Jewish logic. Leaving the insidious envelopes on the floor, I draped myself across Andre's knees.

"We don't own each other," he said.

"Why don't you talk in clichés?"

"'Women are like elephants to me'," he said, ignoring the insult. "'I like to look at 'em, but I wouldn't want to own one.' Quote, unquote."

"Andre, I don't want to play your stupid quote-game."

"*Our* stupid game. C'mon, Frannie. 'Women are like elephants—'"

"W.C. Fields."

"Very good. Give me a kiss."

"'I'd love to kiss you, but I just washed my hair.'"

"Bette Davis. 'I'm probably a cad. Are you by any chance a weak woman?'"

"That's too easy. Humphrey Bogart. Don't leave New York, Andre. 'Forever Asmodeus' takes place in New Jersey, an easy commute. And

Harris says I'll get top money, whatever that means, but I'm sure it'll be more than enough for groceries and—"

"Not the way *you* buy groceries."

He pried my lips apart with his tongue, found my tongue, and performed a tongue-tango against the roof of my mouth. I pulled away. "'It's late,'" I quoted, "'and I'm very, very tired of youth and love and self-sacrifice.'"

"You're sure in a Bette Davis mood tonight."

"Leave me and you'll be sorry."

"Is that a threat, or are you still quoting Bette?"

"Yes. No. I don't know. Hold me, Andre. I drank too fast and the wine is curdling inside my stomach."

"Wine doesn't curdle."

"Cottage cheese does."

"We don't have any more potted palms, and I think Snow went…what's your word?…potty in the last of our philodendrons."

"Potty is Mom's word, Andre, and I'm not throw-up sick. Just sad."

"Let's make the most of the time we have," he said philosophically, un-zipping my jeans.

Straddling his lap, I leaned back until my hair touched the floor. As he fumbled at my jeans and my twisted knickers, he said, "Tell me what you want and then I'll tell you."

"I want to make mad passionate love."

"Say the words, baby."

"I love you."

"And I love you. Say the words, Frannie. Forget inhibitions."

"I can't. Repression's genetic. Speaking of genetic, what's a Jewish American Princess's favorite whine?"

"Yours is Chardonnay."

"No, no, Andre. I wanna go to Miami." *Miami…one of the regional theatre addresses.* "Okay," I said, feeling a sudden chill, wondering if I'd left the bedroom window open. "If Suzanne offers me Asmodeus, I'll turn the part down and travel with you. It's only a double, not a real part."

"Why don't we discuss it later?" Maneuvering my body to the floor, Andre wriggled out of his cut-offs and spread-eagled my hips.

I could no longer smell crock-pot stew, nor incense sticks, just roses. There's no other smell like it…heavy, almost cloying.

Above Andre's shoulder, I could see the Anne Frank poster. Suddenly, dozens, if not hundreds, of beetles cascaded from Anne's frame, fell to the floor, and righted themselves with a thousand clicks.

"Andre." My mouth felt dry and my voice sounded as if there was a burr stuck inside my throat. "Andre, beetles."

"I prefer Ella," he said.

"Beetles, not Beatles."

Shifting my gaze to the mock fireplace, I felt nausea grip my belly like a giant hand.

Emerging from the fireplace was a luminous shadow. His features were hazy…no, obscure…but I could see his penis. The tip glowed red, very red, not unlike my psychic's pulsating brooch.

My flesh crawled, my blood ran cold, and I said the first thing that popped into my head. "Okay, no sweat, I'll do the movie, I promise."

"That's my girl," Andre said. "It's only two, maybe three months. We'll survive the separation."

I squeezed my eyes shut. Then felt like a marionette as someone, or something, pulled imaginary strings and my heavy eyelids lifted.

Someone, or something, turned my face toward the fireplace. The shadow had vanished, but I sensed that the…whatever-it-was…lurked. Still piloted by an unseen director, I darted quick glances left and right until I saw it…him…standing by the merry-go-round horse table. In a mesmerizing rhythm of continuity, he scooped beetles up off the floor and stuffed them inside his pockets.

Except, a naked man doesn't have pockets. So he was stuffing them inside… "Oh, dear, oh, shit," I whispered.

"I will now kiss you in places you have never been kissed before," Andre said.

"Forget kissing," I said, my voice raspy. "Who needs kissing?"

"You do. Isn't that one of Frannie Rosen's canons? Thou shalt kiss before consummation. C'mon, give us a kiss. 'Life is a banquet and most poor sons-of-a-bitches are starving to death.' Quote, unquote."

"Auntie fucking Mame, and I don't want to play your stupid quote game." The wine lapped at the back of my throat, then settled, then sizzled. The room felt ice-cold, but my body burned. Hot. Peppery. Scorching. As Andre penetrated, I shouted, "Eat me, drink me."

"Okay, Alice, let's go straight to Wonderland."

"Yes. Oh my God. I want you, Asmodeus."

"Asmodeus?" Andre withdrew.

"Don't stop, you son of a bitch. Eat me, Asmodeus. Drink me, Asmodeus."

"Jesus," Andre said.

"Oh my God. I'm on fire."

"Jesus," Andre said, and I could feel his body stiffen. But not the part I wanted to stiffen.

The pain was unbearable. I was being cremated from the inside out. Desperate, I curled my fingers around Andre's flaccid penis and tried to guide him inside.

Instantly, as if he'd received a jolt of electricity, he had another erection. "Jesus," he said.

"Now," I said.

"No," he said.

"Ejaculate," I growled.

Somehow, he managed to obey, but his discharge was red-hot. On the verge of losing consciousness, I realized that his fiery fluid had cauterized my burns, and I felt a series of intense bursts, as if nitroglycerin had been wedged inside my body then detonated.

I screamed, "Oh my God. I'm coming."

And heard Andre say "Jesus" for the fourth time.

After he'd finished and I'd finished, I glanced toward the merry-go-round table, then the fireplace, but the luminescent shadow was gone.

Once again, a puppeteer shifted my gaze, this time toward the ceiling, and I saw it…him…floating just below the light fixture.

He was eating beetles.

I heard him crunch them between his teeth.

CLICK. CRUNCH. CLICK. CRUNCH.

Sour wine traveled up my throat.

Before I could spew it out, pain spiked my skull and a different kind of nausea, a fainting nausea, cramped my stomach.

Teetering on the edge of a black abyss, I heard Andre say, "Jesus, Frannie, jeeeesus."

At least he didn't sound gee-I'm-so-sensitive anymore.

FOURTEEN

The next morning I thanked Andre for putting me to bed and vowed I'd never drink wine again, especially on an empty stomach.

To tell the god's honest truth, I had only vague memories of my bacchanalian revelry. I couldn't quite recall the shredded remnants of my nightmare, either; the horrid dream that had followed my drinking spree. Before passing out, I'd scared the bejeesus out of Andre, that much I did know, but he didn't want to talk about it. Correction: he refused to talk about it.

I blocked the ersatz fireplace with our computer desk, then sent *The Diary of Anne Frank* poster, frame and all, down the hallway chute, toward the incinerator. I couldn't fathom why I did these things, but I felt better...safer.

A few days later, I visited Sol's studio. He needed to make a new plaster mask of the demon...with a vomiting apparatus. Since the scene would be shot in profile, tubing stemmed down one side of my face, and that's how I learned that I'd been cast in *Forever Asmodeus.*

Harris called to confirm; I was now "cookie baby."

When my phone rang the following afternoon, I couldn't determine who was calling. The ring sounded persistent, authoritative, so maybe it was my mother, or my aunt Sylvia (Charlene and Marlene's mom), or my Aunt Shirl, the overprotective mother of my stupnagel cousin, Mark. Named for the same dead relative as Marlene, Mark had been my high school prom date. By now, both aunts knew about my "very important part" in a Victor Madison movie.

And yet the repetitive peal didn't have that Jewish-sacrifice quality, hard to explain unless you've been groomed, practically from birth, to become the first Jewish American Princess First Lady.

I picked up the receiver. After a brief hello-how-are-you, Suzanne Burton said *Forever Asmodeus* would be filmed in Houston.

"Texas?" I said.

"The last time I looked at a map, Houston was still in Texas."

"Not New Jersey?"

"Madison has made arrangements to use the Astrodome for Joe Bob's prayer rally. He's shooting the bedroom possession scenes on location, in a sub-division of new model homes south of the city, not far from Galveston. Can you be ready to leave in three to four weeks?"

I said yes while my gaze strayed toward Snow. How could I finagle Mom into boarding her grandcat?

The phone had barely been cradled before I ran to the computer, logged on, and surfed the net.

I had once visited my father's sister, Aunt Estelle. She's retired now, and lives in Arizona, but at the time she ran a souvenir shop in Galveston, Texas. It was Spring Break and I desperately wanted to fly to Fort Lauderdale, where the boys were, but Mom said, "What's the difference, Frannie? Galveston's an island, it has water, sand, a beach, and you won't have to share a crowded motel room."

If I remembered correctly, Galveston also had a dinner theatre.

Bingo. Galveston Dinner Theatre's dramatic webpage included an email link. I typed in Andre's résumé, word for word, except I might have exaggerated a tad when I added one line: *My fiancé, Francine Rose, is starring in a new Victor Madison movie.*

Hitting the send button, I logged off, returned to the phone, and tapped out Bonnie's number. When she answered, I said, "Hi, Bonnie, did you hear about Houston? Did you get the part of Martine? How was your date with Madison?"

"Yes. I think so. Fine."

"You think so?"

"I auditioned for Suzanne, but I'm pretty sure she knew about my date with Victor. She seemed...brusque."

"No, no, Bon, that's her thing. She was brusque with me, too. Don't keep me in suspense. How was Madison?"

"Competent."

"Aw, c'mon, details."

"He was...charming. We dined in his hotel suite, the top floor. It reminded me of *Pretty Woman,* you know, the breakfast scene, a table filled with covered dishes that look like Sterling silver turtles. I pigged out. Champagne, marinated Souvlaki, sautéed veggies, and chocolate-covered pralines."

"Did you sleep with him?"

"Yes, I slept with him."

"I'll bet there was music. What kind of music does he like?"

"There wasn't any music."

"Your voice sounds funny, Bon. What aren't you telling me?"

"He...Victor played videos. He had a suitcase full."

"Wow. X-rated tapes?"

"No. Disney."

"Disney? As in Walt?"

"Correct. Dumbo, Bambi, Tarzan, Snow White, you name it."

I took a moment to adjust to my Prince of Darkness watching Snow White. Then I said, "What exactly did you mean by competent?"

"Victor never seemed to tire. I did, after a while. But he never...well, came."

"Then you don't mean competent, Bon. You mean another tent. Impotent."

"No, Frannie, impotent means incapable of sexual intercourse. Victor was capable."

"Are you sure?"

"Yes. He has a marvelous body and his technique was flawless. The tapes were a bit disconcerting, but—"

"He played Disney while making love?"

"Uh-huh. 'Cinderella.'"

"Well, I suppose famous people have different turn-ons. Right?"

"Right."

"Are you planing to see him again?"

"He's flying back to California tonight."

"Oh."

"Hey, no big deal. The next time I watch Cindy get spiffed up for the ball, I'll picture Victor Madison as Prince Charming."

Inside my head, I heard a simple melody. Cinderella...no, Snow White singing: *Some day-yay my Prince will come.*

"What's new with you?" Bonnie said, then laughed. "I mean, aside from being cast in a major, no-expense-spared movie?"

I wanted to tell her about my nightmare, at least the tattered bits and pieces I remembered, but I couldn't. It would be like a Brady Buncher telling one of her sisters that she'd lettered a poster EAT ME, DRINK ME instead of JAN FOR CLASS PRESIDENT.

So I told Bonnie things were supercalifragilisticexpialidocious.

Later, I remembered that supercalifragilisticexpialidocious was from Disney. Mary Poppins, who, in my opinion, is nothing more than a white, right-wing witch. Call me insensitive, call me an insurrectionist, call me a conservative Republican, but I hate the part of the movie where the mother forsakes her fellow suffragettes to embrace "family values."

Staring at the empty space above my ersatz fireplace, I felt as if my life was a stick of lit dynamite, ready to explode. Everything seemed to be poppin'…except Andre.

Ever since The Night of Wine and Roses, he hadn't touched me.

A Brooklyn Brownstone - 1978

Chaim Mostel stared out the window.

Rose Mostel hot-watered her instant coffee and added three spoonfuls of sugar. Then she returned to the kitchen table, sat in her chair, and stared at the back of her son Chaim's head.

He had his father's hair, she thought, black like a crow. Thank God he didn't have his father's devil-may-care sense of responsibility. Isaac Mostel, may he rest in peace, had been a real sonuvabitch. Dyin' in the street. No life insurance. No money in the bank. No nothin'. Chaim was such a good boy, everyone said so, especially Mrs. O'Connor who lived next door (even if she did call him Kiang). Twenty-two years old, Chaim coulda' left for greener pastures. Instead, he stuck around and took care of his family. Which meant he should be the first to hear, even though, for some reason, the thought made Rose jumpy.

"Peggy's gonna marry Donald Blaustein," she said, drumming her scabbed, swollen fingers on the table top.

Rose worked part time at *The New U Beauty Shoppe.* She didn't wash, cut, color, or even touch the clientele's hair ("Ick, you wouldn't believe the cooties," she always said), but she prided herself on her manicures. Although she tried to hide it, her eyesight was failing and sometimes she'd pierce her fingertips with her sharp cuticle remover.

Thank God she'd never cut a client.

Chaim heard his mother's words, but he continued aiming his movie camera at the window while he collected his thoughts. If he had been gathering Easter eggs, he would have studied each one for its purity of color before he put it in his basket. Outside, the sky was shrouded by chromium clouds. Finally, he turned around.

"Peggy's too young to get married," he said. "She's only fifteen. Donald's what? Thirty? Anyway, Peggy can do better than Donald."

"Better?" Rose stopped drumming. "Are ya crazy, Chaim?"

"Victor, Mother. I told you to call me Victor."

"Donald has an *inheritance*. And a good job, civil service. He can support Peggy. He can support the baby."

Chaim watched five scabbed fingers leave the table top and press against his mother's chapped lips in an oh-shit-I-tattled gesture.

"Peggy's knocked up?"

Silence.

"Is Peggy pregnant, Mother?"

Rose nodded.

"Donald's the father?"

"No. Not yet."

"What does that mean?"

"Chaim, you gotta promise to keep your yap shut."

"Yeah, sure."

"Peggy plans to sleep with Donald. Tonight."

"Was that her idea or yours?"

Lifting the chipped mug to her mouth, Rose seemed to forget what she was doing. "Peggy won't tell who the papa is, Chaim. I think it's that rich sonuvabitch who took her to see *Ain't Behavin'*."

"*Ain't Misbehavin'*. Songs by Fats Waller. Which is kind of ironic when you think about it."

"Peggy ain't fat."

Staring at the tired-looking woman seated on the rickety kitchen chair, Chaim wondered how such a *dummkopf* could have produced a Victor Madison. He knew for a fact that his IQ went off the charts; had figured he'd secure a scholarship to NYU or UCLA. Instead, up until yesterday he'd worked at the A & P, and if he never saw another package of browning hamburger meat or smelled another overripe pineapple, it would be too soon.

The A & P manager was a nice enough guy, even though he wasn't the swiftest horse in the race and probably had the IQ of a Q-tip.

"Sorry, Vic, we gotta letcha' go," he'd said. "Too many complaints. The ladies say you got X-ray vision, like Superman. Mrs. Ginsberg swears you was rapin' her with your eyes. It's all that pretend picture takin'...and it ain't just the customers...the checkers and bag boys say the same thing. Personally, I ain't got nothin' 'gainst ya, Vic. You're a good worker, never came late. You want I should write a recommendation?"

Chaim hated being called "Vic." Almost as much as he hated working in a supermarket. Over the years he'd saved a few bucks, but never enough to finance film school (even with a scholarship), because "emergencies" kept draining his escape fund. Chaim would bet his last dollar, and he didn't have many dollars left, that if you found yourself a dictionary and looked up the word emergency, its definition would state: {Yiddish} : of or relating to Peggy Mostel / *var of* chutzpah.

First, Peggy's piano lessons. The damn house was falling down around their ears, but they had to have what his mother called a "piana."

Then, Peggy's tuition and school uniforms. "Peggy ain't smart like you, Chaim," his mother had said, "and she needs private school, else she'll run wild."

Peggy's tonsillectomy. Peggy's broken wrist (which had killed the "piana" lessons, thank God). Peggy's bas mitzvah, more expensive than a debutante's fancy-dress ball, and kind of funny when you thought about it since she went to a Catholic school.

And don't forget Peggy's fucking ballet lessons. "All the girls take ballet," his mother had said. "You want she should be an outlaw, Chaim?" "The word is outcast, Ma."

Then there was Peggy's theatre gown, so she "shouldn't look like a refugee." She'd worn it to impress her upper-crust date, misbehaved, and now there was a bun in her oven.

Or rather a flaky, rich, crescent-shaped croissant.

Tonight, as Simon and Garfunkle would say, she'd be "Fakin' It."

Would Donald buy premature? Maybe, maybe not, but by then it would be too late. He was crazy about Piglet, and he wasn't bad looking, once you got past the body odor. If he had hair and weighed…oh, say seventy-five to a hundred pounds more…he'd look like Harrison Ford in *Star Wars*.

Donald Blaustein had seen *Star Wars* ten times. Donald Blaustein loved movies. Donald Blaustein had promised to invest the inheritance from his dead grandmother in Chaim's experimental film, *Anthophilous*. If Peggy Mostel became Peggy Blaustein, Chaim could kiss that money goodbye. Peggy would insist that Donald invest in Peggy.

"Where ya goin', Chaim?"

"Victor."

"Where ya goin', son?"

His mother sounded nervous, itchy, so he smiled and held up his movie camera. "I'm going out, Ma. I want to shoot the sky."

Later, he watched his curly-haired, pink-cheeked sister, looking like Disney's Snow-fucking-White, as she sat on the porch steps and waited for her civil service prince. Supper smells—kreplach, kielbasa, souvlaki, fajitas, fried chicken, corned beef and cabbage—drifted through open windows, flavoring the warm evening with the scent of multi-racial, multi - ethnic cuisine.

Someone's stereo blasted *Hot Fun in the Summertime.* The lyrics were meant to sound sly, and they did.

Half-hidden behind a sidewalk tree, Chaim squinted through his camera lens. Peggy made a pretty picture, bathed in the glow from a street lamp. The low-cut bodice of her baby-blue dress, tasteful rather than slutty, enhanced her slender body. Shadows flirted with the deep cleft between her breasts.

She waited and waited. Every so often, she'd glance down at her watch. Then she'd look up and down the street, both ways, as if she were a little kid and needed to cross the street. As Chaim watched, she shook her watch, looked up and down the sidewalk, rubbed her eyes with her knuckles, and yelled, "Hey, Ma, what time is it?"

Some high school girls sauntered by, then backtracked.

"Yo, Peggy, we're goin' to the movies, wanna come?" said one of the girls, flipping long, sleek bangs out of her eyes.

Peggy smiled, her teeth white and straight (her braces had been the biggest emergency of all). "I got a date, Evvy," she said.

A prune-faced Hispanic man stopped near Chaim, blocking his view. "Ain't them Dodgers somethin'?" the old guy said, his accent more Brooklyn than P.R. "Them bums're gonna win the series this year. I been to Ebbets Fields t'ree times a'ready, seen Duke catch a fly an Robinson steal a base, right in'fronna my eyes."

"Them bums moved to *El Lay* in fifty-seven," Chaim said. He wasn't being mean or anything. He just wanted the old amnesiac to move out of the way, move on, shoot the freaking breeze with the freaking street kids playing freaking stickball.

Finally, when the smell of weed and cigarette smoke had replaced supper smells, when James Brown had replaced Sly and the Family Stone, Chaim hunkered down beside his sister.

"Donald's not *coming* tonight, Piglet," he said.

Wincing at her brother's innuendo, she said, "How do you know?"

He grinned.

"What did you do, Chaim?"

"Victor."

"What did you do, asshole?"

He handed her a piece of paper.

"What's this?" Peggy held the smudged carbon copy as if she'd just captured a wasp between her thumb and first finger.

"Donald has the original," Chaim said. "You want I should read it, Piglet?"

"Stop making fun of the way Ma talks. And stop calling me Piglet."

"I'm not making fun, I'm having fun. I've got my glasses, you never wear yours, even though they cost me a month's pay. Do you want me to read what it says? Never mind, I know it by heart. 'Dear Donald, Peggy Mostel is pregnant and she's going to pretend it's your baby.'"

"Bastard. You bastard."

"You want I should pay for an abortion? I'd consider *that* a tangible emergency. You might even say an in-the-flesh emerg—"

"Go to hell, Chaim. I'll call Donald and—"

"Tell him what? That you're *not* knocked up?"

"No. Yes. I'll think of something," she said, rising to her feet.

The phone's not working, Chaim thought, as he heard the door slam.

Much later, hours later, he heard his mother scream. Still half-asleep, he ran to Peggy's bedroom; a pretty room filled with stuffed animals, doll collection, crumpled baby-blue dress, and a nude body stretched out on the ruffled bedspread. A razor blade lay next to the nude body's fingers. Blood from a slit wrist soaked the spread while an empty container of sleeping pills lay on the floor next to an empty container of aspirin. Vomit stained Peggy's face.

Inserted up her vagina was a ceramic Donald Duck. Chaim could see the webbed feet and fan of tail feathers, even a small portion of blue sailor suit, but he couldn't see Donald's face and sailor hat. The miniature duck had once strutted on top of a music box, right next to its friend and faithful companion, Mickey.

Ignoring the bizarre dildo, Chaim felt for a pulse. Wrist...throat... nothing thumped except his own heart.

"Call an ambulance." his mother shouted.

"Phone's dead, didn't pay bill, no money, cashed paycheck, Peggy's shoes," he babbled.

Picking up the music box, he absent-mindedly wound it, thinking a dramatic scene like this required background music. Then, listening to the familiar theme, he began to sing along. "Mickey Mouse, Donald *Duck*, Mickey Mouse, Donald *Duck*—"

"Shut up," his mother cried, trying to staunch Peggy's blood with the baby-blue dress. "You gotta call for an ambulance, Chaim. I can't see the numbers on the—"

"Now it's time to say goodbye—"

"Chaim, borrow Mrs. O'Connor's phone."

"M-i-c, see ya real soon—"

"I think maybe your sister's still alive."

"—k-e-y. Why? Because—"

"Chaim, for the love of God."

"M-o-u-s-*eeeee....eeeee...eeeee...*"

"Chaim, stop screaming and *do* something."

Her hand smashed against his face and his head spun, just like that scene in *The Exorcist*; he'd seen the movie seven times.

Snapping his mouth shut, Chaim bit his tongue. He ran down the stairs and outside, onto the sidewalk. His legs were still churning when he reached Mrs. O'Connor's front door. He knocked until his knuckles felt like raw hamburger meat. She inched the door open, stared at his face, and shook her head no. "Fuck," he shouted, muscling the door ajar and racing toward the phone. Then he waited for the ambulance, his thoughts whirling like a pinwheel.

I think Peggy choked to death on her own puke. If I filmed it, the razor would be more dramatic because, except for The Exorcist, blood plays better than vomit.

His mouth was full of blood from his bitten tongue. Standing beneath a street lamp, he spat, and watched a gob of bright red saliva stain the cracked sidewalk.

Spit on a crack and you'll break your mother's back. Step on a quack and you'll break...

His laugh was half sob as he spat again.

If/when he shot the bedroom scene, he'd have to hold auditions, find the right kid to play Piglet. Too bad Elizabeth Taylor couldn't have stayed young forever; she'd be perfect. In fact, had she not tried to commit suicide, Peggy Mostel could have played herself.

W.C. Fields once said an actor should never work with kids, but the old coot hadn't said anything about a director, and kids were so naïve, so obliging, so...impressionable.

Leaning against the street lamp, Chaim wept, then spat, then wept some more.

FIFTEEN

There's this scene in one of my favorite movies, *When Harry Met Sally.* Everybody remembers the fake-orgasm segment, but the scene I'm talking about is the one where Meg Ryan drags a Christmas tree home to her apartment. It reminds me of my trips to the Laundromat.

"Frannie, why do you always wait until the last minute, when you're out of clean clothes?" Andre has said at least a million times.

"*We're* out of clean clothes," I reply. Jewish subtlety, meaning he has arms and legs and could wash the damn clothes himself. But either I'm too subtle and he doesn't get it, or else he chooses not to.

The Laundromat isn't far, just a few blocks, but the walk home reminds me of Meg/Sally wrestling with that Christmas tree. Except my green Girl Scout duffel bag, filled with neatly-folded jeans, sweats, sheets and underwear, doesn't have sharp green pine needles.

By the time I reach my five flights of stairs, I feel like I'm dragging a corpse, and by the time I reach my bedroom, I'm too pooped to put the clothes away. So the duffel slumps against Nana Jen's genuine, hand-carved dresser, and I end up fishing for clothes, like that carny game where you fish for a prize and you don't care what you win as long as you win something.

Which brings me, in a round about way, to the Night of Wine and Roses. The roses were now dead black petals and the Chardonnay had probably turned to vinegar, but recollections, like clean socks and underpants, kept emerging, one-by-one, from my mental duffel bag.

I wanted to share what I remembered, but with whom?

My best friend would do nicely, only Bonnie, having snagged the role of Martine, had already left for Houston. Madison, she told me, planned to shoot in sequence, starting at the very beginning, before the Robin-Asmodeus possession occurs. Other movies had been filmed that way,

Bonnie said. For instance, *They Shoot Horses, Don't They*, a movie about marathon dancers.

My other best friend spent his days and nights seated in front of our computer, negotiating his Galveston Dinner Theatre contract, emailing friends, and researching rodeos. Andre couldn't care less about beetles and demons. I had scared him, and for a self-professed inhibition buster, he was acting like a polite prick.

That left the police… "Officer, a man, or maybe it was a ghost, broke into my apartment via my fake fireplace. Then he/it ate some beetles. No, not John, Paul, George and Ringo. Deathwatch beetles, the kind that go click. How did the beetles get into my apartment? I'm fairly certain they avalanched from Anne Frank's face."

The nice officer would tell me to hire an exterminator. And/or a psychiatrist.

However, one doesn't need a shrink when one has Ann Landers for a mother. Although I didn't mention the demon by name, or, god-forbid, my bacchanalian revelry, Mom sprayed my hornet's nest, so to speak, with twenty-four words.

"If you've got a dybbuk," she said, "call the Rabbi. Then take some Nyquil and get some sleep. And don't forget to dead bolt the door."

Mom also grudgingly agreed to board Snow.

SIXTEEN

The phone didn't ring so I was unprepared, at a loss for words.

I had picked up the receiver, planning to call my cousin Mark, who—after years of sharing Aunt Shirl's house and closets—had moved in with his long-time lover, a drop-dead gorgeous stockbroker named Troy. I figured I'd give Mark and Troy a housewarming gift, the one or two rafter-plants that hadn't dehydrated yet.

"Hello?" I finally said. "Who's this?"

"It's Mickey Roebuck. Samson. Hey, darlin', I need a big favor."

"Sure."

"Don't you want to know what the favor is?"

"As long as it isn't illegal or fattening—"

"I've received an advance to write an unauthorized biography."

"Unauthorized is the very best kind, Samson. Do you want me to dig up the dirt on a fashion maven? A Broadway star? Donald Trump? The Mets?"

"Nope. Victor Madison. When you told me about your audition I called a California publisher, reminded him that nobody's ever written a Victor Madison bio and it would be a shame to wait till he's dead."

"That's why you sent me the thank-you roses." I wanted to say flowers weren't necessary, but realized I'd sound like my mother. "That's terrific, sweetie. Whoa. Isn't Madison in Houston?"

"I won't interview him until the first draft's written," Samson said, and I could hear the excitement in his voice. "But Madison's ex lover, Catherine Lee Sands, lives right here in Manhattan. She agreed to an interview, then reneged when I turned on my tape recorder. She says she doesn't talk into machines."

"I don't see how—"

"She said she'd talk to you, if you don't record the conversation."

"Me? I've never met her. I've heard of her, of course. Who hasn't? She's won a Tony, and last year she got rave reviews for *Man of La Mancha,* the revival at the Lincoln Center, opposite Richard—"

"It was my idea. I told her you have a memory like a sponge and wouldn't need a tape recorder. People gravitate to you, Frannie. You're like a magnet. I've seen strangers stop you on the street and tell you their life's story. And it's a good chance to get acquainted."

"That's right. She's playing Robin's mother in *Forever Asmodeus.* But...to be perfectly honest, Samson, I don't know how to conduct a professional interview."

"You've seen Jane Fonda in *China Syndrome.* Chat with Sands. Ask her about Madison. See if she'll let loose with a few juicy tidbits."

"Is it very important?"

"I can't answer that until I find out what she says. Madison's a supercilious prick, Frannie, which is why the bio is sure to be a bestseller. So...how would you like to be in my dedication?"

"Is that a bribe?"

"Nope. A promise."

"Please dedicate the book to someone else, Samson. I sort of like Madison." To tell the truth, ever since he'd kissed my forehead at the screen test I'd adored him, but I didn't want to rain on Samson's parade.

"Trust me, Frannie, Madison has it comin' to him. I've already dug up some incredible data. Please? I'll pay a research fee."

"No, Samson. You wouldn't accept a cent when I shared your loft, not even grocery money."

"Invite Sands to lunch and I'll pre-sign the credit card slip. Okay?"

"I guess."

"Tell you what. Take Cat...that's the name she prefers...to that restaurant I'm always ravin' about. I'll make the reservation. Order anything your little heart desires, but taste the *oeufa a la neige.* For dessert."

"The what?"

"Poached egg white floating in sugar and cream sauce."

"Samson, I need to lose ten pounds."

"Thanks, darlin', I really appreciate this. The secret of writing is to know something that no one else knows. Quote, unquote."

"Who is Aristotle Onassis? And it's the secret of *business.*"

"Very good, Frannie."

"'You are a foul ball in the line drive of life.' Quote, unquote."

"Joe DiMaggio to Marilyn Monroe."

"You forgot to put it in the form of a question."
He chuckled. "Who is Joe DiMaggio?"
"Wrong. Who is Charles Shultz? Lucy to Charlie Brown."

SEVENTEEN

Catherine Lee Sands and I shook hands.

Her fingernails were long, oval, polished blood-red. Mine were short, bitten, polished Mets orange.

After brief self-introductions, we descended a small flight of stairs, away from the herd-like bustle of Wall Street's bulls and bullshit.

The restaurant's heavy carpeting and acoustical ceiling muffled our footsteps. Copper ware and ceramics hung above plush scarlet banquettes. Colorful oil paintings transported me to France, and I wished I could step into a painting and join the peasants strolling along the Seine. Lucky peasants. They never had to wriggle their lush bodies into a pair of petite pantyhose.

A penguin-clad maitre d' guided us around a table of cold hor d'oeuvres. I thought of Bonnie when Cat chose *terrine de legumes,* a pate made entirely of vegetables. I chose mussels topped with powdered almonds and screw the calories.

Seated, Cat and I studied our menus. Then we ordered the rest of our lunch—bay scallops with mustard sauce. Unable to pronounce the complicated French wines, I asked for a carafe of the house white.

Catherine Lee Sands defied conventional specification, so I tried to think of something non-cliché. On my mental interview pad, I scribbled: *A forty-ish Natalie Wood riding sidesaddle on a unicorn. Magical. Elfin. Mystical.*

Dark brown hair swept her forehead in thick, pixie-cut florets. Dark brown eyes revealed a fey expression, as if she wore sunglasses that enhanced rather than blocked out the sun. Her ballerina's body had a waist so slender, I could have sworn she'd used a gold choke-collar to belt her white dress.

I had donned a pink mini-skirt and my pink and white audition sweater.

Unlike Lynn Beth, Cat made me feel almost busty.

Our opening conversation was tentative, like a couple of skaters circling a slippery rink, but two glasses of dry white wine broke the ice.

"Your friend wants Victor Madison tittle-tattle," Cat said, "but I'm not sure where to start."

"Tell me about you," I said, "and fuck Madison." It just popped out. The damn wine. Hadn't I sworn on a stack of Ray Milland videos that I'd never drink wine again? Except my promise was that I'd never drink wine on an empty stomach again, and my stomach was well-musseled.

"Please don't take notes," Cat said. "Because if I talk about me, it's off the record."

"I'm not a reporter," I told her, thinking about Jane Fonda in *China Syndrome*. Hadn't her co-star, Jack Lemmon, incurred a slight mishap? "Just start at the beginning, Cat."

"Yes…the beginning. I was born in Las Cruces, New Mexico, christened Mary Catherine Lelia Sanchez. I won't bore you with my early childhood, Frannie. Suffice to say my parents died…car crash. Papa had consumed a goodly portion of tequila, just before he hit a tumbleweed. Unfortunately, the tumbleweed hid a telephone pole."

"Cat, I'm so sorry."

"Thanks. I was very young, no big deal. My two brothers and I were farmed out to relatives. I ended up in Tulsa, Oklahoma. My aunt and uncle were Oral Roberts fans. Make that fanatics. They had no children of their own. They didn't smoke, drink, or…" As the waiter placed our lunch plates on the table, she whispered, "Fornicate."

After the waiter had watched us take a bite and nod our heads, Cat said, "Where was I?"

"Fornicate," I said.

"Right. As I grew older, I wondered who in his, or her, right mind would name a baby boy Oral." She dabbed at the corners of her mouth with a linen napkin. "Due to evangelistic backlash, I tended to rebel. A lot."

"Rebel *with* a cause, huh?" I said, still thinking Natalie Wood.

"Causes, Frannie, plural. Energy conservation, banning the Miss America pageant, saving minks."

"You should hear my mother's zealous commentary on minks, namely coats and stoles. And red paint."

"I was a paint-thrower." Cat chewed a scallop. "To make a long story short, I said goodbye to home, hearth and daily prayers. Then I found the man of my dreams."

"Victor Madison," I breathed.

She laughed, chewed another bay scallop, then said, "Not even close. My dream man managed a gas station. His name was Mike "Dancer" Bleich. He got me off drugs…did I tell you I was hooked on drugs?…and into acting. My biggie was the annual summer production of Oklahoma. I want to barf every time I hear that song about beautiful mornings. Corn as high as an elephant's eye, my ass. 'Corn as thick as an elephant's dick,' Dancer used to say. He was killed during a robbery. I saw the bastards drive away from the gas station in a black pickup with a filthy, mud-encrusted license plate. The cops were sympathetic, but in Oklahoma the words 'black pickup truck' are redundant."

By now I was so fascinated by Cat's narration, I'd forgotten all about Samson's unauthorized biography. I had even forgotten about poached egg whites in sugar.

Cat and I finished our lunch, left the restaurant, and just wandered, no specific direction, until we reached the New York Public Library. Seated on the steps in front of its columnar facade, leaning our butts against the base of a lion, we continued our discussion.

"Where," said Cat, "were we?"

"Tulsa."

"Right. After Dancer's death, I began hitchhiking to California. Enter a quartet I'll call Winkin, Blinkin, Nod and Son. I can't remember their real names, not that it matters. They were three businessmen and one pimply offspring, off on some sort of a hunting trip. The quartet made room for me in a Ford Bronco filled with Dr Pepper, whiskey, and an ice chest that reeked of partially defrosted cow. I surmised that the hunters didn't intend to eat their kill. To make a long story short, Wink wanted me to spend a week in their cabin. If I shared Son's bedroll, Wink said he'd spring for a plane ticket to L.A.X."

(People gravitate to you, Frannie. You're like a magnet. I've seen strangers stop you on the street and tell you their life's story.)

For a while Cat and I sunned ourselves in silence. Then she yawned. "I must be boring you, Frannie. I'm boring me."

"No, really, please go on."

"Where was I?"

"Wink and Son."

"Right. Every morning Wink, Blink and Nod left the cabin with guns and fishing poles, but the only thing they ever caught was a sunburn. Meanwhile, Son and I structured our game plan. You see, Son was…well, let's just say he was asexual. So every night we pretended, with lots of moaning and groaning. Wink was happy and I got my one-way ticket to Hollywood." Cat looked up at the library. "However, with apologies to Ernest Hemingway, I doubt that Son will ever rise."

When I finished laughing, I said, "This is fun, but I'm supposed to be asking you about Madison."

"I've had enough fresh air and sunshine, Frannie. Let's find a shady cave and I'll talk about Madison."

We hopped onto a bus and got off near the Boxing Hall of Fame, an old loft on the edge of the garment district.

"This is probably the most off-beat museum in the city," Cat said.

She and I strolled past display collections of photographs, gongs, timers and pocket watches, all donated by famous sportsmen. Then we passed an array of gloves, punching bags, and championship belts.

The theme from *Rocky* vibrated inside my head.

We finally stopped in front of several showcases that contained fist sculpture. I thought about Sol Aarons as I stared at bronze-colored plaster casts. On the casts, names had been printed in white—Joe Lewis, Rocky Graziano, Floyd Patterson, the great Mohammed Ali.

"Okay," said Cat, "where were we?"

"One-way ticket to Hollywood."

"Right. That's where I met Madison."

"And?"

"I moved in with him. A year later we split, so I shifted my tailbone to New York and I haven't seen him since."

"And?"

"End of story."

"Cat, do you want me to ask questions?"

"No."

"I don't understand."

She stared at Ali's bronzed fist. "I thought I'd give you generalities, Frannie, make stuff up. But you're too nice, not at all what I expected."

"What did you expect?"

"I figured Mickey Roebuck sent you to question me girl-to-girl, pillow talk and intimate details. He looked the type. Mr. Macho."

"Oh no, Cat. I mean, he's macho, but he's also generous and sweet and...didn't Samson...that's his nickname...didn't he tell you that I've been cast in Madison's new movie?"

"No, he didn't." Cat looked startled, but in a nice way.

"I'm doubling for Lynn Beth Sullivan," I said, "after she gets possessed."

"You don't look very demon-ish, Frannie."

"Wait till you see me in Sol's makeup."

"My part's easy. Angst, angst, angst. And, every once in a while, hysteria."

"Angst is easy?"

"It is when you're standing near Victor Madison."

"Speaking of Madison—"

"Frannie, let's get out of here, taxi to my place."

"Sure. Where do you live?"

"The West Village."

She hailed a cab and we traveled down cobblestones, past brownstone buildings, old cafes, street singers, flea markets and fruit stands. Finally, we slowed and halted next to a tree-lined curb.

"Now it's too expensive and chi-chi," Cat said, paying our driver. "But this area attracted poets and artists *en masse* in the fifties. The Village has more shoe shops than any other street in the world," she added, unlocking her door.

I glanced down at my sandals and my Mets-orange toenails, then stared at my new friend's slender form.

She didn't *look* like a white rabbit, but oh, dear, oh, shit…

Was I about to catapult myself into another Wonderland?

EIGHTEEN

Following Cat, I entered into a world of Roy Liechtenstein and American Indians. Liechtenstein's colorful pop art canvases lined the walls. Oak shelves held native American books, crafts and toys.

Above the shelves were masks that Cat said represented the mythical forest creatures whom the Indians believed had powers to cure diseases. By impersonating the spirit, she said, a man who wore the false face gained the power to cure.

"What about a woman?" I asked, remembering my mother's take-some-Nyqil-and-call-the-Rabbi-in-the-morning.

"I don't know, Frannie. I've never put the masks on."

"When did you become interested in Indian artifacts?"

"The day after I could afford to buy 'em." She smiled. "Maybe it's Oral Roberts' backlash again."

"Or maybe it's 'Prince of Darkness' fallout."

"What? Who?"

"Victor Madison."

"Oh. Right. Sit down, Frannie."

I sank onto a white, nubby-cushioned couch. Cat placed a bowl of candies atop a marble-top coffee table. Chewing a chocolate, I sighed, nodded, and said, "*Le Chocolatier*. Behind the tailor shop."

She grinned. "Correct."

I reached for another French-style chocolate, then gave my wrist a slap. "I'm supposed to lose ten pounds. During my first interview with Suzanne Burton, she mentioned a nude scene. Please tell me about Madison. Maybe I'll forget the candy."

"We met. I lived with him for thirteen months. Thirteen used to be my favorite number."

"Cat, you're doing it again."

"Sorry. We met and fell madly in lust. Our relationship was like a see-saw. Up, down, up, down. Remember that thing we used to chant when we were kids? See-saw, Marjorie Daw, Johnny will have a new master? I never did understand what that meant, still don't. But Mary Catherine Lelia Sanchez found herself a new master, and loved every minute of it...until the end."

"Where did you and Madison meet?"

"I waited tables. Madison frequented my restaurant, but he never tipped. One night, royally pissed-off, I told him off, and got my ass fired."

"Good for you. I wish I had the nerve. I wait tables, Cat, at least I did. I quit after my screen test. Sorry, where were we? Madison got you fired. Then what?"

"He took me home with him."

"How romantic."

"Yes. Romantic."

"Tell me about his house. Does it have a gazillion rooms?"

"Have another chocolate, Frannie. Madison lives in a caretaker's cottage, on a large estate. The estate is owned by a very successful Vegas financier."

"Mafia," I breathed.

"Nope. In thirteen months I never saw a hidden shoulder holster, although I once waved at a man who looked like Frank Sinatra."

"It's hard to believe Madison lives in a cottage."

"Why? He's always on location. Anyway, the cottage was posh. Screening room, solarium with hot tub, a guest room, screening room, and a library as big as a bookstore. Rumor has it the cottage is haunted by a ghost who looks like Vivian Leigh. Your face is wonderful, Frannie. You'd never be able to bluff at poker."

"I'm still trying to adjust to a caretaker's cottage, although what you just described doesn't exactly sound like a hole in the wall. Madison has oodles of money, doesn't he? They say he can't win an Academy Award because his films are too commercial, too successful."

"That's only partly true. He's had some *major* flops, and he can be rude, crude and obnoxious. He pisses people off, important people, because he rarely, if ever, plays by the rules..." Cat paused to light a cigarette. "Do you remember his first full-length movie?"

"Sure. It's legend. He shot a low-budget horror film, based on a train monster who devoured commuters. The heroine was a little girl with Mouseketeer ears, an Elizabeth Taylor look-alike. Madison always aimed his cameras at the devour-ees, but he never showed the monster. His background music was Sly and the Family Stone, James Brown, and the sound of snakes hissing. He kept the audience glued to their seats, and no one could enter the theatre after the movie started."

"Madison followed that up with a couple of sequels. Monsters kept breeding anew in Manhattan's underground subway system. The little girl grew older. Last I heard, she was attending Yale."

"It wasn't the movie's plot, per se. That was predictable." Crossing my legs, I reached for another chocolate. "It's the way Madison uses his camera to create moods. And this might sound funny, Cat, but twice I cried when the monster died."

"Did you cry during the last sequel, when the girl died? Madison's backers were furious, and he almost went bust."

Out of the blue, I remembered my mother's question, the one she'd asked on my answering machine, the one where she wanted to know if Madison was as scary as his movies. Before I could stop myself, I said, "What's he like, really? Damn. My poker face again, huh? I'm so afraid I'll sound like a voyeur."

"No problem, Frannie. We kept a low profile, and the paparazzi went batshit. It's hard to explain, but our esteemed director collects wounded animals, especially birds with broken wings." She torpedoed her cigarette into an ashtray. "He changed my name to Catherine Lee Sands, paid for acting lessons, and didn't expect anything in return, even though I worshipped him."

"Cat, I'm sorry. This is none of my business, and Samson will never hear one word, I promise."

"In that case, I'll tell you about our unhappily-ever-after."

(*People gravitate to you, Frannie. You're like a magnet.*)

"I've never told anyone before." She lit another cigarette, and I saw that her hands were shaking. "Victor was at a business meeting when I discovered reels of vintage Disney inside the projection room. Remember that bit with Mickey Mouse as the sorcerer's apprentice?"

"Yes. *Fantasia.*"

"Victor stumbled into the projection room. He was a mess, his clothes torn, his face gashed. Drunk, too. For the first time he became the aggressor, as if he had something to prove. Like an idiot, I didn't leave the room, didn't even try. Then he became amorous, beastly, explicitly lewd. I shoved him away, asked him what had happened, screamed that he needed a doctor, but he ignored me."

"Please, Cat, you really don't—"

"It was so weird, Frannie. Victor stood in front of the screen, his shadow blending with Mickey Mouse's shadow. He...Victor...ripped off my nightgown...I was wearing a nightgown, did I tell you that?"

"Madison raped you, right?"

"Yes. No. I wanted him, but not like that. I'll never forget what he said. He said, 'Mickey's jealous, but no one tells me what to do.'"

"Mickey Mouse?"

Cat nodded. "I was furious. And hurt. Not physically. You just said you were afraid of playing voyeur. I accused Victor of enlisting the aid of an animated mouse to play voyeur. It wasn't pretty, the stuff I screamed...to tell the God's honest truth, it was almost as if I had the devil inside me...like that exorcist movie, or our movie. My voice didn't even sound like me. It was growly..." She took a deep breath. "The next morning I got my walking papers. April Fool's Day, 1989. Victor's lawyer...a huge palimony settlement. I moved to Manhattan. The rest you know."

"Samson will never hear this, I swear."

"Thanks. I don't know why, but I trust you Frannie. And it's a ...relief...telling my bizarre tale to a stranger."

I accepted that premise. Hadn't I contemplated confessing, to a stranger, the bizarre events that had occurred during my Night of Wine and Roses? I might have told Cat about the click-beetles, except by now I'd convinced myself that they were roaches, emerging from one of my apartment wall cracks, then scurrying back inside when I passed out and Andre turned all the lights on.

"I hope I'm not a stranger any more," I said.

Cat smiled. "Give me your life story and we'll remedy that."

I chatted on and on about my so-called career, Andre, and my mother, but Cat only half-listened. She wouldn't make it in a poker game either, I thought, because she's definitely hiding something. At one point, while I was talking about Mom's "subtle" hints for a grandkid, I saw Cat stroke her flat belly.

Had Cat been pregnant when she'd split with Madison?

Had she miscarried?

Given the baby up for adoption?

Or did it exist somewhere away from the limelight?

I couldn't ask. It would be like someone asking Carol Brady if her first husband, the dead one, had actually fathered Marcia, Jan and Cindy. I mean, none of those kids looked alike.

I chewed the last of the *Le Chocolatier* candies to avoid asking personal questions, but my mind raced.

Had Catherine Lee Sands given birth to Victor Madison's son or daughter?

Had Cat given Madison the silver lighter?

To M from S. To Madison from Sands?

It was none of my business. Except Cat...and Bonnie...had made it my business. Why did Madison have this thing for Disney?

Simple explanation. Madison was a perfectionist. So were the animated panels from the Disney studios. Madison used the innocent, exuberant, irrepressible cartoons to alleviate stress, the same way I used The Spa's whirlpool.

Fear had been my off-again, on-again companion ever since the *Forever Asmodeus* audition. I didn't mind Madison's Clark Kent persona, but I didn't want Superman's X-ray vision.

Madison had X-ray vision. He did. He could see into a person's soul, and that scared the shit out of me.

My tongue probed at a tiny piece of cashew, stuck between my teeth. There was no mystery, I thought, no underlying enigma, no skeleton in the attic.

Was there?

The Prince of Darkness is a gentleman.

Only this particular gentleman, stimulated by a virginal waif named Cinderella, had screwed one friend. And he had seduced... make that raped...my new friend, cheered on by a squeaky-voiced rodent who donned red shorts to hide the family jewels.

Hooray for Hollywood. New York pretended to be cool, but Hollywood still employed old-fashioned censorship. Peter Pan was gelded. Tinkerbell wore "me-Jane-you-Tarzan" regalia. Minnie Mouse flaunted panties.

I watched Cat clear away the empty candy dish, her ballerina's grace gone, her movements uncertain. I had stirred up memories like a bitchy witch bending over a crock-pot. *Double, double, toil and trouble, Catherine will have a new master.*

"When do you fly to Houston?" I said, changing the subject.

"I don't," she said.

"You're not taking the part?"

"I'm not flying. If God had meant me to fly—"

"She would have given you wings."

"She would have given me a stomach that doesn't do flip-flops every time it leaves the ground. Have you heard of Charlie Daniels?"

"Of course. Except for John Travolta, he was the best thing in *Urban Cowboy*."

"Charlie's an old pal. He's touring, and he has this comfy bus, so I'm hitching a ride to Texas."

Texas. The stars at night are big and bright, deep in the heart of Michener. Edna Ferber's *Giant*. The movie *Giant,* with Rock and Liz and James Dean. John Wayne. Remember the Alamo.

Suddenly, I remembered the *Urban Cowboy* cowgirl, writhing seductively on top of a mechanical bull while Charlie's bow and fiddle coated everything with breezy layers of *pizzicato* cool.

Hadn't Charlie sung about the Devil going down?

That night I met Samson at Starbucks.

"Sorry, sweetie, no juicy tidbits," I said, having mentally edited my Cat Sands interview until there was nothing left except a detailed description of Madison's posh cottage.

Samson thanked me nicely and paid for my Caffé Latte, but he gave me the same look my mother gives me when I tell her I never forget to dead bolt my apartment door.

A Manhattan Subway Station - 1983

Victor Madison stared at the subway poster—*Torch Song Trilogy*. At the same time, he drummed his fingertips against his black jeans. Inside his head, he heard Lionel Ritchie's *Truly*.

An image came to mind: his mother tap-tapping on table tops, as if she played a "piana." Victor flexed his fingers.

Rose Mostel had died shortly after Peggy's Marilyn Monroe bit...

No. Blue-pencil the Marilyn Monroe comparison. Marilyn's death had been an accident, although she had to know, deep down inside, that she'd never live happily ever after. Shit, that realization would make anybody crack up...unless they admitted to themselves that happily-ever-after was an illusory concept.

Victor had no illusions. He didn't have any guilt, either. Because Piglet's impetuous Kamikaze exploit wasn't his fault. He had merely tried to protect his investment, keep his sister from ball-and-chaining herself to some Phrygian civil service king who'd reverse the Midas touch and turn Victor/Chaim's hard-earned emergency gold into ashy residue.

And if anyone believes that bullshit, Victor thought, *tell them you have a bridge for sale, and it's not far from where you used to live.*

Although she said Peggy "broke her heart," Ma's killer had been a cuticle remover. Ignoring a deep, ugly thumb-gash, the infection had spread to her whole hand, then her arm, then her torso. She must have suffered incredible pain, but (shunning the synagogue) she spent her days and nights inside a neighborhood church, finding Jesus, and when she finally saw a doctor she was terminally gangrened.

To Victor's surprise, while he'd been paying for Piglet's piano and ballet lessons, orthodontist, private school tuition, and amoral theatre dress, Ma had been paying the premiums on a life insurance policy. The compensation wasn't a fortune, but there was enough for film school, and once he'd sold the Brooklyn brownstone to Mrs. O'Connor's divorced-but-not-really-divorced-because-she's-Catholic daughter, he could "emergency" himself for a change.

Following Peggy's duck-dildo number, Donald Blaustein had given the words "Jewish guilt" a whole new meaning. He'd also given Peggy's big brother the money to shoot *Anthophilous*, a little film about a priest trounced by the Antichrist. Manhattan-in-miniature was set aflame while grotesque gargoyles gnawed on roasted flesh. There was even a brilliant playground scene where vultures pecked at a swinging corpse whose white panties flashed every time her swing swung.

Victor's professor graded the short subject C+,

("Fuck film school, I quit," Victor said)

but it won a few minor awards and became a cult favorite. The cultists branded Madison heir apparent to Orson Welles. The *Times* wrote an article lauding Madison's cinematography.

Thanks to the *Times* article, and the fact that his film made an oodle (he would have preferred oodles) of money, the financing for his low- budget feature-length movie, *D-Train To Hell*, had been no sweat.

He was only twenty-seven, and he wished the A & P manager could see him now.

Christ on a crutch. Orson's heir-apparent hadn't finished shooting *D-Train*, and already his investors were talking about *Express Train To Hell*—a fucking sequel and his second full-length feature.

With a grin, Victor punched the button on his tape recorder. A trip to the Bronx Zoo's reptile house with a state-of-the-art, borrowed tape recorder and—*viola*—the flawless blend of rhythm and blues, early California rock, and snake-hiss. The snakes sounded nicely sibilant, like the spray of water from a defective shower head.

Loud, obtrusive, his background music would spawn shivery sensations, and he felt a congratulatory erection build. But the turgid swelling diminished when he glanced down at his script. Why had the goddamn writers named the monster-slash-antagonist Clootie? Kids would mentally translate it into Cootie.

("Ya got cooties, Omar Chaim?" his schoolmates had taunted, after Ma discovered body lice and shaved his head.)

Victor looked up and down the subway tracks. Another train, a local rather than an express, was due any moment, and he needed exterior shots. For those shots, he'd use real passengers, a few paid extras, and...

Snapping his fingers, he nodded toward the script girl. She scurried to his side, her face a mask of fearsome anticipation, her unfettered breasts bobbing beneath her Angora sweater.

"Strike out all references to Clootie, sweetheart," he said.

"Why?" Taking a few steps backward, she leaned against another subway poster. *Cats*. Black background, yellow eyes.

Too bad the nest of dark hair between her legs didn't match her platinum Farah-Fawcett-curls. Too bad her brains were as thick as her ankles. Too bad he had taken her to bed and kept his slightly altered promise—a *job* on his first movie rather than a part in his first movie.

"I've got my reasons," he said. "First, call Sol Aarons."

"Ya wanna see him?"

"Yes, you idiot. Set up a meeting."

"Oh-oh-okay," she stammered. "For when?"

"Yesterday. Move your butt, sweetheart. Tell Sol 'ASAP.'"

I won't show the monster, Victor thought, *so he doesn't need a name.* Christ, was he a genius or what? A genius whose resurrected erection threatened to burst through his jocks.

He focused on one of the extras. Tall. Lovely blue-green eyes. Long, red-tinged hair. And a mouth that looked as if it could suck a corpse until a formerly flaccid body part became dilated with blood.

Victor beckoned, then pointed to his director's chair.

Leisurely strolling toward the chair, the extra's motions were lithesome, no scurry, no fear.

Interesting, Victor thought, drumming his fingertips against his jeans. Inside his head, he heard his *D-Train To Hell* soundtrack.

NINETEEN

Leaning across Andre, gazing through the small porthole, I thought about singing *Good Morning Starshine* (from the musical *Hair)*. Only it wasn't morning and there were no stars.

Our plane was sandwiched between Houston and Heaven, and I wondered if God cut the crust off clouds. If only I could have traveled by bus, with Cat Sands and Charlie Daniels, because, to be perfectly honest, airplanes make me hyper, tense, *high*-strung. Which movie plot served up the tainted fish that caused the flight crew and half the passengers to flounder between life and death? *Knock, knock, who's there? Juliet. Juliet who? Juliet the fish so she can't land the plane.*

We roller-coastered and all the fasten-your-seatbelt signs lit up. Consumed with an almost epileptic fear, I jostled Andre's script.

He gave me one of my mother's patented martyr-sighs and said, "Frannie, try to relax. Visit the cockpit and ask Peter Pan Pilot if he'll teach you how to fly."

"Very funny. And while we're on the subject, would you like to explain where cockpit got its name?"

"Grow up," he mumbled.

Time for a change of subject. "You'll have your part memorized before the first rehearsal, Andre."

"Not if you keep interrupting."

"Switch seats with me. I'll look out the window and count the stars."

Andre didn't respond; probably hadn't even heard me. He'd been doing that a lot lately. I could say: *ohmigod-the-apartment's-on-fire.* and he'd say: *what's-for-supper-Frannie?*

As we shifted, I wriggled my tush provocatively. Andre didn't rise to the bait, didn't even give my tush a conciliatory pat.

And yet, recently, he'd been in a great mood. Galveston Dinner Theatre, also known as GDT, had softened the blow of his soap opera demise. The fiancé bit hadn't been necessary; GDT's owners were overjoyed to hire a bona-fide Tee-Vee star. They'd scheduled *Bus Stop* for their first production, and Andre would perform the lead role of the naïve cowboy, Beau.

Coincidentally, GDT's resident director was an old friend.

"Remember Richard Dean?" Andre had asked while we were shrouding our furniture with sheets...definitely a WASP tradition. Mom would have "protected" the furniture from day one, even the barber chair. With plastic. That way, the plastic gets dirty while the furniture stays clean, and usually the plastic stays clean because nobody wants to sit on it. The only exceptions to what I call the "Rosen plastique" are Mom's kitchen, Daddy's workshop, the basement's washer, dryer, freezer, Ping-Pong table, and ironing board (for Mom's cleaning lady), my bedroom—now a guest room—and the patio barbecue.

"Richard Dean," I repeated. "Didn't he once appear on your soap? As a doctor or something?"

"Close. Veterinarian. Remember that dumb dog who slobbered all the time? When Trish slipped on dog drool, they fired the mutt and stuffed the vet's story-line. Anyway, he...Rick, not the dog...owns a duplex in Clear Lake City, not far from Galveston. Rick lives in one half, the other half's vacant. I can have it for utilities and—"

"We'll split expenses, right?"

Startled, he said, "Won't *your* crew be based in Houston?"

"Yes, but they're shooting my scenes south of Clear Lake City. If I stay with you, I can bank my per diem? Isn't *that* a good idea?"

"Yeah, sure," Andre said, but it sounded like *frankly-my-dear-I-don't-give-a-damn.*

"Honey, let's talk about this," I had pleaded, meaning the Night of Wine and Roses, knowing he'd know what I meant.

He said, "What's for supper, Frannie?"

When I tried to bring it up again, he said, "Forget it, Frannie."

However, I couldn't forget my psychic's prediction: *Everything will begin to happen in a festive atmosphere. Be careful. There are negative forces possessive toward others and jealous of your success.*

I pictured Mrs. Carvainis levitating a few inches above the plane's wing, her gold tooth challenging the sun.

Our flight attendant could have doubled for *Wheel of Fortune*'s Vanna White. Leaning across Andre, her breasts shaded his eyes like a visor as she looked into *my* eyes and asked if I wanted steak, chicken, or fish for dinner.

"Definitely not fish," I said, but she was indulging in airline humor. My menu options were peanuts or peanuts…and booze. Daddy had given me some emergency grocery money, so I handed Vanna a twenty, pocketed the change, and slurped a couple of vodkas. On the rocks.

Andre looked up from his script.

"Slow down, lil lady," he drawled. "I don't wanna haf'ta' carry y'all through the airport like a piece of gol-dang luggage."

"Y'all is plural," I said, "and I'm not Wendy. I hate flying."

Defiantly, I pressed Vanna's buzzer and ordered another Smirnoff. Had they been hedge clippers, her breasts could have trimmed Andre's hair as she leaned over to hand me the miniature bottle. This time, I could make out the letters on her nametag: FAITH.

I finally un-stressed. To have faith is to have wings.

TWENTY

Three days later, I watched insects spatter the windshield of my borrowed stick-shift. Richard Dean, who looks like Shakespeare's Puck, had impishly bestowed a name upon his old, dented, yellow car. Yoda the Toyota. Cute.

Before lending me the car, Rick had given me a quick lesson in how to clutch, then complimented me on my hand-foot coordination. I didn't bother telling him that my flexibility came from years of dancing the hokey-pokey, the bunnyhop, and the hora. Weddings and bar mitzvahs were especially big on the hora, an Israeli circle dance where the music increases, speed-wise. Most people corkscrewed their feet, but practice makes perfect and I'd had way too much practice (Charlene, Marlene, and Mark, from my mom's side of the family, were married, engaged and significantly-othered. All, of course, had been bar mitzvahed and bas mitzvahed. Meanwhile, Daddy's side of the family included dozens of first, second and third-rate cousins).

Clutching the slippery steering wheel, I tried to remember the directions to the *Forever Asmodeus* get-acquainted party without sneaking a peek at the piece of paper buried inside my purse. I had driven my father's car all over Long Island, from Great Neck to West Babylon, but Texans speak a foreign language, including the words: North, South, East, West. New Yorkers never give directions that way. If one is not driving into Manhattan via the Queens Midtown Tunnel or Paul Simon's groovy Fifty-Ninth Street Bridge, directions pinpoint shopping centers, churches, synagogues, a McDonald's or three, and stoplights. Example: "When you get to the McDonald's on the corner, don't do anything. Go to the next stoplight and hang a left."

Ordinarily, I could deal with compass directions *and* Houston-style humidity. But Yoda's air conditioning was on the blink, and even with all the windows open, I felt sluggish, as if I were trapped inside an esoteric, George Lucasonian sauna.

The car radio worked...one station...Golden Oldies, or Oldie Goldies, or Songs Goldie Hawn Might Have Sung, or whatever the heck the retrospective was called. Its DJ promised commercials on the half hour, time and weather every fifteen minutes. Judy Collins sang about making her entrance again with her usual flair, sure of her lines.

Send in the damn clowns, send in Frannie Rosen. Sweat streaked my makeup, my nose flaunted a sunburn, the traffic was bumper to bumper, at least ten of the bumpers stated: GUNS DON'T KILL, PEOPLE KILL, Yoda's transmission groaned in protest, the road's white dividing line wavered in the heat, I wasn't sure of *my* lines, and Jeremy Glenn would be at the restaurant...Madison's Guest of Honor.

Swell.

On TV, Jeremy clobbered bad guys into submission or car-chased them into oblivion. But he needed no weapons to subdue bad girls. He simply charmed them to death.

Once upon a time Andre had charmed the socks off me, not to mention the rest of my clothes. His melt-Oscar smile, however, was wearing thin. Tonight he rehearsed in Galveston.

I'd met a few *Bus Stop* cast members and crew. Prominent among the stage hands were twins, Bambi and Fawn. They shared angelic faces and what my Uncle Lars would have called Scandihoovian-blonde hair. Four mammary protuberances stretched their elastic halter tops while a couple of rounded butts threatened to split the seams of their cut-offs. My mother would have baptized them Goyim Slut One and Goyim Slut Two. Andre thought they were adorable.

He and I hadn't consummated our safe arrival. By the time we'd completed the long drive from the airport to Rick's duplex, I was what my Australian pal Gordon would have called "pissed as forty cats."

Entering the living room, staring at its fireplace, swigging from my umpteenth miniature vodka bottle, I'd sung who's afraid of the big bad demon, the big bad demon, the big bad demon. Andre had swept me up into his arms, navigated the stairs a la Rhett Butler, deposited me on the queen-size bed, and exited stage left.

Ever since, Andre had spent the majority of his time at *Bus Stop* rehearsals. I had spent the majority of my time sunning myself on a redwood deck, re-reading my dog-eared copy of *Forever Asmodeus*, and petting Rick's dog Ginger, whose name had been inspired by the *Gilligan's Island* movie star, or as my psychic would say, "Gilligan's ecktriss."

The party locale—a seafood restaurant—was supposedly ten minutes from Rick's duplex, fifteen max. I had been driving for twenty minutes.

Braking Yoda at a stoplight, I fumbled inside my purse and retrieved my directions.

TWENTY-ONE

Woodcock's Wharf roosted on the edge of the Gulf, amidst seafood retail shops and tourist-oriented bars. When I arrived, the setting sun looked like a huge, newly-minted penny.

After curbing Yoda, I strode through a parking lot covered with finely-ground seashells. Then I introduced myself to the cop who stood by the front entrance. Security was as tight as my mother's pink panty girdle. A few Jeremy Glenn groupies grouped, but most were bivouacked outside his Houston hotel.

I passed my identity quiz with flying colors, and the cop waved me inside. Taking a deep breath, actually several deep breaths, I climbed a flight of stairs and walked into a large room.

A plate-glass window framed seashore and nightfall. To my left was a polished mahogany bar. An authentic jukebox squatted against one wall. At the far end of the room, a piano bar was flanked by a dozen brown-cushioned stools.

Thirty cast and crew members, maybe more, mingled, but all I saw was Jeremy Glenn. Straight white teeth. Dimples that deepened when he smiled. Dark hair, professionally tousled. His eyes…I spun an imaginary color wheel and the imaginary arrow landed on cobalt blue.

He wore khaki slacks and a Denver-Broncos-blue golf shirt. Short sleeves revealed bronzed forearms and an almost Herculean dedication to weight lifting. Snakeskin boots added another couple of inches to his over-six-feet height.

Christ, no one could be *that* perfect. Maybe the tousled hair was a toupee. Maybe the eyes were colored contacts. Maybe the bulge between his thighs was a rolled-up pair of socks.

"Frannie, yoo-hoo, over here, I saved you a seat." Lynn Beth Sullivan indicated an empty Captain's chair, pulled away from a wood-plank table.

I smiled and walked toward her. Jeremy stood at the head of the table. As I passed him, our bodies collided and I dropped my purse. We both bent down to retrieve it…and bumped foreheads.

He helped me rise, his fingers loosening the white silk blouse I had tucked into my black Calvin Klein crepe evening pants.

Tall, I thought, *he's so tall, taller than Andre,* and I wondered if, looking down, he could see the cleavage I'd desperately tried to enhance with a Victoria's Closet underwire bra.

"Hello," he said. "Any permanent damage to your head?"

I searched my brain for a scintillating reply. "It is better to be knocked over," I said, "than knocked up."

"What?"

"Sorry. I was paraphrasing Mae West, who said 'It is better to be looked over than overlooked.'"

I knew my nose looked like a clown's, but were my cheeks now patched with crimson? What's black and white and red all over? My stupnagel cousin Charlene would say an embarrassed zebra, but she'd be wrong. Unless she took a wild guess and said, "Cousin Frannie."

Jeremy's dimples flashed. Then he turned and headed toward the piano bar.

I continued my trip around the table. Lynn Beth wore a yellow sundress and cork-soled wedges. Sliding my tush over polished wood, I said, "What do you think of Jeremy Glenn, in person?"

"He'd baaaad," she said, sounding like Mary's lamb. "When he hugged me I almost fainted."

A waitress materialized, jostling my elbow as she placed a platter of raw oysters on top of the table. Her name tag stated: KELLY. She had the body of a clarinet. No breasts. No tush. Her expression was vacuous until she glanced over at Jeremy Glenn.

He's baaaad, I thought, *and bad is good.*

Carafes of white and red wine garnished the table. I poured some white into an empty glass and washed down a few oysters.

"Yuk," said Lynn Beth, drowning a shrimp in blood-colored sauce. "How can you eat that, Frannie? It looks like Asmodeus throw-up."

I laughed. "What are you drinking, kiddo?"

She held up a toothpick, speared through a cherry and pineapple wedge. "A pina colada…virgin. Mommy would kill me if I drank wine."

"Been there, done that," I said. "Once I sneaked a few sips during a family celebration and got grounded for three weeks."

"I'd probably get grounded for life. Mommy's mad as hell tonight because Shelly didn't come with us."

Lynn Beth's *Mommy* was still jarring, and I pictured Faye Dunaway as Joan Crawford, insisting that her adopted daughter call her Mommy Dearest. "Sheldon Giglia?" I said. "Our assistant director?"

"Uh-huh. They had a big fight." Lynn Beth twisted a ginger-colored curl around her index finger, then let it spring back to join the mass of hair that framed her face like a fancy bathing cap. "I hate it when Mommy breaks up with her boyfriends. Would you order me another shrimp cocktail, Frannie?"

I summoned Kelly, and saw Victor Madison chatting with Jeremy Glenn, who now stood near the piano player. I could have sworn Jeremy nodded toward me and Madison shook his head, but maybe my overactive imagination was acting up again.

The Prince of Darkness wore black jeans, a black shirt with silver threads, and a black Stetson. Thanks to Cat and Bonnie, I no longer thought: *Clark Kent.* But I remembered Samson's apt description: *His eyes seemed to flash black lightning.*

A few more people sat at our table, and I excused myself to use the restroom, which had a Mermaid on the door.

As I pressed my palms against the Mermaid and opened the door, party sounds receded and I heard the now-familiar *click-click-click.*

TWENTY-TWO

Standing in front of a wall-mounted hand-dryer, Bonnie drip-dried her wet hands. As I watched, she *click-clicked* the dryer's start button, rejuvenating the warm whiff.

Apparently, she'd just finished brushing her hair because her ebony strands seemed to crackle with static. She wore white tailored slacks and a sleeveless blouse in various shades of violet and gold. A charm bracelet encircled one slender wrist. I had given her the sweet-sixteen charm that hung from its chain-linked middle.

"Hi, Bon," I said, as she began to retrieve her purse.

Her black-rimmed, pansy-flower eyes met mine in the mirror above the sink. "Frannie. Oh God, Frannie, it's so good to see you."

"You, too. We haven't talked since New York. I tried to call you at the hotel, but—"

"I know. I'm sorry. I got your message…messages, but I've been so tired. Victor added more Martine scenes, and he never shoots one take. I swear, Frannie, we're lucky if he gets the scene he wants in fifty takes."

Momentarily, I felt green with envy. Bonnie had a real part; she didn't double for someone else. Bonnie had slept with Victor Madison, even if the experience had been a tad weird. I hadn't slept with Andre since the Night of Wine and Roses.

"What's wrong?" Bonnie said. "Your face is all scrunched up."

"Nothing. I suddenly letched for your Martine role, that's all."

"You couldn't play Martine," she said with a wink. "Because the only French you know is *Le Chocolatier.*"

"True." I gave her a smile and a hug. "Tell me about you and Madison. Tell me about the shoot. Tell me everything."

Her dark-winged brows merged. "There's been no publicity, Frannie, none at all. It's unbelievable, considering how many people are involved.

Aside from Cat Sands, Lynn Beth, me, and a dozen high school students, there's the crew. Surely one person—"

"What are you talking about?"

"The accidents."

"What accidents?"

"Cat hurt her back. We all had mild food poisoning. Filming was held up by what the locals fondly call a tropical storm...I'd call it a hurricane....and we didn't have electricity for two days. Then one of the electricians almost shocked himself to death. And there have been little things, missing props and a diamondback rattlesnake who—"

"Whoa. A real, honest-to-God rattlesnake? You're talking fangs and forked tongue?"

"Absolutely."

"Where did it come from?"

Bonnie gave me the ghost of a grin. "An egg, I think. Don't mama snakes lay eggs?"

I recalled, in detail, my bus ride to The Spa—the "Birdman of West 56th. Street" and the heavy woman's pet carrier. "Please tell me where the snake came from, Bon. It might be important."

"I'm not sure where it came from, Frannie, but our technical advisor removed it."

"Technical advisor? Asmodeus has a technical advisor? Who is he? A priest? Evangelist? Presidential candidate?"

"Not even close. Madison met this young black woman while he was in New York, or she met him, or they bumped into each other...who knows? He's enthralled with her, and after the first few accidents he flew her to Houston. Frannie, she's a witch. You don't believe in Satanism or covens, but I do, and—"

"Tenia," I breathed, then watched Bonnie's face turn one shade lighter than a honeydew melon.

"That's right," she gasped. "How did you know?"

I heard an echo: *Ain't got no cat. Snake.* "Tenia and I 'bumped into each other' the day after my birthday, on a bus, following my psychic session. A man who looked and acted stoned gave her his seat, the only empty seat on the bus, which happened to be next to my seat, and Tenia said she had a pet snake."

Bonnie just stared at me.

I said, "It's got to be a weird coincidence. Right?"

"I guess."

"You guess?"

"Of course it's coincidental," Bonnie said, her voice too New York. Unless she's agitated, she has no discernible accent. Now, she sounded like *The Sopranos.*

"Do you think Madison structured the accidents, Bon?"

"Why would he do that?"

"To make his actors nudgy, scared, in the mood."

"Get real, Frannie. He ate the tainted food, too. And he couldn't order up a tropical storm, could he?"

"How long has Tenia been a member of the crew?"

"A week."

"When did the snake appear?"

"Her second day. Damn thing slithered onto the set as if it wanted to audition. Cat christened it George W. Tenia picked it up and carried it away. Far away, I hope, like maybe the Houston Zoo."

"Have the accidents stopped?"

"Yes."

"Is Tenia here tonight?"

"No." Bonnie giggled. "She's attending this voodoo convention at a downtown hotel."

"A voodoo convention? You're kidding, right?"

"Frannie, they have name tags. The kind you stick above your breast. No...no pins." Clutching the sink for support, Bonnie giggled helplessly.

"Hey," I said. "It's not all *that* funny."

"No pins, Frannie. What are they going to use to pierce their little doll effigies? Laser beams?"

"Bonnie, hey, cut it out."

"Sorry...tension. I'm okay. Really." She wiped at tears with the back of her hand. "How's Andre?"

"Fine." I bit my lower lip, stifling the urge to tell her the truth. If I did, we'd spend the whole night inside the Mermaid bathroom.

Instead, I brought her up to date on everything else. I told her about Rick and his duplex and Yoda the Toyota. I told her about the introductory cast party at Rick's, where I had met the twins, Bambi and Fawn. I didn't tell Bonnie that after the party I had tried to initiate sex. I didn't tell her that Andre had mumbled something about drinking too much, sorry, couldn't get it up. I didn't tell her that I wanted to un-zip Jeremy's fly and determine if his bulge was as authentic as the restaurant's jukebox.

I ended my brief recitation with a question. "What's your opinion of

Jeremy Glenn, Bonnie?"

"Epicurean," she said.

"Yeah," I said. "Wild. Orgasmic. *Bad.* I hear he's straight."

"As an arrow."

"Married?"

"Once. A long time ago. Usual cliché. The wife couldn't cope with Jem's success. Divorce City. No kids."

"Jem?"

"Wipe that look off your face, Frannie. I'm not his type."

"Who's his type?"

"Madonna."

"*The* Madonna?"

Bonnie shook her head. "Sorry. I always get them mixed up. I meant Mary-Magdalene, the model who graced last year's *Sports Illustrated* swimsuit cover. Mary-Mag visited our set the same day we found George W. Evidently Mary-Mag's not a big fan of snakes because she packed her cosmetics case and said she was flying home. Jem's gorgeous, Frannie, but he's not *my* type."

"Who's your type, Bon?"

"Victor Madison."

"Wait a sec. I thought—"

"Yes, I know. I can't explain it. Despite his idiosyncrasies, he has this seductive charm."

Silently, I agreed. Except seductive charm wasn't what my mother would call "the whole megilla." How about magnetic omnipotence?

Bottom line: there was something inside Madison that attracted even as it repulsed.

Aloud, I said, "How does he behave when he's around you? I mean, any chance of an encore performance?"

"It wasn't a performance, Frannie. He was totally sincere. Now, I crave his attention. But he's been the perfect gentleman."

The Prince of Darkness is a gentleman.

While Bonnie waited, I peed, washed my hands, and conducted an imaginary orchestra under the flatulent dryer. As we returned to the party, she said, "I saw your friend, Samson."

"Where?"

"He was scanning the hotel lobby. I waved, but he didn't wave back."

"Samson's been doing research for a Victor Madison bio, Bon. He said it was unauthorized, so he's probably lurking, sleuthing around for juicy tidbits, and he doesn't want to be acknowledged. I'm fairly certain he'll try and get in touch with me, though."

Actually, I wasn't fairly certain at all. After our tête-à-tête at Starbucks, I hadn't heard from Samson; not one word; not even a *see-you-in-Houston-darlin'*.

"If Samson does get in touch with you," Bonnie said, "Please don't mention my Madisonian fling."

With a wink, she headed toward Madison's entourage. Walking toward my table, I saw Jeremy Glenn holding court near the jukebox, charming every female in his galaxy, including a pregnant calico cat who flashed me a feline smirk as she rubbed against Jeremy's ankle.

Lynn Beth and her mother, Dawn Sullivan, leaned against the piano bar. They, along with a few others, sang, "You'll never know dear, how much I love you…"

"Please don't take my sunshine away," I sang, standing where Jeremy Glenn had stood, prior to our head-on collision.

I swallowed a half dozen raw oysters, gulped down a white wine chaser, and was about to join Lynn Beth and Dawn when I sensed someone, or something, standing behind me.

TWENTY-THREE

"Oysters intensify desire, eh?"

Jeremy huffed into my ear, his breath generating shivers.

"Want some?" I clutched my wine glass for support. "Need some?"

"I'm not an oyster kind of guy," he said, grasping my elbow and leading me away from the table.

"My name's Frannie," I said. "I'm doubling for Lynn Beth in the possession scenes. What kind of guy *are* you?"

"For starters, I like girls with long hair."

"I've got long hair."

"Hard to tell with it pinned up like that."

"I thought it made me look taller, but I'll take it down if you feed me more oysters, outside on the deck, in the dark, where we can be alone."

Dear God, I was flirting. I've never played a flirt in my whole life. I'm simply not a bat-the-eyelashes kind of girl.

What kind of girl are you, Frannie?

Well, for starters I like guys with tousled hair.

Jeremy hadn't introduced himself. Why bother? Unless I'd been locked inside a Jewish convent for the last several years, I'd recognize that famous voice and countenance. Nevertheless, I said, "You're Jeremy Glenn, right?"

"My friends call me Jem. Why do you want to look taller, Fanny? You're cute as a button. Can I buy you a real drink?"

"The name's Frannie, Jem. What do you mean a real drink? Wine's not real?"

"Wine's too mellow. No quick kick, eh?"

"Tell that to my mother."

Mom had gotten drunk on wine one Passover, when I was just a little kid. She'd sobbed something about Gracie, poor dead Gracie. I, along with everyone else, assumed she meant Grace Kelly, her favorite Gentile American Princess. But now, for no apparent reason, I recalled what my New York psychic had said, and I wondered if Mom could have been blubbering over a stillborn child.

"What's wrong, Fanny?" Jem said, and I remembered Cat's *you'd-never-make-it-in-a-poker-game* remark.

"It's Frannie," I said again, "and I'd like a Cape Codder please."

Maybe vodka and cranberry juice would blot out the memory of Mom and poor dead Gracie. As Jem walked toward the bar, Madison whistled through his fingers. "I've got a surprise," he announced. His voice, like a switchblade, sliced through multiple monologues. "A preview. We've edited some of the film from the screen tests and..."

The rest of his speech was drowned out by loud cheers, not to mention my involuntary gasp. Had Madison edited me?

Of course not. I wasn't important, a mere double. He'd show Lynn Beth Sullivan or Jem. Jem had screen-tested. So had Bonnie...

The room dimmed. A beam of light projected images on a screen, and Robin, in full makeup, appeared.

Was that Lynn Beth or me? Definitely me.

No, not really. It was a conglomeration; Lynn Beth, me, and Asmodeus.

Whoa, kill the Asmodeus bit, I told myself. Because the demon wasn't an independent entity. He didn't have a separate, distinct existence. Or even a conceptual reality.

As I stared at the screen, my palms moistened. My forehead felt clammy. Even my toes sweated. Instinctively, I began to duplicate the demon's gestures, so I found a vacant chair and sat on my hands...until Jem removed one hand and wrapped my fingers around a tall glass. He stood directly behind me. While I sipped from the glass, he caressed the nape of my neck, but I didn't know if my spasmodic shivers were generated by Jem's warm touch or Madison's edited screen test.

Probably both. I swallowed a moan. And more vodka. The bartender had added a mere splash of juice. Before you could say forever Asmodeus, I felt a rush. Heat zig-zagged toward my brain, sizzling rhyme and reason, leaving behind tendrils of satyrical lust.

In other words, I had Andre's concupiscence.

Jem removed the empty glass from my fingers. "Don't move," he said. "I'll be right back."

Move? Was he kidding? I couldn't move a muscle. Mesmerized, I stared at the screen, stared at that demon on the screen, stared at conceptual reality. I felt a growl rise in my throat, and drowned it with vodka when Jem pressed another glass against my sweaty palm.

With an effort, I resisted the urge to hurl my drink toward the demon, blot out that Frannie-Robin-Asmodeus character. Who was wonderful. Awful. Awfully wonderful.

This time, the bartender had forgotten to add ice cubes.

"Bartender forgot ice," I told Jem, as screen images finally faded.

"Sorry, Fanny. Want me to fetch you a new drink?"

Shaking my head no, I watched party guests crowd around Lynn Beth. They were smiling, praising, kissing…hey, unfair. That was me on the screen. I played the demon.

"That was me," I told Jem, "on the screen."

"Sure, Fanny."

"It was." Lurching to my feet, I stumbled toward the well-wishers. "Gonna tell 'em."

Grasping my elbow again, Jem propelled me out onto the wooden deck. Round white tables with stupid umbrellas stood guard. Empty tables, because everyone was inside. Everyone was paying homage to Madison, exalting Lynn Beth, when they should have been worshipping me. Huzzah, Frannie.

"You don't want to hassle Madison right now," Jem said.

"But I'm the demon."

Stars blinked, and in the distance water *whooshed* against a rocky shoreline. I drained the last of my drink, tossed the glass over the railing, and, still furious, turned to face Jem.

"You're not a demon, Fanny," he said, stroking my cheek with his first finger. "You're an adorable imp."

"My name's Frannie," I shouted. "With an R. Like the 'r' in Lucifer, Lord of Vermin, Prince of Darkness."

"Okay, take it easy." Tilting my chin, Jem lowered his head and kissed me.

His kiss was professional. Wet. Warm. Sincere. His hands were everywhere; under my breasts; on top of my nipples; cupping my buttocks; crushing my crepe evening pants; unpinning my hair; between my thighs.

"Stop," I said, around his thrusting tongue. "Somebody'll see us."

But my actions belied my words as I pressed my legs together, trapping his fingers.

Jem maneuvered us to the darkest corner of the deck. I felt an explosion inside my body. Sinking to my knees, I unzipped his fly.

Vaguely, I heard the jukebox. John, Paul, George and Ringo were singing about holding hands. I traced Jem's emphatic trail of belly hair until I had him fully in my grasp of my hand.

"I knew it," he said. "I knew the moment I saw you. Something in your expression…"

I flicked my tongue.

"…something in your eyes."

I flicked again.

And heard: *Click. Click. Clickclickclick.*

No. Oh, no. Twisting my head sideways, I stared at the opposite end of the deck, where thousands of beetles were avalanching from the railing, falling to the deck floor and righting themselves with a decisive click. As one entity, they crept toward Jem and me, covering the deck like a living, breathing, undulating carpet.

I wanted to run as fast as I could, toward a shelter, *any* shelter. Was the inside of the restaurant safe? Except, once again I couldn't move. Then my intuition kicked in. The beetles tended to ignore me when I was sexually aggressive.

"Say the words, superstar," I growled, dropping Jem's penis and sitting back on my heels.

"More, baby, please."

"Tell me what you want. Say the words." Dimly, I realized I had played this scene before. But hadn't the roles been reversed?

"I want you to suck, baby. And swallow. Do you swallow?"

"Yes." Staggering upright, I tugged my pants down. The beetle carpet was oscillating closer, but Jem didn't notice…*or couldn't see it.*

Should I point it out? Or continue the seduction? "You first," I said, choosing the safest course. "Eat me, drink me."

Jem knelt and crushed my hips with his hands. This time *his* tongue flickered. My legs tensed, then quivered. Jem stood up and gave me a kiss that virtually drained all the breath from my body.

A voice called, "Jeremy Glenn, are you out here?"

Victor Madison.

"Shit," Jem swore.

I yanked my pants up. Jem's tall body hid me from sight, but I had to stifle a cry when I felt the deck's railing dent my backbone.

"I'm over here, Madison," Jem said. "One of your actresses had herself too much to drink. She's a bit under the weather, eh?"

As if on cue, vodka and cranberry juice lapped at the back of my throat. I swallowed convulsively, then gagged.

"Good girl," Jem whispered. "Pretend you're sick."

Pretend? I felt a shadowy claw tickle my neck. A finger parted my lips and inserted itself. I bit the finger and my teeth came together so hard my head rocked with pain. Against my ear, a voice hissed: "I want you to try and keep your teeth apart so the mouth is structurally sound."

Sol Aarons. Somebody mimicking Sol Aarons. I gagged again.

Madison's voice: "Can I help you, Jem?"

Jem's voice: "No, thanks. She'll be fine. It's all my fault. I'm the bastard who got her drunk."

Madison: "I warned you, damn it. Who is it this time?"

I didn't hear Jem's reply. The finger thrust all the way down my throat, scratching, tickling. A disembodied voice said: *Vomit his kiss.*

Sweat and tears streamed down my face as I resisted the urge to throw up. Despite Jem's words to Madison, I wasn't drunk. I should have been, but I wasn't, even if my whole body felt like the rubber band on the end of a slingshot.

Turning abruptly, I leaned over the railing and tried to spit out the finger. It probed deeper.

I heard the hissing voice again. *Vomit his kiss.*

"Why?" I managed between clenched teeth.

He's not the one.

"Who?" I said, the word paving the way for a guttural retch.

Son of Mad. Son of Mad.

I heard Jem say, "Christ, you really are sick," as my waist caught on the railing and my toes left the deck.

"Catch her." Madison shouted. "She's going to fall."

I heard the jukebox. I want...*click-click*...to hold...*click-click*... your hand...*click-click*.

Had beetles invaded the jukebox, or was the needle stuck?

My throat unstuck. Wine and oysters and vodka and cranberries gushed as I finally gave in to the demon's finger.

The sky spun until it merged with the water. Breakers crashed against the shoreline and I smelled decaying fish.

Or did I smell decaying flesh?

That thought gave new impetus to my stomach's ejective powers. Disgorging with a vengeance, I wanted to die.

The demon laughed. Grasping the soles of my sandals, it hefted me up over the railing.

I felt my body descend, and with horrific relief, welcomed the gaping black void.

TWENTY-FOUR

An overhead fan sounded like one of those dicey slice-and-dice appliances.

Was I in hell?

Beneath my silk blouse and crepe pants, I felt a vinyl couch.

Slowly, I blinked open my eyes…and saw Bonnie's fake-gem-studded harem slippers. She perched on the edge of a scarred wooden desk, her legs dangling. Above and beyond her head, taped or hooked to the wall, were pictures of food, a calendar, a catalogue for non-slip shoes, coffee mugs, a clock shaped like an overripe tomato, and several clipboards.

I shook my head to clear spider webs, checked my body for broken bones, didn't find any, and said, "Am I fired?"

She chuckled. "Most people would say 'where am I?'"

"I'm obviously inside an office. This is just an educated guess, but it's the restaurant manager's office, right?"

"As rain."

The ceiling fan's blades were filthy, but sharp. I watched one blade nudge an obese, Texas-size fly, probably a horsefly.

With a shudder, I sat up and said, "Tainted food."

Bonnie's face scrunched. "What do you mean, tainted food?"

"Earlier, inside the Mermaid bathroom, you said the cast and crew had food poisoning…an accident. Maybe my fall was another accident."

"What fall?"

"From the deck." Stiffening my fingers, I made a diving gesture.

"Frannie, you didn't fall. You passed out."

"But…but…" My breath escaped in short gasps and my head whirred faster than the fan. "But I wasn't drunk, Bonnie, I swear."

She smiled. "Yeah, right."

"Oh God, what happened on that deck?"

Her smile faded. "You don't remember?"

"Tell me."

Abandoning the desk, she slid her tush next to mine. "First of all, Jem accepted all responsibility. He bribed the bartender, told him to make your drinks ninety-nine percent vodka."

"Read my lips, Bonnie. I was *not* drunk."

Or was I?

My mind raced as I tried to reconstruct events.

Oysters and white wine.

A double-strength Cape Codder with a splash of cranberry juice.

Madison's edited screen test.

A triple-strength Cape Codder with no ice.

My compulsion to tell the party guests that Frannie Rosen, not Lynn Beth Sullivan, had played the demon.

Sailing outside onto the deck, my anchor Jeremy Glenn's hunky hand, attached to his hunky wrist and arm.

Deck events were…blurrier. But unlike the Night of Wine and Roses, I had a sneaky suspicion it wouldn't take me days to remember details. This time, in time, probably a short time, I'd remember everything. Because this time I didn't *want* to remember.

"Madison wasn't upset," Bonnie said, rising. She walked to a wall hook, retrieved a pretentious Lone Star mug, poured coffee from an insulated Thermos, and handed the mug to me. "In fact," she continued, "he sounded amused. And sympathetic."

"Omigod. I ralphed in front of Jem and Madison." At the thought, I placed my sloshing mug on the floor.

"Frannie, read *my* lips. You passed out."

"I didn't throw up?"

As if speaking to a small child, she said, "You leaned over the railing. You had an Alfred Hitchcockian attack of vodka-inspired vertigo. You passed out. Jem caught you before you fell. Madison summoned me. Jem found the manager, who unlocked the office and said to take all the time we need. He, the manager, wanted to call 911, but Madison said no. Then he, the manager, said there was a trash basket near the desk, if you woke up puking."

"He sounds like my mother," I interjected, "only she would have said if I puked in my sleep."

"Jem wanted to stay and apologize." Bonnie was still talking very slowly, very distinctly. "But Madison said no again. End of story. Unless you feel like 'ralphing' now. Do you?"

I shook my head from side to side, then pressed my thumbs against my pounding temples. "Wait a sec...the voice...the finger."

"What voice? What finger?"

"A voice hissed in my ear, told me to vomit his kiss."

"Who's kiss?"

"Jem's kiss."

Bonnie patted the hands I'd clasped in my lap. "Your voice of reason," she said, "wanted you to barf that potent poison inside your system."

"My 'voice of reason' doesn't hiss or growl or tell me to vomit a *kiss*. I think it was the screen test."

"What do you mean?"

"Long story."

"We've got time. They're dancing the Cotton-Eyed Joe out there."

"Jem? Madison?"

"Jem's dancing too, just one of the guys. Madison...I don't know."

I took a deep breath, then told Bonnie everything, starting with my erotic audition. "So you see, Bonnie, I get an allergic reaction."

"Oh, great. You're suddenly allergic to acting."

"No...not acting. I think I'm susceptible to the demon. Or maybe it's a dybbuk."

Bonnie looked mystified so I said, "Jewish folklore. Dybbukim are wandering souls who enter and control a person's body. They're like doppelgangers...you already know about them. My cousin Charlene used to scare the living daylights out of me by talking about dybbukim. *My* dybbuk, or doppelganger, enters and controls me temporarily whenever it wants to, or whenever it's...provoked. At the audition I couldn't perform. In my apartment I said something about turning down the 'Forever Asmodeus' role. Tonight...well, I don't know what brought it out tonight. Shit, Bon, maybe I imagined the whole thing. Maybe it was the vodka. Maybe the beetles were Beatles. Maybe—"

"Frannie." A small hand pushed open the office door. A slender body literally burst inside. "Are you okay?"

Cat Sands exuded the scent of perfume, humidity, and unicorns.

Unicorns? Whoa... How did unicorns smell?

With their noses, I thought, stifling the urge to giggle hysterically. If I started, I'd never stop.

"Except for my sunburned clown-nose," I said, "I feel fine."

"Hi Bonnie." Cat turned to me again. "I just got here, Frannie, and heard about how you almost plunged into the Gulf."

"From whom?

"Dawn Sullivan."

"If I had plunged, Cat, I would have landed on seashells." Glancing at the tomato clock, I said, "Why are you so late?"

"I'm afraid curiosity consumed the Cat. You see, Madison hired this fascinating technical advisor—"

"Tenia. Yes, I know. Bonnie told me."

"And tonight she attended—"

"A voodoo convention."

"Not voodoo, Frannie, witchcraft. Anyway, I decided to follow her. Are you sure you're okay? You look funny. Strange."

"I know that look," Bonnie said, "and I don't like it."

At the same time I said, "I'm fine, Cat, really. Please go on."

"I didn't have a name tag, so I stationed myself in the hotel lounge. I was at the bar, smoking a cigarette, when I overheard a conversation between Tenia and another woman, a slinky blonde who could have doubled for that Canadian model, Jem's girlfriend, Mary-Magdalene. Anyway, for what it's worth, several convention members are planning to hold a Black Mass tomorrow night. Tenia noticed me eavesdropping, grabbed the blonde by her skinny arm, and walked away from the bar."

"A Black Mass," I said. "Yup."

"What do you mean, yup?" Bonnie's question sounded rhetorical.

"If they plan to hold a Black Mass," I said, "I plan to be there."

"Why?"

"It'll be...educational. I can use my reactions for the Robin-Asmodeus scenes."

"Bullshit."

Cat's eyebrows merged. "Hey, what's going on? What did I miss?"

"Frannie wants a spell to ward off demons," Bonnie said. "But a Black Mass is a perverse combination of sacrilege and sensuality. Frannie doesn't need to fall into a trace. She needs to fall out of one."

I said, "Do you know where they're holding the Mass, Cat?" She didn't reply, a definitive yes. "Hey, you guys, I don't believe in all that crap, but I was a Girl Scout and should be prepared, fight fire with fire. That damn demon has finally met its match."

"Okay, I'll go with you," Bonnie said.

"Me, too," Cat said, then laughed.

Bonnie and I stared at her.

"I'm good at puns," Cat said, "but Frannie's a pro."

"Puns?" Rising from the vinyl couch, I performed an upper-torso aerobics stretch.

"Fire. Match." Cat laughed again.

Bonnie and I joined in, even though, in retrospect, it wasn't funny.

Because my demon was determined to have the last laugh.

A Los Angeles Restaurant
January, 1988

Victor Madison couldn't stop staring at the waitress.

He hated her.

No. Hate was too strong an emotion. He didn't hate her.

She wore a name tag on the pocket that would have stuck out had she boasted a breast.

M A R Y

Her name was Mary. Mary...plain as any name could be. George M. Cohan had hit the proverbial nail on the proverbial head. Plain Mary.

Except...she wasn't plain. All she needed was a make-over. Then she'd be...exquisite? Stunning?

First, he'd send her to a professional stylist and get rid of that hair. Too long, almost waist-length, the profusion of sienna strands minimized her ragamuffin face and dark brown eyes. On the other hand, Natalie Wood could get away with long hair, and Mary looked a little like Natalie in *West Side Story*...at least she did when she smiled.

She never smiles at me. If she smiled just once, I'd leave her a tip that would knock her socks off.

Her panties, too.

Christ, what was he thinking? He didn't need a woman right now, not even a one-night stand. The extra he'd enjoyed nine years ago, during the filming of *D-Train to Hell,* had come back into his life, uninvited but not unappreciated. Then there was The Stalker.

The Stalker had a first, last and maiden name. Victor had met her twice. An aspiring actress, he'd never balled her...never even hinted that he might ball her. She had a kid, or kids, and that took her out of the ballpark. His strict rule, *no mothers*, was absolute.

Sometimes she followed him and watched him from a distance. Sometimes she raided his trash. Sometimes she sent him love letters, unsigned, mostly bad poetry. It was creepy, but he didn't deem her pathological, and one had to maintain one's sense of humor when it came to un-fatal attractions.

He sipped from his glass of Il Fratello. A cheap wine, but he liked the taste; fruity, with accents of chocolate, blackberry and spice.

Shit, was he going Hollywood or what?

Wine was wine. He only drank it when he ate Italian; red with beef and veal, white with fish and chicken. Fuck accents.

"Will that be all, sir?"

Victor eyed the waitress. Mary. *She* had an accent, a regional twang. Nebraska? Oklahoma?

With a scowl, he shoved his plate toward the edge of the table.

"You didn't finish your Veal Parmigiano, sir," she said.

She made the word "sir" sound like *you-son-of-a-bitch*. He could have been watching an Italian movie where an astringent Sophia Loren says "Prego" and the subtitle reads: "Have a nice day."

Mary's uniform didn't fit. Granted, she was thin…almost scrawny… but surely the restaurant had another, smaller, nondescript dress. Her breast pocket handkerchief looked as if it hadn't been used since Custer's last stand. Her bobby socks cut her legs in half, thirds when she bent over, and when she bent over she had a *very* nice ass.

The foot inside her chunky, rubber-soled, black waitress shoe was tapping impatiently. At the same time, she surreptitiously glanced toward her other tables. She'd asked him a question…

"The veal was fine," he said. "But you, Miss Mary, give me indigestion."

"Really." She shoved her hand inside her skirt pocket, pulled out a small tin of Tums, and tossed the tin toward the salt shaker. "Here," she said, "on the house."

Along with the tin were a few coins, scooped up with the Tums.

Instinctively, Victor pried the coins loose from the tablecloth. Extending his hand, he said, "Here, on the house."

"Keep it," she said. "You need it more than I do."

"Now just a minute."

"Dessert, sir? Our special tonight is amaretto cheesecake."

"Why are you so hostile?"

"What's hostile about amaretto cheesecake?"

"How old are you, Mary?"

"Over twenty-one," she snapped. "How old are *you*?"

He almost said *over-twenty-one*, which would have been juvenile. He had guessed her age at twenty-three. "I'll be forty-two next month. Do you have any children, Mary?"

"No," she said. "Not that it's any of your business...sir."

"Why do you always call me sir as if you hated me?"

"Would you prefer Mr. Cheapskate, Mr. Madison?"

"Aha. Now we get to the crux of the matter. Your tip."

"What tip? You never leave a fucking tip." With a shaky hand, she finger-combed the bangs away from her angry eyes.

Perversely, as her voice grew louder, he dropped his voice lower. "Do you know what the letters t-i-p-s stand for, Mary?"

"Do you, Mr. Madison?"

"'To insure proper service.'"

"Are you saying I don't give proper service? How *dare* you. Every week you walk in here like you own the place. You demand a table in *my* station, then you glare at me as if you wanted my intestines on the side, rather than spaghetti. You spend forty to sixty dollars, depending on whether you order a bottle of Il Fratello, Giovanni Dri Refosco, Estate Bottled Sterling Chardonnay, and/or a slug of Gran Marnier on your fucking canoli. Not that I remember, *sir*, but the most you've ever left me was fifty-fucking-cents, the change from three twenties."

Victor saw the restaurant manager waddling toward the table, his belly one car-length ahead of his thick legs and saggy behind. If the manager had been a dragon, his nostrils would have ejected tendrils of smoke. His mustache reminded Victor of Laurel, or Hardy, the fat one. His name was something Italian. Rocky? No. Tony. Tony Dippolito.

"Is there a problem, Mr. Madison?" he said.

"No," Victor said.

"Yes," Mary said. "This liar, this *bastard* says I don't give him proper service."

"I didn't say you don't give me proper service."

"You should see his table when he leaves, Mr. Dippolito. He's worse than a rug-rat. Stains everywhere. He drinks a whole bottle of wine, and he's so fucking smashed by the time he pours the last glass, there's wine all over the—"

"Miss Sanchez."

"I don't care, Mr. Dippolito. He asks for my station, spends money like it's going out of style, and never tips."

"Please lower your voice, Miss Sanchez. Mr. Madison doesn't have to tip. You know that. We don't even *talk* about tips."

"Are you out of your fucking mind? Of course we talk about tips. How do you think we tip out the bartender and bus boys? How do you think we pay our fucking rent?"

"Miss Sanchez, you're fired. Collect your things and leave immediately."

Stunned, she took a few steps backwards. "I...I can't leave, Mr. Dippolito. I have three other tables."

"Miss Gluckman will serve them. I want you out of here right away or I'll call the cops."

"And charge me with what?"

"Stealing."

"But I didn't steal anything."

"Who do you think the police will believe, Miss *Sanchez*?"

Although her eyes looked stricken and her lower lip quivered, she said, "Fine, Tony, great. You can take this job and stick it up your ass."

Everyone in the restaurant applauded. Mary burst into tears and fled, heading toward the kitchen. Victor tried to follow, but was waylaid by the manager's bulk.

"I can't apologize enough," Dippolito said. "Your next meal is on the house, Mr. Madison."

On the house. Victor scooped up the Tums tin and strode outside. He had a feeling she'd leave by the front door, rather than slink out the back door, and he was right. As soon as she appeared, as if her exit had been a script cue, it began to rain.

She had changed into her street clothes, a faded blue denim shirt with an embroidered Tigger on the pocket, and a pair of skin-tight jeans that sculpted her butt and legs.

"I thought you might need these," he said, pressing the Tums against her palm.

"Thanks," she said, her voice colder than a frozen cappuccino, her eyes feral, "but I haven't eaten yet."

"I can remedy that. What kind of food do you like?"

"Anything but Italian," she said. "And you, Mr. Madison, can go straight to hell. Do not pass go. Do not collect—"

"Do you have a car, Mary?"

"No," she spat. "Do you?"

"No. But I've got a limousine, and you're beginning to look like Audrey Hepburn in that last sappy scene from 'Breakfast at Tiffany's.'"

"Don't be stupid," she said, her voice suddenly weary. "I'm not wearing a trench coat and I don't have a cat."

"George Peppard carried the cat."

"You're wrong." Once again her lower lip quivered. "George gave the cat to Audrey, and I've always given you proper service."

"T-i-p-s," he said. "To insure proper smiles."

"Smiles aren't on the menu, Mr. Madison."

"*Victor* Madison."

He waited for some sign of recognition, but she merely said, "I don't care if you're Victor fucking Mature. You have no right—"

"To act like a pompous asshole. I couldn't agree more, Mary."

Her eyes grew big as saucers and her mouth dropped open, and he couldn't resist. Pulling her hard against him, his tongue darted between lips that were wet from the rain, lips that seemed glued to his. He felt her heart pound, heard her say, "Please...I...can't...breathe."

When he let her go, she said, "Kisses aren't on the menu, either, and you look like a drowned *rat*."

"You look like a drowned bird," he said. "So fragile...so goddamn fragile. As for kisses on the menu, Mary, you don't work here anymore."

He could have reinstated her; a few words to Dippolito and she'd be back where she belonged, slinging pasta.

Instead, he took her home with him.

And no one was more surprised than Victor Madison when she was still there, ensconced inside his cottage, thirteen months later.

TWENTY-FIVE

When I was a little kid I had nightmares about flying monkeys.

Those dreams were followed by a nightmare in which I skipped rope and chanted: *S, my name is Sandra and my husband's name is Sam, we come from South Carolina, and in our basket we carry snakes.* At which point, the jump rope would become a snake. Then I kept dreaming I walked into the boys' bathroom by mistake. After I actually did it, the dreams stopped, although to this day I scrutinize bathroom doors at least three times before I enter, and I hate the ones that have cute euphemisms like Femme and Hombre or Neptune and Mermaid.

One of my worst nightmares put me in the bleachers at a high school basketball game. A naked cheerleader who had my mother's face shouted, "Two bits, four bits, six bits, a buck; all for Frannie stand up and holler."

A marginally better dream had me naked, sitting next to a naked Woody Allen, eating popcorn and watching *Night of the Living Dead.* In that dream, Woody leans over and quotes Albert Camus: "The absurd is sin without God."

I suppose I continued having bad dreams once I'd reached adulthood. However, upon awakening I couldn't remember them.

Until the Night of the Cast Party.

That night I dreamed Nana Jen was alive, tangible. She wanted to tell me something important, but I couldn't find her.

She kept saying, *Inside the mirror, Frannie, inside the mirror.*

The directions were clear enough. I knew she meant her genuine, hand-carved, French beveled glass mirror, and I knew I could step through the beveled glass; Frannie in Wonderland.

And yet I was afraid to face my dear, sweet, precious Nana. How would she look? Porcelain skin or putrescence? Cucumber slices shielding her bright blue eyes, or dark sockets—like the nighmare-people in *Fiddler on the Roof*?

Suddenly, I was at the Tony awards. Whoopi Goldberg told a joke, but I couldn't hear her, so I held up my hands and tried to shush the audience. I saw Matthew Broderick in the first row. He was laughing and applauding. I'd had a crush on him practically forever, and my heart thrummed. The other actors in the audience were faceless, but they all wore formal clothes; evening gowns and tuxedos. I, of course, was naked. Ignoring the TV cameras, pushing Whoopi aside, I grabbed the microphone and said, *I want to laugh, too.*

Someone, not Whoopi, said, *Go to hell.*

The curtain rose and Cat Sands sang, *Matchmaker, matchmaker, make me a match.*

I lit a match.

Holding it to the wick of a bayberry-scented candle, I inhaled several times, as if I were Shelley Winters getting ready to swim underwater.

Then I walked through Nana's beveled glass mirror.

Except for my small circle of candlelight, the darkness was impenetrable. I didn't sense any demons nearby because I knew Nana wouldn't have gone to hell. Not that she believed in heaven or hell, but nothing is absolute, and Woody Allen is fond of saying that when he dies he plans to bring along a change of underwear, just in case.

I exhaled when I saw that Nana didn't look like a *Fiddler* nightmare person. She looked like...Nana. Slender save for a little bit of stomach, she wore her favorite purple velveteen bathrobe, belted. Underneath, she wore a long white nightgown with teensy purple flowers.

We could have been getting together for one of our "womanly" tête-à-têtes, only Nana's feet didn't touch the ground. That, I thought, killed the authenticity.

I know this is just a dream, I said, *but you want to tell me something. Right?*

As rain, she said, sounding like Bonnie.

Nana walked on ether, moving closer, and I could smell Cherry Lifesavers.

This is just a guess, I said, *but you want to talk about the demon. Or the dybbuk.*

What demon? she said. *What dybbuk?*

Asmodeus, I said.

Who's Asmodeus? she said.

Stumbling backwards, I bumped into the mirror and dropped my candle. Nana followed me, still walking on air. A radiant nimbus defined her silver braids, bright blue eyes, and the diamond earrings she'd promised I could have when I turned twenty-one. Mom had insisted the earrings be buried with Nana's ears.

Mom. I had a sudden thought.

Gracie, I said. *You want to tell me about Gracie. Right?*

Nana nodded, and to my horror I saw that her neck wasn't attached to her body. Nevertheless, I said, *Mom had a stillborn baby named Gracie. True?*

This time Nana didn't nod, and her head stayed put.

Grace Ingrid Rosen, she said. *I'm going to give you a spell, Frannie sweetheart, an incantation that'll get rid of Grace.*

Get rid of Gracie? But...but she's dead."

Don't argue, princess. Listen carefully and learn it by heart. You have a memory like a sponge, so you won't need a tape recorder, Nana said, sounding like Mickey Samson Roebuck. *You must chant this every morning, as soon as you get up, before you go potty even.*

I breathed a sigh of relief. Nana sounded like Nana again.

Frannie, sweetheart, stop kibitzing. Are you listening to me?"

Yes, Nana.

You must say, 'Palas aron azinomas.'

What does that mean?

Never mind what it means. Say it, sweetheart.

Palas aron azinomas.

Good. Very good. This time Nana sounded like Victor Madison. *The next one is a little harder, like a day-old knish,* she said, sounding like Nana again. *And you must chant it every night before you go to sleep. 'Bagahi Iaca Bachabe.'*

Bagahi Iaca Bachabe.

Good. All right, darling, the last incantation is very important."

Nana, I can't remember all this, I cried.

Say the first two, sweetheart...now.

Palas aron azinomas. Bagahi Iaca Bachabe.

Yes, oh yes, that was terrific, she enthused, sounding like Suzanne Burton. *The last one is easy, princess,* she said, sounding like Nana again. *It's in English, and it doesn't matter when you say it as long as you think of Grace, first.*

Can I think of Gracie instead, Nana?

She hesitated, then said, *Of course, darling. Here's what you say. You say, 'Gracie Ingrid Rosen, go hence, ghost of my ancestors.' Frannie sweetheart, you're not listening.*

Sorry, Nana. I just wondered...I mean, I assume the Ingrid is for Grandpa Irving, but I was trying to figure out which dead relative's initial Mom used for Gracie.

Nana began to laugh. Quickly, she raised her hands to cover her mouth.

However, she wasn't quick enough. I saw spaces between her teeth, and the teeth she did have were...

Fangs.

I had caught a glimpse of Nana's anterior fangs, looking like a picture in my college Zoology text, a picture of...

A poisonous spider.

You're not my Nana, I said, probably the understatement of the century.

Of course I am, she said.

But she was already evolving into a creature with four pairs of legs and a red, hourglass-shaped mark on the underside of her black belly.

No, you're not, I screamed.

The 'G' is for God, the spider said, as more laughter erupted, along with several noxious breath-puffs.

Usually spiders scare the shit out of me, especially if they're five feet tall. But for some strange reason, I didn't feel the least bit scared. Maybe because part of me knew I was dreaming. Maybe because...

Jenny Rosen, I said, *go hence, ghost of my ancestors.*

This time I didn't need a beveled glass mirror. I found myself back at the Tony awards. Instead of Whoopi, Woody Allen stood in front of the mike. He must have been cracking wise because the faceless audience was convulsed with heehaws and Matthew Broderick knuckle-wiped tears of laughter from his eyes.

Woody waited until the heehaws became chuckles, the chuckles giggles, the giggles an occasional snicker.

Then he said, *Showing up is 80 percent of life.*

Apparently, an actor hadn't shown up to collect his or her Tony.

I wished I hadn't shown up in my own dream.

Then, as if God or someone had read my mind, I *woke* up.

TWENTY-SIX

Thump.

Something inside the duplex had fallen over, and as I struggled to a sitting position I saw that my pillow was soaked with perspiration.

So was I.

What the hell had happened to fearless Frannie? Maybe five-foot spiders scared the shit out of me, after all. And just for grins, how did that bitchy arachnid get its abdominal spinnerets on Nana's earrings?

"They were paste, not real," I said, and almost laughed at the incongruity. Dreaming about my Nana, I'd surely include the earrings Grampa Louie had given her on their Diamond Anniversary. If Mom died, godforbid, and I dreamed about her, I'd include her most prized possession—a genuine, paint-spattered mink stole.

"It was just a dream," I said, as sweat-centipedes crawled down my face, slid across my neck, and inched toward my meager cleavage.

The thumpy noise, however, was no dream.

I looked around for a weapon. Incantations wouldn't ward off burglars, and demon hocus-pocus wouldn't shoo away people who raped people in their sleep.

"People...people who rape people," I sang softly, paraphrasing Streisand, hoping Rogers and Hammerstein's whenever-I-feel-afraid philosophy would calm my ragged nerves.

At the same time, I reached for an oversized *Les Miserables* teeshirt. Before putting it on, I gazed at the sad-eyed waif on the front.

Which made me think of Cat Sands, who had called earlier to tell me that Madison had scheduled a meeting for cast members. I figured a mere double Demon could skip the meeting, especially since the time clashed with Tenia's Black Mass. Cat made me promise not to attend the Mass alone. Crossing my fingers behind my back, I promised.

Technically, I wouldn't be alone. I'm not sure how many folks consti-tute a Black Mass, but I'm fairly certain it's more than one.

I finally found a weapon, Rick's golf clubs. Although I couldn't care less about golf, I've watched Tiger Woods at least a million times. So if there really was an intruder and I swung one of the woods like Tiger—

Another *thump*, this one slightly muted, then a howl of pain.

"Fuck," said a voice that sounded like Andre's.

"Andre," I yelled, "what happened?"

Silence.

"Hey," I yelled, "I heard a noise, two actually, and I'm already awake, so you don't have to worry about waking me up."

Silence.

"Andre," I yelled, "what did you knock over?"

"That stupid wooden statue," he yelled back. "It won't sit straight on its base, and this time it fell on my fucking foot."

"What's your definition of stupid?" I yelled. "Rick paid a fortune for that statue."

"He was robbed," Andre yelled back. "It has no arms or legs."

"Neither does Venus de Milo."

"Who?"

"Why don't you come upstairs where you can hear me better?"

"Because I'm drunk, Frannie, and frankly, my dear, I don't—"

"Give a damn?"

"Want to sleep with you."

"But I need you, Andre. We don't have to make love. Just hold me. I had this horrible nightmare and I'm still scared. Please?"

My throat hurt from yelling, but I couldn't move.

Because I was suddenly afraid to confront the man I loved.

Was I still dreaming?

Would Andre turn into a spider, too?

He entered the bedroom like a man, not a spider. His blonde hair was mussed, his chin boasted designer stubble, and he looked adorable. All my original feelings for him washed through me, and I was one caress away from an intense orgasm. Had he touched my shoulder, I would have dis-solved into a throbbing heap of protoplasm.

"Did you plan to take up golf at three o'clock in the morning?" he said. "Or are you playing the female equivalent of OJ Simpson?"

"What? Oh. No. I heard a noise and thought it might be the spider."

"You were going to kill a poor defenseless spider with a 9-iron?"

Taking the wood...the iron...from my hand, Andre placed it in the corner, against the wall, beneath a scenic watercolor.

"The spider wasn't defenseless," I said. "It was hu-huge. Five feet. Maybe more. I had this hor-horrible nightmare. About a giant black spah-spah-spider."

Andre wrapped me in his arms. "Hush," he said. "Don't cry. Hush Frannie, it's okay. I'm here."

"Please, Andre," I sobbed into his chest, "please make love to me."

"I can't. I told you. I'm drunk."

"You don't look, sound, or smell drunk."

"Okay, I'm exhausted."

I pulled away a little. "Then why did you say you were drunk?"

"I'm fulfilling your mother's prophecy."

"That's so unfair, Andre. Mom has her faults, but she's never, ever accused you of—"

"Let's not go there, Frannie. I'll tuck you into bed and stick around until you fall asleep. Is *that* fair?"

"Stick around? Were you planning to go out again?"

"Yes. Rick found this rodeo star...ex rodeo star. He's gonna' teach me how to twirl a lasso."

"At three o'clock in the morning?"

"Yes. No. He...the rodeo guy...lives a couple, maybe three hours away. Rick wants to get there early, before sunrise, so we can be back in time for our noon-thirty rehearsal. We're taking the dog...Ginger...so that means stopping along the way to...uh, walk her."

For an actor, Andre made a lousy liar. My hand dipped between his thighs and began to stroke. "This is me, honey," I said. "You don't have to deal with that crazy Frannie who invaded our apartment, after my screen test. This is me, not her."

"Prove it," he said, but I could tell he was weakening. For one thing, his voice was 75% tease. For another, his erection practically burst through his jeans.

"'There are two reasons why I'm in show business," I said, "and I'm standing on both of them.' Quote, unquote."

"Betty Grable. 'They say a man is as old as the woman he feels.'"

"George Burns?"

"No. Groucho Marx." As he gave me a fathomless kiss, Andre's hand roved beneath my teeshirt. "I think you're losing weight, babe," he said, abandoning my lips. "Your breasts feel bigger."

"Breasts grow when you lose weight?"

He actually laughed. "Hell, I don't know," he said. "The rest of you shrinks, so maybe your breasts feel bigger."

"That feels so good," I said, arching into his fingers and fumbling at his fly. "I've missed you, Andre. I've missed...*ohmigod.*"

Pressing my hands against my mouth, I ran for the bathroom.

And made it just in time.

The finger that had tickled my throat...on the deck...when Jeremy Glenn initiated his "Fanny seduction"...finally finished its mission...its assignment....its function.

This time there was no liquor in my system.

This time I didn't lose consciousness.

Kneeling, hugging the toilet bowl, I retched.

And kept retching, over and over again.

My wretched retching blocked out everything, sound-wise, except the slam of the front door. Like Elvis, Andre had left the building.

The finger, however, wouldn't leave. It ebbed just long enough to let me take a breath, then plunged down my throat again. And tickled again. And choked me again.

I retched and gagged.

The finger tickled.

I gagged some more.

The finger plunged deeper. And deeper...

Until I gave a desperate moan and my stomach turned inside out and the world turned upside down.

I heard the hissing voice: *He's not the one.*

TWENTY-SEVEN

In my circle of friends it's not cool to admit that one is an atheist. But it's chi-chi to say that one is an agnostic, which not only kicks butt, metaphorically speaking, but also covers one's butt. If there really *is* a God, we haven't denied his/her existence, and if we want to bargain with God...for example, during an audition...that's perfectly acceptable. My mother, of course, thinks my logic is as twisted as a French cruller.

Now, however, I was pissed off. Because agnosticism went out the window when it came to my demon.

Call it a doppelganger, call it a dybbuk, call it a nudist who stuffs beetles inside its belly without swallowing. I only knew that if a tree fell in the forest and hit a Mime, no one would hear (or care), but if it hit my demon, the echo of its eerie screech would reverberate left and right, up and down, from the Bronx Zoo to Bloomingdale's, from the Brooklyn Bridge to the Guggenheim Museum. Then the demon would pick itself up, brush itself off, and visit a Houston forest.

Why me? That's what I couldn't understand. Why an uptight Jewish "ecktriss" from Long Island?

Did the demon have a warped sense of humor?

"Let's choose Frannie Rosen, who won't even put a you-know-what in her mouth," the head honcho tells his legions, "and let's make her sexually promiscuous. Wouldn't that be a hoot?"

Which didn't explain the hissing voice.

Vomit his kiss. He's not the one. Son of mad, son of mad.

Rising from my bow-backed kitchen chair, I poured myself a mug of Mr. Coffee coffee, added a splash of milk from a carton inside the refrigerator, then walked into the living room and sank down upon a couch whose clawed feet fondled wooden balls.

Mad could be...probably was...Madison, I mused. Or taken literally,

Victor Madison's son. Madison, fifty-something, could have sired a son who was now in his twenties or thirties. Except, to my knowledge, based on a *Rolling Stones* magazine interview and an A&E Biography, Madison didn't have a dad, mom, sister, brother, wife, ex-wife, or any offspring.

Both bios had mentioned Cat Sands, briefly, and I remembered my conjecture during my visit to her brownstone. I had talked about my mom's desire for a grandkid and she had rubbed her belly and I had thought she might have been pregnant when she and Madison split. But, assuming my presumption was correct, where the hell was Madison's son?

Or if the demon meant Madison himself, it was way off base. I pictured Bonnie inside the Mermaid rest room, where we had talked about Jem. "He's not my type," she had said.

I wasn't Madison's type, not even close. There was no chemistry between us. He'd no sooner take me to bed than fly to the moon.

Even if we didn't need chemistry, even if I merely scratched an itch, there was a definite roadblock—Madison's Disney obsession.

Despite her dark hair and dark eyes, Cat resembled Tinkerbell. Bonnie could have posed for Aladdin's girlfriend. Or Pocahontas.

At best, I looked like Simba's gal-pal in *The Lion King*.

Yet, an image came to mind. Jem and Madison standing near the restaurant's piano bar, Jem gesturing toward me and Madison shaking his head.

But that could have meant any number of things. Madison might have been telling Jem not to get involved with a cast member. Madison might have been telling Jem that his 99%-vodka-ploy would make me puke my guts out.

Which brought me, in a round-about way, to Andre. I was pissed at him, too. He could have stuck around. He could have held my head. Christ, how often had I held his?

Well, to be perfectly honest, once—the night he up-chucked four quarts of Madeira into our potted palm. Still, that counted. Andre owed me at least one head-holding.

After he held my head, we could have *rationally* discussed recent events. The click-beetles. The finger. The hiss-voice. The spider dream. My fortuitous promiscuity. Andre might have suggested a visit to the Betty Ford Clinic, where I could rid myself of demonic addiction. The thing is, Andre can almost always make me laugh, and I desperately needed laughter to eliminate the doubts and fears that were spreading faster than zits before a prom.

According to the living room's ship-shaped wall clock, it was five a.m.

From Rick's duplex, I heard Ginger bark. Then I heard Rick shout, "Shut up, you bitch." Which meant that he and Andre were *not* on their merry way to the retired lasso twirler.

So where was Andre? Surprisingly, I didn't care. I had blown my breakfast, lunch and supper, but Andre had blown his chance at a forever love, and I felt sorry for him. He might find another woman to wash, dry, even iron his clothes, but he'd be hard pressed to find one who possessed a mental encyclopedia of nostalgic movie quotes.

So why did I feel like crying?

I returned to the kitchen and poured myself another mug of coffee. My throat felt raw and it was hard to swallow, but I didn't want to go back to sleep. If I slept, I might dream. Which was why I decided to sit on the living room's hardwood floor, mentally compose rap lyrics, and wait for sunrise.

Someone, or something, must have slipped decaf into my 100% pure caf coffee beans. As I gradually curled into a fetal position and closed my eyes, I remembered my psychic's prophetic words: "I see cameras and people. Travel. Romance with a tall, dark man."

Jeremy Glenn was tall and dark, but I didn't think she'd meant Jem. Despite the *he's-not-my-type* justifications, despite the lack of sexual chemistry, she'd meant the Prince of Darkness.

TWENTY-EIGHT

I slept for eleven hours.

I didn't dream.

But my throat was still sore when I awoke, which made me wonder how I'd simulate the demon's voice.

Sol Aarons had finished refining the Asmodeus makeup, and Madison would soon shoot the first possession scene.

Andre had programmed the answering machine and it blinked like a freaked-out rabbit. Christ, I'd slept through the ringing of the phone. The first message was from Andre. No apology regarding his abrupt departure. He'd leased a car, he'd be driving to rehearsal, he'd be back late. His voice assumed its gee-I'm-so-sensitive groove as he said he'd sleep on the couch so as not to wake me, and he wouldn't knock over any statues, ha-ha. His laugh sounded forced.

The second message was from stagehands, Bambi and Fawn.

"This is for Ann-dray," they said.

"Ann-dray, are you there?" a twin said.

"He's not there," the other twin said.

"Ann-dray, when are you coming?" they both said, then giggled.

The third message was from Rick. He would drive to the rehearsal with Andre, so if I needed Yoda the keys were in the visor. And would I feed Ginger, please?

I heaved a sigh of relief. Yoda took care of my transportation, the one and only Black Mass obstacle.

"This is Sheldon Giglia," the fourth message began. A limo would pick me up tomorrow morning at five-thirty and drive me to the Asmodeus set. Makeup would commence at six, and Madison wanted to discuss a spider sequence with me.

A spider sequence? What the hell did *that* mean? There were no spiders in the book. With a shudder, I listened to the fifth message.

Mom had dipped into her mah-jongg fund to call me long distance, and she sounded irate as she blamed my absence on "schmoozing with movie stars." Charlene had begun her second trimester and Marlene was still engaged to that "nice Negro." Nettie Lieberman had eloped with an Italian. His last name had an etti in it, like spaghetti, so she'd be Nettie Spaghetti, wasn't that funny? Daddy missed me, but Mom told him he shouldn't expect someone who lived near the Alamo to remember her parents. Even though, if it weren't for Daddy's seed (for an instant, I thought she said "semen"), I wouldn't be in Texas making a movie. She hoped I hadn't taken up smoking, after all John Wayne died from lung cancer, and the kosher butcher, Mr. Plotnick, wanted an autograph. Could I sign a picture from the movie, please, and send it to him? And while I was at it, could I send one to Daddy? Then she gave me Plotnick's address.

The last message was from Bonnie. She reiterated Cat's warning. I must *not* attend the Black Mass alone. And Madison had said something about hiring an actor to do Asmodeus voice-overs. Bruce Willis, Debra Winger, and Angela Landsbury were on his short list.

Well, that solved my sore throat problem.

It was time to go potty, shower, and don proper clothes.

While pantyhose and heels were suitable for Rosh Hashanah and Yom Kippur services, my mother would have given an enthusiastic thumb's up to my Black Mass ensemble—black stirrup slacks, one of Andre's black teeshirts, and a motorcycle jacket I'd found at a garage sale. The Prince of Darkness would have upped his thumb, too.

The effect I strove for was somewhat ruined by white socks, white sneakers, and the jacket's Harley logo. However, I successfully stuffed my hair underneath a black Stetson, then slid a small but sharp pair of scissors into my pants pocket. I didn't think I'd need a weapon, but a Girl Scout, even an ex-Scout, should always be prepared.

After feeding Ginger, I toasted some stale-but-not-yet-moldy bread, smeared a ton of peanut butter across the slices, and cut off the crusts. That took care of my empty stomach. Thirsty, I wondered if I dared drink any-thing more potent than Diet Pepsi. Compromising, I downed a Diet Pepsi and two Lone Star beers. I went potty again, then filled a Thermos with cranberry juice. And vodka.

I knew I was drinking too much, but this was a special occasion; a Jewish agnostic about to witness a mock Christian mass.

Before leaving the duplex, I used the bathroom again, just in case the Black Massers didn't have a Port-a-Potty handy.

TWENTY-NINE

Yoda's gas gage read: EMPTY; my first omen.

I stopped at a gas pump and had one hell of a time inserting the nozzle into Yoda's gas tank.

As it turned out, that was my second omen.

Had I seen the handwriting on the wall (or in this case, billboards), I would have hung a U-turn, squashed Yoda's accelerator against the floorboards, and hightailed it back home…all the way to Manhattan.

Cat Sands had scribbled the Black Mass address on a piece of paper. I had shown the paper to Rick, who gave directions like a New Yorker. Thus, I soon found myself parking Yoda along a Godforsaken road, near a fenced pasture inhabited by horses and bordered by a fortress of trees.

Sunset battled Night for dominance. Before Night won, I was able to make out the name and address of the pasture owners—Daniel and Aretha Pearlstein—printed on the mailbox that squatted atop a wooden post at the entrance to a gravel driveway. Strung above the mailbox were black balloons, just in case one of the witches had misplaced her reading glasses.

Cresting a hill was an edifice that could have been an illustration for Grimm's *Hansel and Gretel*. I wondered if Pearlstein's aggrandized gumdrop foundation, Nestle's-Crunch-stucco walls, and red-licorice roof harbored a demon. If yes, implementing Grimm's termination technique would prove virtually impossible, since the demon would surely *emerge* from Pearlstein's oven.

Not that I planned to kill anything. I just wanted to watch and listen and learn. Only half fibbing when I told Bonnie I'd use my reactions for the Asmodeus possession scenes, I knew there had to be a perfectly logical explanation for the mirror, fireplace and deck episodes. Maybe the Black Mass would be an eye opener; an "Occult Visine."

So far, my reactions were trepidation, anxiety and dread, and my sane self told me to re-start Yoda and drive away…like a bat out of hell. My right sneaker hovered above the accelerator pedal while my left sneaker pressed against the clutch ped—

Get a grip, Frannie. Pretend you're auditioning for Macbeth.

I pulled my feet back, placed the rim of the Thermos against my bottom lip, and chugged down its contents. With luck, any booze-induced false courage would last through the Mass. Plus, I'd found a treasure trove on Yoda's back seat; a small Styrofoam cooler with a couple of six-packs; Coke and Coors.

A loud screech shattered the silence. Had the sacrificial portion of the Mass begun?

Nope. From inside the house, a CD player blared at the top of its electronically-generated, stereophonic lungs. In all honesty, I expected my eardrums to be detonated by *That Old Black Magic*, a demonic rap song, or even the cast album from *Phantom of the Opera*. But the Pearlsteins liked Elvis. And/or teddy bears.

The house seemed to burp, and thirteen Satanic worshippers emerged from its mouth—which in this case was a doorway.

My throat felt dry, my heart knocked explosively against my ribs, and I damned Madison for his ill-timed meeting. I needed Bonnie's pragmatism and Cat's caustic humor.

Employing Elvis (now singing Gospel) as their background music, the black-robed, scarlet-shod witches marched down to the pasture, single file. From a distance, they looked like an October thirty-first kindergarten class on its way to recess.

I couldn't pick Tenia out of the pack…coven?…because I couldn't see faces…or hear voices. Damn, I'd have to leave Yoda and wend my way closer.

One of the Pearlsteins killed Elvis and turned on a radio or TV. I heard the crack of a bat, followed by cheers, and remembered that the Mets were playing the Astros, a twilight game. Had I been in New York where I belonged, I'd be sitting in Shea Stadium, spending grocery money on indigestible hot dogs.

Since there was no accessible hot dog vendor, I thumbed open a Coors and poured half down my throat.

Yoda's yellow exterior was out of sight, sheltered by a weeping willow. But a hot, electrified breeze had whipped up, and the willow's oscillating branches made a weird noise, akin to a rustling wail.

It sounded like a warning.

Ignoring all portents and premonitions, I chugged down the second half of the warm Coors and stepped out of the car.

Now what?

I reminded myself that I didn't believe in witches, and anyway, these witches weren't expecting a gate crasher. I scratched my brain, trying to picture every war movie I'd ever seen. I was in pretty good shape; without actually dieting I'd lost excess pudge; and, there was no reason why I couldn't slither across the pasture like Audie Murphy or Tom Hanks, using my elbows and knees for propulsion and, hopefully, momentum. The loose sleeves of my jacket would be an impediment. I took it off and left it in the car.

Circumventing steamy piles of horse shit, scraping my elbows on bare pasture patches, thanking God for horses who didn't want to use me as a hoof-stool, I crept closer and closer. Only to find that the witches were gone. Mashed grass and a trail of Almond Joy candy bar wrappers extended into, and doubtless beyond, the fortress of trees.

Bad news, good news, I thought. Totally exhausted, I'd have to slither again. However, a tree or foliage might conceal my slacks, tee, and Stetson. Stetson? No way. I took it off and hung it from a fence post.

My pores sweated like a lawn sprinkler. Not that it was especially hot, or even humid. In fact, an icy chill permeated the forest.

Providentially, a fat oak stood sentinel, as if it had been planted a hundred years ago, just in case Frannie Rosen wanted to watch a Black Mass and remain undetected.

Forget Alice and her rabbit hole; that was New York. I'd landed inside a Gothic novel. As a kid I used to love reading about the naïve but gutsy governess who explores the dark, dank cellar. My shaky hand would try and hold my flashlight steady as I propped my book against the pillow and played the part of Jane or Mary or Miss Whomever, prim and proper on the outside, brimming with courage on the inside.

Crouched behind my oak shield, feeling the moist darkness settle around my shoulders like a Jane Eyre cloak, I didn't brim with anything. Because this semi-feminist didn't have Lord Comely fidgeting in the wings, dying to rescue her derrière.

Vodka and beer lay heavy in my stomach, probably the reason I had to go potty again.

The Mets-Astros game had ended. I didn't know, nor did I care, who'd won. After a rousing rendition of Jim Morrison's *Wild Child,* all din from the Pearlstein house had abruptly ceased. And yet my ears still strained to hear something, anything, as the words *silent as a tomb* reverberated inside my head.

I took a deep, unsteady breath, peeked around the tree trunk, and saw Tenia.

She held a slender black candle whose glow illuminated her round, cafe au lait face. Instead of a long brown skirt and proverbial teeshirt, she wore a long black robe, decorated with esoteric symbols. Instead of a pet-carrier-constrained snake, she was shadowed by a gray, white-mittened cat.

Tenia and her fellow witches stuck their black tapers into a couple of menorahs—at least they looked like menorahs to me—then emptied three pillow cases. I couldn't make out all the items, but I saw twigs and ashes, a mirror, a small lamp, a drum, bones (hopefully chicken, not human), something that could have been a bird's wing, and a baggie filled with mud. Or feces.

I wanted to leave, but it was too late. I wasn't at all certain I could slither backwards, especially with a full bladder.

Twelve witches sat helter-skelter, but Tenia stood.

"If I command the moon," she said, "it will come down. And if I wish to withhold the day, night will linger over my head. And if I wish to embark upon the sea, I need no ship. And if I wish to fly though the air, I am freed from my weight."

For some reason, probably nerves, that last line struck me as funny. Tenia had to weigh over two hundred pounds. *What a terrific diet,* I thought, picturing a late-night Infomercial. *All you have to do is call 1-800-SORCERY, agree to pay four installments of $29.95, give the operator a credit card number, and adopt witchy precepts.*

Trying to prevent a terminal case of the giggles, I clamped my mouth shut, bit my tongue, and drew blood.

The urge to giggle didn't help my desire to pee. In another moment I'd wet my pants, so I really had no choice.

As my body begged for a chiropractor, I used one of my agnostic emergency cards and prayed to God.

God apparently considered my request legit. I made it, unseen, to a small patch of ground, encompassed by leafy saplings and flat rocks.

First, I spat tongue-blood. Then, I pulled down my pants.

I had witnessed enough, nothing beneficial, and I wanted to get the hell out of Dodge.

Contemplating a return slither through the pasture, I heard castanets.

THIRTY

Click. Click. Click-click-click.

Something lurked within the tangled underbrush, and it wasn't Tarzan. Wishing my head could rotate like that girl in *The Exorcist,* I looked left and right, up and... "Oh my God," I whispered, holding back a scream.

My spit dried up, my hand clutched at my chest, and a newspaper headline swam before my eyes: ACTRESS FELLED BY HEART ATTACK.

A snake.

A rattlesnake.

A diamondback rattlesnake.

One of my high school buds, Artie Borst, had evolved into a fashion photographer. He asked me to pose for a calendar titled: "A Day At The Zoo." I postured in front of lions and tigers and bears, oh my, then we entered a dimly-lit Snake House. Artie ran out of film. Stepping outside to reload his camera, he left me alone....except for a gazillion snakes. Reminding myself that Snake House visitors were protected by glass, I didn't really believe it. When the rolls of film were developed, every post-snake photo included a pair of haunted eyes, filled with shock and terror. Artie re-shot the calendar, using a professional model, and last I heard it was out-selling the Sierra Club.

As I brought my attention back to tonight's coiled horror, I silently warned myself that I should remain perfectly still; no tremors, no tics.

The rattlesnake looked startled, too. It probably hadn't expected a New York "ecktriss" to go potty near its rocks.

I recalled my chat with Bonnie, inside the Mermaid rest room. Could this be the rattler whom Cat had christened George W?

My legs ached. If I continued to crouch motionless, would the snake slither away?

No, damn it. The snake stayed put, flicking its forked tongue.

My tongue hurt even worse than my legs, and I wanted to spit.

Instead, I swallowed blood and a second scream.

The interlocking joints at the end of the snake's tail made a threatening click that was actually louder than castanets.

I swallowed my third Jamie Lee Curtis scream, not wanting to alert Tenia and her fellow witches. I truly doubted they'd come to my rescue, but if perchance they did, they might have other nifty tortures in mind; for example, human sacrifice.

Maybe the snake was a witch. I'd heard or read somewhere that a witch could disembody herself and—

The rattler's mouth gaped open and two long, slender fangs appeared.

I'd squeezed my eyes shut during *Indiana Jones*, and that was just a movie. Now I thought I'd lose it; nose-dive toward the diamondback's fangs. Activating every memory cell, I tried to revive the dream spider's dicta. I was fairly certain the ancestor bit wouldn't work, so I decided to give one of the alien phrases a go. "Palas aron azinomas," I said.

Which had no effect whatsoever on the snake.

I'd have to make a run for it, or shriek at the top of my lungs, or—

The ghostly apparition from my New York apartment walked through the saplings. Literally.

He had the same luminous quality, the same shape, the same hazy, imperceptible face, and the same red-tipped penis.

This time I couldn't hold back a scream. Except, I suddenly felt so cold my teeth chattered, so my scream emerged as a throaty hum.

In New York the apparition had stuffed beetles inside his body. Now, his weightless foot pinioned the rattler.

As I watched, mesmerized, he wound the snake around his neck like a lozenge-patterned stole, then simply walked away.

After several deep breaths, I decided I couldn't get enough air, and blacked out.

When I came to, my head felt lighter. Dizziness aside, my brain told me I'd dropped a few ounces from my skull.

Glancing around, I saw human hair on the ground. Next to the hair was a pair of scissors. Slowly, I raised my hands.

Shorn. I'd been shorn. Well, technically, I'd been trimmed. My own fault. After all, who'd put the damn scissors in my pocket?

The question was, who'd taken the scissors out? And why?

Had the owners of the house, Daniel and Aretha Pearlstein, found me and cut my hair? Was this the way they treated trespassers in Texas? Or had

I slipped into a fugue and cut my own hair? The uneven strands beneath my fingers suggested that might have been the case.

Too frightened to cry, I staggered to my feet.

The hot electric breeze had died down, but now a stronger wind, a gust actually, propelled me toward the witches. I fought the gusty wind as hard as I could, digging my heels into the ground, windmilling my arms. Then I just...gave up.

I'm dreaming, I thought with profound relief. *I passed out from too much beer and vodka. I'll wake up in the car, and my hair will be uncut, and I can tell Cat and Bonnie that I skipped the Black Mass.*

Except...I hadn't skipped the Black Mass.

The relentless special-effects wind swept me behind my original oak shield, and I suddenly knew the reason for my shorn hair. Earlier, the moon had been hidden by clouds. Now it shone brightly, and the shimmer of my long, pale gold hair would have been a dead giveaway.

Obviously, I had failed to catch some of the incantations. But to my eyes, the gathering looked like...Girl Scout camp. The witches sat around a small campfire. In another moment they'd toast marshmallows and sing *One Hundred Bottles of Beer on the Wall.*

Whoa. There were only nine witches. Maybe the other four had to go potty, too.

I couldn't have been more wrong.

When the missing witches returned, three had their arms draped around number four, who was either drunk or drugged. Slumping, her head sloped downward, as if it were attached to a Slinky toy. Her mop of hair, tangled and twig-infested, was a dull auburn, and the knotted strands veiled her features. She wore a robe, but something seemed out of sync. My gaze traveled down to her feet. No scarlet shoes.

The stupefied woman's robe fell from her shoulders, and I stifled a gasp. Forget shoes. How about no clothes at all?

"Tenia, I'm fr-r-r-eezing," she slurred.

Tenia rose to her feet and said, "Shut up."

Then she slapped the naked woman's face, and all but one witch laughed. The witch who hadn't laughed said, "Maybe this isn't such a good idea."

Tenia said, "Do you want to take her place, Aretha?"

When Aretha shook her head, Tenia picked up a goblet and pressed it against the naked woman's lips until she opened her mouth.

"For Satan's sake, drink it down, it's an aphrodisiac," Tenia said.

I remembered Bonnie saying that Madison was enthralled by Tenia and I wondered why. I also wondered why I had been so frightened.

Because this wasn't a Black Mass. This was a Black Comedy. *For Satan's sake?* Give me a break.

The three non-drugged witches lowered the dazed woman to the ground, not far from the campfire. After some rearranging of lethargic limbs, her arms and legs formed the shape of a cross. Tenia placed two candlesticks next to the nude woman's outstretched hands. The candlesticks held flaring black tapers.

Disgusted by the whole charade, I desperately wanted to leave, but someone or something wanted me to stay. I felt chained to the oak, as if I played freaking Houdini, shackled to the wooden bars of a jail cell.

Apparently, I wasn't the only person who'd experienced revulsion. Aretha refused a sip from a second goblet, filled with an aphrodisiac, or crushed qualudes, or whatever. Then she and another witch stood up, moved away from the campfire, and sat down. They were only a few feet from my oak, within hearing distance, and I struggled to control my raspy breath.

The moon's spotlight shone on Tenia. "Satan and Asmodeus," she said, after raising her hands and signaling for silence. "I beg you to accept the sacrifice of this woman whom we now offer to you, so that we may receive the things we ask for."

"I wan' wha' I assed for," the drugged woman slurred.

"The things that we and *she* ask for," Tenia amended.

In a low voice, Aretha's companion said, "I know who Satan is, of course, but who's Asmodeus?"

"My dear Mary-Magdalene," Aretha said. "According to Hebraic legend, he's the king of the demons, and he's usually represented pictorially with three heads, goose feet, and a snake's tail."

I didn't know that.

S.B. Eisenberg, the author of *Forever Asmodeus,* had conveniently disregarded that little tidbit, probably because it would have been a tad gauche for a three-headed, goose-footed, snake-tailed demon to blend in with a crowd.

"Tenia will now give everyone a White John," Aretha said.

The novice witch, Mary-Magdalene, said, "What's a white john?"

"The host, my dear."

"Host?"

"The Eucharist bread."

"What kind of bread is that?"

"*Communion,* Mary-Mag. A spiritual communion with…hush. Forget the White John. Here comes the best part."

I heard a vicious dog-growl, and darted a glance toward the gray cat…who serenely paw-washed its whiskers.

Some shrubbery separated. A black and tan rottweiler appeared, followed by a tall, naked, skeletal man. The man's legs were reedy, but the penis that dangled between his thin thighs looked to be the size most guys like to brag about. His gaunt face was bland—balding forehead, sparse eyebrows, bifocals, and nondescript nose. A salt and pepper mustache garnished his upper lip. He didn't have goose feet.

The dog growled again. The skinny man held up one finger and the dog sat. "Stay, Dashwood," the man said.

"Daniel named him Dashwood after Sir Francis Dashwood," Aretha told Mary-Magdalene. "Sir Francis was the leader of the Hell Fire Club."

Mary-Magdalene said, "Ooooh, could I join that club?"

Aretha said, "Sure, once you find a way to travel back to the seventeenth century."

The skinny man, in all likelihood Daniel Pearlstein, walked over to the drugged woman, who wasn't cross-shaped anymore. Her fingers had begun kneading her breasts and pinching her nipples.

"Somebody tie her arms down," Tenia said. "Sorry, Daniel."

"That's okay," Daniel said, his voice raspy. "That's okay, Tenia. Leave her alone."

"But it's not part of the ritual."

"Fuck the ritual," Daniel said.

The drugged woman pressed her palms against the ground and pushed. She didn't rise very far, just far enough to glance around. Momentarily, her gaze seemed to perforate my tree, and I felt as if I'd been punched in the stomach. The woman looked familiar. Very.

Daniel shoved her back to her prone position and licked his lips. His penis was firm, turgid, dilated with blood, and his face didn't seem bland anymore.

Aretha, Mary-Magdalene, and a handful of other witches began to masturbate.

Mary-Magdalene had an orgasm, and she resembled…more than resembled…the woman who'd recently graced my *Cosmo* cover.

Holy shit. Mary-Mag was Jem's model girlfriend.

Discarding her robe and clothes, Tenia slurped down something from a golden chalice, spilling half the blood-red liquid on her porcine belly. As she dropped the chalice and fondled her pendulous breasts, a witch knelt, encircled Tenia's butt, and lapped at her belly.

Christ, I'd witnessed enough. More than enough.

I must have seen what I was supposed to see because I didn't feel like a shackled Houdini anymore, and the witches were so preoccupied, they wouldn't have noticed me if I stood on my head, played an accordion, and sang *The Yellow Rose of Texas*.

All of them were naked. A few danced lewdly. But most watched Daniel Pearlstein mount Dawn Sullivan.

Dawn writhed, and Pearlstein had trouble penetrating, and I suddenly recalled the gas pump's nozzle.

This time, when I turned and ran back to Yoda, no gusty wind tried to stop me, and I'd almost reached Clear Lake City before I realized that I'd left my Stetson on the fence post.

Madison's Cottage
Los Angeles - 1999

Victor Madison stared at the plump scarecrow.

He knew from his research that her broom-textured, straw-yellow hair had once been pumpkin orange, sea-green, Prussian blue, and puce. Hell, her split ends *still* looked as colorful as Joseph's biblical coat. He also knew that she'd made an appointment to visit a cut-rate cosmetic surgeon.

Today, however, she'd compromised with cosmetics. Black kohl masked the circles beneath her hazel eyes, navy blue mascara spiked her lashes, and rose colored pie wedges slashed her cheekbones.

In an effort to look younger than fifty-six, her pierced ears sported a total of fifteen earrings. Her left wrist boasted a snake tattoo…with fangs …and the same tattoo artist had engraved a crimson-pigmented Pegasus above her right breast.

As a guest on CNN's Larry King, Victor had said he liked Disney because every single animated feature included elements of hostility and terror. Taking his words to heart, Stefani Bergen (real name Stevie Eisenberg) had stuffed herself into tight jeans, emblazoned with Mickey Mouse. A night chill permeated the air, yet she wore a cotton, spaghetti-strap tee-shirt. As Victor watched her raise a glass of champagne to her glossy red lips, 101 Dalmatian puppies romped across unfettered breasts that should have been fettered, and if she said the goddamn bubbles tickled her nose one more time, he'd kick her abundant butt out the front door.

Except he couldn't boot her from his cottage. Because, damn it, he needed her.

"I drank a whole bottle of champagne all by myself as soon as I finished the book," she said, "but it was cheap shit. This stuff tastes like a million bucks…" she paused to giggle "… and it tickles my nose."

"Would you like another hundred thousand dollars worth?" he said sarcastically, retrieving the Dom Perignon from a Sterling ice bucket.

"I really shouldn't." As she extended her glass, her expression turned coy. "And I don't mind being tickled, if you know what I mean."

Yes, he knew what she meant. From the moment she'd swiveled her hips into his living room, he could see the word "groupie" branded across her forehead, as if printed with visible rather than invisible ink.

First, she'd scrutinized the framed photos on his wall. She hadn't been turned on by Victor, circa 1986, schmoozing with Ronald Reagan. But she'd practically creamed her jeans over pictures of Paul Simon and Victor, Paul McCartney and Victor, Paul Newman and Victor, The Stones and Victor, and Redford and Brad and—

She had tapped her fake fingernails against the non-glare glass that protected a British rock group. "I made it with him," she said. "We fucked in Philadelphia. Well, I think it was Philly. I remember eating Philly cheesesteak sandwiches before we ate each other."

Then she had arched one hoop-earring-embellished eyebrow, as if she hoped he'd ask for references. When he didn't respond, she said, "I made it with Charlie Sheen...*we* ate hoagies...and the Grateful Dead and Robert—"

"Do you need to use the bathroom?" he had asked, cutting her off at the pass. "There's a whole wall of celebs above the bidet."

And yet, despite Stevie Eisenberg's abrasive language, despite her brash bravado, she possessed an impressionable insecurity.

Victor knew her background, had in fact made it a point to find out everything he could before their tête-à-tête. Just like *his* father, hers had been an unemployed, part-time drunk. Her mother had divorced and remarried, but Stevie left home at sixteen when her stepfather, playing Jack Nicholson in *The Shining*, broke down a locked bathroom door and violently raped her.

She, in turn, had knifed him.

Fleeing to Colorado, she married a man who combined the worst qualities of her father and stepfather. When he tragically burned to death, no one could *prove* that Stevie set the fire. As a matter of fact, she elicited more sympathy than suspicion, since the flames seared her left leg, leaving her with an ugly scar and a permanent limp.

Victor employed the best private detective agency in the business, yet her trail over the next several years had grown colder than the ice-swan centerpiece at Peggy Mostel's bas mitzvah. Ostensibly, Stevie traveled throughout the country, following the Grateful Dead.

Then, all of a sudden, she re-emerged in Denver.

Renting a small apartment, she worked as a pet groomer. Nights, she wrote romance novels. On her wall, she tacked a map of the United States. Starting with Colorado, she set each of her books in a different state. By the third state, she'd made her first sale.

Her heroines were young, beautiful, un-scarred. Her heroes were handsome and sensitive. Her love scenes pushed the envelope, but never quite broke the seal. She won a Lifetime Achievement Award from *Romantic Times* magazine and a couple of Romance Writers of America plaques. Then she married the stud who'd posed for three of her book covers, and they moved to Los Angeles.

She could deal with her husband's bar bills and gambling debts, but when she found him screwing everything but the dog (and she wasn't sure about the dog), she paid him off and kicked him out. The divorce drained what little remained of her savings.

Depressed, she gave away the dog and dyed her hair magenta. Her publisher, who didn't give a shit about clinical depression, told her to meet her deadlines or send back the advance payment, and would she *please* stop giving her heroines nervous breakdowns. Ultimately, Stevie severed all ties with her agent and publisher.

By then, she was pushing fifty-five. In a *Playboy* interview, she boldly and incautiously admitted that she could no longer write about "vapid virgins with secret babies, who have multiple orgasms at the first sight of a fucking cowboy." The remark didn't make her universally loved, especially among her fellow romance authors, and she spent the next thirteen months hibernating. When she finally came up for air, her hands were suspended above her keyboard, and she had just finished typing THE END on the last page of a 1,507-page horror novel.

Which was why Victor needed her. To put it bluntly, his last two films hadn't broken any box office records. If he didn't produce another hit movie soon, they'd be saying: *Madison who?*

Throughout his musings, Stevie had sat motionless, quiet as a mouse. Her bravado was gone, along with her coy expression, and nothing but her raw, almost anguished, vulnerability remained.

"So what do you think?" she said. "Will *Hell Hath No Fury* fly?"

"Do you want strokes or an honest opinion, Ms. Eisenberg?"

"Call me Stevie, please, and I want the truth. My bank account is overdrawn and there's barely enough ink in my printer to print a query letter.

Not that those bastards in New York have sufficient balls between them to play a game of tennis." She gave him a tight-lipped smile that was 90% Elvis. "Sorry, sir. I really shouldn't bad-mouth—"

"Madison. No first name, just Madison, and I hate being called sir."

"Yes, sir. I mean, Madison." She nodded toward a couple of reams of paper, stacked neatly on top of a Chippendale table. "Okay. I sent you my manuscript un-repped, which isn't fucking de rigueur, and ever since I got here we've made small talk...I've made small talk. I know you don't like me, and you obviously don't want to fuck me, so you must like my book. Am I right, or am I right?"

"I think it shows promise," he said.

"What?" Rising from her chair, she limped over to the antique Singer sewing machine that Cat Sands had found at a flea market and turned into a coffee table.

"I think it shows promise," Victor repeated. "Which word didn't you understand?"

"Fuck you, *sir.*"

Surprised, he said, "That was supposed to be a compliment."

"Well, you can stick your compliment up your ass, *sir.* I showed *promise* when I submitted my first manuscript. Which, for your information, became my tenth book. And when it was published, I hadn't changed one fucking word."

"Sit down." Grasping her by the shoulders, he steered her back to the chair. "How dare you play the brat with me? One more *fucking word* and I'll summon my driver. He'll dump you off in front of your trailer. Which, for *your* information, has been rented, following your second eviction notice, and the new tenants move in next week."

Sinking into the chair, she reached for her champagne glass.

"Put that down. I don't care how drunk you get, lady. I don't care if you chug the entire bottle and puke your guts out inside my celebrity-infested bathroom. But you won't drink another drop until I finish what I have to say. Is that perfectly clear?"

"Yes."

"Good. Your book shows promise, Stevie, but it's too long and you use the word 'fuck' every other sentence. Your male characters react like a herd of horny romance heroes, your teenage girl is a spoiled brat, and her mother is unbelievably stupid. In fact, the mother is one big cliché. I understand Yiddish, but your average reader won't."

"Now just a min—"

"Shut up. The only *feasible* character is Asmodeus. He's brilliant, well written, well developed. In fact, he could have been in the room with you, looking over your shoulder, spinning the planchette on your Ouija board."

"I don't own a fucking Ouija board."

"Take it easy. That's another compliment. I didn't mean to suggest …what's the matter now?"

"I thought I saw something. Bugs. I hate bugs."

Victor hunkered down. "Please don't pull that shit with me. I know you have a drinking problem, Stevie, but you haven't reached the I-see-bugs stage yet. And if I have anything to say about it, you never will."

Tears brimmed, then overflowed. "Do you want to option my book?" she whispered.

"Yes. I have the papers all prepared and notarized, ready for your signature. But you won't see one penny of the option money, my dear, until you revise your manuscript. From scratch."

"I can't. I told you. I'm out of ink. I don't even have the electricity to run my printer, or my computer, because I didn't pay the bill."

A shiver coursed through Victor as he remembered another city, another room, another lifetime. His sister Peggy lay bleeding to death and his mother told him to call an ambulance and he said he couldn't because he hadn't paid the phone bill.

Rising, Stevie's tear-drenched eyes displayed more grief than animosity. "Thanks for nothing," she said. "Christ, what a bummer."

Rising, Victor gently pushed her back down. "I have a vacant guest room," he said.

"I don't take charity, Mr. Madison, and I'm not a whore."

"With all due respect, and using your favorite expression, Stevie, I don't plan to fuck you."

"Then why the guest room?"

"You can have the whole damn cottage, except for my bedroom. Here's the deal. I'll buy you a new computer and printer. You'll get eight hours of sleep every night. You'll follow a healthy, balanced food program, and you won't drink booze or take any drug except aspirin. I suggest you use my exercise equipment to stimulate your brain, and my hot tub to relax your body, but that's only a suggestion, not an order."

"And in return?"

"In return, you'll write a bestseller."

"And the catch is?"

"I'll expect you to be disciplined and—"

"I *am* disciplined."

"Yes, I know. But you've never revised a book, my dear, and you have an explosive temper."

"If you call me 'my dear' again, I'll call you sir."

"Is your real name Stevie?"

"Yes. My father wanted a boy."

"What's your middle name?"

"Belle, as in belle of the *ball*. There's a certain irony in that, don't you think? Why are you grinning?"

"Belle is the name of Beauty, in Disney's *Beauty and the Beast.* You don't look like a boy, so I'll call you Belle." He gave her a mock-bow. "If that's okay with you."

"Sure, but I'm still looking for the catch. There's got to be a catch."

He grinned again. "Of course there's a catch, Belle. If I tell you to make changes—"

"Changes?"

"For instance, the title."

"You don't like my title?"

"*Hell Hath No Fury* is a romance title. I prefer something with Asmodeus in it. After all, he's the main character."

"He is not. Robin's the main character."

"Well, Belle, there's the catch. If you throw a tantrum, or argue, or ignore my editing, the deal's off."

"What a bummer. When does the deal start...*Beast?*"

"Tomorrow morning. You can stay here tonight. I'll be happy to buy you a new wardrobe, but, if you prefer, my driver will collect your clothes."

"How do you feel about cats?" She smiled at the expression on his face. "I don't need my clothes...you can burn them, for all I care...but I have a cat named Eros, and if I can't have Eros, the deal's off."

"You can have the cat."

"One other little thing."

"The cat isn't a little thing."

"Okay, big thing. Maybe I can give up drinking forever, Beast, but I can't give up sex forever."

"There you go. There's our title. *Forever Asmodeus.*"

"I don't like it."

"Isn't *that* a bummer? Don't worry, Belle, you'll get used to it."

Victor fetched the film option contract and a contract that made him sole rep of her book. He couldn't care less about the commission, but he didn't want her taking the finished product, *his* finished product, to a literary agent.

Especially when she realized that he'd optioned her book for a pittance.

After she had signed the contracts, she said, "The deal starts tomorrow, right?"

"Right."

Defiantly, she drank the rest of the champagne. Then she prowled around until she found his wet bar, whereupon she broke the seal on a bottle of Johnny Walker Red.

Around midnight, he heard her in the bathroom, puking her guts out, but after that she never touched another drop of liquor.

And by the time she'd finished the *Forever Asmodeus* revisions, her hair was a velvety brown, she'd dropped thirty-five pounds, she looked ten years younger, and she hated him with a passion.

THIRTY-ONE

"I want whatever you're taking, Frannie. You look gorgeous. In fact, if you weren't so short you could be a super-model."

Bonnie was, of course, lying through her perfect teeth.

Once I'd evened out the strands, my cropped hair looked okay, a smidgen longer that Mia Farrow's when she starred in *Rosemary's Baby*.

But I had gazed into the mirror this morning, and as the witch said when she gave the poisoned apple to Snow White: "Mirrors never lie."

A raccoon would have thought I was gorgeous, especially around the eyes. My lovely tan had faded because Sol Aarons applied my makeup before sunup and removed it after sundown. Madison had shot three bedroom sequences. Four days

(*and nights, Frannie, don't forget the nights!*)

had passed since the Black Mass.

Every night I dreamed about Tenia. Every night I dreamed about Daniel Pearlstein and Dawn Sullivan. Every night, in my sleep, I heard Elvis singing about teddy-bears and Dawn Sullivan singing *you are my sunshine,* until the loud pounding of my heart drowned them out. Then I'd see a wooden signpost, one arrow pointing to Clear Lake City, one to Never-Never Land, one to Houston. The biggest arrow of all read: SALEM, MASS. A scarecrow with an evil smile pointed in that direction, so I followed the MASS arrow, and when I woke up my pillow was soaking wet and my face was as white as the proverbial ghost.

The movie's evangelist, Joe Bob Lancaster, had met "Ellen"— Robin's mom—during a Billy Graham-ish rally at the Astrodome. Joe Bob hadn't appeared in any of the house scenes yet, but every morning a crowd of ever-hopeful Jeremy Glenn addicts surrounded my limo. I'd hear cries of "It's not HIM," and "Who's SHE?" Which didn't bother me…much. But once my Demon-face had been applied, I didn't care to leave the house.

Bonnie took her breaks outside, and I wished there was some way she could capture the sun, stick it in her pocket, and pull it out like a handkerchief. Beneath my demon makeup, my eyes squinted, my nose was stuffed with steel wool, and I always felt the urge to sneeze.

I didn't look "gorgeous." On the contrary, this morning's mirror reflection had looked dreadful; if I didn't know better, I'd have sworn Sol had forgotten to remove last night's makeup. Furthermore, I suffered from some weird stomach virus; couldn't hold down breakfast, then became ravenous by lunch time. I'd think: *pregnant*, except Andre and I hadn't made love since the Night of Wine and Roses.

An off the wall supposition occurred, even though recent events hadn't exactly been on the wall. First, I thanked Bonnie for the compliment. Then I said, "Tell me about the deck again."

"The deck?"

"Sorry." I reached for a plate of doughnuts, set out for the cast and crew, but stopped when I realized it was only seven o'clock. I couldn't tolerate another volcanic tummy eruption, even though Madison had called and told Sheldon Giglia to cancel the shoot. "Sorry," I repeated. "Please tell me what happened on the restaurant deck."

She did. When she'd finished, I said, "Was I ever alone?"

"Define alone," Bonnie said.

"Madison summoned you, and Jem went looking for the manager. Did they both leave at the same time?"

"They must have, Frannie. Jem said he and Madison put you on a table—"

"They wrapped my body around an umbrella?"

"No. There was a long plank table. Jem didn't want to carry you inside because the inside tables were cluttered with food and he would have drawn attention to your…condition. Personally, I think he was embarrassed because he'd gotten you drunk."

"I wasn't drunk."

"Hey, Jem felt guilty, so what's the difference?"

Weaving my hands through what was left of my hair, I said, "How long did it take Madison to find you, and how long did it take Jem to find the manager?"

"I was in the rest room. The manager was in the kitchen, calming a stressed-out cook. Jem said he wanted to hit the cook over the head with a frying pan, so I guess it took Jem more time to fetch the manager than it took Madison to fetch—"

"How much time, Bonnie? Ten minutes? Fifteen? Twenty?"

"I don't know, Frannie. I only know that Jem was frustrated and Madison was edgy and...why is it so important?"

"I've been feeling shitty," I said.

"And?"

"And I thought maybe I'd caught a chill," I fibbed.

"Frannie, it was *hot* outside."

"Not really. There was a breeze from the Gulf and—"

"Frannie. I need you." Madison propelled himself forward. In one hand he clutched a McDonald's wrapper. Biscuits, ham and sausage, from the smell. My stomach lurched, then settled.

"It's good to be needed," I said, thinking of Andre.

Who slept on the couch, if/when he bothered to come home at all. Who had found the time, or someone else, to wash his clothes. Who, after one double-take at my shorn hair, had said, "PMS, Frannie?"

Which was a joke, considering I hadn't had my period since the day before my Cat Sands interview.

But my periods have always been erratic, I justified, the hairs on the back of my neck prickling. It's a Jewish tradition. It's in the genes.

My mother had suffered from random menstrual periods, which had led to her hysterectomy, the reason why she couldn't have a second child. Her mother, my Grandmother Esther, had borne three daughters before she hit twenty-five, then—with relief, I suspect—had scheduled what she and my mom called "The Big Operation" or "The Big H."

I felt Bonnie poke my ribs, and realized that Madison had asked me a question. I'd been listening but not listening, and I tried to mentally knit the words of his request together.

The perfect high school had suddenly become available. It was Teachers' Day, when kids stay home. Madison wanted to shoot the scene where Robin, possessed and physically metamorphosed, attends a basketball game...as a cheerleader...definitely out of sequence since we were still shooting the "mutation" scenes.

Problem was, Madison needed another cheerleader and he didn't have time to audition a stray, stay-at-home kid.

Bonnie, who'd actually been a cheerleader, couldn't play one; the audience would recognize her as Martine. However, since I wore demon makeup...

"Do it, Frannie," Bonnie urged. "You've always wanted to be a cheerleader."

I said, "Would the cheerleaders have to cheer, Madison? I mean, would they have to perform cartwheels and stuff?"

He said, "Yes, of course they would. That's the point of the scene. Christ, you've read the book."

Of course I'd read the book. At least a gazillion times. "But I can't do cartwheels and splits," I said. "I don't have the..." *suppleness, elegance, grace* "...coordination."

"Yes, you can," Bonnie said. "C'mon, Frannie, try."

So, I tried. My legs vehemently protested the split, but managed to stretch far enough. The cartwheel was a breeze.

"Frannie, Frannie, you did it." Bonnie jumped up and down, as if she rode a pogo stick. "Isn't she perfect, Madison? Isn't she gorgeous?"

He looked startled. Then a strange expression briefly transformed his face; not exactly bestial, but undeniably deviant. I felt both frightened and flattered.

"I'll put you on top of the pyramid," he promised.

Holy shit. Frannie Rosen on top of the cheerleader's pyramid.

Just where I'd always wanted to be.

And I didn't even have to bargain with a demon to get there.

THIRTY-TWO

Neil Armstrong High School reminded me of Bayside High School, my old alma mater. The same trophy cases. The same up and down staircases, their banisters sticky with perspiration and hair spray. The same hall posters, except the names of the events had changed. For our dances we'd used "Under The Sea" and "Over The Rainbow." Neil Armstrong had embraced the electronics age. The most simplistic poster read: "MNEMONIC VAMPIRE BALL - BRING DATE AND BYTE."

The hallways smelled the same, too; cheap perfume, chalk dust, and Spearmint-Juicy-Fruit-gum. I expected Mr. Lash, from the Science Department, and Mr. Frankle, art teacher, and Mr. Neiman, English Department, to step out from the classrooms and shout: "Where's your hall pass, Frannie Rosen?"

I wouldn't have been the least bit surprised to see my old Principal, Dr. Moskowitz, suddenly appear—played by a stern-but-paternal Morgan Freeman.

Walking into the gym, I was transported back in time. Same shiny basketball court. Same wall of windows; multiple panes that looked like colorless Rubik Cubes. Same double nets and backboards. Same accusatory time clock.

I pictured Mike Seidman wearing a white booster sweater with its Capital B, brandishing a megaphone, whipping the spectators into a frenzy: *"Hey. Hey. Take it away. Take it down the other way."* I could see Pat Lash (daughter of the aforementioned Science Department's Mr. Lash), standing on top of a human pyramid, supported by Kathy Miao, Deena Cohen, Eileen Albany, Peggy Adler, Sandra Allik, and my best friend, Bonnie Sinclair. I had made fun of cheerleaders, the same way one makes fun of super-models, but—oh God!—how I envied them.

Glancing up at the bleachers, I thought: *Today I won't splinter my tush.*

Today I'll flip my short skirt and show off my tush.

Today I'll stand on top of the pyramid.

Eight "cheerleaders" used the girls' locker room to don socks, sneakers, blue stretch panties, and short white dresses that boasted orange and blue space shuttles across our breasts. The felt-lettered name on the back of my uniform read: MARIANNE. Most of the extras had already appeared in crowd scenes, and they chatted together as if they were old friends. Again, I was transported back in time, and I felt like a McMurtry outsider…until Lynn Beth Sullivan gave me a hug.

"Isn't this exciting, Frannie?" she said, her ginger curls practically leap-frogging, her amber eyes aglow.

I could understand her glee, poor baby. Thanks to her ambitious mother, Lynn Beth hadn't delved into many extracurricular activities.

My mind returned to the Black Mass, where a drugged Dawn had "sacrificed" her body in order to get what she asked for. What exactly had she asked for? Her daughter was starring in the biggest movie of the year. Wouldn't that be enough for any normal, red-blooded stage mother? Sure it would. Unless…

I remembered the edited screen tests, shown at the restaurant. I had focused on The Demon, even though there were other scenes, most of them with Lynn Beth and Jem. Cat Sands hadn't auditioned.

But Dawn Sullivan had.

Now, clear as a bell, I saw Dawn. She'd tried out for the part of Robin's mom, Ellen, and she'd actually been pretty good. However, Cat had already been chosen. Correction: Cat had been asked. So it made perfect sense for Dawn to screen test, just in case Cat said no.

But Cat said yes.

Had Dawn been dickering with the devil? Should I warn Cat?

If I did, I'd have to confess that Frannie Rosen had attended a Black Mass…alone…and that was one secret Frannie Rosen meant to keep.

In any case, Pearlstein wasn't Satan. He was just a horny old man, who got his kicks by screwing a narcotized, bedeviled woman in front of Tenia-the-Snake-Goddess and eleven naked witch wannabes. Including his own wife.

Had the rattlesnake been real? Probably. Had the luminescent shape been real? Doubtful. After all, as my Aussie friend Gordon would say, Frannie Rosen had been pissed as forty cats. How drunk was she? Well, she'd gone into an alcoholic fugue and cut her own hair.

Bringing my attention back to Lynn Beth, I heard the echo of my mother's voice: *It's a wonder you didn't cut off your nose to spite your face.*

"…and I really, really like your hair," Lynn Beth said, then paused for breath.

"Thanks, kiddo," I said, zipping up the back of her uniform.

She zipped up mine, and together we entered the gym.

THIRTY-THREE

Due to time constraints, Madison couldn't shoot scenes over and over, ad nauseam. Forget fifty takes. Three seemed to be the max, and he appeared to be satisfied with every actor...except one.

The kid who played Robin's boyfriend.

Physically, the kid fit the part, and I could understand why a Texas-based casting agency would pull his photograph and resume from the heap, then pat themselves on their overworked, underpaid backs.

Davy Crockett Brakowski was a high school senior. He'd never be *baaaad,* like Jeremy Glenn or John Travolta, but except for his dark hair, he resembled William Katt in *Carrie*. The sensitive type. Just what the doctor ordered. Just what Madison wanted.

The kid's experience, if he had any, was probably a bit part in a high school production of *Romeo and Juliet*. Or *West Side Story*. He could have played Romeo...or *West Side Story*'s Tony...except Davy Crockett Brakowski couldn't act worth a damn.

He'd memorized his lines, and confidence oozed from every pore, until our esteemed director began cutting him down with sarcasm. Had Madison yelled, it would have been better. I had a feeling Davy often endured yelling, even triumphed over the occasional this-hurts-me-more-than-it-hurts-you disciplinary drubbing...with a belt...or a broom handle...or maybe a horse whip; after all, this was Texas.

His father, who sat in the bleachers, looked the type. I hate to categorize, but Mr. Brakowski sported a beer belly, a stubbled double chin, and a quart of Pennzoil beneath his fingernails. Every time Madison chastised, Mr. Brakowski glowered at Davy. Every time Mr. Brakowski glowered, Davy forgot another line.

Lynn Beth kept saying things like: "That was my fault" or "I gave Davy the wrong cue," but it didn't help, and by the time Madison signaled for a lunch break, poor Davy looked as if he wanted to burst into tears.

Except he couldn't cry, not with his father still glaring and baring tobacco-stained teeth in a rabid wolf-snarl. Davy headed for what I assumed was the boys' locker room, maybe to cry, maybe to re-learn his lines. I had never felt so sorry for anyone in my life, and I damned Madison for his insensitivity.

Since I was powerless to alter the situation, I headed for the school cafeteria, my tummy growling with peckish anticipation, and ran smack-dab into Madison.

"Frannie," he said, "I need another big favor."

He put you on top of the pyramid, I reminded myself. And yet I knew my reply would sound brusque, if not downright rude. "What favor?" I snapped.

"That kid, the one who plays Robin's boyfriend…"

"Yes?"

"Could you find him and tell him I'm not pissed-off?"

I didn't say anything, but my expression must have said: *Find him yourself, dipshit.*

Still facing me, Madison put his hands on my shoulders, and I felt a not-unpleasant electric current course through my body. Confused, I turned my gaze away from his dark, earnest eyes.

A little farther down the hallway was the cafeteria, double-doors propped open by two chairs. I saw tables topped with cutlery, napkins, soft drink cans, and humidity-streaked water pitchers. Glancing out the window to my right, I saw caterers carrying sandwiches, salads, and plates heaped with yummy-looking pastries.

One of the caterers stood under a tree, not far from the window.

He looked like my friend Samson.

Holy shit. He *was* my friend Samson. If I hadn't shared his loft for nine months, I'd never have recognized him.

He wore a white kitchen jacket. A chef's hat hid his long hair. Lost in thought, he negligently flicked a lighter. I'd begun watching James Bond movies when I was knee-high to a Munchkin, and Samson didn't smoke, so I knew the lighter concealed a tiny camera. Samson was still furtively stalking Madison—for the unauthorized bio. It occurred to me that I could do my friend a favor, make up for the skimpy Cat Sands interview. Maybe, just maybe, I could set up a Victor Madison interview. That would make the bio an *authorized* bio, much more valuable than un, a shoe-in for the *NY Times* non-fiction bestseller list. Logic, however, told me I'd have to do Madison's favor first.

His fingers had left my shoulders to tilt my chin and caress the curve of my cheekbone. Again, I felt a sensual thrill. I sighed and said, "What do you want me to do for you, Madison?"

"Victor," he said, his voice a caress.

"What?"

"You can call me Victor, only not in front of the cast and crew."

"Okay...Victor." Briefly, I thought about his Disney obsession. Hell, I could always play Thumper.

He maneuvered my body against the wall opposite the window, so that, to anyone passing by, it would look as if we merely conversed. His hands reached beneath my short skirt and he began to sculpt my tush. His first finger edged along the elastic at the bottom of my blue stretch panties. My legs quivered. Instinctively, I spread them...just far enough for his finger to rub.

In another moment, less than a moment, I'd come. But I couldn't push away the thought that he'd slept with two of my friends, one of whom still craved his attention, so I pushed Madison away.

"The fa-favor," I stammered, trying to catch my breath. "You want me to do something for you."

"Yes, please." He straightened up, all business. "I need you to work with that kid, Robin's boyfriend—"

"Davy."

"Right. Davy. Cue him. 'Direct' him. I can't do it, he's scared of me. Meanwhile, I'll talk to Lynn Beth. Give her a few more lines, so she can fill in if the kid forgets his lines again. I'm running out of time here."

"I'll do it, Victor, but only if you get rid of Davy's father. Move that bastard out of the bleachers, out of the goddamn *school*, or you'll never get any kind of performance from Davy."

Madison nodded. "No problem," he said.

He gave me a quick kiss on the lips, then turned and walked away, and I thought it would be just my luck if Davy brooded inside the boys' locker room.

The boys' locker room isn't the same as walking into the boys' bathroom, I told myself. *And even if it is—*

My thoughts were interrupted by a new thought.

Witnessing Tenia's Black Mass had been like my old dream of walking into the boys' bathroom by mistake...only worse.

THIRTY-FOUR

I needn't have worried.

Davy Crockett Brakowski wasn't inside the locker room.

He was in the gym, standing at the foul line, shooting hoops.

Every time he shot, he missed. Every time he missed, he shouted, "You're such a fuckin' freak, Brakowski."

He wore a basketball uniform, and his orange-numbered shirt with JEROME on the back was still damp from nervous perspiration.

His non-movie street clothes were on the floor, neatly folded behind the foul line; black suit jacket, black slacks, white tee, and a leather belt with a huge silver armadillo belt buckle.

Davy's basketball hit the backboard and missed the net by a good eight inches. As he retrieved the ball, he shouted, "You're such a fuckin' freak, Brakowski." Then he saw me walking toward him.

"Mr. Madison sent you to fire me," he said. "It's okay, Frannie. I didn't want to be in the stupid movie anyway."

"No, Davy, you're wron—"

"I'm puttin' together a motorcycle, and as long as they pay me for today, I can buy more parts."

"Whoa, wait a min—"

"My dad thinks I'm crazy, buildin' a cycle from scratch. He says I'm wastin' my time. He says if the cycle don't run, he'll..." Davy paused.

Beat the shit out of me, I finished. Aloud I said, "You're *not* fired."

"Well, I'm gonna be." He twirled the basketball on top of his index finger, like a white Harlem Globetrotter. "Last night I knew the part perfect, Frannie. My dad even bragged to his friends 'bout me bein' in the movie. Today I don't know nothin'. I'm supposed to kiss Lynn Beth...Robin...but why would she want to kiss a fuckin' freak like me?"

"First of all," I said, "you're not a freak. You're a good-looking kid."

"I'm not a kid. I'm seventeen."

"Right. Sorry. I think I know what the problem is, Davy,
(*the problem is your fucking freak of a father*)
and I can fix it."

Hope flared in brown eyes that reminded me of Bambi's. "How can you fix me, Frannie?" he said, his voice negating his eyes.

"I can't fix *you,* Davy. You're not a broken toy. The problem is, you're not thinking like Jerry, Robin's boyfriend."

"How can I think like Jerry? He's captain of the Rockets. I can't even shoot a goddamn basket."

"That's exactly what I mean. Maybe Davy can't shoot a basket, but Jerry can. You've got to be Jerry inside your head. Jerry wouldn't have any reservations about kissing Robin. He's probably slept with half the cheerleaders."

"No, I ain't. My dad thinks I have, but—"

"Please listen, Davy." I led him over to the Rocket's bench, sat him down, then sat next to him. "The point is, you've got to shed your skin like a snake."

"A snake," he repeated, and I gave an involuntary shudder.

"Or, if you prefer, a caterpillar. Davy isn't into sports, but Jerry is. Davy gets good grades—"

"Yeah, so what? My dad don't give a shit if I pass or flunk."

"Then *use* your father for Jerry. Jerry's father smacks him around," I said, and this time Davy gave an involuntary shudder. "Jerry knows a college basketball scholarship will get him out from under his father's thumb and…I've got an idea. Try this, Davy. Pretend Jerry writes poetry and the only person he's ever shown his poems to is Robin. He's liked her all along, because she's the only one who appreciates his sensitivity. But when she suddenly turns drop-dead gorgeous, he's a little shy, knowing she's read his poems, afraid she might be laughing at him behind his back."

"So when he starts to kiss her, he's not sure she'll kiss him back," Davy said. "He thinks she'll laugh in his face."

"Very good, except I think Jerry knows Robin will kiss him back. So instead of giving Robin his usual *Splendor in the Grass* kiss…have you seen *Splendor in the Grass*?"

"Yeah, on TV."

"Okay. What Jerry feels for Robin is love, not lust. So he'd kiss her very gently, pull away, then kiss her again with more passion."

"Because she doesn't laugh in his face, right?"

"Right. Well, sort of. Look, I've got another idea. Sometimes my boy-friend..." I hesitated, picturing Andre who slept on the couch, then Jem who wanted to know if I swallowed, then Madison who wanted me to call him Victor. "My ex boyfriend," I amended, "would cue me, tell me if/when I said something wrong. Will you let me cue you?"

"I didn't bring my script, Frannie, 'cause I knew my lines."

"I have a memory like a sponge, Davy. I know all the lines."

It was a good half hour before I felt that Davy Crockett Brakowski could successfully, if not brilliantly, portray Jerry.

No one had entered the gym. *Everyone is too busy feeding their faces,* I thought, wishing I could feed mine.

And yet, helping Davy had helped me. For the first time in weeks I felt like my old self, rather than some unorthodox puppet in a far-fetched morality play.

Bottom line: every recent occurrence had been generated by my drink-ing. In New York I rarely, if ever, chugged down wine and beer. I didn't even like the taste

(*what about the audition, Frannie?*)

of liquor, unless it was diffused by lime juice,

(*the audition inside Madison's hotel suite, Frannie!*)

like maybe a nice salty margarita, or vodka and

(*you didn't drink before the audition, Frannie!*)

cranberry juice. Shit, anyone would hallucinate if they drank enough booze.

Turning to Davy, I said, "You'll be fine, but I'll give you something for luck...a talisman." *Dumbo's feather,* I thought, as I reached behind my neck and unclasped my Star of David. "I have a sneaky suspicion you're not Jewish, Davy, so you don't have to wear this 'round your neck. Maybe you can put it in your sneaker. The important thing is to know it's there."

"Thanks, Frannie. I'll give it back after I'm finished."

Rising to his feet, Davy grasped my hands and pulled me from the bench. I felt the star's six sharp points dig into my palm. Worse, my legs were full of acute, knifelike pins and needles.

I staggered forward. Davy, still holding the necklace, caught my shoul-ders. We hadn't rehearsed the Robin kiss, but "Jerry" had learned his lesson well. Removing one hand from my shoulder, he traced the contours of my face, then bestowed a gentle kiss upon my lips.

I smiled, said, "Perfect," and Davy turned animalistic. His hands were everywhere, squeezing my breasts, pulling my body against his, painfully kneading my tush like bread dough. Vaguely, I saw that he'd dropped the necklace. Still stunned, I felt him bend his knees until his groin was on a level with my panty-clad vagina. He pressed me closer and began jerking back and forth, but his penis wasn't hard enough to make a dent.

"Stop it, Davy," I yelled. "What the hell do you think you're doing?"

Which had to be the second most inane remark I've ever made, the first being my response to the dream spider when I saw it wasn't Nana Jen. Because Davy knew perfectly well what he was doing—trying to screw me through my clothes.

He loosened his grip at my words. I pulled away, and laughed. I don't know why I laughed. Yes, I do. In my whole life, no one has ever thought me juicy enough to initiate a violent seduction. Andre had come close, the day we played our "John-Mary" scene inside my dressing room. But, to be honest, I initiated the Andre seduction. In fact, except for the Night of Wine and Roses, I've initiated *all* his seductions.

A cameraman ducked into the gym, but turned tail when Davy shouted, "Don't laugh at me, Frannie. Don't you dare laugh at me."

"Calm down," I said. "I wasn't laughing at you. This isn't the time or place, Davy, and a guy should ask a girl if she's in the mood first." I couldn't resist adding, "You can use some of what you just felt when you play Jerry, but not when you kiss Robin."

"Okay, Frannie, sorry," he muttered, retrieving the necklace. His cheeks were as red as twin stoplights. "If you'd been in the mood, would you have said yes?"

"Absolutely," I fibbed sincerely.

As I walked toward the gym's double doors, I glanced over my shoulder. Davy had a goofy grin on his face. My "absolutely" had salvaged his wounded pride, and I was fairly certain his performance this afternoon would be *better* than satisfactory.

Strolling down the hallway toward the cafeteria, I wondered if I should go back and ask Davy if he wanted to join me for lunch.

No. He might run into his father, who'd nullify my coaching.

My neck felt strange without my Star of David. Maybe I should have "Dumbo-feathered" Davy with an earring. I'd worn my favorite pair, diamond studs, not unlike the studs Sol Aarons sported. Instinctively, my hands reached up to touch my earrings.

Shit. An earring was missing. It must have fallen off during my scuffle with Davy.

My mother equated pierced ears with waitresses, musicians, and "those

colored people in *National Geographic,*" but Daddy had given me the diamonds, a don't-tell-Mom birthday present, so finding the stud would have
to be my number one priority...well, maybe number one-and-a-half.

Sandwich first, I thought, increasing my pace. *I can eat the sandwich on
my way back to the gym.*

I scooped up two sandwiches, ham and cheese, then smeared the bread
with mustard. Bonnie leaned against Madison. She looked purry. As I
headed for the hallway again, I feigned external indifference.

Hopefully, Davy had already spotted my earring. Because once the cast
and crew resumed filming, the odds of me finding my diamond stud would
be the about the same as me pocketing a winning lottery ticket.

Speaking of pockets, where would I put the damn sandwich crusts? My
cheerleader outfit didn't have pockets.

I'm eating the crusts, Mom. Hope you're happy.

Except for my missing earring, I felt happy...

Until I opened the gym door and stepped inside.

A shaft of sunlight from the gym's Rubik Cubes windows shone on
Davy's armadillo belt buckle.

I screamed at the top of my lungs. Then, raising my fists toward the ceiling, I cried, "It was just a kiss, an innocent kiss, it didn't mean anything.
Why didn't you make me vomit *his* kiss?"

Summoned by my scream, the cast and crew entered the gym and
stopped short, jostling each other. Madison ran toward me and pulled me
into his arms. I said, "It's all my fault," then sobbed uncontrollably.

Murmuring words of comfort, Madison stroked my back.

My head rested sideways against his chest, my eyes open, and I saw
Madison...*Madison?*...standing by the double doors of the Neil Armstrong High School gymnasium, his arms around a grief-stricken Bonnie
and a stony-faced Tenia.

As I tried to absorb the tableau, "my" Madison's hands left my back,
fading away with the rest of him, until my face rested against nothing,
unless you consider air something.

In the split second before I pitched forward and fell, unconscious, to the
floor, my frantic gaze touched upon the body that swung from the scoreboard.

THIRTY-FIVE

The cops called it a suicide.

I knew better, but they wouldn't have listened to me, even if I could have told them.

Davy Crockett Brakowski hadn't hanged himself with his belt. Davy had been killed by a demon. Or a human. Or a human demon.

Motive: He had kissed me. It didn't make any difference if the kiss was a prelude to nothing. The demon didn't know that, and Davy *wasn't the one*. There was no doubt in my mind, except...why? WHY didn't the demon make me vomit Davy's kiss? WHY kill the boy?

The film's on-site doctor had resuscitated then escorted me to the principal's office, and I felt the same way I used to feel when I was a recalcitrant student at Bayside High. Guilty. Contrite. Apologetic.

Introduced to a couple of police officers, I felt even more penitent. The interview, however, was a mere formality. The cops, it seemed, had an air-tight case. When I insisted that their case wasn't air-tight, they told me why it was.

One, Davy had been castigated, by Madison, over and over again.

(*"But he was 'up' when I left him,"* I told the cops. *"He had his lines memorized and was looking forward to the shoot."*)

Two, Davy was anti-social, a loner, and his classmates called him a homo...or worse.

(*"Bullshit,"* I told the cops. *"He had low self-esteem because his father treated him like dirt."*)

Three, Davy had repeatedly threatened to kill himself so that everybody, especially his dad, would be sorry.

(*"He was building a motorcycle from scratch,"* I told the cops, *"and excited about buying the parts he needed."*)

Four, a member of the crew had heard Davy say: "Don't laugh at me,

Frannie, don't you dare laugh at me."

How could I explain, without sounding narcissistic, that my "absolutely" had assuaged Davy's wounded pride? How could I explain that an icy finger made me puke everyone else's kiss, but not Davy's? How could I explain Tenia? Or novitiate witches? Or a ghost who ate beetles and wore a diamondback stole? How could I explain anything "woo-woo" to a couple of world-weary, skeptical cops?

The cops who questioned then released me were polite, as if they'd taken sensitivity classes where they had to watch *Law and Order* reruns ad nauseam. But they obviously thought I had contributed to Davy's suicide and wanted to mitigate my guilt by conjuring up a make-believe murderer.

If Madison had any guilt, he didn't show it. Discarding his usual hermitic façade, posing in front of mikes and TV cameras, he said that *Forever Asmodeus* (starring Jeremy Glenn and Catherine Lee Sands) would include a dedication to Davy Crockett Brakowski. During the credits, Madison said, at the end of the movie.

Funny how he suddenly remembered the kid's name, I thought, as Madison continued.

He had dozens of takes, enough film so that movie-goers could see how beautifully Davy had played the part of the handsome but tormented high school student, not unlike James Dean in *Rebel Without a Cause.* Davy was another James Dean, his promising career cut short by unforeseen circumstances. And, in essence, just like James Dean, Davy would never die.

Christ. I saw a few reporters, men and women both, wipe tears from their eyes. They didn't know, as I knew, that Madison planned to insert another kid, another basketball player, seen from the back or not seen at all, easily filmed off-location. During the lunch break, Madison had re-written the Jerry-Robin kiss so that Lynn Beth had 90% of Davy's lines. Of course, he'd keep the close-ups that revealed Davy's confusion. And anguish.

However, the James Dean bit was brilliant. I had to give Madison that, but I didn't have to give him anything else. My body, for instance.

Aside from his blatant promotional tactics, aside from his ability to turn Davy's death into a *Forever Asmodus* asset, I blamed Madison for "the kid's" execution. If he had been a little more compassionate, a little less disparaging, I wouldn't have sought out Davy and he'd still be alive.

Or would he still be alive? Everything I told the cops was true, but the echo of Davy's *you're-such-a-fuckin'-freak* kept reverberating inside my head. Maybe he'd shifted back into freak-mode as soon as I exited the gym. No. He had Dumbo's feather. He believed in Dumbo's feather.

He did, didn't he? Or did *I* believe in Dumbo's feather?

The police had found my Star of David necklace in Davy's jock strap. If he had put the necklace in one of his sneakers—taking the shoe off then lacing it up again—would he have had enough time to change his mind? Or had he unhesitatingly thrust the necklace into his jock strap, scooped up his belt, and headed for the scoreboard?

My earring hadn't been found, but I couldn't have cared less. If only I'd gone back to search for the diamond right away. If only—

"Frannie. I've been looking all over for you."

As I stared up at Bonnie, I realized I still warmed a bench inside the locker room. I even wore my cheerleader's uniform. Which didn't have blood on it, but should have.

"Sorry, Bon," I said. "I'm not in a very good mood."

"Everyone's feeling down. We thought we'd hit a bar, not too far from here. The limo drivers said they'd wait. We've all decided to get smashed …" She paused. "Frannie, is Andre out of the picture?"

"I guess. Why?"

"Jem said he'd take care of you."

"What time is it?

"Late. The police are finished and they plan to lock up the school."

"Change…clothes," I mumbled, not moving, still drugged by guilt.

"Wake up, Frannie. Grab your clothes and change later." She squinted at her watch. "Dammit, move."

I moved. After the Black Mass, I'd sworn never to drink again, but what the hell. If the demon appeared, I'd ask him why he hadn't made me vomit Davy's kiss…

A new thought occurred.

Madison had kissed me. In the hallway, near the cafeteria.

Granted, it wasn't a deep sucky kiss, like Jem's kiss or Andre's kiss. In fact, Madison's kiss was no more aggressive than Davy's kiss. But I hadn't vomited, and as far as I knew, Madison was still alive.

"Bon," I said, as we ran toward the exit. "You were with Madison during the lunch break. Did he ever leave you?"

"What do you mean?"

"When we broke for lunch, did he meet you inside the cafeteria?"

"No. We walked to the cafeteria, ate together, and returned to the gym. On our way back, we ran into Tenia. Then we heard you scream."

"He never left? To talk to someone else? Or use the mens' room?"

"No. Why do you ask?"

"Hurry, Bon, I need a drink. I need to drown myself in a bottle of vodka. If I do, maybe things'll make more sense."

I pictured my New York psychic and heard myself saying: *By the way, Mrs. Carvainis, do you believe in spirits?*

I saw her blood-red brooch and heard her reply: *Doppelgangers.*

Oh, dear, oh, shit. Doppelgangers...

Ghostly counterparts of living persons.

THIRTY-SIX

I didn't drown, but if there had been a beer vat large enough to fall into, I would have.

"My kisses are jinxed," I told Jem, "but you can do anything else."

I was so drunk, I felt numb as well as uninhibited.

"Feel me up, Jem, feel me down, even put your you-know-what in my—"

"Frannie, watch your mouth," Bonnie said, as drunk as I, although Bonnie doesn't usually drink very much.

We both thought *watch-your-mouth* was the funniest remark in the history of the world, and we laughed so hard I almost peed my cheerleader's uniform.

"Watch your mouth," Bonnie said again, but it wasn't as funny the second time.

"I'm Marianne," I told Jem and Bonnie, removing one of my elbows from the bar's surface. My first finger managed to find my back and tap the felt letters. "Marianne doesn't have to watch her mouth. Marianne can do anything she fuckin polices."

"Fuckin pleases," Bonnie said, although she hardly ever uses the F-word.

"No, no, Bonnie, police. They wouldn't listen to Marianne. They believe she…" I paused to belch. "They believe I killed Davy."

My words hit a wall of silence. Everyone had paused for breath or was sipping/gulping down their drinks. The bartender was changing a tape, so even the music had stopped.

"You didn't kill Davy," Jem said. "She's drunk," he told the room.

Everyone nodded and began to talk again. The music blared…The Byrds…*Lay Lady Lay.*

"Marianne says turn down the music," I told the bartender.

"You got it, Marianne. I wouldn't want you to kill me."

The bartender meant it as a joke. Nevertheless, I told him to shut the fuck up, then said, "Why is Marianne talkin' in third person, Bon?"

But Bonnie was gone, sitting at a table. Correction: sprawled across the lap of Jon Rubenstein, the hunk who played the fictional Rockets' basketball coach.

"Bonnie hoped Madison would be here," I told Jem. "That's why she's drinkin' so much. Do you know where he is?"

"Sure, Frannie. He's at the hotel. Booking a flight to L.A."

"Call Marianne Marianne, Jem. Why is he flyin' to L-freaking-A?"

"Because tomorrow he'll meet with Stevie Eisenberg."

"Why?"

"Madison and Stevie will revise the script and give Robin a new boyfriend," Jem said. "Frannie, my little kumquat, you need fresh air, eh?"

"Marianne kumquat," I admonished. "Do you think Marianne can kiss Jem, Jem? She wants to awful bad, and maybe the demon'll be fooled 'cause she's Marianne, not Frannie."

As Jem helped me off my stool, I began to cry, and that's the last thing I remember.

I didn't pass out, but I have no idea what happened when Jem drove me home, just the two of us, inside an empty limousine.

Well, empty except for the driver.

I must have given the driver directions, which is incredible when you consider how out of it I was, because he found Rick's duplex. I don't remember what happened when Jem walked me inside. I think he might have stayed a while because the hands on the shipshape clock traveled round and round…like a movie telling time. I think Jem took off my cheerleader's uniform, even though I kept telling him I was cold and needed a sweatshirt. I think he put me to bed. I don't remember if he joined me there. I don't think he did. I think he said, "Goodnight, Frannie, goodnight, Marianne, and thank you."

Marianne was as drunk as Frannie. I don't think either of us knew why Jem was thanking us…

Until hours later, when I woke up and let the icy finger do its thing.

"Okay, you've made your point," I said to the empty bathroom. "He's not the one. I've vomited Jem's kisses, you bastard. Now, for Christ's sake…*for Satan's sake*…why don't you leave me the fuck alone?"

Madison's Cottage - Los Angeles

Hollyhocks brushed against her knees as the dark-haired woman spat on her handkerchief. After rubbing the hanky across a piece of window, she stared into the cottage.

He wasn't there, but that was okey dokey, smokey.

She tried to keeps tabs on him (*isn't tab a soda?*) and knew he was someplace that started with a "T" (*Tennessee? Toronto? Timbuktu?...Tab is a diet soda; I drank it for years, dammit...Texas. That's where he is.*)

Usually she had trouble remembering things, but this time she'd remembered.

"Could be worse," she told her window reflection. "A lot worse, they say. For instance, if I had that forget-disease...Alzheimers? Ah well...I remembered Tab, didn't I?"

Her reflection nodded agreement.

She had seen a movie once called Shirley...(*Dammit...dammit... dammit...some kind holiday. Mother's Day? Shirley Mother? No...that doesn't sound right. Valentine's Day...that's it*) and Shirley talked to walls.

Everybody, especially Nurse, thought that part of the movie was hilarious.

(*What's so funny about talking to walls? At least they don't talk back. And if you ask questions, you can make up her own answers, which can be fun.*)

And Dr...(*his name...dammit...what's his name?*)

"I can't remember his name because he's new," she told the window. "My real doctor died of old age. They said: Oh, God, heart attack...but he died of...Dr. Feldman. That's the name of the new doctor.

"And he says it's all right to talk to walls. Or windows, if you prefer. Or the mirror. Dr...oh, hell...the one who died, wanted me to write everything down in a book called a…dairy? No…that doesn't sound right. Oh, I hate this.

"Caruth. That was his name. And it's diary…not dairy."

She had drunk Tab because she didn't want to get fat. Way back then, Madison drank Coca-Cola. Once he had said, "Every single day you see the word 'Coca-Cola' on signs, on TV, in the stores, on a menu, even when you're not looking for it. I wouldn't be so presumptuous as to think people will see the words 'Victor Madison' every day, but when they see a horror book or a horror movie, I want them to associate it with my name."

"How come I can remember that when I can't remember diary or Dr. Caruth? Anyway…why did I come here?"

Madison (*who wanted everyone to see his name every day*) had something she wanted to see, and he wasn't home, obviously. Well of course…the *L.A. Times* said so. The *Times* said he was in…Texas, and someone had died, and there was a big picture of Victor Madison standing in front of a school, and there was a little picture of the kid who died. It should have been the other way around. The kid who died should have gotten the big picture.

When Dr. Feldman died he got a small picture. (*No, not Dr. Feldman. Dr. Caruth. Why the hell can't I keep them straight? Dr. Caruth was the old doctor and Feldman is young. When I first met him, Dr. Caruth was young…maybe that's why I keep getting them confused. Nurse says that when you forget a name, you should go up and down the alphabet. A, B, C…Caruth. D, E, F…Feldman.*)

Anyway, the *Times* said Madison was in…R, S, T…Texas, so this morning she'd given Nurse the slip.

That's what they called it on TV, even though everyone knew a slip was something you wore under a pretty dress. But she watched Jeremy Glenn every week, even the reruns, and he called it slip. She had no trouble remembering Jeremy's name because she loved his show.

"Are the doors locked?" she asked the wall, then made up her own answer. "Of course they're locked."

She could say open-sesame like A…Alan Ladd. No. A… Aladdin. But that was a little kid's story, dammit, so it probably wouldn't work.

Maybe she'd go through Victor (*who wanted everyone to see his name*) Madison's trash can, first.

* * *

Victor stared at the flight attendant.

Black. Denzel in Glory.

Graceful, with finely-honed muscles.

Probably played college ball but didn't go pro.

Wide receiver? Fullback? Tight end?

Years ago, the A&P manager had accused Victor of raping people with his eyes. At the time Victor had thought it a compliment, and he still did. Stripping away flesh, he scrutinized the flight attendant's bone structure. Nice. Very nice. "Denzel" was maybe twenty-five, and he didn't wear a wedding band. Straight? Gay? Hard to tell, but by the time the fucking plane landed in L.A., Victor would know.

If it ever landed. The plane had taken off two hours late—engine trouble or some such bullshit. Stevie was always saying he should buy a private jet. "You can afford it, Beast," she'd say, and she was right. His literary agent's contract, the one he'd included in order to protect his film rights contract, had netted him a small fortune. And when he held an auction for S.B. Eisenberg's *Forever Asmodeus* sequel, the bids had, first tiptoed, then hurdled, then rocketed into Stephen King territory.

Problem was, she refused to work on the new novel unless she could use her title, *Birds Can't Fly*. A stupid title, it had something to do with Robin, whom she still considered her protagonist. Victor wanted *Asmodeus II,* but he didn't have 100% control over Stevie anymore. Unless he took her to bed, he didn't have any control at all. He knew she hated him and loved him, and he could have dealt with that, but she was jealous, her claws as sharp as her cat Eros, who continued to live at the cottage...because S.B. Eisenberg continued to live there.

She behaved at interviews, but privately she insisted on calling the first horror book *Forever Robin*. She also insisted that she'd written *Forever Robin* at the cottage and didn't want to incur "bad luck" by changing her locale. He didn't frequent the cottage all that often, and didn't give a shit if she took root, but he'd recently learned that she answered phone calls with: "This is Stevie Eisenberg, Victor's fiancé."

They'd have to talk about that...after she revised the script.

Stevie had a knack for script writing. She'd learned the computer program in less than an hour, and had finished the *Forever Asmodeus* screenplay in three weeks.

And it was the best first draft Victor had ever seen.

If she finished the revisions tonight, he could fly back to Houston at the crack of dawn, losing one day and one day only. No big deal; he'd canceled today's shoot so that everybody could mourn the kid.

Stevie could have faxed him the revisions, but he wanted to be with her. His presence had a *Streetcar Named Desire* effect. Raw sex. Raw power. Kim Hunter wending and strutting her way down the stairs so that Marlon Brando could fuck her senseless. Brilliant in the movie, it played pretty well inside the cottage too. At least it did when Beast, not Belle, directed the scene.

He hated wasting the time it would take to satisfy Stevie's voracious appetite (she hadn't been kidding when she said she wouldn't give up sex) and he loathed flying. But he couldn't take a chance on something else going wrong.

The tropical storm, the shocked electrician, Cat's sprained back, the tainted food, the rattlesnake…and now this latest disaster.

Why hadn't the kid…Davy…*waited* a few weeks? Frannie could have walked him through his part. Victor could have used the James Dean bit, but dodged the revisions and bedroom aerobics.

Frannie. Now there was one lucky break. He'd hired her because, in demon makeup, she looked like Lynn Beth. And because her audition and screen test had both been out-fucking-standing. He hadn't intended to use her for all the demon scenes, but Lynn Beth couldn't do them. Frannie could act up a storm and she never complained. And although it had escaped his notice at the first interview, she was beautiful. He liked her Mia haircut. He surmised that her light golden hair was natural, which meant…

Which meant nothing. He didn't screw around with his cast. He had enjoyed Bonnie, and knew she wanted a repeat performance, but once she'd accepted a part in his movie, an encore was verboten. The extra in his first film had taught him a good lesson; it took months for his lacerated face and body to heal.

Talk about a fatal attraction.

His un-fatal attraction had been another lucky break. He'd met Dawn Sullivan years ago, at a cocktail party. She had been an aspiring actress, her greatest asset a luxurious mane of auburn hair that cascaded down her back to her butt. She had stalked him for a while, then given up. Little did he—or she—know that her daughter would one day star in Victor Madison's most ambitious film.

"Denzel" kept sneaking covert glances toward Victor's first-class seat. The flight attendant's Lion King eyes revealed an interest that was impossible to miss. But now Victor wasn't interested. Because, if he played his cards right, everything would come up roses. Or, to be more precise,

Rosen. Frannie Rosen.

She didn't know that he'd fallen in love with her. She didn't know that, staring through the lens of his camera, devising the perfect shot angles, he'd often felt intense heat course through his body. He, himself, hadn't recognized his true feelings until he'd asked her to play a cheerleader. Now, thinking back, he realized he'd begun to crave Frannie when she questioned him about his Picasso sculpture. Then, her incredible audition. Christ, if Suzanne Burton hadn't been there, he'd have joined Frannie and...

After *Asmodeus* wrapped, he'd buy a house in Connecticut or an apartment in Manhattan. Maybe he'd buy a chunk of Utah from Redford. Or, if Frannie preferred, a goddamn mansion in goddamn Beverly Hills.

He'd never felt this way about a woman before, not even Cat. Frannie was Circe. She had a sensual aura...and, with Frannie, he wouldn't use condoms. If she got pregnant, so be it. He'd never wanted children before, but now he wanted a son, a miniature Victor Madison. He even had a name picked out. Orson Welles Madison.

Stevie Eisenberg stared at *Birds Can't Fly.*

The half-finished manuscript was two-hundred-and-sixty pages of pure, unadulterated crap. Almost as bad as the four-hundred-and-fifty pages she'd already shredded. Seven-hundred-and-eleven pages, one and a half reams of paper, thirteen months of her life—gone.

God, how she hated to give in to Victor. But when you're right, you're right. Right?

And just for grins, why the fuck was she trying to kill her career again? Why did she stubbornly insist that Robin was the protagonist?

"Robin isn't the heroine," she told Eros. "If any human is, it's Daisy, Robin's sister. Maybe I should call the damn book 'Flowers Can't Grow.'"

Eros gave her arm a lick with his sandpaper tongue. Damn, she didn't want the cat's tongue. She wanted Victor's tongue. Or else she'd never be able to write *Birds Can't Fly,* or *Flowers Can't Grow,* or even *Asmodeus II.*

Stevie knew she was addicted to sex, the same way she had once been addicted to liquor and pot. Her own fingers provided a small amount of relief, but what she really needed was the tongue of the Beast. And soon, thank God, she'd get it.

She had finished the *Forever Asmodeus* revisions (screenwriting was a piece of piss) but Victor didn't know that. When he arrived, which should be any minute now, she'd be sitting in front of her computer, scowling at the screen.

"I'll tell him to inspire me," she said, scratching the cat's chin. "I'll tell him to inspire me with his tongue."

As if on cue, she heard someone at the front door.

Victor had hung a small mirror on the wall, near her computer desk, so that while writing Robin's physical transformation, Stevie could see her own. Now, she studied her face. Her eyes were clear, her complexion unblemished (except for a few scars, thank-you gifts from her stepfather and model husband), and her just-washed hair curled below her shoulders. A few stray gray hairs had invaded the mink-brown strands—*what a bummer*—but a tweezers took care of that.

Why didn't Victor walk inside? She rarely, if ever, locked the door because the estate owner had a security guard who carefully checked the I.D. of anyone entering through the front gate.

Limping over to the door, she cracked it open. A dark haired woman with pink-patched cheeks stood on the welcome mat. The mat had been shredded by Eros' claws, and Stevie kept meaning to throw it into the trash can out back.

As the woman said "Open sesame," Stevie recognized her.

"Come in," Stevie said, flinging open the door. "I'm expecting Victor any moment, and I'm sure he'll be happy to see you."

Like hell he will, she thought, but merely said, "Would you like something to drink? How about a Coke?"

"A Tab would be nice, Miss…sorry, I can't remember your name."

"Stevie. Stevie Eisenberg. Victor's fiancé."

Briefly, Victor though about calling Stevie from LAX. He was now running three hours late. The plane had circled above the airport…and by God, he'd start shopping for a private jet as soon as he returned to Houston.

On the other hand, if Stevie was working on script revisions, she shouldn't be interrupted. She'd want to take a break the moment he set foot inside the door; what she called an "inspirational interlude."

Surprisingly, he didn't want to "cheat" on Frannie. As Stevie would say, what a bummer.

His driver had waited while the damn plane circled endlessly, and

Victor had no luggage to claim. For once the freeway was unclogged by breakdowns, mud slides, and/or construction, so he reached his cottage in record time.

Exiting the car, stretching his cramped muscles, he saw that Stevie had left the door wide open. How many times had he told her to keep the damn door shut and locked? A security guard watched over the front gate, but even security guards had to take a whizz every once in a while. And if somebody wanted to trespass badly enough, he or she could enter the estate by hiking through a wooded area behind the main house and cottage.

"Damn it, Belle," he said, entering the living room, "I'd turn you over my knee and paddle your butt, except you'd probably enjoy it."

Holy Christ. The living room. Mess would be an understatement.

Cushions had been slashed. Pictures had been pitched or hurled to the floor, leaving a trail of broken glass everywhere. The three Pauls were okay. So was Ronnie Reagan, Madonna, and as far as Victor knew, all the other superstars...

But in each and every photo, *Victor Madison* had been mutilated.

Fear rendered him paralyzed. Then, aware that this was the reaction he sought from his audience (*pounding heart, watery legs, raspy breath*), he stepped into Stevie's office.

A tornado had hit.

For starters, every file drawer had been emptied. In the midst of scattered papers and file folders, Victor spotted a manila envelope.

Asmodeus Revisions.

Thank God.

Swiftly, Victor checked the other rooms. They had all been thoroughly ransacked, and where the hell was Stevie?

Outside, you idiot. She's hiding. She ran to the main house for help. Where the fuck do you think she is? Do you think she stuck around while somebody turned the cottage into a fucking war zone?

"Mr. Madison."

His driver. Alvin. Alvin was the epitome of cool...

"Mr. Madison, come quick."

...but Victor wasn't surprised to hear an urgent fearfulness in Alvin's voice.

Stevie lay face down in the hollyhocks. If alive, she was snacking on garden dirt. Near her right hand was a claw-shredded welcome mat.

Victor checked her neck pulse. Then he stood up and said, "Alvin, call 911. Use the car phone, not the phone in the cottage. The police might want to dust for prints."

"She's dead?"

"Very."

I shouldn't touch anything, Victor thought, *but the cops won't mind if I retrieve a certain manila envelope and stick it inside my briefcase.*

He prayed the envelope contained film revisions, not book revisions.

Fuck. Or, as Stevie would say, what a bummer. Now she'd never write her *Forever Asmodeus* sequel.

THIRTY-SEVEN

It was five days after Davy's suicide, and I had never felt less like playing a spider.

Despite three aspirins and a Diet Pepsi, my latest hangover hung around. Thanks to S.B. Eisenberg's broken neck, the press hung around too, optimistically waiting for the next *Forever Asmodeus* disaster, confident the film was cursed.

Furthermore, Madison's attitude toward me had changed.

As the tech crew attached a harness and piano wires to my body, I remembered my tête-à-tête with Andre, following my Spa visit. I had said Peter Pan was a chauvinist who wanted Wendy to mend his shadow and mother the lost boys.

Madison now treated me like Wendy.

Except he called me Circe, and while I'm no mythological expert, I do watch *Jeopardy*. Circe changed men into swine. And some god…Odysseus, I think…make her change them back.

Was Madison playing a boar or some goddamn god?

Every time he touched me, I wanted to scream: "Hands off." But directing is a hands-on transaction. He'd mold me into an Asmodeus pretzel, or tap my shoulder to get my attention, and I'd feel that strange, unauthorized, electrical current surge through my body. It made me yearn to rub against him like a hungry cat, and he could have rooted me stupid (as my Aussie friend Gordon would say) but he didn't even try. When I told him to stop calling me Circe, he called me "Peg"—after the pound bitch in Disney's *Lady and the Tramp;* the mutt with the Veronica Lake bang over her eye.

Evidently, he himself didn't care for Peg, so he switched to "little Frannie." He said my name as if he coated a doughnut with powdered sugar, and I felt like singing: *Little Orphan Frannneee.*

Which probably would have sounded a lot better than: *he's a tramp (woof, woof,* arf*), but I love him—*

"Frannie. Is the harness too tight?"

"Huh?" I stared at Bob, head technician, who bore a striking resemblance to Santa Claus. Bob had once told me that his name spelled backwards was Bob, ho-ho-ho.

"The harness, Frannie. How does it feel?"

"Okay, I guess."

Actually, the harness felt tight. But that was okay; I wanted tight.

Bob had rigged the harness and piano wires so that I could comfortably *(ho-ho-ho)* flip over on my back...like a turtle. Starting at the top of the staircase, another tech would go down the steps with me. As I slid away from him, all I had to do was move my arms and legs. The tech would "marionette" me, Bob would supervise, and the speed of my descent would be directed by Madison.

The crew had christened me "Itsy Bitsy Spider."

I wished I could itsy-bitsy-spider myself up a water spout, rather than down the stairs. I had been told, by Bob, that my rig was "as seaworthy as the Titanic, ho-ho-ho." Which, in tech-speak, meant: "Chill out, don't worry, you'll be fine."

We tried a run-through. Even from an upside-down perspective, Madison looked disgruntled. He lit a cigarette, and if he'd been a dragon, the fire from his silver lighter would have flashed from his nostrils.

The problem was my harness. Through the eye of the camera it looked like the rotten blotch on a pear, and Madison said, "Take a break, little Frannie."

You betcha. I was more than happy to shed the breath-stealing harness and retreat. Slaying dragons didn't coincide with my mood.

The house, our set, was a two-story that reminded me of my own house—except, of course, there was no plastic on the furniture. The upstairs included a master bedroom, Robin's bedroom, and a nursery for Daisy, Robin's sister. Briefly, I thought about catching twenty winks inside the master bedroom, but the smell of coffee beckoned.

Entering the kitchen, I saw Lynn Beth. Since we weren't playing The Demon, she wore a nightie, white with tiny purple flowers, similar to the gown Nana had sported in my spider dream. I wore a duplicate nightie.

Seated at the table, Lynn Beth had propped a paperback against an empty mug. Miniature Buddy Holly glasses adorned the bridge of her nose, and she reminded me of someone. An old classmate? A Bayside High School pyramid cheerleader? My cousin Mark? Lynn Beth looked up, took her glasses off, and the fleeting image faded.

"Hi, Frannie," she said, placing her glasses next to her book.

"What are you reading, kiddo?"

"*Misery's Return* by Paul Sheldon," she said, then blushed. "It's a romance."

"Wow," I said, pouring myself a cup of coffee that looked more like mud. "I devoured all the Misery books, couldn't put them down. Paul Sheldon's responsible for my C in geometry."

"Really, Frannie? Mommy says they're crap."

"Where is your mother, sweetie? I haven't seen her."

Not since the Black Mass.

"She flew to L.A. My brother's in trouble."

"I didn't know you had a brother."

"He's actually my step-brother. When Mommy married my dad, he already had a son. His first wife died. Mommy adored my brother...my step-brother, I mean...but then her marriage started coming apart and I think she got pregnant with me so she could hold on to my dad."

"Oh, I'm sure that's not why—"

"It didn't work. He left, anyway, after a big fight. He said Mommy was fooling around with Mr. Madison. Mommy cried, and I couldn't hear everything they said, but my dad was wrong. Mommy met Mr. Madison at a party, two years before I was born. She told me he liked her, but they never, you know, got together. Mommy wouldn't fool around, even if she wanted to. I mean, she was already married to my dad. He sends me birthday cards..." Lynn Beth shrugged.

"And your step-brother?"

"He and Mommy are still very close. She says he's a 'free spirit.' He's divorced, no kids, and he's always getting into trouble."

"Are you staying alone at the hotel?"

"No. I'm sharing Cat's room. Cat sings me lullabies..." She blushed again. "I know I'm too old for lullabies, Frannie, but Cat has such a beautiful voice. Cat bought me this book and...I think they're calling you." She waggled her fingers like a spider. "Have fun."

Smiling, she put her glasses on, anxious to get back to Misery.

As I headed toward the staircase, I thought about what Lynn Beth had just told me, especially the "already married to my dad."

I didn't believe, for one moment, that a small impediment like matrimony would bother Dawn, and I was equally certain it wouldn't fluster "Mr. Madison."

So what? An *affaire de coeur* between Dawn Sullivan and Victor Madison…assuming one even existed…didn't have anything to do with me. And yet, inside my head, I couldn't help paraphrasing Peggy Lee's Lady-Tramp song.

She's a tramp (woof, woof, arf), but she loves him…

THIRTY-EIGHT

During one of our trivia marathons, Andre had said that Oscar- winning director George Stevens discharged blanks during the filming of *The Diary of Anne Frank*. George wanted to provoke startled reactions from his cast, and it worked. Except, I can't watch the damn movie anymore without trying to guess when and where the gun goes off.

I knew Madison had the same ploy in mind. Cold, I'd searched for a sweater. Inside a bedroom closet, I saw a gun…and a box of blanks.

He hadn't used the gun yet, of course, but it was just a matter of time. And what better time than the spider sequence?

I would do my turtle-on-its-back walk half-way down the stairs. Then Madison would cut to Robin's mom, who was throwing a party. Then he'd cut to Lynn Beth. On all fours, flicking her tongue like a snake, Robin would crawl toward the party guests. *Bang*. Startled reactions.

Madison had promised to shoot my spider sequence in one take. I didn't believe him, but if true, maybe I could leave early. I felt queasy, exhausted, but most of all I wanted to see Andre. This morning I'd left a message on Rick's cell phone. "Andre, we have to talk," it began. I told him I'd be filming all day. I told him I'd wait up for him. Sounding like my mother, I asked if he could "spare a few minutes." Then I left a second message. "Disregard last part of first message," I said, trying to make my voice sound seductive. "Just come home, Andre, please."

My game plan was to clean the house and bake some peanut butter cookies—Andre's favorite. I needed to repair the rift in our relationship. My strange reaction to Madison could be sex deprivation. How many times had *Cosmo* told me that a woman's sex drive was as strong as a man's? I felt I could now give Andre what he wanted— uninhibited sex. And if the demon didn't like it, he could lump it.

While the cookies cooled, I'd take a nap.

Stifling a yawn, I strolled through the living room.

Cat had arrived, looking drop-dead gorgeous in her Ellen party gear. The extras mingled. Bonnie, who'd arrived with Cat, was chatting with ...*ohmigod.*

Bonnie was petrified of guns. Her father had been shot and killed when she was five years old. I needed to tell her about Madison's gun. Now. Plunging through the crowd, I was stopped by a familiar grip on my arm, as Madison said, "We've revamped your harness, little Frannie."

At that very moment, had I looked up "surreal" in the dictionary, it would have stated : having the intense irrational reality of a dream FRANNIE ROSEN FELT ~. I didn't care if the living room had wall-to-wall people. I wanted Madison's hands to paw beneath my nightie. I wanted him to do his sculpt-butt thing. I wanted his index finger to—

"Come on, Frannie, we're running out of time here."

Madison's words brought me back to rational reality, and I thought: *If I had a dollar for every time he's said we're-running-out-of-time-here, I'd never need grocery money again.*

Revamped harness, my ass. Bob had rigged piano wires to a white belt. He must have caught my expression because he didn't say anything about the Titanic. "We've tested this twice," he said, "with a sandbag that weighs 115 pounds."

"Bob," I said, then hesitated. I've never, ever verbalized my true weight; even my drivers license fibs. "I think...shit, I know I weigh more than one-fifteen. Try one-twenty-one."

"Ho, ho, ho," he said. "Dripping wet, you can't weigh more than 105."

"Hurry, we're running out of time here," Madison said.

With a shrug, I let Bob attach the belt.

The strobe lights felt hot.

Madison had cameramen shooting from all angles.

I did my spider walk, halting half-way down the stairs.

Madison didn't yell cut, so I knew Lynn Beth was in position.

A shot rang out.

I had been sort of expecting it, but my tech man hadn't.

He dropped the wires. I tumbled down the stairs. Correction: I fell down the stairs on my back.

It hurt to turn my head, but somehow I managed, and saw Bonnie crying hysterically while Cat tried to comfort her. The party extras looked as if a VCR had stopped on PAUSE.

Except for one obese lady with red, silicone lips. Her lips formed vowels and consonants as she said, "The media's gonna love *this*."

Bob said, "Don't move, Frannie."

Madison didn't say anything. He ran his hands over my body, testing every inch for broken bones, and I almost purred like a cat.

Then pain, rather than desire, throbbed…and I felt as if I'd been thrown to the lions.

THIRTY-NINE

Nothing was broken, thank God, but the on-site doctor said the X-word, as in rays, and Sol Aarons volunteered to drive me to the emergency room. Madison would have taken me, but he had to shoot Lynn Beth's "spider" close-ups. Sheldon Giglia, the ass director, had been fired. I didn't know why, but suspected terminal ineptness.

Once I was comfortably (*ho-ho-ho*) seated inside Sol's car, I begged him to drive me home. Yes, I understood insurance would cover the hospital. Yes, I understood the producers wanted to cover their butts, just in case I was badly hurt. Except I wasn't badly hurt. According to my mother, my head was as hard as a rock, and a slug of vodka with aspirin would take care of my ribs. Please, Sol, please.

He said, "Frannie, you've got to cut down on your drinking."

"Why?" I said, startled. "Is it affecting my work?"

"No, but it's affecting your eyes. Half the time they look dazed, the other half scared."

I tried for humor. "Only a makeup man would notice that."

Silence.

"Hey, Madison hasn't said anything."

"He's been preoccupied. First Davy, then Stevie Eisenberg."

"Was he close to her, Sol? I mean, he didn't seem all that upset."

"He shed a few tears for the TV cameras."

"Yes, I know. But he sounded like the President after a Mideast catastrophe. 'The bombing of 20 Israeli citizens is unconscionable, and tomorrow we'll hold our annual Easter egg hunt in the Rose Garden.' At least Madison didn't compare S.B. Eisenberg to F. Scott Fitzgerald. But then, Fitzgerald isn't as big an icon as James Dean."

"Sometimes Madison hides his true feelings. That's what you're trying to do with your drinking. But it won't play in Peoria, sweetheart. Your eyes are too expressive."

"My eyes are always hidden by makeup, and what's the difference if I drink a little vodka? Christ, it's not as if I'm playing a real part."

"Don't kid yourself, kid. The Demon is real."

"*What?*"

"The Demon's a real part. Lynn Beth couldn't do it, even if Dawn hired the best drama coach in the business. You've got an instinct for acting, Frannie. You're holding our movie together, and don't think, for one moment, that Madison doesn't know it."

I blushed at the compliment, then said, "Is that why he's been so lovey-dovey recently? Toward me, I mean?"

"No, sweetheart, 'lovey-dovey' isn't his style. And as far as I know, he's never messed around with anybody in his cast. Before the shoot, maybe. After, frequently. But never during."

I pictured the high school hallway, Madison's hands molding my tush. If I hadn't stopped him, would we have found a broom closet and messed around? Whoa…Bonnie said she and Madison spent the whole lunch break together, so how could he have fondled me?

Doppelganger, doppelganger, doppelganger reverberated inside my bruised head.

No. Bonnie wasn't infallible. She could have forgotten a brief potty recess.

Then how come, later, Madison stood by the gym door and held you in his arms at the same time, Frannie?

A voice that sounded like my Nana Jen's answered my silent query. *You were bowled over by the sight of Davy hanging from the scoreboard, princess. The sun hitting his silver armadillo belt buckle blinded you, darling. And don't forget, you went into a state of shock.*

I heard my mother: *Stretch your imagination too far, Frannie, and it will snap back at you.*

Then my stupnagel cousin Charlene: *Most accidents happen accidentally.*

My psychic put in her two cents. *You're an ecktriss, Miss Rose. An ecktriss has an overactive imagination. 'The lunatic, the lover, and the poet are of imagination all compact.' Quote, unquote.*

"Who is William Shakespeare?" I murmured.

"Frannie. Are you okay?"

"Yes, Sol." With relief, I saw that we'd passed a hospital. However, Sol looked as if he wanted to hang a U, so I decided to change the subject. "Sol, do you know why Sheldon Giglia was fired?"

"No, not really. I've heard rumors..."

"What rumors?"

"Shelly was...shall we say keeping company?...with Dawn."

I wondered if Shelly, or Madison for that matter, knew about Dawn's other company—Daniel Pearlstein, Tenia, Aretha, and *Cosmo* cover-model, Mary-Magdalene, just to name a few.

Aloud, I said, "Why would Madison care about that?"

"Ordinarily, he wouldn't. But some say Shelly campaigned relentlessly for Dawn to play Ellen. There's even a rumor that Cat's sprained back was due to Shelly's deliberate screw-up."

"Jesus."

"The cruncher came when he showed an interest in you."

"Me? Shelly hates me."

Sol shook his head. "Bob said Shelly told him, in detail, what he'd do to you when he got you alone. Shelly told Bob that he couldn't stop thinking about you, that he'd make you 'love him back.' Bob's no prude, Frannie, but the crew adores you. You're their itsy bitsy spider, and they don't want to see you get stepped on. So Bob went to Madison. Bob says Madison told him to get back to work and mind his own business, but Bob says Madison's eyes glittered like 'two pieces of hot coal.'"

"Did Bob add ho-ho-ho?"

"What?"

This time *I* shook my head, and felt a stabbing pain. "I'd hate to be the reason why someone gets fired, Sol."

"Shelly didn't blame *you,* Frannie. From what I heard, he threatened to kill Madison, then threatened a lawsuit."

I caught a quirky quality in Sol's "threatened-to-kill-Madison." Glancing at his hands, I saw that he clutched the steering wheel the same way he'd clutched the Tsingtao bottle during our first makeup session, inside the CBS studios. It was none of my business, of course, but not asking Sol would be like my mother not asking me if I had remembered to dead-bolt the door. Or not asking me if I'd had my period...god-forbid I should get pregnant before I was legally married. (*As opposed to* illegally *married, Mom?*)

So I asked.

"Sol...what have you got against Madison?"

He stayed silent so long, I was afraid I'd blown our friendship.

Then he said, "Madison's a bastard," and I surmised he didn't mean an illegitimate child. Wisely, I didn't ask him to clarify.

"I wish I had the guts to kill him myself," Sol said, then swung the car toward the curb. If he'd been thinking clearly, he'd have known the sudden motion would cause waves of agony to wash over my body. In fact, I almost passed out. If I had, I would have missed his next remark.

"I'm in love with his sister," Sol said.

My mind (*like a tape recorder, right Samson, right Dream Spider?*) undigested everything I'd ever seen or read about Madison. A&E's *Biography*, *Rolling Stone* magazine, *People* magazine, *E!*, the *Houston Chronicle*.

Stupidly, I said, "Madison doesn't have a sister."

"That's what he wants everyone to believe," Sol said.

"Why?"

"She's...different."

I waited.

"Sometimes she has memory glitches," Sol said.

I waited some more.

"Madison was responsible for her...condition," Sol said, leaving the curb, inching his car in between a pickup truck and a pickup truck.

"What did he do?" I breathed.

"He didn't *do* anything. What happened was pure Frank Capra, only in reverse. There's this scene in *It's a Wonderful Life*...at a cemetery...where the ghost...the Angel..."

"Clarence," I clarified.

"Right. Where Clarence tells Jimmy Stewart that his brother died because...um...Harry?"

"George. Harry's the brother."

"Because George wasn't there to save Harry. That was George's wake-up call. It made him realize life was wonderful, after all."

"I love that movie, Sol. We didn't celebrate Christmas, but every year we'd watch *Wonderful Life* on TV. Then my mom would run up and down the street, yelling 'Merry Christmas, Mrs. Merewether, Merry Christmas, Mrs. Wagner, Merry Christmas, Vera, Merry Christmas, Betty.' And everyone yelled back, 'Merry Christmas, Mrs. Rosen,' or 'Merry Christmas, Miriam.' Mom looked so cute in her fuzzy blue bathrobe and black galoshes...uh, sorry, please go on."

"First, allow me to savor the image of your mother's fuzzy blue bathrobe and black galoshes."

Maybe that's where Fuzzy-Wuzzy's hair went, I thought. *Maybe Fuzzy-*

Wuzzy's not a bear at all. Maybe he's a childhood memory that makes you smile.

"If Victor Madison had never been born," Sol said, his voice bitter, "his sister wouldn't have tried to kill herself."

"Oh my God. How—"

"She slit her wrist. Thank God it wasn't fatal. But she lost her unborn baby and suffered a small stroke. The stroke left her with a memory impediment. When I first met her, I thought she was naïve, impressionable, like a foreign visitor, or the Mermaid in Disney's *Splash*. Which is kind of ironic when you think about it..." He paused.

"Because Madison has a thing for Disney?"

"No. Because the Mermaid's name is Madison."

"How did you meet her?"

"Despite his recent press conferences, Victor Madison has always tried to keep a low profile. People don't recognize him on the street, like...oh, say Spielberg."

"True. When I first saw him, I felt let down. He looked so normal, so Clark Kent-ish."

"For the last twenty or so years, Madison has kept his sister in a home. Not a hospital, a nice house, owned by a middle-aged, childless couple. He doesn't want her to be a part of his life, but he's not a monster. So he'll take her out to dinner, a movie..."

Sol cleared his throat. "One night, three years ago, they were at a restaurant. I happened to be there, too, sitting in the corner, listening to Maxine Nightingale's *Lead Me On*...the restaurant had wall jukeboxes at every table. I had worked with Madison, but he didn't acknowledge me, so I kept drinking my coffee and pigging out on blueberry cheesecake." Sol smiled. "Peggy...that's her name...loves cheesecake. She stood up and drifted over to my table, so Madison had no choice. He invited me to join him, introduced me to his sister, and—"

"It was love at first sight."

"Not quite. But I did want to see Peggy again. Only Madison made it very clear that she was off limits. Truthfully, Frannie, Peggy didn't seem all that...outlandish...to me. She has trouble remembering things, but she's warm and sweet and...I guess what I'm trying to say is that my feelings for Peggy, right from the start, were stronger than mere chemistry.

"When Madison went to the mens' room," Sol continued, "I asked Peggy where she lived and...isn't this your duplex?"

"Yes."

"Do you want me to carry you inside?"

No, tell me more, I thought. But I had a feeling Sol was finished. All I knew for sure was that Madison had meddled, maybe even done something horrific, and Sol despised him.

In any case, I wanted to call my mother, tell her I loved her, thank her for the hours she'd spent driving back and forth to the city, taking Girl Scout leader courses so my friends and I could have a troop. I also wanted to thank her for the fuzzy-wuzzy bathrobe smile.

"I'm okay, Sol," I said. "Honest."

Which was true. A heating pad would take care of my bruised ribs, and my headache had become a dull throb.

Sol insisted on walking me to the door. His eyes looked sad.

As he drove away, I heard Ginger bark.

Entering the duplex, painfully navigating the carpeted staircase, I thought: *Cleaning's out, but I can still bake peanut butter cookies. First, a long hot bath. Then I'll call Mom. Why is the bedroom door closed?*

Maybe a capricious breeze had slammed it shut.

Drawing closer, I heard voices, and my next (dumb) thought was: *Andre bought a TV and he's watching his old soap.*

Then I had an out-of-body experience. I heard a squeal, followed by: "Ann-dray, you're baaaad." I watched my hand grasp the knob, turn it to the right, and open the door. My feet dug into the hallway's shag, but Frannie entered the bedroom.

Three faces swiveled toward her/me. All three faces were topped by tousled "Scandihoovian-blonde" hair.

Correction: one face possessed tousled German-blonde hair.

"Oops," said Fawn. Or Bambi.

FORTY

In a movie, the tongue-tied heroine would clutch at her bosom. Demi-Moore-tears would spring to her eyes and stream down her pale cheekbones. Then she'd turn and run away.

I didn't do any of those things.

First, my tongue wasn't tied. "'Oops' is a malapropism," I said. "I believe you mean 'Fuck.'"

Second, I couldn't run, not with my bruised body.

Third, I had nowhere to run *to*.

Exiting the bedroom, I shut the door and made my way back down the stairs. At least I could wrap up part of my game plan.

To my surprise, Mom had installed an answering machine.

"Hello whoever's calling," the machine said. "This is Miriam Rosen, Frannie Rosen's mother. Frannie's starring in a Victor Madison movie. I'm probably out shopping, spending Frannie's money, so leave a message at the sound of the beep."

Why did I always forget that my mother has a sense of humor?

"Mom," I said, after the beep. "Buy yourself a fake fur, something that looks like mink, and I'll pay you back. I owe you so much..." I paused, swallowing a sob. "I'll call again, I promise, but don't call me here. I'm moving to the hotel..." I tried to remember the name of the hotel but couldn't. "I just wanted to thank you for...well, lots of things. I know you'll say I'm *meshuga,* but...Merry Christmas, Mom."

As I hung up, I sensed a presence. The ghost of Christmas past?

Close. Andre stood behind me, his body wrapped in a towel.

"Is it deer hunting season?" I said.

"I'm sorry, Frannie."

"Oh, good. That makes everything peachy keen, Andre. Apology accepted. Now get the fuck out of this room." He didn't move. "I'm not kidding. Can you say k-i-l-l? Can Bambi or Fawn say malapropism?"

"Your message, Frannie, the one you left on Rick's cell phone…you said you'd be filming all day."

"Oh, I get it. What happened upstairs is my fault."

"In a way."

"What? In case you haven't noticed, Andre, I'm a tad angry."

"In case you haven't noticed, Frannie, my play opened."

"When?"

"Five nights ago."

Five nights ago? Where was I?

Playing Marianne, drowning myself in vodka, mourning Davy's suicide, vomiting kisses.

"And in case you care," Andre continued, "the reviews were fantastic. I'm up for the TV remake of *Bus Stop*. And, another soap."

I took a deep breath. "Why didn't you tell me?"

"Why didn't you ask? For starters, I left a note on the fridge."

"I didn't see a note."

"Maybe your ghost destroyed it."

"Not ghost, Andre, demon. And for the record, I bet that's exactly what happened."

"Oh, give me a fucking break."

"There *is* a demon, Andre, and he's jealous. Why do you think I threw up the night we almost made love?"

Looking like Scrooge's Ghost of Things To Come, Andre pointed.

My eyes followed his finger, and I saw an empty vodka bottle next to a half-empty bottle. Christ, Sol was right. No wonder my eyes were always dazed and/or scared.

"Frankly," Andre said, "I would have invited you to several parties, but I didn't want a repeat of Rick's party."

"What did I do at Rick's?"

"What didn't you do?"

"I'm serious, Andre. All I remember is you telling me you were too drunk to get it up."

I took a few steps forward and almost pitched to the floor. Andre caught me before I fell, then dropped his hands as if he'd touched a hot potato, and I caught his look of disgust.

"I'm not drunk," I cried. "I fell down the stairs, at work. They wanted to take me to the hospital…what did I do at Rick's?"

"You were fine, Frannie, until you went to the bathroom. When you came out, you said it was too cold in there and that Rick should turn the air-conditioning off."

"I don't see what's so wrong about—"

"You weren't wearing anything except panties, and you were all goose-bumps. I tried to cover you with my shirt, but you growled at me."

"Growled like a dog?"

"No. More like that girl in *The Exorcist*. You…"

"What? I what?"

"You said you were Robin and you wanted to make baby demons."

"Christ, Andre, I don't remember any of that."

"Then you lay on the floor, out of it."

"Passed out?"

"No. You played with your breasts and spread your legs. The guests were embarrassed, but they figured you were drunk. Rick laughed. After a while, he told me to carry you outside and sober you up, the guests were complaining. You fought me tooth and nail, until we got home. Then you asked if we could make love, sweet as sugar, but all I wanted to do was put you to bed."

"And go back to the party."

"Yes."

"To sleep with Bambi and Fawn."

"No…not that night."

"None of those things happened," I screamed. "I'd remember if they did. I drank one beer, one crummy beer. No way did I take my clothes off. No way did I play with myself. *No way.* What I can't understand is why you're making it all up. Why, Andre? Why?"

"He's not makin' it up."

Whirling around, I hugged my ribs so they wouldn't fall out. The twins stood on the stairs, looking down into the living room.

"He's not makin' it up," Bambi or Fawn repeated. "We were there. I hate to say this, Fran, but you were actin' real slutty."

"Please don't call me Fran, and at least I don't sleep with someone else's boyfriend. That's my definition of a slut."

"Bitch," said Fawn or Bambi. "*You* brought a guy home. We were at Rick's, with Ann-dray, after the show, waitin' for the papers, and we saw you, drunk as a skunk. This guy helped you walk, coppin' a feel every now and then—"

"You were wearin' a cheerleader's uniform," Bambi or Fawn interjected.

"I bet you hardly got the door shut," Fawn or Bambi continued, "before he was eatin' pussy."

"Shut up," Andre said. "Go over to Rick's and wait for me...please."

As the twins swiveled their butts down the stairs, I recalled my conversation with Jem. I had finally summoned the courage to ask him about the night of Davy's wake. Jem said I got out at the curb. He swore up and down he hadn't walked me inside, hadn't stuck around, hadn't said thank you, Frannie, thank you, Marianne. Yes, we kissed in the limousine. No, we didn't have intercourse. I didn't want to, not "in front of the driver." That sounded like me, and I believed Jem.

"Bambi," I said, "the man you saw...what did he look like?"

"Didn't see his face," one of the twins replied, her voice churlish.

"What kind of car did he drive?"

"Don't know."

"What was he wearing?" *Dumb question, Frannie. Can you remember what Jem wore?*

"Black," Bambi said, then followed her sister outside.

"Andre..."

"Enough, Frannie. I don't want to talk about this anymore."

"Would you make me a sandwich?"

"A sandwich?"

"I'm hungry. There's a fresh loaf of bread and a can of tuna. Please?"

"Hey, I'm not Wendy," he said softly, his voice an echo from the recent past. Still wearing his stupid towel, he headed for the kitchen.

I made my way over to the phone again, remembered the name of the hotel, and called Bonnie...who wasn't there, damn it. My life had just changed radically, but everything (and everyone) else was so goddamn normal.

Ho-ho-ho. Define normal, Frannie. What's normal about a director firing a gun filled with blanks while a five-foot-two-and-a-half-inch itsy bitsy spider climbs down the staircase spout?

Shit. Cat would be at the set, too. How about Jem?

The hotel operator had been told not to put any calls through to Jeremy Glenn, sorry. Unless, she said, I knew the special password.

Jem had given it to me. Password...password...

"Moosehead," I said.

Using one of my emergency God prayers, I heaved a sigh of relief when Jem picked up the phone. He said he'd collect me ASAP.

One detail down, I thought. If the hotel didn't have a vacant room, I'd bunk with Bonnie. Or Cat, assuming Dawn had returned to Houston and "collected" her daughter.

As I tried to swallow my dry, no mayo, no celery sandwich, Andre said, "You're looking good, Frannie. You've lost more weight, but in all the right places. And your breasts—"

"Are bigger. Yes, I know. I think I'm pregnant, Andre."

I didn't mean to blurt that out. But it's hard to unshackle oneself from one's best friend, even if one's best friend has used one's bed to make love to a couple of slutty stagehands.

Andre's sandwich had been halfway to his mouth. Putting it down with a shaky hand, he said, "Is it mine?"

"No, it's not yours."

"Is *he* the father?" Andre nodded toward the phone.

"Jeremy Glenn? No."

"Then who?"

"I don't have a clue."

"Jesus, Frannie."

"It's not what you think, Andre. I haven't slept around. Despite what Bambi and Fawn said, there's been no one but you."

"So that means *I'm* the father."

"Hey, I'm not even sure I'm pregnant. I've skipped a couple of periods, that's all."

Relief washed over his classic features; not as classic as Jem's, but close. "That sometimes happens when you lose weight," he said. "I once dated a gymnast. She was twenty-three, over the hill, and had to watch her weight. She never got her period, which made me very nervous. So I…we…finally split. Up."

"I'll bet she was low maintenance?"

"What?"

"Your gymnast. She probably didn't eat very much." I'd finished my boring sandwich, even the crusts, and still felt ravenous.

Andre said, "Do you need help packing, Frannie?"

I wasn't sure I could make it up the stairs again, but didn't want to appear needy. So I said, "I'd rather avoid our…your bedroom, Andre. Throw a few things into a suitcase, undies, toothbrush, stuff like that, and I'll get the rest another time….after you've changed the sheets."

Waiting outside for Jem, my mind focused on what the X-rated Bobbsy Twins had said.

Bambi (or was it Fawn?) had said a guy helped me inside the duplex, but she hadn't noticed his car.

Wouldn't she have noticed a *limousine?*

I remembered my mother's Nyquil remark. Maybe, instead of a rabbi, I'd call 1-800-EXORC'ST.

FORTY-ONE

As Jem's limousine approached, I saw that Bambi and Fawn were scrunched together, peering out of Rick's window.

Jem wore khaki pants and a white shirt, open to the waist. He hugged me gently, and I made certain my back faced the window so the twins could see *Jeremy Glenn*. I pictured their trashy mouths open, drool accumulating at the corners of their trashy lips.

On our way to the city, I asked Jem to stop at a drugstore. Telling him I needed shampoo and a mild pain killer, I purchased a home pregnancy kit. Then I dozed against his heroic chest until we pulled up to the hotel entrance.

Jem said he was running late for a *Houston Chronical* interview.

A doorman took my suitcase while I thanked my knight in shining khaki. This time I gave him a hug, careful not to kiss him, knowing my ribs would never tolerate another vomit-his-kiss session.

The woman at the registration counter could have doubled for one of The Spa nymphets. Perky as all get out, she told me I couldn't get in. I tried to explain that I didn't own a credit card because my father was my VISA, but could barely make out her reply. She spoke Texan rather than high school Southern. However, the bottom line was: "Get lost."

A familiar voice said, "Find her a room, a nice room, and put it under *my* name, on *my* credit card."

"Yessir, Mistah Aarons," the nymphet replied.

"Thanks, Sol," I said, "but that's not necessary. I have some cash and my checkbook, and I'm sure my dad'll wire me—"

"We'll settle up later, sweetheart. Okay?"

"Okay," I said, and burst into tears.

Sol led me into the hotel's art deco lounge. After three Cokes and one Andre-vent, I felt much better. Better enough to invite Sol to my room—for purposes he couldn't fail to understand.

"I'm honored," he said, swiveling on his bar stool to caress my cheek and wipe away my last tear with his thumb. "But..." He smiled. "Color me old-fashioned, Frannie, but I believe love comes before sex."

Rejected again, I said, "Don't tell me you haven't messed around since Madison's sister."

He nodded. "However, if I should decide to mess around, you'll be my first choice."

"Sol, I'm sorry. No, I'm not. I love you Sol, the same way I love Frank Capra, and love means never having to say you're sorry."

A familiar voice (from my recent past) said, "Who is Erich Segal? Or, if you prefer, what is Ryan O'Neal?"

I swiveled my bar stool, endangering my ribs, then grinned and said, "Sol Aarons, Mickey Roebuck. Samson, this is the greatest makeup artist in the history of the world."

"She exaggerates," Sol said.

"I do not."

"It's a pleasure," Samson said. "I've seen your work."

"Haven't you experienced my work? Weren't you in Madison's debut film?"

"Lord, you've got a good memory."

"It's hard to forget a six-foot-four Texan with hair down to his butt."

"It wasn't quite that long," Samson said. "If I had cut it, Victor would have given me a speaking part. *C'est la guerre.*"

"Samson speaks four languages," I bragged.

"Five, if Latin counts. What are you drinking, Frannie?" He summoned the bartender. "How about you, Aarons?"

"Coke," I said. "I'm off the sauce, on the proverbial wagon."

"And I'm off to talk to Madison, assuming he's back from the shoot." Sol abandoned his stool. "Nice seeing you again, Roebuck. Frannie, don't forget room service. You really should rest those ribs."

"Barbecue, dry, or spare?" Samson said, adopting Sol's stool.

"I fell down some stairs and bruised my ribs. No big deal. Bonnie said she saw you sleuthing. How's the bio?"

"Just about finished. I should be leaving soon, flying back to L.A."

"L.A.? What happened to New York?"

"Godzilla ate it."

"Matthew Broderick. Be still my heart. Seriously."

"L.A. is where my publisher staffs his office. He, himself, doesn't seem to do anything except sleep till noon, attend previews, smoke cigars, and mutter 'Long live Charlton Heston' while he cleans his guns."

"Cute. Would you like to interview Madison, Samson? I think I can arrange—"

"No, thanks. The bio's done, Frannie. It's been fun playing sleuth, but I have to leave."

"To find a new project?"

"Yup. I like your hair. Can I call you Mia?"

"Only if I can call you Willie Nelson. Who's taking care of your cats?"

"I gave them away."

"All of them?"

"Yup. *Cave canem.*"

"What does that mean?"

"Beware the cat."

"*Canum* means cat?"

"Actually, it means dog."

"You're such a nut. Speaking of sleuths, I saw you at the high school."

"What high school?"

"Neil Armstrong, not too far from Clear Lake City."

"You didn't see *moi.*"

"Yes, I did. You were with the caterers."

"Frannie, I've never catered anything in my life." He waggled his eyebrows a la Groucho. "People cater to *me.*"

"Okay, but the man I saw could have been your twin. Speaking of twins..." I told him about Andre.

"Sorry," he said, not sounding sorry at all.

"I guess I'd better lie down now, Samson. I've got a headache the size of Godzilla and...why are you looking at me like that?"

"What's wrong, Frannie?"

"I just told you. Andre Vaughn is history." I made a slice across my throat with my index finger.

"Bullshit. That's not all of it."

Tempted to tell him about the demon, I clamped my mouth shut, unwilling to risk another *give-me-a-fucking-break.*

Samson's eyes were more green than blue as he said, "Why are you clutchin' your handbag as if you're afraid something will fall out?"

My pregnancy kit. "Samson, I always clutch—"

"What do you have in there?"

"Samson, a woman's purse is as intimate as a woman's boudoir. That's from *Cosmo* so it must be true."

"Is it Madison's room key?"

"What? Are you crazy? Why would I have Madison's room key? Here…" I thrust the handbag at him. "Look for yourself."

"Okay, forget it, sorry. I was worried about you, that's all." He tousled my shorn hair. "You wouldn't believe what my research has turned up. Trust me, Frannie, you would not, repeat *not* want to get involved with your director."

"I do trust you, and there's no way I'll get involved. What has your research turned up?"

"My workin' title is 'Love Them and Leave Them and Let Them be Lonely.' Is that clear enough?"

"Great song," I said. "Great movie. Doris Day and James Cagney." I gave him a rueful grin. "All a director has to do to get a woman is say he's a director. It's an aphrodisiac. Quote, unquote."

"Saul Bellows. And it's *writer,* not director."

"Very good. But you forgot to put Bellows in the form of a question."

Gingerly climbing down from my stool, I hugged Samson's rugged body. Then, exiting the lounge, I rode the elevator to my floor and checked the room number on my plastic "key."

There were at least five uniformed maids with rolling carts. They swarmed up and down the hallway, and my first thought was: *bumper cars at an amusement park.* That image was reinforced when I bumped into one cheerful maid and said hi.

"*Saludo,*" she said. "Is chew the movie star in…in…" Perusing her mental dictionary, she gave me a rueful shrug. "In *la cinta del diablo*?"

I didn't need Samson to translate.

I remembered what Sol had said in the car, his comment about me holding the movie together.

"*Si,*" I said, trying to sustain a demure demeanor. "I'm one of the stars in the devil movie."

Despite my bruised ribs, despite my throbbing headache, despite my split with Andre, the maid had made me feel good. No. Better than good. Like a movie star who commands ten million dollars per film, then modestly says: "Golly-gee, Diane-Barbara-Leeza-Katie-Oprah, I'm not in it for the *money.*"

FORTY-TWO

I pedaled my stationary bike, going nowhere. I'd already done 45 minutes on the hotel's treadmill, my sneakers going nowhere.

Strange as it sounds, I've never stayed at a hotel before. Not even an old, opulent hotel, built when dinosaurs roamed the earth, renovated in 1998. Stick a flag-pin into a map at random, any state except Alaska, and the pin'll land on the house of a relative. Or the relative of a relative. Or the house of a "she's always been like a sister to me." I'd almost made it to the overcrowded Spring-Break Florida motel, but opted (*ho-ho-ho*) to stay with my Aunt Estelle and soak up some rain. And when the Rosen family hit the road during summer vacations, we stored a carton of hostess gifts—wrapped with generic paper and leftover Chanukah ribbon—inside the trunk of our car.

Thus, I truly appreciated nifty things like a balcony-with-a-view. Room service. Maid service. Swimming pool. A vast, glass-enclosed area with more exercise equipment than The Spa. And, especially, the lounge. I discovered that booze is a depressant, but Cokes have enough sugar to out-hyper Mick Jagger. I discovered that cast and crew members didn't exclude me, once I un-stressed.

Best of all, I discovered I wasn't pregnant.

The home pregnancy test came up negative, but just to be 100% certain, I bought a second kit. Positively negative.

I still had "morning sickness" and my breasts were sore, but Andre was probably right; my weight loss had played havoc with my menstrual cycle. There was no disputing I'd lost weight. None of my clothes fit, except denim coveralls that had once been snug.

Did I mention that my nifty hotel sported a clothing emporium?

Not that I needed new clothes. Even when I wore my old coveralls, I got hit on. A Sean-Connery-clone from Tulsa, a scriptwriter from San Francisco, a couple of Continental Airline pilots, a guy named Rex (his muscled arms and chest enhanced by a teeshirt lettered: *Murder by the Book*), one of the lounge bartenders, you name it. I didn't get propositioned by women; my "sexual aura" was definitely male-oriented. However, I was off men. Not for the duration of my life—God forbid!—but for the duration of the *Forever Asmodeus* shoot.

Madison wasn't shooting demon possession scenes, so I had a few days to enjoy the sheer luxury of a first-class hotel. Which was fine by me, since my body needed to mend, to get over its weird flu or virus or whatever the heck it was. I hated wolfing down a room service breakfast of eggs, biscuits and gravy, grits, coffee and orange juice, just to flush every delicious, expensive, regurgitated bite down the toilet.

Bonnie thought I'd turned bulimic. She hovered, especially during and after meals. Or maybe she hovered because Madison's interest in me hadn't waned. If anything, he'd become more intense, more "lovey-dovey." Bonnie said, somewhat bitterly, that the tech crew had established a Frannie jackpot, a human football pool. Only instead of guessing the score, they guessed when Madison would score. Hell, I wished I could wager. I'd guess "never" and win. Samson's warning resonated inside my head. Even more significant, Bonnie was jealous, and her friendship meant more to me than another love-me-leave-me relationship.

With that last thought, I climbed down from my bike, said goodbye to my fellow biker (who was avidly reading *Bait* by C.J. Songer), and rode the elevator to my floor. I'd take a quick shower, change into a pair of jeans Cat had loaned me, then join the lounge lizards. It was almost five...happy hour. John, my favorite bartender, would be there, and he never charged me for Cokes or appetizers. Maybe this evening I'd have raw oysters, topped with margarita salt and olives. And a bagel. A bagel sounded good, topped with both cream cheese and peanut butt—

Why is my room door open?

Deja vu all over again. Except last time, at the duplex, the door had been closed.

Three maids were staging their bumper-car act. Maybe one had garnished my room with fresh towels and forgotten to shut the door.

I always left a light on in the bathroom so I'd never be greeted by darkness. Not that the sun had gone down, but...*oh, dear, oh, shit.*

The drapes were drawn. Had I drawn them? I never drew them, even though I constantly heard Mom's voice in my head. An intruder, she'd say, would scale the hotel and rape me in my sleep. But Mom, my head would reply, I like the view, and the open drapes make my room look bigger.

Now, my room looked small.

And dark.

Should I ask a maid to escort me inside? No. Because a maid had probably drawn the drapes, and later the merry maids would laugh. At me. In Spanish.

Don't be such a scaredy-cat, I told myself. *What's the bottom line? If it's a rapist, you'll scream. Or exit stage left. Or hit him over the head with Jack and Jill's pail...which, in this case, is an ice bucket.*

Taking a deep breath, I walked inside. All my senses were as fine-tuned as a Gibson guitar. The bathroom smelled like the soap I'd left in the shower. I tasted my fear. I heard shallow breathing. The wall near the light switch felt bumpy...

As light flooded one half of the room, my half, I saw a shadowy shape in the corner, huddled against the wall.

FORTY-THREE

"Is someone in here?" I said, the third dumbest remark I've made in the last few weeks, surpassed only by *what-are-you-doing-Davy?* and *you're-not-my-Nana-Jen.*

Because there was definitely someone in my room.

I flicked another light switch, and as my eyes adjusted to the glare I saw a woman. With her dark curly hair and pink-patched cheeks, she looked like Disney's Snow White, only older. Actually, it was difficult to determine her age. Somewhere between 35 and 50.

Could you be a tad more specific, Frannie?

Why? I asked myself. What difference did it make? The poor girl looked more frightened of me than I of her, and that's what counted.

She wore glasses with tortoise-shell frames, a loose, white, ankle-length dress, no accessories, and suddenly I knew exactly who she was. Or thought I did.

"You're Peggy," I said. "Sol's Peggy."

The girl bobbed her head up and down. I kept thinking of her as a girl, not a woman. She was ethereal, ageless, and very pretty. The kind of pretty that transcends age, like a Meryl Streep or a Barbra Steisand.

I said, "Would you like to sit on the bed, Peggy? I won't hurt you."

"Okey dokey, smokey," she said. "But where's Sol?"

"I don't know. Oh my God. You thought this was his room because it's under his name. One of those idiots at the desk gave you this room number. They're not supposed to give out...Peggy, I can find Sol for you. Sol Aarons. He's my friend."

"*My* friend."

"Yes, I know. He told me all about you. You're Victor Madison's sister."

"Chaim."

"Excuse me?"

"Chaim Mostel's sister."

Her expression changed. Fear? Anger? It made her look older.

"Piglet," she said.

"What?"

"He calls me Piglet. Chaim does. I like Tigger and Eeyore and Pooh, but *not* Piglet."

"Okay, I'll call you Eeyore. You look blue, sad, just like Eeyore. If you smile, I'll call you Tigger. And if you get off the floor and sit on the bed, I'll give you a candy bar, a Baby Ruth."

That got a smile.

"Not babyruth...Caruth," she said. "Dr. Caruth. No, he was the old doctor...the new one is...A, B, C, D, E, F...Feldman. Dammit, dammit, dammit...I hate these memory glitches."

She started to get to her feet, but almost immediately her legs gave way and she grabbed at the drapes for support.

"Pins and needles, Peggy?

She looked confused. Then she said, "Nurse gives me needles."

"Shots?" I mimed a huge hypodermic needle plunging into my arm. Eventually, my thumb pressed against a vein.

"Yes. Little needles too, with colored wool and a sampler. Oh, I *really* hate that. I'd rather do...dammit...wait, I remember...needlepoint. Sol bought me a kit. The picture on the...canvas...was mostly words. There were lots of red hearts and the words were written by...by...A, B, C ...Cow...Cowper. 'With all thy faults, I love thee still.' Isn't that pretty?"

"Very pretty. And true." I thought of my mother.

"After I embroidered the needlepoint, the words *and* the hearts, Nurse said *good girl.* But then she gave me a *baby* sampler and said it was from my brother...a pink Piglet." Once again, her face scrunched.

As she sat on the bed, I handed her the Baby Ruth and a can of Coke, for good measure. Then I said, "How'd you get here, Peggy?"

She cocked her head like an inquisitive bird.

"Here...Texas...Houston," she said. "Oh...by airplane, of course. Who *are* you?"

"I'm Frannie. Sol's friend. You came by yourself?"

"Sure. I picked up a bundle of money at Chaim's house, and it was easy after that. The lady...oh, her name's gone now...wasn't happy about me taking the money, but it was just lying there on the table, and if he'd really needed it, it would have been in his pocket, right?"

I nodded, thinking I'd opened a whole new can; not Coke, worms. Had Peggy visited her brother's house *before* or *after* Stevie Eisenberg's murder? There'd be cops *after*, right?

"Peggy," I said, "did you see the police at your brother's house?"

She shook her head. "No...just the lady. Q, R, S...Stevie. She had a cat. Did I remember to tell you that?"

"Peggy, this is important. Was there anybody else there? Besides Stevie, I mean."

"The cat...does it count?" She sighed and slumped back onto the pillows. "Gee, but I'm tired. What's it called? Jet lag? I didn't think you could get jet lag going north and south, but—"

"Just a few more questions, sweetie."

"Peggy. And they can wait." She took off her glasses, carefully placed them on the bedside table, then rubbed her eyes. "Is that okey dokey, smokey...uh, Frannie? You see, even without the meds, I can't always think straight. Not when I'm..." she yawned "...exhausted."

Then she was gone. Out like a light and just as quick. I had never, ever, seen anyone do that before, at least not that quickly.

Walking around the bed to the phone, I dialed Sol's room number. He answered on the first ring, and I told him to get his butt to my room ASAP. He didn't say anything, not one word, just hung up.

I waited by the door, saw him round the corner, and said, "How did you know?"

"Her nurse called me. I always leave an address and phone number, for emergencies. That's how Peggy found out where I was staying, the name of the hotel. She can be very devious. Is she okay?"

"She's fine. Hungry, sleepy, a little scared at first...but fine."

Sol sagged against the wall. "I gave her description to every hotel employee, including the doormen, thinking they'd hold on to her. It never occurred to me they'd give her your room number."

"She walked right in. My guess is that the maids were adding towels...I like lots of towels. Does Madison know?"

"Yes. But this time I won't let him talk me into sending her back."

"This time? She's done it before?"

"Once, in the beginning of our...relationship. But Madison said she had to go back, that she needed full-time care. Doctor, nurse...the whole enchilada. He said she could get violent and..."

"And?"

"He said she tried to kill him."

"Oh, I can't believe that."

"Neither can I. But I had no reason to believe he'd lie, and her doctor—"

"Caruth."

"Right. Dr. Caruth said it would be disastrous for me to take her away, that she *was* violent. But I think Madison paid him to say that because her new doctor—"

"Feldman."

"Right." Sol gave me a lopsided grin. "Dr. Feldman said it would be good for her to visit…maybe even stay with me." Sol's eyes were very blue, and starry, like the bunting on an American flag. "I'm talking permanently, Frannie."

"Cool." I wondered if he knew about the needles, which had in all likelihood kept Peggy doped up for years. "Don't you want to see your wayward child, Sol?"

"She's no child, she's a woman, my woman, and yes I want to see her."

I meant to tell him his woman was asleep, but he'd barely stepped through the door when I heard Peggy's voice.

"Sol, Sol, I rode an airplane. All by myself. I gave Nurse the slip again, even though, boy oh boy, was she mad the first time I gave her the slip. I took a taxi to the airport…L, A, X. I know the letters stand for something, but I told the driver L, A, X, and he drove me right to the door. After that, it was easy. People are always taking airplanes on TV, so I knew what to do. I showed the…dammit, what's she called? The reservations lady, yes. I showed her a picture of me and gave her money and said Houston. She told me the number of a gate and said hurry, and there were signs to the gate, and they let me on the airplane as soon as I showed them my ticket. When the airplane came down, I wasn't sure what to do next. I guess I looked scared because a nice colored man who works for the airport asked me if I had bags and when I said no he asked me if I wanted a bus or a taxi or a…shuttle. I said taxi, and he showed me where they were. I wanted to give him money for being so nice, but he wouldn't take any, so I got in the cab and told the driver the name of your hotel and…well…here I am. Sol, I love you, and I rode the airplane all by myself."

"What a clever girl," he said, his voice a caress. "But I swear, my love, you'll never have to ride by yourself again."

At which point, I decided I would visit the lounge in my workout clothes.

Victor Madison's Hotel Suite

Houston

Victor Madison stared at the TV screen, where a Disney bitch was royally pissed at the King and Queen. The next frame depicted the baby who'd grow up to be one hell of a drowsy princess, you might even say the quintessential sleeping beauty, and the baby looked so fuckin' Disney, as if she didn't dare shit her diaper. Or spit up. Or cry.

Peggy Mostel had done all those things; shit, spit, cry. Father, may he rest in Hell, had escaped to the nearest saloon, and Ma couldn't cope. Chaim had been such a good baby, she kept saying; Chaim never cried.

So *Chaim* (who never cried) had changed Peggy's muddy diapers and scrubbed infant-puke from his clothes. Every night he paced back and forth, Baby Piglet squealing against his eight-year-old shoulder. He tried to soothe her by singing songs from *Snow White.* Someday your prince will come and whistle while you work...

Nothing worked.

She cried and spit and cried and shit and cried, while Papa got drunk and Ma slept through it and Chaim thought he'd lose his mind.

So why did he want to make a baby with Frannie?

Because *Victor* would have a nurse-in-residence. Because *Victor* would buy a house large enough to muffle the baby's cries. Because *Victor* wanted to watch his son nuzzle Frannie's beautiful breasts.

He'd never filmed a *normal* family scene, and planned to record every stage of Orson Welles Madison's growth, from babyhood to...

Holy Christ. Maybe he'd find a nurse who looked like Crawford. Or even better, Bette Davis. And weren't Joan and Bette a couple of savvy actresses? Past their prime, they'd segued into horror films.

He'd dress Orson's nurse in an old-fashioned uniform, hemline below the knees. Her face would be hidden by shadows. That way, the audience would see a healthy baby boy but feel an evil presence.

Black and white. He'd shoot the opening scenes in black and white, the only color a red splotch of blood on Nursie's white uniform.

Why would parents hire a nurse with blood on her uniform? Hell, he'd figure something out. Maybe, when the parents weren't looking, the wind would blow open Nursie's old-fashioned cape and...

Speaking of nurses, he should have fired Peggy's years ago.

Shifting in his chair, his elbow nudged the notebook that lay on the table. He'd been scribbling *Forever Asmodeus* observations. Transcribed, the hen scratches would become a legible cast/crew critique. So why had he scribbled the word "Piglet" across an entire page?

Because he couldn't get her off his mind.

How had she managed to fly to Houston? Where the fuck had she gotten the money for the ticket? From her new doctor? Christ almighty, Victor had known from the get-go that Feldman couldn't be trusted. Caruth was easy to control; a physician who favored the same shots he gave his patients was infinitely persuadable. Had Piglet killed Caruth? The last time Victor had seen her, at the cottage, she'd insisted over and over that Caruth didn't die of a heart attack. Stevie had asked how he died, and Piglet had clammed up. When Victor repeated the question, she'd said, "Don't call me Piglet." End of issue. End of focus.

What the hell. She was Sol's problem now.

Ripping the "Piglet page" from his notebook, he stuck it inside a bed-side copy of *Forever Asmodeus.* Then he propped himself against the bed's headboard and focused his thoughts on Frannie. The chemistry was there; every time he touched her, she practically melted at his feet. However, he felt as if he were Chaim Mostel again, spending hours creating a Valentine's Day card for the pretty girl who sat in front of him at school. She'd given him a card in return, one of those cheap cards you bought at the drugstore, 200 cards for a buck, and his heart had soared. Until he found, on the floor, in the corner of the classroom, a crumpled note she'd written to one of her girlfriends.

OMAR CHAIM IS UGLY, she'd written, then drawn a crude picture of a frog. With an erect penis. Even in Brooklyn, especially in Brooklyn, fifth-graders knew what an erection looked like. Today he would have been flattered by the length of her representation.

Last year he'd hired a P.I. to check her out. Her abusive husband managed a pizzeria. Her favorite music: country. Her favorite movies: *Titanic* and anything starring Julia Roberts. Her favorite TV show: *Survivor.*

He'd sent her a Valentine's Day card. Inside, he wrote: "You have to kiss a lot of frogs before you find your prince." Her husband had probably given her one hell of a beating, assuming he read the card.

Victor had mailed the heart-embellished envelope to the pizzeria, but he carefully printed *her* name on it, which should have insured that she, not Hubby, opened the envelope…right?

He hadn't needed Tenia for that caper. However, when it came to Frannie, Tenia was his insurance policy. Or perhaps collaborator would be a better designation. Victor accepted necromantic precepts. If he hadn't believed in the supernatural, his horror comics would have been trashed by the age of ten. Long live the Grim Reaper. Werewolves. Vampires. Witches.

Tenia had been told to prepare a potion; Victor's insurance, just in case Frannie's "melting" came from fear rather than desire. He'd asked his witch-on-retainer for a simple love potion, nothing that required eye of newt or wing of bat, something that could be slipped into a drink or sprinkled on top of the oysters Frannie consumed by the dozen.

So far, Tenia had come through for him. A couple of requests, a couple of incantations, and he'd found a new scriptwriter, right here at the hotel. After one night in Victor's suite, Norman Daniels was eager to begin scripting Victor's next film project. Best of all, Norm hailed from San Francisco and planned to stay there. No cottage shenanigans.

Then, a fax from a Canadian author…Nicola. If Victor would send Stevie's disk and notes, Nicola would ghost-write the *Forever Asmodeus* sequel. Victor liked her chutzpah, and he really liked her sample chapters, also faxed to the hotel. He called his lawyer. Stevie Eisenberg had one living relative, her mother, who was more than happy to sign over all *Asmodeus* rights for $50,000. Christ. Assuming Nicola worked out, Victor Madison could become another V.C. Andrews.

The only goddamn fly in the goddamn ointment had been his verbal blunder. He'd told Tenia that, after the love potion, she was finished. She'd more than earned her retainer, and he'd keep her in mind if he needed her again. Of course, he'd fly her back to New York.

His motive had been simple. He sensed Frannie didn't care for Tenia, was, in fact, repulsed by her.

Tenia had been furious. She would *not* leave Houston, she said. Equally angry, he said he wouldn't pay her hotel expenses. She said she'd board with a family—Ruby, or Pearlstein, or Diamond, something like that—and she wouldn't even charge him extra for the love potion because Frannie deserved everything she got.

Yes she did, and he'd make sure she got everything she deserved. He had a few necromantic...and *ro*-mantic...tricks up his own sleeve.

Champagne, for starters, then scented oils. Musk for passion. Jasmine for love. And flowers. From what he'd read, violets and red roses and pink geraniums.

Not that he'd need it, but a mandrake root in his pocket would ensure his sexual prowess.

Stopping the tape, he clicked off the TV. Tonight he'd have his own sleeping beauty, whom he'd kiss awake. As Leonard Bernstein and Stephen Sondheim would say: *Tonight there will be no morning star.*

FORTY-FOUR

Clothed in a black leotard and white tights, I smelled my own sweat. Soon I'd call my room. Surely Sol and Peggy were gone by now.

John the bartender kept serving me oysters and Cokes. Despite The Beach Boys' *Fun Fun Fun*, I could hear rain pelting the patio.

Too bad my odor didn't bother Tenia. She straddled the bar stool on my left, flashed her I.D. at John, then ordered two frozen margaritas—one for me. I didn't want a drink, and ever since the Black Mass I'd tried to avoid Tenia. However, I couldn't turn her down without hurting her feelings, and a few minutes with Tenia-the-Witch wouldn't hurt *me*.

In any case, she looked as if she was waiting for something or someone. Madison? The spider sequence had been successfully edited and he'd promised to join the cast and crew for a celebratory dinner at a nearby steak house. Maybe I'd go, maybe not. It was raining pitchforks, and, without me, Bonnie could perform her own magic on our esteemed director. Bottom line: I didn't want Victor Madison and Bonnie did.

A second margarita appeared at my elbow. Tempted to accidentally knock the glass over, I saw that John had scribbled something on the beverage napkin: **NO TEQUILA**

"Hi Frannie, and thank you." Sol claimed the stool on my right.

"You're more than welcome." Swiveling, I hugged him.

"Hi and bye Sol," Tenia said. "I gotta go. How about one last toast, Frannie?"

"Sure." I picked up my virgin margarita. "Here's to…what?"

"Love," Tenia said, clicking my glass with hers.

"Works for me," I said.

"Me, too," Sol said.

Tenia wended her way through the crowd to a table, then sat next to Jem and…*oh, dear, oh, shit*…Mary Magdalene, novice witch. Should I warn

Jem? *Warn him about what?*

Sheldon Giglia occupied the same table.

Gesturing toward Jem's group, I said, "What's Giglia doing here?"

"My guess is that he's still sleeping with Dawn," Sol said.

"Lynn Beth told me her 'mommy' took off for L.A."

Sol shrugged. "Shelly looks like a drunk thundercloud. Madison had better watch his back."

"Don't be silly. I felled our ass…our ex ass director with one blow."

"You did? When?"

"During my screen test. You were putting makeup on Lynn Beth."

"I still say Madison should watch his back. Shelly gets belligerent, especially if he's drunk…a combination weasel and Bantam rooster."

Scooping up my empty glass, John the bartender said, "There was no tequila in the first margarita, either. You never drink, Frannie, but if I guessed wrong I'll make you two more. With tequila."

"You didn't guess wrong, John. Thanks."

"Go on, Frannie," Sol said. "Have one drink. You've been…" He grinned again. "A good girl."

"Okay, John, one." I swiveled my stool toward Sol. "How's our Peggy?"

"She's asleep in my room, after a huge room service meal. A balanced meal, I might add. Vegetables, dairy, and fruit. Corn on the cob and cheese-cake with blueberries. Not to mention ice cream with whipped cream, strawberries, *and* cherries."

"I think corn is a starch, Sol."

"I still can't believe she's here."

"Hey Sol…I have a stupid question."

"There are no stupid questions, just stupid answers."

"My mother would disagree," I said, thinking I hadn't called Mom back yet. "Peggy was at Madison's house before Stevie Eisenberg's murder, maybe even during. That's how she got the money for—"

"Yes, she told me."

"My question is, how'd Peggy find the cottage?"

"She gave her nurse 'the slip' and took a bus. She had bus money. Madison gives her an allowance, for candy, Kotex, books, whatever. Dr. Feldman's idea. He wanted Peggy to feel 'independent.'"

"Okay, but the security guard didn't see anyone."

"There's a wooded area behind the estate. It's a long trek, but Peggy's familiar with the terrain. She's been to the cottage a dozen times, usually via the gate, but she's roamed through the woods, even picnicked there. She's slow, Frannie, but not stupid, especially when her shots wear off."

Sol looked so enraged, I thought: *Christ, I'd hate to have him mad at me.*

"Apparently," he said, his voice deceptively calm, "that fucking nurse has been over-tranquilizing her."

"Yeah, I figured. Why was she at the cottage?"

"She saw something on TV, Jem's show, the usual storyline…missing will…murder…so Peggy wanted to find her mother's will."

"Why?"

"No reason. She saw it on TV."

"When did her mother die?"

"Years ago. She left everything to Madison. Before her mother's death, Peggy was sent to a public institution. Which, in my opinion, really fucked her up."

Now, *I* felt Sol's rage, and wondered if I should continue the Stevie Eisenberg thread.

"After Peggy and I met," Sol continued, "I had a long talk with her doctor, the first one, Caruth. I believed him when he said Peggy could become violent. I was such a bloody fool."

"Hey, don't blame—"

"I saw her as often as I could…stupidly, I thought Madison would be grateful to get his sister off his hands."

"It's hard to believe he was afraid she would tarnish his image."

"He's a control freak, Frannie, but I think it goes deeper than that. I think it has to do with his whole background, the Chaim Mostel years. He'll tout his films, but camouflage his private life. Even Larry King…all he could get out of Madison was the reason behind his Disney fixation. And wouldn't the tabloids have fun, airing Madison's dirty laundry?"

Samson's bio, I thought. *Soon a whole clothesline of dirty laundry would be aired, despite Madison's convoluted precautions.*

Carefully, I considered my next words. "Madison's cottage was trashed, Sol. The cops said the motive was robbery. Stuff was missing. Jewelry. Madison's silver lighter. His Golden Globe award."

"The nurse said Peggy came back empty-handed," Sol said, reading my mind.

"Okay, but she could have ditched the stuff. Is she strong enough to trash the cottage?"

"Probably. Look, I asked her straight out if she killed Stevie. She said no, and that's good enough for me. Peggy doesn't lie. Anyway, Stevie's always been nice to her and…Frannie, what's the matter?"

"Nothing. I feel…a little…dizzy…"

"Christ, you're so pale. Are you planning to be sick? Pass out? Put your head between your legs."

"No. I'm okay now. Honest, Sol, it passed, the dizziness. Sorry, I didn't mean to scare you. Get back on your stool, I'm fine. Hey, John."

"Yo."

"You said…here we go again…room spinning…John, you said no tequila."

"That's right. Shit. What's wrong with her, Aarons?"

"I don't know. Frannie?"

"Yes?"

"Are you okay? Is the room still spinning."

"No. For a moment there, I felt as if an evil merry-go-round had captured me. One margarita, John, then I'll change my clothes."

"You mean one more."

"No. One. With tequila."

"Frannie, you just drank it."

"I did? God, I'm so tired. I must have pedaled a gazillion miles on that exercise bike."

"I'll escort you to your room," Sol said.

"That's not necessary, sweetie. Besides, you have someone waiting in *your* room."

"Peggy will sleep till morning. I gave her half a sleeping pill, not that she needed it. She's exhausted. But I wish now I hadn't promised to join the crew for dinner."

"I'm going to skip it. After all, I might be contagious."

Sol placed his palm against my forehead. "Cool as a cucumber. You haven't got a fever."

"I'm just tired, and I desperately need a shower. Would you make my excuses…please, Sol?"

"Sure, but I still think I should walk you to your room."

"No, thanks." Dismounting from my stool, I performed a pirouette. Then, using the bar as a barre, I flexed my leg muscles. "Ballet lessons."

John applauded, Sol gave me a smile, and The Animals sang *House of the Rising Sun* as I exited the lounge.

Walking past a florist shop and "my" clothing emporium, I stopped in front of the elevators, pushed the up button, and saw Dawn Sullivan.

"Hi, Dawn," I said. "Did you just get back from L.A.?"

"Uh-huh." Hefting her suitcase, she staggered a little. "They make drinks strong here," she slurred. "Bartender wantsa' big tip."

"Not really. John always makes his drinks strong. I drank one margarita and felt dizzy. We…Sol and I…didn't see you…but then the lounge was jam-packed. Do you know about the steak house, Dawn? The crew—"

"Heard 'bout it, Frannie. Gotta brush hair an' change clothes an' get 'brella 'cause it's pourin' out."

I didn't think she'd make it back down to the lobby, but wisely held my tongue while waiting for an elevator. Although renovated, the hotel was old, built before the year of the flood, and it only had two elevators.

Finally, one stopped. The doors slid open and I saw Madison inside. So did Dawn, who perked up. In fact, she looked like a tipsy coffee percolator, shifting from foot to foot, the color in her cheeks flashing from red to white to red.

Madison stepped out, and the freaking elevator took off again.

He looked frightened, his face deathly pale, his eyes as black as my cat Snow's fur. However, *he* perked up when he saw me.

What happened next was a tad three stooges.

"Madison, I've got to talk to you," Dawn said.

"I think the steak house party is waiting for you in the lounge," I said at the same time.

"It's important," Dawn said.

"We need to talk, Frannie," Madison said, ignoring Dawn, who looked as if she wanted to bop him over the head. Or cry.

Taking pity on her, I said, "The group's waiting for Dawn, too."

Madison laughed and said, "So am I, Frannie. By dawn I hope to have accomplished lots of…things." He scrutinized my black leotard. "I assume you plan to change into something more appropriate."

"Absolutely," I said. "Pajamas."

"Me, too," Dawn said. "I bought a bran' new outfit while I was in Bev Hills an' thought I'd get dressed up for dinner."

Lighting a Marlboro, Madison said, "What do you mean, pajamas?"

"I don't feel well," I said. "Tired. Woozy."

"Did you see Tenia when you were in the lounge?"

"How'd you know I was in the lounge?"

"I was in the lounge," Dawn said. "I thought you couldn't smoke in the lobby." Pawing through her purse, she pulled out a crumpled pack of Camels, extracted a cigarette, and waited for Madison to light it.

"You just said the cast and crew were waiting for me there. Dawn, get that fucking cigarette out of my face. Did you see Tenia, Frannie?"

"Yes, Madison. She's with Jem and Mary-Mag—"

"I saw Tenia," Dawn said. "She gave me marg'rita."

"She gave me one, too," I said. "Which is probably why I feel so woozy. I haven't been drinking lately and my tolerance—"

"They make drinks strong here," Dawn slurred, dropping her unlit cigarette, then stumbling into Madison and clutching at his body like a Jules Verne squid. He disentangled her tentacles, his dark eyes probing my face.

"Don't look so worried," I said. "By tomorrow morning I'll be okey dokey, smokey."

"Ah," he said. "You've met Peggy."

Dawn said, "Who's Peggy?"

"Here comes the elevator," I said. "If you'll excuse—"

"I'll escort you to your room," Madison said, grounding out his cigarette with his heel.

Walking into the elevator, he reached for my arm. I took a few steps backward, not wanting him to touch me. As his foot wedged the elevator door open, I played Greta Garbo.

"Madison," I said, "I want to be alone."

"Frannie," he said, "I have something for you."

"I know what you have," I said, staring at his black jeans. If Jem's bulge looked like a pair of rolled-up socks, Madison's looked like a fat snake. "And there's no way we'll spend the night together. *No way.*"

Then, quick like a bunny, I hopped into the second elevator.

FORTY-FIVE

The best thing about room service is that they deliver the food.

While that might sound gospel, or simplistic, it's an opulent luxury to a struggling actress who waits tables and lives on the fifth floor of a five-floor walk-up.

Someday I'd perpetually fly first class and consistently stay at a first-class hotel and endlessly order from room service…even if I wasn't hungry. But tonight I *was* hungry, and I regretted my decision to forgo the steak house. I felt much better, as good as new, and the rain had changed to a pitter-patter, hardly forceful enough to muss one's hair.

Especially my hair. After a long, hot shower, the pale gold strands clung to my head like an upside-down tulip.

Speaking of tulips, a profuse bouquet decorated my dresser, placed in front of the mirror so that the flowers doubled. Not that they needed doubling. There were no tulips, but violets and red roses and pink geraniums filled a cut-glass vase, and the To-Frannie-From-Victor card read:

All thoughts, all passions, all delights
Whatever stirs this mortal frame,
Are but the ministers of Love,
And feed his sacred flame.

Keats? Byron? Coleridge? I couldn't remember, and didn't care. What did Madison's flowers mean? Why did he talk of love? I thought he simply wanted to take me to bed. If he wanted more, I'd have my first-class flights and hotels…anything my little heart desired. I knew, from Cat, that Madison was very generous. I also knew that I'd never have to worry about a film role again.

God, it was tempting. And I guess somewhere in the back of my mind I thought of Andre and his two dearies. Picturing a year from now, I heard myself say: "Andre Vaughn for my co-star? I don't think so."

Of course, I might have blown any chance of a love affair during my elevator moratorium. I may be wrong, but an emphatic "No way" isn't the best foundation for a long-lasting relationship.

Hadn't Sol said that Madison didn't mess around with his cast?

Well, I'd simply wait and see what happened next in the continuing saga of "Frannie and the Bachelor"...co-starring a naïve New York ecktriss and a blasé Hollywood horror film director.

Right now I waited for Room Service, having ordered a grilled cheese sandwich, fruit salad, a slice of pecan pie and...damn.

I wore a sheer red robe, dotted with minuscule red velvet hearts. The robe was supposed to fall to the top of my thighs, but at five feet two (and a half), it fell to the middle of my thighs. Andre had given me the diaphanous robe, a Valentine's Day present, except I'm not a lingerie kind of gal. Nor had I ever worn the matching red thong panties. They reminded me of the macramé I'd knotted at Girl Scout Camp, and one coarse string stealthily invaded my buttock's cleft.

Madison's flowers and poem had...aroused...me, and the lingerie felt like a breath of fresh air against my hot body. But I didn't want room service to see me semi-nude, so I covered my translucent robe with the hotel's one-size-fits-all terrycloth robe, which I could purchase for $99.95 plus tax.

And just in time, too. The polite knock on my door suggested that a rolling cart, topped with goodies, awaited my pleasure.

I couldn't have been more wrong.

FORTY-SIX

Enshrouded by white terrycloth, looking like Disney's Dopey Dwarf, I opened the door.

"Hello, Frannie."

"Madison."

"Won't you please call me Victor?"

"No."

"May I come in?"

"No."

Whereupon, Madison proceeded to give me a detailed critique.

Standing in the hallway, he mentioned some of the things I'd done wrong, acting-wise, and how to fix them. I blushed at his praise and mentally catalogued my mistakes. I was getting an on-the-spot acting lesson from one of the greatest directors in the history of the world. I couldn't shut the door on his words, and he knew it.

Still talking, he placed one foot inside my room.

I didn't care. I wanted to re-shoot the Asmodeus possession scenes, screen-test for a new movie, audition for a Broadway show. Most of all, I wanted to express my gratitude by throwing my arms around Madison.

Sensing my capitulation, he cradled my face between his palms.

If the flowers and poem had aroused me, his touch sent an erotic sizzle throughout my entire body. I thought fleetingly of Bonnie, Cat and Peggy, but my nipples betrayed me by swelling against two red velvet hearts. "Come in," I said.

"Thank you." Dropping my face, he pulled a suitcase-on-wheels through the doorway. "I have the whole evening planned," he said.

"I'll bet you do. First, tell me more about acting."

He laughed, and his face looked so young, so joyous. "First," he said, "champagne." Reaching into the suitcase, he retrieved a silver wine bucket and placed it next to the flowers.

"No, please...Victor. I don't want anything to drink. You drink it."

"I've never cared for wine, except with Italian food. My downfall is Tsingtao beer."

"That's the beer Sol drinks."

"I know. Sol's addiction came from me." He rummaged through his suitcase. "I've got pralines and a box of *Le Chocolatier*."

"How'd you know I love *Le Chocolatier*?"

"There's not a woman alive who doesn't."

"Victor, I appreciate the chocolates, but I ordered dinner from room service and I don't want to ruin my appetite." Inside my head, I heard: *Jesus, Frannie, you sound like your mother.*

He said, "When the server knocks on the door, tell him to leave your dinner in the hall. Or would you rather wait until after he delivers the food?"

"Wait for what?" I said, the fourth dumbest remark I've uttered in the last few weeks. I knew what he meant, and I didn't care if my grilled cheese fell down an elevator shaft. Thinking he would either laugh again or believe I was too naïve to bother with, I watched him attach a VCR to the TV. "Did you bring your Disney videos?" I asked.

"Yes." He reached into the suitcase. "And how'd *you* know that?"

"Bonnie," I said, leaving Cat off my short list.

"These tapes are...different." He inserted one into the VCR's slot, hung a Do Not Disturb sign on the doorknob, then shut the door and locked it. "Why are you wearing that robe, Frannie? It makes you look like a bowl of tapioca pudding."

Except for moving out of his way when he and his suitcase entered, I'd stood rooted to the spot. If I stirred, I might play the Robin role I'd perfected at Rick's cast party; sink to the floor and spread my legs and tell him to make baby demons.

"It's cold," I replied, which was true. My body might be hot, but the room felt frigid.

"I'll turn down the air-conditioning," he said, "and turn up the heat."

I pinched my wrist. "Ouch."

"You're not dreaming," he said with a grin. "I'm real, little Frannie. This is real. Everything else is an illusion."

"Tell me what you want, Victor."

He walked over to me and un-knotted my sash. Drawing terrycloth from my shoulders, he let the robe drop to the floor. "This is what I want," he said, leading me toward the mirror above the dresser. "Do you have any idea how beautiful you are?"

Mom always told me that beauty was in the eyes of the beholder. Staring into the mirror, my eyes beheld a beauty. My hair had dried, and the curly wisps were as downy as a new-born chick. My eyes looked somnolent, while a natural blush stained my cheekbones.

To be perfectly honest, it was the vision of my body that anchored me to the dresser. Even though I hadn't suddenly sprouted "tall genes," I felt I could hold my own on a New York, maybe even Paris, runway.

Victor could afford to dress me in designer gowns, but that wasn't why I pressed my tush against his groin. He was, in two words, if you include a hyphenated word as one word, drop-dead gorgeous. Looking over my shoulder, he studied my reflection. I shifted my focus to his mirror image, and for the first time noticed that his face was lightly pockmarked. Chicken pox scars? No matter; it only made him more attractive. He wore a black, long-sleeved turtleneck, with a white, embroidered manufacturer's logo above his collarbone—a tiny hourglass, full of sand on top, and the words: Docendo Discimus.

I'd never heard of that name or brand. But then my knowledge of foreign labels is as limited as my knowledge of foreign films—though undeniably subversive, I'm not into sub-titles—and Victor would surely stock the most expensive European clothing.

Following my gaze, he said, "It's Latin, Frannie, and means 'we learn by teaching.'"

"Oh, I thought it was a brand name."

"It is. It's my brand, my crest."

"How did a Brooklyn boy learn Latin?"

"How did a Long Island girl learn acting?"

"I studied a little, but mostly it was instinct."

"Right. Me, too."

"You learned Latin instinctively?"

"*Fata viam invenient.*"

"Something about fate, right?"

"'The fates will find a way.'"

"Is that what happened to us, Victor? Fate?"

"Absolutely."

I wanted to ask him more, get to know him better, but his arms had encircled my body and his hands cupped my breasts. My fault. I'd semaphored him by pressing against his penis, which was now as hard as the proverbial rock.

"Victor," I said. "Kisses first…please."

Apparently, a couple of booze-inspired demon possessions hadn't squelched my inhibitions.

"Bed?" I suggested, shamed by the timidity in my voice.

"Of course, little Frannie, we have all night."

Victor released me. I raced my shadow across the room, and won. Hitting the mattress, pulling the covers up to my chin, I watched him devour a few chocolate-covered pralines and chug down a Tsingtao chaser. Then he took off his clothes and retrieved his TV remote.

A knock sounded and a voice said, "Room service."

"Please leave it outside the door," I said, admiring Victor's tall, lean, well-endowed body. "I'll take care of your tip later."

"The tip's already been added, Ms. Aarons."

"Ms. Aarons?" Victor raised an eyebrow.

"Long story. Registration hassle. Sol came to my rescue."

"Good for Sol. Do you want your dinner right away, Frannie?"

"No, Victor, I want you."

An echo inside my head said: *Eat me, drink me.*

Not now, I told the echo. *Please, please, please don't do your demon thing now.*

Joining me in bed, Victor placed his glasses on the bedside table. Then, he clicked his remote.

This is nice, I thought. *Normal.*

I can't even count the number of times I've made-out in front of a TV. Except I've never petted and pawed in front of Disney; mostly it was Steve McQueen, Arnold, Keanu, Harrison, and/or Samuel L. Jackson.

Curious, I waited to see what tape Victor had chosen. *Bambi? The Little Mermaid? Beauty and the Beast?*

I was half right. The Beauty half. Victor had brought *Sleeping Beauty.*

Leaning against his shoulder, feeling his arm snake around my back, I stifled a gasp.

Then, I un-stifled.

FORTY-SEVEN

If Victor's video had been rated, it would have been rated X.

Or XXX.

I'd seen *Sleeping Beauty* before, and remembered that Disney's version included a soirée that extolled the birth of a royal princess. An evil witch who hadn't been invited cursed the kid. In usual Disney fashion, there were some funny fairies and, eventually, a handsome prince who looked like Leonardo DiCaprio.

Victor's version stripped away every single piece of clothing, probably not very difficult to do if one knew what one was doing and one had access to the latest computer equipment. Everyone at the party was naked, including the king and queen, the witch, even the fairies. Everyone was anatomically correct. Everyone performed explicit acts.

My first thought was: *Black Mass.* My second thought was: *Holy shit, a Black Mass.* My third thought was: *If Disney knew this tape existed, Madison would get the shit sued out of him. Talk about copyright infringement.*

Victor said, "Frannie, are you all right?"

I realized I'd gasped again. "Yes. I guess so."

"We can turn it off," he said.

"No. No, it's…interesting. Different. Definitely."

"My collection is called *Disneyland After Dark.*"

"Really. I wonder what charming outfit Cindy's fairy godmother whipped up for the Prince's ball. Can you say leather?"

"How do you feel, Frannie?"

"I'm not sure, Victor. Your video reminds me of…" I almost said Tenia's Black Mass, almost said that two of the copulating celebrants reminded me of Daniel Pearlstein and Dawn Sullivan. "An orgy."

"It *is* an orgy, but how do you *feel*?"

How did I feel? Repulsed? Aroused? Both?

One thing for sure. If Beauty fell asleep naked, her awakening would involve more than a kiss.

For the third time, Victor said, "Frannie, how do you feel?"

Suddenly, I knew exactly how I felt. "Awake," I said.

"Good," he said. "That's what I wanted to hear." Lowering his mouth to one breast, he teased my other breast with his fingers.

Silently, I vowed not to flinch. Hell, if he was a breast man, so be it. I'd endure, give him pleasure, and...

That was my last coherent thought, at least for a while.

I urged him on by arching my back and thrusting, first one breast, then another into his mouth. The clock on the bedside table digitized minutes...five, ten, fifteen...until I finally screamed, "Stop."

He did, immediately.

"Oh, God, Victor," I cried, "my nipples hurt."

"Your nipples are swollen, Frannie, that's all. When you're ready for more—"

"I can't, Victor. No more. My breasts are on fire."

"Do you want me to put the fire out?"

Glancing at the TV, I pulled my arms from the sleeves of my red robe, then wriggled out of my stupid piece of macramé. "No," I said with a whimper. "I want more. Please, Victor, please."

"Of course, little Frannie, we have all night."

This time, when I focused on the clock, another fifteen minutes had flown, and I realized my breasts didn't hurt. My ribs hurt, from arching my back. Again, I asked him to stop and he did. Again, I told him I was on fire and he said, "Do you want me to put out the fire?"

"Yes. No. Victor, the tape re-wound. I missed the awakening. What are you doing?"

"Fast-forwarding the tape. Watch and learn."

"*Docendo Discimus.* 'We learn by teaching.' You teach, I learn."

"Correct. Watch the tape, Frannie. Watch Beauty."

Victor placed my fingers between my legs. Then he rose from the bed and walked toward the dresser.

"Don't leave me," I cried.

"Watch the tape, Frannie. Don't take your eyes from the screen."

I heard what sounded like a gunshot—or the pop from a champagne cork—but kept my gaze riveted to the TV, and soon my fingers began to move in a mesmerizing rhythm of continuity.

"Very good," Victor said, as if I were auditioning. "Spread your legs as wide as you can, Frannie, but don't look away from the screen."

I obeyed, and felt the splash of something cold and sticky.

Victor said, "I put the fire out. Now I'll build it up again."

I sensed what he planned to do. After all, weren't Beauty and her prince doing exactly the same thing?

My mom would have had a long "talk" with Beauty. My mom would have said that men never marry the girls they "sleep around with." My mom would have said that a Jewish American Princess should never allow anyone…even a Prince…such pervasive intimacy.

Get real, Mom, I thought. *Beauty isn't American.*

My Prince of Darkness placed his knees on both sides of my head so that his lower body was directly above my face. Fronting my toes, leaning forward, he used his tongue to cleanse away the champagne.

I wrapped my mouth around his erection, and forgot everything my mother had ever told me.

FORTY-EIGHT

As a Girl Scout, I attended Camp Laughing Water, where every Scout tried her damnedest to accumulate badges. Mine included arts and crafts, diving, canoeing, even sewing, but they should have fashioned a chevron for sex education. I would have shaped it like the Nike swoosh, then proudly stitched it onto my green bosom banner.

My bunkmates and I would sit around a campfire. There, we'd sing *I've Been Working on the Railroad* and toast marshmallows and talk sex. A couple of Scouts had already "done it." We spoke in euphemisms. A penis was a "you-know-what" or "his thing." An orgasm was "the big O."

Fourteen-year-old Marion Bloch was the only Scout who said "fuck." She pissed off the counselors by saying it, then cried when she didn't get any badges. After the ceremony, I gave her my sewing badge.

During campfire soirées, I always sat next to Marion. Scorching my marshmallows, I lied like a trooper. Not only had I *done it,* but I'd experienced *the big O.* My actress instincts came in handy. Everyone believed me, even Marion, who wanted to know what the *big O* felt like, and if I had put his fucking *you-know-what* in my mouth?

Yes, I'd put his thing in my mouth, I told my avid listeners. And the *big O* felt like a Coney Island roller coaster…which I'd actually ridden once, sharing (at my stubborn insistence) the first car with my stupnagel cousin Charlene. After the ride, my mother hustled me over to a trash can, then helped me maintain my balance while I threw up a Nathan's hot dog, an ear of sweet corn, and a large lemonade. Charlene, who never forgave me, had to be carried to the First Aid Station, where she spent the rest of the afternoon puking her guts out—assuming her guts consisted of *two* Nathan's hot dogs, *two* ears of sweet corn, lemonade, and the cotton candy she'd refused to share with me.

In truth, this innocent Scout had hit the proverbial nail on the proverbial head. An orgasm with Andre did feel like a roller coaster. However, compared to Victor Madison, Andre was a kiddy coaster. With Victor, you could add a Ferris wheel and parachute jump, carousel and watershoot. The *biggest O* I've ever experienced.

Correction: the biggest *multiple O.*

And…Madison WAS the one. No bathroom tiles scraped my knees. No icy finger tickled my throat. No voice hissed: *vomit his kiss.*

Instead, Victor turned off the TV and said, "Go to sleep now."

"Will you wake me with a kiss?" I said, smiling like Scarlett O'Hara.

"Close your eyes, Frannie, and thank you."

His thank you sounded familiar. To my knowledge, Victor never thanked anyone. Had I heard him say it to me at our first interview? How about the screen test? And why did his thank you bother me?

"Thank *you,*" I said, and fell asleep…and dreamed I was at the Academy Awards.

I sat in the audience, Victor Madison on my left, Joan Rivers on my right. I wore my red robe, a red bra, translucent harem pants, and my macramé thong. My hair had grown long again, all the way down to my tush. People kept leaning over my seat and saying *good-luck-Frannie.* Joan Rivers whispered, *Who fits in anymore? I was invited to a pot party and I brought Tupperware.*

Why are people wishing me luck? I asked Joan, feeling I could trust her. Outside, in front of the TV cameras, she'd told me I looked like Cher.

That's a good one, she said, nudging me with her elbow. *Because of you, they've added a new category. Best performance by a Demon. Your only real competition is Al Pacino.*

On the stage, Robin Williams stopped clowning around long enough to announce one of the songs from the best song category.

Jim Morrison, who hadn't died after all, sang *Love Me Two Times,* then encored with *Touch Me.*

Morrison waited until the applause died down, then stepped up to the mike to announce the best performance by a Demon, and I realized I hadn't written an acceptance speech. *Don't forget Mom, don't forget to mention Mom by name,* I kept thinking, as I waited for Jim to announce the winner.

Problem was, I couldn't remember Mom's name. Marion Bloch? Miriam Bloch? What the hell had my name been before it got changed to Frannie Madison? I began to sweat bullets.

And the Oscar goes to Lynn Beth Sullivan, Jim Morrison said.

Wearing a cheerleader's uniform, Dawn Sullivan sat on Victor's lap.

They make drinks strong here, she said, *an' now I feel like Sleepin', Beauty. Two bits, four bits, six bits, a dollar, all for Lynn Beth, stand up and holler.*

Hey, I played The Demon, I said, tears blurring my eyes.

You fucked the Demon, Dawn said.

Victor, tell that bitch I played the Demon.

Take it easy, he said, *or you'll lose the baby.*

What baby? Looking down, I saw that my stomach was huge. Christ, I had to be eight, maybe nine months pregnant. I felt a sharp pain. Then another. As Lynn Beth said, *I want to thank Frannie, my inspiration,* amniotic fluid flooded my seat.

Victor, I moaned. *Our baby's coming.*

He pointed to the stage, then guided my fingers beneath the waistline of my harem pants, between my legs, directly above my macramé. *Watch the screen, Frannie,* he said. *Watch and learn.*

There were several screens, all showing Jim Morrison and Lynn Beth and Oscar. My Oscar. As my gaze flickered from screen to screen, a TV camera honed in on Madison, then me, then my fingers.

Lynn Beth said, *Mommy, make her stop, I haven't finished thanking people.* Her microphone screeched, hurting my ears.

The high-pitched squeal woke me up.

Light from the bathroom spawned a nimbus around Victor. Clothed, he carried his suitcase. Gone was the VCR, the silver ice bucket, the candy... Only his flowers remained.

As I focused on the bedside clock, I heard him say, "Sorry, Frannie, this time I didn't *mean* to wake you."

"I just had the weirdest dream, Victor. We were at the Academy Awards, I almost won an Oscar, and I was having your baby."

He smiled. "Maybe that'll happen someday."

"I hope you mean someday I'll win an Oscar...not the baby part."

"*Fata viam invenient.*"

"Well, I sure hope the Fates hurry. I'm not getting any younger."

"You're the perfect age, Frannie."

"For an Oscar?"

"For a baby."

"Don't even joke about that, Victor. I want a career first." Glancing at the clock again, I said, "Why must you leave so soon?"

"I have to go, Frannie. I wish I didn't."

"But you said you'd stay the night."

"I thought I could."

"It's only midnight."

"Yes."

"Victor, what is it? Did I do something wrong?"

"No." Dropping the suitcase, he walked over to the bed and knelt by my pillow. "You did everything right."

"You're not disappointed?"

"On the contrary, I've never been happier."

"You don't look happy."

"Hush. Go back to sleep."

"Not without you," I said, then watched him stand up, walk to the suitcase, unzip it, and pull out a fresh bottle of Dom Perignon.

"This is room temperature," he said, "but it'll have to do."

Actually, room temperature was pretty cold, and I made a mental note to call the desk and tell them about my broken heat regulator.

"I don't want champagne," I said. "I never ate dinner. My stomach's empty. I'll pass out."

"That's the idea. Here, this will make your stomach less empty."

He pressed a chocolate against my lips. I managed to say, "Oony ifoo airit."

"Only if I share it? Gladly," he said, and practically suctioned my tongue. "Now, the Dom Perignon. We're running out of time here. Open your mouth, Frannie."

Like a baby bird, I opened my mouth and let him pour champagne down my throat. To this day, I don't know why. Maybe I thought he'd stay. Maybe I hoped he'd "awaken" me for the fourth...or was it fifth?... time. Maybe I was thirsty.

After several swallows, I felt a buzz. After half a bottle, I was singing Morrison's *Touch Me*. I think Victor touched me all over, as if memorizing my body, but I'm not sure. I don't think I finished the whole bottle, but I'm not sure about that either. I'm only sure about three things. The bottom half of the embroidered hourglass on his turtleneck was full; outside, the rain fell like pitchforks; and, I passed out cold.

Just before I passed out, Victor said, "Thank you, Frannie"...and I suddenly remembered where and when I'd heard it before.

FORTY-NINE

Victor had given me the biggest "O" I'd ever experienced, and the next morning I experienced the biggest hangover in the history of the world. Having seen *The Philadelphia Story* with Katherine Hepburn at least a million times, I now knew how Tracy Lord—the character Hepburn plays —felt after her nighttime fête with James Stewart.

Except James Stewart hadn't "done it" four, maybe five times.

Tracy Lord couldn't remember being carried up to her bed, and I couldn't remember my last thought before passing out. It was on the tip of my tongue...something about being polite.

I tried to shower away the champagne's after-effects, although I can't imagine what made me think soap and water would liquidate a hangover. *This is all Victor's fault,* I thought. *Everything was supercalifragilisticex-pialidocious until he insisted I drink the damn champagne.*

Wondering if he'd ever denuded *Mary Poppins,* I toweled my body and walked over to the air vents beneath my window. The sun poured through glass panes while heat streamed from the vents. Beads of perspiration dotted my forehead and...whoa. Victor had said he'd turn up the heat, but the room had felt cold before he'd exited stage left, and even the "room temperature" Dom Perignon had tasted chilled. Maybe the thermostat had switched over on its own.

Turning off the heat, I turned on the air, and a blast from the vents goosefleshed my legs. If it ain't broken, I thought, *don't fix it.* Except something was broken, and somewhere on my bedside table—hidden by a copy of *Forever Asmodeus,* an empty Tsingtao bottle, a water glass, a lamp shaped like a gargantuan kidney bean, a radio-clock, and my discarded red macramé—was the phone.

I reached for the receiver, then hesitated. I could always call mainte-nance later. Victor had given everyone the day off, cast and crew, and I craved an encore.

As I shed my towel and opened the bureau drawer, I felt a Moby-Dick harpoon pierce my head. Christ, I'd never drink champagne again, not even at my wedding, assuming Victor wanted to marry me before…or after…he impregnated me.

Men don't marry the girls they sleep around with, Frannie.

I'm not a girl, Mom, I'm a woman…especially after last night.

I looked at the clock…7:05. Victor might still be asleep, but he'd surprised me by appearing spontaneously, and I wanted to return the favor.

Donning shorts and a denim shirt, I slid my key-card into my shirt pocket, shut the door, and slanted a glance at a tray filled with covered dishes. I thought about scarfing down last night's pecan pie, but, instead, navigated the hallway, clogged with Room Service trays and free copies of *USA Today*. Then, I summoned the elevator.

When Victor opened his door, I'd quote Mae West: "It's not the men in my life that counts—it's the life in my men." Or, even better, Henry Miller: "Sex is one of the nine reasons for reincarnation…the other eight are unimportant."

Then, I'd fall into Victor's arms.

Or maybe I'd stand in the hallway and critique his performance.

Except…there was nothing to critique.

I heard the echo of Bonnie's voice: *It wasn't a performance, Frannie. He was totally sincere.*

Bonnie. I had betrayed my best friend, but if I had it all to do over again, I wouldn't change a thing. I couldn't, even if I wanted to. One touch from Victor and I'd be lost, beyond hope.

His door knob sported a Do Not Disturb placard. Well…two thirds of a placard. The other third was stuck between the door and the door frame. Which meant the door was open.

Unless Victor had locked it from the inside by sliding the safety chain… "Oh, sweetie," I whispered. "We won't tell my mom you don't dead-bolt your door."

Now, I had three options. One, knock. Two, shout his name. Three, hit the bed and show him how much I'd learned.

Actually, there was a fourth option that made me giggle.

"Room service," I said, stepping into the suite and reaching for my shirt buttons.

Silence.

"Room service," I said louder. "Hey, my darling, do you or do you not wish to be serviced?"

Silence.

Could Victor be in the shower? Or had he already left the room?

Damn. Maybe I should have called, first. Maybe he was a deep sleeper. Maybe he wore ear plugs.

His travel companion, the Picasso sculpture that looked like a winged baboon, graced a gate-legged table. I remembered the first time I'd seen the Picasso, seen Victor. I had compared him to Clark Kent. How wrong can you get? Try Superman.

Deep in thought, smiling inside and out, I opened the bedroom door, walked into the room...and reeled against the dresser.

The room reeked; a sharp, coppery smell, as if I'd stuffed pennies up my nostrils. I couldn't believe my eyes, and yet I felt as if images were being burned into my retinas. My stomach churned. Choking back the sour acid that rose in my throat, I hugged myself to keep from gagging, then gave the loudest scream in the history of the world.

My second scream sounded like Jamie Lee Curtis.

My third scream could have been assimilated into the soundtrack for *Psycho*...the sequence where Jamie Lee's mom gets stabbed with a knife.

FIFTY

Blood is brown.

Not red.

At least, it isn't bright red when it's had seven-plus hours to coagulate.

In the Rosen household, blood never has time to turn a rusty brown. Immediately, if not sooner, it's soaked in white vinegar, club soda, and/or salt water.

Which was probably why I kept telling the cops to soak Victor and Dawn's blood-spattered bodies in white vinegar, club soda, and/or salt water.

Instead, they summoned the hotel doctor, who gave me a sedative. Unfortunately, the doctor's goodie bag didn't contain a drug that would erase the nightmare trapped behind my eyes.

While sedated, I overheard the medical examiner guestimate the time of death…make that deaths…as midnight.

The guestimation had to be dead wrong. Victor had been with me—*not Dawn*—from 8 p.m. to 12 a.m. He wouldn't have had time to exit my room, wait for one of the two rinky-dink elevators, ride it to the top floor, walk down the hall, enter his room, shed his clothes, and fuck Dawn, assuming Dawn had been fucked.

No way. Unless he really *was* Superman.

The cops had asked me some who-why-what's-your-room-number questions. Now they said they'd talk to me again, after I felt better.

"I feel fine," I said, sitting primly in my chair, staring at the winged baboon and trying not to puke. Just in case, I said, "Did you know that you can remove vomit stains, as well as blood stains, by soaking 'em in white vinegar, club soda, and/or salt water?"

The cops were shadowed by a homicide detective who looked like an armadillo. My mom would say he "walked like he had a load in his pants."

He kept making jokes, and he had mean, squinty eyes.

"Someone help the movie star to her room," he said, his voice dripping with sarcasm. "I'll question her later."

He pronounced star "stah."

FIFTY-ONE

Still somewhat groggy, I showered for the second time, as if I could scrub away the memory of Dawn and Victor's bloody bodies.

Tears mingled with the water that pelted my face, until I had no tears left. In fact, I felt as if I had no *face* left.

Stepping out of the shower, I roughly toweled my body until it looked madder-red.

Someone knocked at my door.

Dropping my towel, I scooped up my white terrycloth robe.

The frenetic door-thumps continued.

"Hold your horses," I whispered, trying to knot my robe's sash and turn the door knob at the same time.

Finally, I managed to yank open the goddamn door.

I fully expected to see the detective who looked like an armadillo, but Bonnie lowered her arm. Her lips quivered, her face scrunched, a sob caught in her throat, and her eyes welled up with tears.

Staring at my face, Cat said, "You've heard about Victor." It wasn't a question, but I nodded. Then she said, "May we come in?"

All I could do was nod again. At the same time, I saw that the bumper-car maids had removed last night's Room Service tray.

Bonnie hugged me. Her arms felt like iron bands as we stumbled inside.

Cat trailed us. Her gaze swept the room, and I felt my face flush. Victor and I had "done it" everywhere; on the floor; in the chair; draped across the desk where tourists usually wrote postcards...*Having a fab time, wish you were here.* A damn dog couldn't have marked its territory more thoroughly.

Victor had cleansed me after every orgasm, so washcloths and hand towels garnished multiple surfaces. My red robe diffused the light from a standing lamp. Christ, the room probably *smelled* of what we Scouts had euphemistically called a man's "come-uppance."

Releasing me, staring at the bedside table, Bonnie said, "When did you start drinking Tsingtao beer?"

I slanted a glance at the bottle. "I drank champagne, Bon, not beer. Didn't want to, but he insisted."

"Who insisted?"

"Victor."

"When did he…visit…you?"

She placed a bet in the Frannie-Victor-consummation-football-pool, I thought, stupidly. My next impulse was to fudge a little and change Victor to someone else; John the bartender, or a Continental pilot, or Rex with the muscles (who wore a *Murder By the Book* teeshirt).

"He visited me last night," I finally replied, sticking to the truth. "What I don't understand is how he could have been with me and *her*."

"Victor," Cat said, "had an active…libido."

"No, no, I meant at the same time."

"Victor's death is all my fault," Bonnie screamed, drowning out my *at the same time.*

Cat patted Bonnie's shoulder. "It's *not* your fault," she said.

The phone rang. With a shaky hand, I picked up the receiver.

A woman who identified herself as "Marva Hickler from KHOU-TV" asked for Sol Aarons.

Shit, I thought, *those loony-tunes at the front desk are still confusing my room with Sol's.*

"He's not here," I told the loony-tune on the phone.

As soon as I hung up, the phone rang again. This time, a chainsaw-voiced reporter from News 2-Houston wanted a Victor Madison quote. I knew she meant a we'll-miss-him-so-much quote, but I said, "A Victor Madison quote? Okay. 'We're running out of time here.'"

Then, pressing my thumb against the disconnect button, I slid the receiver underneath the *Forever Asmodeus* paperback .

New tears coursed down Bonnie's face. "I saw you in front of the elevators, Frannie, with Victor and…and Dawn. I was headed for my room to get a raincoat, and I heard what you said. Then he…Victor…found me inside the lounge. He said he had videos and champagne and wanted to come to my room. But I was his *second* choice. You said no, so I said no. He walked over to Jem's table, grabbed Tenia by the arm, and dragged her out on the patio, where they could be alone. But I could see them through the glass, and they were arguing, and Tenia slapped him."

As Bonnie paused for breath, I said, "Cat's right, Bon. It's not your fault. How could it be?"

"If I had let him come to my room—"

"He came to *my* room."

"No, Frannie, he took Dawn to *his* room."

"She couldn't have stayed very long, Bon. Victor showed up at my door around eight o'clock and—"

"She stayed long enough to get herself killed," Cat said.

True. I had never felt sleazier in my life. Victor had apparently gone from Dawn to me, or from me to Dawn. Unless...

"She was drunk," I said. "Maybe she followed him to his room and passed out. He made her comfortable, came to me, and she was still there when he—"

"No," Bonnie said. "After his fight with Tenia, he headed toward me again. He looked angry, confused, and I was about to tell him I'd changed my mind when Dawn intercepted him. He kept walking. She clung to him like a vine, and I was glad Lynn Beth had decided to go back to Cat's room. Then he stopped short and said, 'Okay, I don't want to ride the elevator alone, and after all those trash bins I probably owe you a good fuck.' Just like that. Right in front of everybody. Dawn didn't care. She looked like she'd won the lottery."

"What did he mean by trash bins?"

"I don't know."

"But Dawn still could have passed out, Bon."

"I don't think so, Frannie. She'd sobered up. No slurred words. And except for when she clung to Victor, she walked perfectly straight."

"Then he must have left her alone when they reached his room. Why are you shaking your head?"

"Cat and I met for breakfast. That's when we heard about the murders. The news spread faster than a brush fire. According to the coffee shop waitress, Victor called room service twice. He ordered food at eleven-thirty—"

"That's impossible. He didn't leave here until— "

"—and nine-forty-five."

"No way, Bon. Room service had the time wrong, just like the desk thinking my room is Sol's room. This hotel hires idiots."

"Room Service couldn't be wrong twice," Cat said.

I felt the room whirl. Bed, dresser, desk, chair, everything looked like those pinwheels that change colors as they spin faster.

Thank you, God, I thought. If I fainted then regained consciousness,

Victor would be knocking on my door, and I'd say come in, and he'd join me in bed, and we'd talk about the baby I'd have at the Academy Awards ceremony, and he'd kiss me...

Except, he hadn't kissed me. He'd spurted his seed four (or five) times, and we'd pretzeled ourselves into every position imaginable, and when I moaned he'd told me I was good, very good, but he'd never kissed me, not once. Even when we'd finished—and why wasn't I sore from four (or five) penetrations?—all he said was *thank-you-Frannie.*

Yes, oh yes, that's what I couldn't remember, what a relief. His voice had sounded exactly like the voice at Rick's duplex, the night I played Marianne. Victor was the man in black, the man who'd walked me inside, the man who'd stayed with me while the hands on the ship-shape clock spun round and round. Only I'd been dead drunk, not awake...not awakened. He had said: *Thank you, Frannie, thank you, Marianne.* Then he had encored with the video, when I wasn't drunk, when I was *receptive,* when I could

(*good, Frannie, very good!*)

give as good as I got.

"Frannie, are you planning to faint?"

"No, Cat," I fibbed. "If only the room would stop spinning. Holy shit. Room spinning. Tenia put something in my drink."

"What do you mean? When?"

"Last night. At the bar. Obviously, it wasn't poison."

"Frannie, I think you'd better lie down. Bonnie, help me."

Cat and Bonnie wound their arms around my waist as I began to sag, and I had deja vu all over again. The Black Mass. Tenia had given me whatever she'd given Dawn at the Black Mass...

An aphrodisiac.

FIFTY-TWO

I didn't faint.

Partly because I knew Victor wouldn't appear, once I'd regained consciousness. Partly because I knew that, if he did appear, he'd look like roadkill. Or, even worse, something out of a Stephen King novel.

Lynn Beth, mildly sedated, was with Sol. Cat wanted to get back to her, but first, she said, we'd make a list. Because, she said, there had to be a *logical* explanation. Bottom line: Victor Madison couldn't be in two places at the same time.

"Yes, he could." Staring at the kidney-shaped lamp, I spilled the beans; told Cat and Bonnie about the high school gym and the night I played Marianne. "I don't remember much about that night," I said, "but I do remember Jem saying that Madison was in *Houston,* booking his flight to L.A."

"Frannie," Cat said, "you were crazed with grief. Suppose, just for argument's sake, that you imagined Victor's arms around you? Suppose Victor changed his mind, hit the bar, saw you leave with Jem, and followed you home?"

"I can 'suppose' the first premise, Cat. But why would Victor mess around with someone who was falling-down drunk? He can...could have any woman he wants...wanted...with the snap of a finger. Oh, God, Bon. I'm sorry."

"That's okay, Frannie. I feel numb."

"Me, too. Disconnected...like the phone."

"List," Cat said, retrieving a hotel pad and pen, then sinking to the floor and sitting cross-legged. "Forget the gym and duplex, for now. Let's concentrate on last night."

Bonnie and I followed suit, and I felt like a Scout again, minus the campfire.

"First," Cat said, staring at my face, "are you absolutely positive Victor showed up around eight?"

"Yes. But since Room Service seems to keep such good records, we can always check it out. He arrived shortly after I called them."

Cat scribbled on the pad. "Bonnie, what time did he leave the lounge with Dawn?"

"I'm not sure. But the steak house reservations were for eight, and the crew was gearing up to depart. I felt crummy, sorry I turned Victor down, so I went to my room."

"Didn't *you* notice the time?" I asked Cat.

"No. I wasn't there. I decided to skip the restaurant and join Lynn Beth. I ordered from Room Service around 7:45. Lynn Beth and I ate dinner in my room, then watched *An Affair to Remember* on TV."

An affair to remember, I thought. *How apropos.*

For the record, that movie has always bugged me. Cary Grant should have called every hospital in the city when Deborah Kerr didn't show up for their big date. Why did he simply assume she'd changed her mind? If Madison had filmed it, King Kong's cousin would have flung Cary from the top of the Empire State Building and...

Shit. How could I nonchalantly sit here, deciphering motivational problems in a fucking script, pissed off at Cary Grant? Two people were dead. I hadn't liked one of them, and Dawn certainly hadn't cared for me, but yesterday she'd been alive, with hopes and dreams and...*don't think about that now. Stay numb.*

"Dammit, Frannie," Cat said. "I don't know what else to write, except for what time Victor left your room."

"No, Cat, there's lots more." Sneaking a peek at Bonnie, I gave a mental shrug. "When Victor touched me, I felt a sizzle. Not the usual 'make out in the movies, oooh I'm getting turned on' kind of jolt. I'm not sure I can explain it, except it's been happening for quite a while."

"What does that prove? Victor 'jolted' me, too. That's why I lived with him for thirteen months."

"You knew him better than I, Cat, better than almost anybody. Did he have pockmarks on his face?"

"Pockmarks?"

"Scars, very light, hardly noticeable. Acne scars, maybe."

"Victor once told me he never sprouted pimples, but he paid a dermatologist to clear up his sister's face."

"Okay, write that down. The man who visited my room last night had a pockmarked face. Bonnie..." I could hear my voice grow cold, analytical. "When you slept with Victor, did he play an X-rated tape?"

"No. I told you. *Cinder—*"

"Had the tape been altered?"

"What do you mean?"

"Was Cindy's fairy godmother clothed? Were the freaking women at the freaking ball wearing freaking ball gowns?"

Christ, don't lose it now, I told myself. *Stay numb. Stay focused.*

"Yes," Bonnie said. "Of course they were clothed. Why?"

"Because the man who visited me last night had an X-rated version of a Disney classic. I guess it's possible to fiddle around with a tape, if one has up-to-date computer equipment, but—"

"Why do you keep calling him *the man* who visited?"

"Because the man I saw last night wasn't Victor Madison."

There. It was finally out in the open. I could have said the man I fucked wasn't Victor Madison, but later I'd play around with *that* concept, decipher the motivational problems in *that* particular script. Right now, I needed to stay numb and focused.

"Oh puh-leeze," Cat said. "Next you'll tell us that Victor had a brother who looked exactly like him, except for the scars on his face. You've been watching too many soaps, Frannie."

I ignored Cat's sarcasm, thinking she hadn't shown any outward grief over Victor's death and she had to be suffering. Holding up my hand, counting on my fingers, I said, "One, the scars. Two, the sizzle. Three, the video. Four, he knew exactly what turned me on, and, according to my mother, practice makes perfect."

Bonnie said, "Practice?" She looked alert now, tears gone, and I could sense the wheels in her head turning.

"Yes. Starting with Rick's cast party. Maybe it started after the screen test. No," I corrected myself. "Andre came that night, not Victor's double. Holy shit. They weren't two separate entities. The demon has always been Victor's double."

Bonnie was still attentive, but Cat's face registered confusion, not to mention disbelief.

"Then," I continued, "the restaurant deck. Bon, you said Madison and Jem left me alone out there. Then, the duplex…the night I played Marianne."

Stay focused, Frannie.

I wiggled my pinkie. "Five, last night my room was cold enough to chill champagne." I held up my other hand. "Six, he never kissed me."

"Christ on a crutch," Cat said. "What have cold rooms and kissing got to do with anything?"

"I've felt chilled every time I encountered what I believed was a demon.

As for kissing, Victor's double smiled and laughed and spoke, but I never really saw his teeth up close. Maybe they were pointy, like a spider's fangs. Maybe he had bad breath. Maybe his dental records would reveal..." *Numb,* I thought, *stay numb, stay focused.* "Seven, he left my room at the very same time Victor Madison died."

"Frannie, you're giving me goosebumps," Cat said, her pad and pen forgotten. Reaching into her shirt pocket, she retrieved a pack of cigarettes.

"That's another thing, Cat. Number eight. The man who visited me last night didn't smoke."

"This...this is a...a non...non-smoking room," she stammered, stuffing the pack back inside her pocket.

"That wouldn't have stopped Madison. He even smoked in the lobby, by the elevators. Nine, and most important of all, before he left he said time was running out—"

"There. You see? Victor *always* says that. 'We're running out of time here.' You even quoted it, before, on the phone."

"And the bottom half of his hourglass was full."

"*What hourglass?* Bonnie, say something, do something."

"No, Cat. So far, Frannie's making perfect sense."

"Jesus Christ. You've both lost your minds."

"The embroidered hourglass on his shirt," I said. "I wouldn't swear on a stack of bibles that the top of the hourglass was full when he arrived, but then I'm an agnostic so I don't have to. I would, however, swear on a stack of Dean Koontz novels."

"If it wasn't Victor Madison," Cat said, "who was it?"

"A doppelganger," Bonnie said. She met my eyes, and I nodded.

Cat's eyes implored the ceiling. "What the bloody hell are you talking about?"

"Doppelgangers," Bonnie said, "also known as doubles. An etheric counterpart of the physical body which may temporarily move about in space and appear in various degrees of density to others."

"Please don't tell me you woke up one morning and said, 'Gosh, I wonder what a doppelganger is, I think I'll look it up in the dictionary.'"

"Not quite, Cat. I took a course at NYU."

"Oh."

"There are many examples, just like there are many examples of ghosts who inhabit houses. A guy named Maxwell, Dr. Joseph Maxwell, studied a woman who was entrusted with the bringing up of a child from birth. The woman saw a luminous shadow with features more formed than that of the child. The shadow was always by the child's side, and seemed to gradually penetrate into the child's body."

"The shadow I saw in New York was luminous," I said. "So was the shadow who captured Tenia's rattlesnake."

"When did you see Tenia's snake?"

"At the Black Mass." My hand shot up like a school crossing guard. "Don't chastise, okay? Victor's doppelganger was there. He saved me from the snake and *made* me watch the Mass. Tenia's coven included Dawn. To make a long story short, Dawn 'bargained' with Satan…she wanted to sleep with Madison. Victor's doppelganger hoped I could stop that from happening, but I didn't 'get it.' If Victor had escorted me to my room last night, both he and his double would still be alive."

"Or you'd be dead, too. Call your mother, Frannie."

Consumed with guilt, I stared at Bonnie. "Why?"

"Didn't you say Mrs. Carvainis told you about a stillborn baby? Call your mother and ask her. Now."

I stood up, retrieved the receiver, and tapped out Mom's number.

Please be home, I prayed. *Please don't let that stupid answering machine get this call. Please…*

"Hello?"

"Hi, Mom," I said, as my legs, already rubbery, almost gave way.

"Frannie. Why didn't you reverse the charges?"

"They'll put it on my hotel bill, Mom, so don't worry about—"

"And when are you coming home? Sarah Bloom…she's my bridge partner, remember?"

"Yes, Mom, but—"

"She asked me only yesterday when you were coming home. I said, 'I'm not a mind reader.' But now he's dead, it was on the news, every channel, they even interrupted Oprah. You can't make the movie, so when are you coming home?"

"Mom, you're priceless. My director gets murdered in his sleep, and all you want to know is when I'm coming home."

"You didn't kill him, did you?"

"Me? No."

"So they'll find whoever killed him and it'll be on the news. I miss you, Frannie."

Holy shit. For the first time in the history of the world, Mom (not Daddy) missed me.

"Ask her about the baby," Bonnie whispered.

"What baby?" Mom said, which verified what I've suspected all along; my mother has selective hearing.

I took a deep breath and said, "Gracie."

Mom exhaled the breath I'd inhaled. "Who told you about Gracie?"

"My psychic," I said, and for the first time in twenty-four years heard my mother use the F-word. "Please tell me about Gracie, Mom. It's very important."

To give credit where credit is due, my mother didn't equivocate. "You were born a twin," she said.

My rubbery legs gave way, and I hit the bed with my tush. "And my twin was stillborn?"

"Yes."

"Why didn't you tell me?"

"It's not something you talk about, especially with the daughter who lived."

"Why? Did you think I'd feel guilty?"

"Yes. You've been guilty your whole life, Frannie, ever since the first time you wet your training pants. You tried to turn them inside-out, and when that didn't work, you sat down in a puddle. On purpose."

"Pretending my pants got wet in a puddle isn't the same as a twin sister, Mom."

"I thought if you knew about Gracie, you'd act *meshuga,* like Elvis."

For Bonnie's benefit, I said, "So I had a twin sister, stillborn, named Gracie. Just out of curiosity, whose initials did you use?"

"I used the 'G' for George Harrison."

"George Har...*the Beatles?*"

"I had a thing for George Harrison. So sue me. Your father said okay, as long as I used Frances for his mother's mother."

"Mom, I've got to go. I'm fairly certain the police will be here soon, and they'll want to ask me questions about Victor Madison."

"Why?"

"Because I spent last night with him," I said, and waited for one of her pithy clichés.

"Before he got killed?"

"Of course." I bit my lip to keep from laughing...or crying.

"Will your name be in the newspapers?"

"Maybe. But don't believe everything you read. Okay?"

"If it's good, I'll paste it in the scrapbook."

"You have a scrapbook?"

"I've got two scrapbooks. I'm your mother."

I told Mom we'd get together soon, do lunch, my treat, and hung up.

Then I called the desk and asked them not to put any calls through …with the exception of Sol Aarons.

"But you're Sol Aarons," the girl said.

"Right," I said. "If the *other* Sol Aarons calls, put him through. No one else." Hanging up the receiver, I looked at Cat. "Sol knows you're here, right?" She nodded. "I figured you'd be worried about Lynn Beth," I said, crossing my legs and sinking to the floor. "Bon, did you get the gist of the conversation?"

She wriggled her denim-clad tush closer to the bed, making more room for me. "That was my guess, Frannie, before you spoke to your mom. No wonder you're so susceptible to a doppelganger. You have elements of a double inside your own body."

"You've lost me." Cat stared at Bonnie. "Are you saying that Victor has…had a double?"

Bonnie nodded. "Not only that, but I think he, himself, saw it. In the lounge he told Dawn he was afraid to ride the elevator alone, and—"

"He looked scared when he stepped off the elevator," I interjected. "No, petrified."

"It's rare, but sometimes people see their doubles before they die. Catherine of Russia saw hers seated upon her throne, and ordered her guards to fire on it. I'll bet Madison—"

"I don't *believe* this. You two sit there, calmly discussing doubles, gossiping about some Russian bitch, and Victor's d-d-dead."

Good, I thought, *Cat's finally grieving.*

"A flesh and blood killer stabbed Victor, not some goddamn ghost or fucking double," she cried, "and I don't know what to do about Lynn Beth."

"Maybe you can adopt her," I said, mainly because it was the first thing that came to mind.

"Oh, that's fuh-funny." Still crying, Cat began to laugh. "You can't imagine how fuh-funny that is."

Bonnie and I exchanged a Rosen-Sinclair shorthand look that said: *She's hysterical, should we slap her?*

"Lynn Beth is mine," Cat said. "My daughter. Victor didn't want kids, so I resolved to blame my pregnancy on that night I told you about, Frannie, the night with Mickey Mouse. But we parted company the next day, so I decided to give the baby up for adoption."

"No," I said. "I believe in six degrees of separation, but that's too much of a coincidence. Next you'll tell me you knew Dawn Sullivan."

"Dawn was Dancer's wife." Cat turned to Bonnie. "Mike 'Dancer' Bleich was my boyfriend, my first love. He left Dawn for me. After the divorce, she moved to New York. So did I, after my split with Victor. I waited tables and Dawn ate at my restaurant. I was pregnant, had just started to show, and she said she was happily married but couldn't have kids and desperately wanted a baby. I felt culpable, responsible for her divorce from Dancer, so it seemed only natural that I give her my baby. She never knew it was Victor's."

I said, "Did Lynn Beth tell you about—"

"Dawn trying to keep her marriage intact? Yes. She must have pretended she was pregnant, told her husband it was *his* baby. She's actually a very good actress. I checked Dawn out before I gave her Lynn Beth. Her husband was gainfully employed, I hadn't hit it big on Broadway yet, and I told myself that my baby deserved a family."

No wonder Dawn insisted Lynn Beth call her Mommy. It was a constant, if sick, affirmation of a lie. Aloud, I said, "You only did what you thought was best for Lynn Beth."

"But how do I tell her I gave her up? She'll *hate* me."

We all jumped at the sound of a knock on my door.

The cop who looks like an armadillo, I thought. *Now that I'm sane and rational, ho-ho-ho, how do I tell him I spent a goodly portion of last night with Victor Madison's double?*

Maybe it would help if I helped solve the real Victor Madison's murder…which might even help me stay numb.

I remembered one of Jem's cop shows. I had performed my usual role, standing (and looking horrified) behind the yellow crime-scene tape. Then, with a gazillion close friends, I'd watched "my" show. Jem had car-chased two suspects, charmed a couple of others, and almost blown one away, before he solved the heinous crime.

The incriminating evidence had been a lighter engraved with the killer's name.

"Cat," I said, "did you give Madison his silver lighter, engraved 'To M, From S'? And if you didn't, do you know who did?"

FIFTY-THREE

Homicide Detective Armadillo hadn't knocked on my door.

Unless he'd metamorphosed into a wolf in sheep's clothing with a chin that boasted designer stubble.

"Hi, Andre," I said. "I'm a tad busy right now."

"Frannie, I've got to talk to you."

He walked inside. Then, looming over my two friends, who still sat on the floor, he said, "Hello, Bonnie."

"Andre," she said, her voice as frosty as a fudgesickle with freezer burn.

Rising to her feet, Cat said she had to get back to Sol's room.

"I'll go with you." Bonnie rose with a grace that belied her earlier anguish. "Frannie, let's meet in the lounge as soon as you're finished."

She didn't add *with Andre forever,* but it hung in the air as she and Cat exited stage left and shut the door.

Reluctantly, I faced my blonde wolf. "How'd you get my room number, Andre?"

"You look cute in that robe, Frannie."

"I look like a bowl of tapioca pudding. How'd you get my room number?"

He gave me his melt-Oscar grin. "I charmed the girl at the desk."

"Oh, great. All of a sudden, they know who I am."

"What?"

"Never mind. Find a chair or a piece of bed and sit down. I've got to get dressed."

"Frannie, I came to apologize. There's no excuse for my betrayal—"

"Betrayal, Andre? Try double fuck-up."

"—and I miss you."

"So does my mother."

"I'm serious. I miss the way you cut the crusts off your bread. I miss the way your nose crinkles when you're pissed off. I miss the fact that you can never decide what to wear."

"Andre, you're paraphrasing Billy Crystal in *When Harry Met*—"

"And how you always call our balcony a patio." He patted his left pec (where everybody thinks the heart is), then extended his arms in the traditional come-to-me-baby. "If I swear Bambi and Fawn will never happen again, can we give 'us' another try?"

"No, Andre. There will *always* be another Bambi and Fawn. It's in your genes."

"Low blow."

"Sorry."

"But I probably deserve it." When he realized I hadn't fallen into his arms, his lowered them. "Frannie, I got the part."

"What part?"

"The 'Bus Stop' part. I didn't even have to audition. My agent sent them Galveston Dinner Theatre tapes and—"

"Congratulations."

"I told them you'd be perfect for the Marilyn Monroe role, and they want *you* to audition."

"Thanks, Andre. That was sweet."

"You don't sound very excited."

"I've got a lot on my mind."

He nodded. "Victor Madison. But that's no big deal, right?"

"What do you mean?"

"From what I've heard, everyone's glad he's dead."

"Not Cat, not Bonnie, not me."

"Another director will probably finish shooting the movie, although they say it's jinxed."

"I'm not worried about the movie, and who's they?"

"The TV reporters."

"Fuck the TV reporters."

"Why are you so upset?"

"I'm not upset. I'm angry."

"Why are you so angry?"

Because I loved Victor, loved his double, and how dare you say it's no big deal.

"Because I don't know what to wear. How does one dress for a cop interview? On Jem's show, suspects always look scruffy, and they say 'eh' a lot, as in 'I didn't spend last night with Victor Madison, eh?'"

Andre sat on the edge of the mattress. "Frannie, did you spent last night with Victor Madison?"

"No."

"Then you have nothing to worry about. The cops will ask you a few questions and—"

"Right. Except, I found the bodies, and there's this detective who walks as if he has a load in his pants, and he hates 'movie stahs.'"

"*You* found the bodies? God, Frannie, I'm sorry. The TV didn't identify—"

"Shit. If the girl at the desk gave you this room number, I'm not Sol anymore, and soon the media will thrust hand-mikes under my nose. I may be wrong, but in my humble opinion, the clerks at this hotel can be bribed with more than a smile. So, for that matter, can the bumper-car maids. What'll I tell the reporters? They're sure to ask me why I was in Victor's room. Will they believe I merely wanted an encore, that I planned to Room Service him?"

"Frannie, I didn't understand one word you just said."

"What didn't you understand, Andre?" Plunging into the closet, I began to rearrange hangers.

"For starters, the encore bit? Does that mean you fucked Madison? Please step out of that closet and answer me."

"Cat's jeans will do nicely," I said from the depths of the closet, which was actually pretty shallow. "They're designer scruffy, just like your chin. Where's my new top? Here it is. Shows my belly-button. Can't get much scruffier than that, eh?"

"Frannie, are you going crazy again?"

"Again? When did I go crazy before?"

"All that demon talk."

"There *was* no demon."

Briefly, I wondered if I should tell him it was a doppelganger. Nah. Why bother?

"Frannie, did you or did you not sleep with Victor Madison?"

Fully clothed, I stepped out of the closet, then slid my feet into a pair of sandals. "Andre, I've got to meet Bonnie. If it makes you feel better, I haven't slept with another human being since the day we met. In fact, long before that. Despite your snotty comments, Samson and I never screwed around, not even when I shared his loft. Oh my God. Holy shit."

"What's the matter?"

"Mickey. Mickey Mouse."

FIFTY-FOUR

Had I raced Bonnie to the lounge, I would have won.

Because she wasn't there yet.

The bar opened for drinks at noon, so the lounge was empty.

Except for John the Bartender, who was working the day shift.

Right now, he held a phone to his ear.

Straddling a bar stool, I let my thoughts meander.

Stevie Eisenberg's death and Victor Madison's death were linked…but I couldn't figure out how.

Shelve that one, Frannie.

Tenia had argued with Madison, even slapped his face, but she'd never stab him. She'd stick pins in a voodoo doll. Or send an email to Satan.

Sol hated Madison, but he'd been given the green light as far as Peggy was concerned, so his impetus would be a tad un-kosher.

Apart from Sol's *she-never-lies* assertion, Peggy could have killed Stevie Eisenberg. And once the sleeping pill wore off…half a sleeping pill…Peggy could have killed her brother. But why kill Dawn?

I refused to believe Cat and Bonnie had anything to do with the murders.

Sheldon Giglia was the most logical suspect. Sheldon Giglia had threatened to kill Madison, and Sheldon Giglia had been in the lounge, sitting at Jem's table, when Dawn accepted Madison's crude invitation.

Mary-Magdalene had been at Jem's table, too, but I didn't think there was any connection between Mary-Mag and Madison. Unless she was Tenia's instrument of destruction.

Shortly after Andre had knocked on my door, Cat had said she didn't know the name of the person who'd given the silver lighter to Victor. It had been a gift from an extra who appeared in his first movie. Victor said the extra described him as having eyes that flashed like black lightning. Victor loved that phrase, Cat said.

Eyes that flashed like black lightning.

In my humble opinion, the 'S' on Victor's lighter was none other than Samson, and the Mickey who'd been responsible for Madison's rage and Cat's rape had *not* been Mickey Mouse.

Samson had said he was leaving for L.A., but he might have stuck around. Samson had become agitated when he believed I had Madison's room key in my purse. Samson could have obsessed over Madison for years, the reason why I never saw him with a lover…man or woman …while sharing his loft. And hadn't his loft included a Victor Madison dart board?

Calm down, I told myself. Except for Coffee Shop scuttlebutt and the medical examiner's time guestimation, you don't know shit. The cops could have found fingerprints, a bloody shoe print, the murder weapon. At which point they'd say, "Aha. It was a Crime of Passion, and Sheldon Giglia, ass director, dropped his Rolex."

Staring at shelves filled with liquor bottles, I tried to write a cop-show script. How much harder could it be than rap lyrics?

PAN CAMERA across Victor Madison's hotel suite. ANGLE ON a five-foot-two (and a half) ectriss/stah, hidden behind bedroom drapes. No. Behind a closet door, slightly ajar.

ANGLE ON killer…

Not Giglia.

Not Sol.

Not Bonnie, Cat, or Peggy.

Not Tenia or Mary-Mag.

Who, then?

Mickey Samson Roebuck.

Jeremy Glenn, supercop, would say, "Mickey Mouse and the lighter are 'circumstantial.' They'll never hold up in court."

His partner, Francine Rose, might agree. But then, in a burst of brilliance worthy of Sherlock Holmes (or Kinsey Millhone), Frannie would remember that Samson had said something…something important…the last time she saw him.

Forsaking the mental script, my mind, like a tape recorder, rewound and played. Sol had said, "It's hard to forget a six-foot-four Texan with hair down to his butt." Samson had said, "It wasn't quite that long. If I had cut it, Victor would have given me a speaking part."

No one on our set called Madison "Victor"—not Cat, not Bonnie, not even Jem. Outside the high school cafeteria, Madison (and I was now fairly certain it was Madison, not his double) had said, "You can call me Victor, only not in front of the cast and crew."

Mickey Samson Roebuck had been an extra in *D-Train to Hell*. Had Madison allowed his cast to call him "Victor" way back then?

Once again, I rewound and played.

A&E's *Biography*. Comments by D-Train's cinematographer and the girl with the Mouseketeer ears and an extra who'd become a superstar. All of them had referred to Victor Madison as "Madison"...even the superstar.

"Would you like a Coke, Frannie?"

Startled, my gaze shifted to John. "Coffee, please," I said. "I need to kill this hangover, stay focused."

"You got yourself a hangover from one margarita?"

"Long story. But I need you to do me one hell of a big favor."

"Anything."

"Find a room number for me."

"Anything but that. I'll get my ass fired."

"John, let's say a guest ran up a big tab. He charged it to his room and signed his name, but didn't put the room number down. Couldn't you check with the desk?"

"No. My manager would. Unless he wasn't here."

"Is he?"

"Not until later. I called for back-up. The press is all over the place, and they'll invade—"

"Would you check a room number for me, John? Please?"

"Will you have dinner with me tonight?"

"You bet."

"Okay. What's the name?"

"Mickey Roebuck. R-o-e-b-u-c-k. If it's not under that, check Samson Roebuck."

Drumming my fingers on the bar, I waited for John's return. It didn't take long. "Colleen...one of the girls at the desk...couldn't find anything under Roebuck," he said. "So I asked her to look up Samson. She found M. Samson, Room 1030. But he's already checked out."

"When?"

"Fifteen, maybe twenty minutes ago."

"Did she see him leave the hotel?"

"No. He might be in his room, Frannie. He called the desk and asked for someone to pick up his luggage."

"They would have collected it within twenty minutes."

"Not really. It's a mess out there, because of the murders."

"God, you're clever."

"God, you're beautiful. Don't forget dinner."

"I won't. One more favor, John, this one legal. Bonnie should be here any minute. You know Bonnie, right?"

"I've never met her, but I know what she looks like."

"Okay. Please give her the room number, 1030, and tell her I think maybe Samson killed Madison. Then ask her—"

"What did you say?"

"Please ask Bonnie—"

"*Who* killed Madison?"

"Mickey Samson Roebuck. Please ask Bonnie to find some cops and—"

"Frannie, *I'll* get you cops. Stay right here. That's an order."

"No, John. If Samson's about to leave, I've got to hurry. Explaining everything to the cops would take a gazillion hours. Anyway, Bonnie's more credible, and she's due any minute. Also, see if you can get through to Sol Aarons."

"Please, Frannie, at least let me go with you."

"No. I need you for Bonnie and Sol. Whoa…you don't have Sol's room number, and the desk might patch you through to my room."

"Actually, I do have his room number. He's always buying drinks for people and must have signed a…what's your word?…gazillion tabs."

"Damn, you're smart."

"Frannie, don't go to that guy's room."

"You're supposed to say damn-you're-beautiful."

"Frannie, please."

"I'll be okay. Samson wouldn't hurt me. He treats me like one of his stray cats. Anyway, there's no reason for him to hurt me. If I'm right, everyone will know, including you, Bonnie, Sol and the cops."

John pointed toward the blackboard, where bartenders chalked the daily drink specials. The blackboard was at the entrance, near a host podium.

"I'll try Aarons," he said, "and if Bonnie's still not here, I'll leave her a note on the board, where she can't miss it. In fact, nobody'll miss it. Then I'll find a *gazillion* cops."

"Deal," I said, and headed for the elevators.

FIFTY-FIVE

Waiting for an elevator, leaning against the wall, I had an off-the-wall thought.

Would I see my own doppelganger inside the elevator?

If I did, I'd return to the lounge and let the cops confront Samson.

Yeah, sure. Could one truly change one's fate?

Fata viam invenient. The fates will find a way.

An elevator opened its doors and a family stepped out, dressed for the pool. They were followed by a Japanese businessman and a woman who looked as if she suffered from nicotine deprivation. I nodded, smiled, said hello three times, and stepped inside.

No luminescent double lurked…a good sign.

Samson won't hurt me, I kept thinking. I also kind of hoped he wouldn't be there.

His door was open. I said, "Samson?"

"Frannie, is that you? Come in."

Said the spider to the fly.

Now for a fib that sounded plausible. *You're an ecktriss,* I told myself, *so act like one.*

"Bonnie swore she saw you going into this room," I said, strolling through the doorway. "I told her that was impossible, that you'd already left for L.A. So we made this stupid bet."

"What did you bet?"

"The usual. Dinner. I don't think I ever thanked you properly for treating me and Cat to that incredible lunch. Maybe I'll take Bonnie there…I mean, once we get back to New York. We don't know yet about the movie, if or when they'll continue shooting, because of Madison…you've heard about Madison, right?"

I'd started out fine, the bet idea brilliant, but now I babbled.

Staring at my face, Samson said, "What gave it away?"

I glanced around the room, similar to mine. Samson had packed up everything except his laptop, open on the desk where tourists usually wrote postcards. Maybe tourists didn't write postcards anymore. Maybe they sent emails, along with a webpage address for Texas or Florida or Acapulco. Wish you were here, check out www.fabvacation/wishyouwerehere.com.

Did Samson's luggage contain bloody clothes and a knife?

"Frannie, answer me." He shut the door and locked it.

Oops. Not a good sign. I said, "What gave what away?"

"Has anyone ever told you that you have a lousy poker face?"

"Yes. Cat Sands." My temper simmered, then boiled over. "What I really want to know is *why*?"

"First, tell me what gave me away."

"Ah, so now it's me, not it."

"Frannie, what gave me away."

"You called Madison 'Victor.' In the lounge, when you talked to Sol and me. No one calls Madison Victor, Samson, unless they've had, or they're having, a personal relationship with him."

"And?"

"And you've been stalking him for a bogus bio."

"Wrong." Samson pointed to the laptop. "The bio's real. It's my publisher who's bogus."

"But you said you were going back to L.A. because your publisher... Holy Christ. Stevie Eisenberg."

"Frannie, get out of here. Now."

"Okay."

I made it halfway to the door before Samson caught me by the scruff of my neck. Correction: the scruff of my shirt. Which made it marginally easy to slip out of my shirt and head for the door again. But this time he encircled my waist and said, "I can't let you leave."

"Sure, you can. What's the point of keeping me here? I've already told three people about you."

Releasing me, he said, "Dammit, you're lyin' again."

"No, I'm not. All right, I told one person. But I told him to tell a couple of others. And the cops."

"What exactly did you tell your one person?"

"That you killed Victor Madison."

"Did you tell him how you came to that conclusion?"

No. I hadn't. It was all in my head. "Of course I did."

"Jesus, Frannie, you can't bluff worth shit."

"And you can't do anything to me, Samson. It'll just prove I was right about you."

"True enough, darlin'. I'll have to use Plan B."

"Which is?"

"Another suicide."

"*Another* suicide?"

"You're much too sharp, Frannie. I really should watch what I say around you."

"Oh my God. It really *was* you at the school. Why, Samson, why? What did that poor kid ever do to you?"

He opened a suitcase and pulled out a manuscript. It's title page, neatly formatted, read: *Love Them and Leave Them and Let Them Be Lonely* by M. Roebuck. "It's all in here," he said. "It'll never be published, at least not while I'm alive, but it was fun to write."

"May I read it?"

"Not on your life. Wait. There's an idea. I'll let you read the manuscript, darlin', but only if you write your own suicide note."

"You've *got* to be kidding."

"Well, then, I'll write it on my laptop. That way it doesn't require a signature. Meanwhile, you can read my manuscript. Deal?"

"'When choosing between two evils, I always like to take the one I've never tried before.' Quote, unquote."

"Who is Mae West? Sit on the bed, Frannie, so I can stay between you and the door."

"Why am I going to commit suicide, Samson?"

"Andre."

"Excuse me?"

"Your break-up with The Incredible Hunk."

"But…" I almost told him that his motivation sucked, that Andre had not only visited me, not only asked for a reconciliation, but had dangled a major role in a high-powered TV production as bait. "Just for grins, Samson, *how* am I supposed to kill myself?"

"My room has a balcony, like that balcony in *Pretty Woman*." He made a diving gesture with his hand. "Wasn't that a fun movie, Frannie? Except for its sappy ending."

I glanced toward the balcony. "Very clever, Samson."

"Yes, I have my moments."

His turquoise eyes sparkled and he looked adorable, in an I'll-show-you-mine-if-you'll-show-me-yours kind of way. Frankly, I had to remind myself that he probably looked the same when he pulled the wings off flies. "Okay," I said. "I'll read while you write."

"I'm not stupid, darlin'. I know you're tryin' to stall. But it won't take me very long to write your suicide note, so you'd better skim."

With that, he handed me the manuscript.

I sat on the bed and propped a couple of pillows behind my back...

And skimmed.

FIFTY-SIX

The manuscript needed editing.

Samson had written it stream-of-consciousness, a la Alice Walker. But while Alice Walker is a genius, her *Color Purple* one of my favorite books, M. Roebuck didn't come close to excellence. In fact, had his publisher not been bogus, I doubted his book would have flown.

Bogus publisher.

Flipping pages, I found the Stevie Eisenberg chapter. Somewhere after Victor Madison's early childhood as Chaim Mostel, Samson had switched to first person, written from his personal viewpoint, the pages dotted with "I" did this or "I" did that.

"I" (Samson) had called Madison's cottage. Stevie had answered with: "This is Stevie Eisenberg, Victor Madison's fiancé." Several paragraphs followed, dripping with self-pity. "I" (Samson) had given Madison the best years of his life. Cat Sands had been bad enough, but Mickey (as if he were another person) had taken care of that little episode by beating Victor to a bloody pulp. When "Mickey" heard Stevie on the phone, he saw red...

Jesus, I thought, *what a cliché.*

...and had taken care of Stevie.

I (Frannie) glanced over at Samson, a hunt-and-peck typist—*thank you, God.* How much time did I (Frannie) have, and why wasn't I (Frannie) figuring out an escape route?

Just the same, I (Frannie) flipped back to the Davy Crockett Brakowski segment. Samson was Mickey again. I read a few pages, couldn't believe my eyes, and couldn't help saying, "Wrong."

"What's wrong?"

"Samson, you suggest...hell, you *state*...that Davy had an affair with Madison."

"He did. How do you think the little snot got cast in the movie?"

"A casting agency. Madison had nothing to do with it. Jesus, Samson, Davy was only seventeen."

"I was barely seventeen when I first met Victor."

"But the kid couldn't act worth a damn. Do you honestly believe Madison would sacrifice his movie by casting an amateur?"

Samson shrugged. "Okay, so I goofed. You've only got a few more minutes, Frannie. But it's pretty good, huh? My book, I mean."

"I can't read anymore. I feel sick."

"Don't pull that crap with me, darlin'. That's what *she* did."

"Who?"

"The bitch who was fucking Victor."

"I can't help it, Samson. Do I have your permission to puke?"

"If you must. But do it here, not the bathroom, where you'd lock the door. Mickey kickin' the bathroom door in wouldn't exactly lead the police to believe your fall was suicidal."

Samson handed me a wastepaper basket, but all I could think of was: *Oh, dear, oh, shit, he's Mickey now.*

FIFTY-SEVEN

By the time I finished throwing up, Samson had finished the suicide note.

"How should we do it, Frannie?" he said, opening the French doors to the balcony and placing the wastepaper basket outside . "Do you want to jump, or do you want Mickey to push you?"

"That's a stupid question."

"Push you, huh? Mickey won't mind, but I think Samson was hopin' you'd jump."

"Knock it off. If you're planning to toss me from the balcony, do it as Samson."

He looked wounded. "Samson would never hurt you, darlin'."

"And don't call me darlin'."

"Are you ready? Another stupid question, huh?"

Where the fuck was John? Bonnie? Sol? The cops?

"Samson, this whole *game plan* is stupid. Once they discover you killed Victor—"

"Mickey killed Victor. Samson left false evidence."

"What kind of evidence?"

"Sol Aarons' diamond earring. I know all about him and Peggy. Victor told me. Aarons hated Victor. Motive and opportunity, Frannie. Aarons has no alibi. I saw him go into his room before Mickey killed Victor. And in case you're wonderin' why your cops aren't here, I made a phone call. Said I was a hotel guest who'd seen a man slip into Victor Madison's room around midnight. I gave a description, includin' the mustache, and said I'd seen the same man in the lobby and someone called him 'Sol.' I would guess the cops are grilling Aarons even as we speak."

"How did you get...oh my God. The gym. That was *my* earring. You found *my* earring when you killed Davy. It looks like Sol's."

"Don't shit me, Frannie."

"I swear. My father gave me diamond earrings for my birthday. There goes your evidence, Samson. And your motive. Why would *I* kill Madison?"

"You were jealous?"

"Of whom? Dawn? I don't think so. In any case, your suicide note won't ring true. If I was jealous enough to kill Madison, why would I care about breaking up with Andre?"

"I'll think of somethin' else, and revise the note."

"It'll never fly, Samson. You told the police you saw a *man* slip into the room around midnight, and they know Madison was killed between 11:30 and midnight because he called Room Service at 11:30."

As relief washed over Samson's face, I wondered what the fuck I'd said wrong.

"No problem, Frannie. You killed Victor at 11:45, before Sol hit the room. That''ll fly. It couldn't have taken Mickey more than ten minutes to stab Victor and his bitch. And while that's cuttin' it close, I did say *around* midnight."

"Okay, rewrite the damn note while I puke again."

He shook his head. "It's time you jumped. I'll change the note after Mickey takes care of you."

Christ. There was nowhere to run, nowhere to hide, and overpowering Samson was out of the question. How could a five-foot-two (and a half) New Yorker thrash a six-foot-four Texan?

Despite my fear and angst, I heard *click-click-click*. It sounded like my cat, Snow, when he wants to go out onto the balcony.

Or come in.

Reflexively, I looked around. No beetles appeared. Why would they? Click-beetles usually heralded the appearance of the demon/doppelganger, at least they had when he wanted to frighten me rather than love me. Anyway, the clicks sounded like fingernails tap—

"Let's get this over with, Frannie."

Samson's voice sounded so sad, I dismissed beetles from my mind. All I wanted to do was soothe his pain, by word or gesture, and I had to remind myself that he planned to kill me.

As he grabbed my arms, a luminescent form materialized. Gliding on air, it emerged from the balcony.

Victor's doppelganger?

Impossible. A doppelganger was the ghostly counterpart of a *living* person.

I blinked several times, but the phosphorescent shape didn't go away. Maybe I was dreaming or imagining...no. Because Samson saw it, too. He dropped my arms and backed up against the dresser.

There could be only one conceivable, or maybe not so conceivable, answer...

It was *my* doppelganger.

Mesmerized, I watched the shape became distinctly female. And although she didn't have much substance, she had strength.

Picking Samson up in her arms, ignoring his screams of terror, she carried him through the open balcony door and tossed him over the railing...and I knew the echo of his last horrorstricken howl would haunt my dreams forever.

As the radient shape began to dissipate, I heard clicks again. This time, it was the laptop's keyboard. Somehow, I made my legs move and walked over to the desk.

On the laptop's screen, in big letters, it said: HI FRANNIE, I'M YOUR SISTER GRACIE.

Even though I was safe, undamaged, no longer threatened, my life flashed before my eyes...at least a small portion did.

A gazillion weeks ago, back in New York, I had finished rehearsing for the *Asmodeus* screen test and Bonnie had phoned me. As my mind played tape recorder (or sponge), I distinctly heard her words: *But then I saw a glow around you, an aura, so I called to tell you that everything's okay. Your good angel is protecting you.*

Gracie wasn't my doppelganger. Gracie was my good angel.

More clicks sounded, and I focused on the laptop's screen.

Almost as if my mother had spoken, Gracie wrote: PUT YOUR TOP ON, FRANNIE, YOU'RE ALL GOOSEFLESH. Then: I LOVE YOU.

As Gracie's message deleted itself, new letters appeared.

I KILLED VICTOR MADISON AND PLANTED FRANNIE'S EARRING, the screen screamed. FRANNIE FIGURED IT OUT, SO I'M GOING TO JOIN VICTOR IN HELL. MICKEY ROEBUCK.

Stupidly, I waited, staring at the laptop, until I realized that my sister, like Elvis, had left the building.

"Wait," I cried. "Please, Gracie, don't go."

But I couldn't hear anything, and tears rolled down my face as I listened to the sounds of silence.

Epilogue

A major New York publisher published Samson's book, and it became an instant bestseller.

Jem married Mary-Magdalene. Tenia was her bridesmaid.

No studio attempted to finish *Forever Asmodeus.* Maybe it really was cursed. Maybe they didn't dare. Maybe they didn't care.

I couldn't have cared less. Having captured the "Marilyn Monroe role" in the TV adaptation of *Bus Stop,* I was nominated for an Emmy…along with Andre, whom I date every now and then.

Bonnie was crushed when they chose to close down *Forever Asmodus.* Her angst, however, was somewhat mitigated by John the bartender. Still based in New York, Bonnie often flies to Houston. John is studying to become a lawyer, and he's very persuasive. He even talked me into forgiving him, after I learned the reason for his…shall we say tardiness? Bonnie hit the lounge on that dreadful day nine months ago, still upset over Madison's murder, still blaming herself. John comforted her, fell in love, and time lost all meaning.

Actually, he *had* tried to contact Sol, who was being grilled by Homicide Detective Armadillo, and when John heard that, he felt I was in no immediate danger.

Little did he know, little did anyone know, and little will anybody ever find out. Mom kept my good angel, Gracie, a secret for twenty-four years. I can keep a secret at least that long.

Speaking of time, Lynn Beth did hate her real mom. For about fifteen seconds. They're together now, in California. Madison left half his fortune to Catherine Lee Sands, the other half to Peggy Mostel. Lynn Beth has quit acting. Cat's last letter said that her daughter was "into clothes, causes, and boys."

Tonight I'll see Cat and Lynn Beth for the first time since Houston.

They're flying into Manhattan for my Awards show, sitting next to me as I wait for my category to be called—Best Performance by an Actress in a Dramatic Role.

To tell the God's honest truth, I think my best performance took place inside a certain hotel room, with an X-rated Disney movie in the background.

There, my forever love directed me in the art of *making* love.

Too bad he was a doppelganger.

Although I didn't sit next to Matthew Broderick, who sat next to his Emmy-nominated wife, I couldn't have been happier.

I sat next to Cat, who sat next to Lynn Beth, who sat next to Bonnie. Sol and Peggy had surprised me by flying in for the show. Surrounded by friends, I didn't even care if they called my name.

Instantly, I pictured Disney's *Pinnochio*. Okay, so I did care.

But only because of Mom, who had stuffed everyone she knew into the Rosen's plastique living room. There, she watched the show on TV.

Pinnochio's nose grew longer, and I giggled.

"Something funny?" Cat whispered.

"It's been nine months since Victor's death, and I can't seem to get rid of Disney images."

She squeezed my hand and said, "You look gorgeous."

"I look like a beached whale."

"Hush. They're up to your category. God, I'm excited."

"Me, too."

With a big grin on his handsome face, Jeremy Glenn stood in front of the microphone. He announced the nominees, then said, "And the Emmy goes to…Frannie Rosen."

"Francine Rose," I murmured.

Cat laughed. "Go get your prize, sweetie."

As I stood up, pain coursed through my body. "Shit," I said, "I think the baby's coming."

Cat's beautiful eyes widened. "When did your labor pains start?"

"Around noon-thirty."

Deja vu all over again, except I was at the Emmys, not the Oscars.

I heard a voice say: *Maybe that'll happen someday.*

Twenty minutes later, I heard Cat's voice.

"It's a girl, Frannie, and she's not happy. Listen to her scream. She's going to be a little devil. What are you planning to call her?"

"Victoria," I said…and smiled.